JOSEPH CONNOLLY

The Works

ff

faber and faber

First published in 2003
by Faber and Faber Limited
3 Queen Square London WC1N 3AU

This paperback edition published in 2004

Phototypeset by Intype London Ltd
Printed in England by Mackays of Chatham plc

Joseph Connolly is hereby identified as author
of this work in accordance with Section 77
of the Copyright, Designs and Patents Act 1988

A CIP record for this book
is available from the British Library

ISBN 0–571–21728–1

2 4 6 8 10 9 7 5 3 1

THE WORKS

Joseph Connolly is the author of seven acclaimed novels: *Poor Souls, This Is It, Stuff, Summer Things, Winter Breaks, It Can't Go On* and *S.O.S.* He has also written several works of non-fiction, including admired biographies of Jerome K. Jerome and P. G. Wodehouse, as well as the standard work on book collecting, *Modern First Editions*.

by the same author

fiction

POOR SOULS

THIS IS IT

STUFF

SUMMER THINGS

WINTER BREAKS

IT CAN'T GO ON

S.O.S.

non-fiction

COLLECTING MODERN FIRST EDITIONS

WODEHOUSE

JEROME K. JEROME: A CRITICAL BIOGRAPHY

MODERN FIRST EDITIONS: THEIR VALUE TO COLLECTORS

THE PENGUIN BOOK QUIZ BOOK

CHILDREN'S MODERN FIRST EDITIONS

BESIDE THE SEASIDE

ALL SHOOK UP: A FLASH OF THE FIFTIES

CHRISTMAS

To the Family
(and the way it works)

My father is dead. I simply can't tell you how happy this makes me. Can I say more? I'm not really sure. But let me, at the outset, be thoroughly clear, here: all the people who wholly admire me, are dazzled and look up to me (all the people, then, that are common to me, one could easily say), would have little hesitation, I feel quite sure, in joining together to pressingly assure you that it is *rare*, you see – oh, right up to the very brink of unknown, for me, Lucas Cage, to be found even close to the region of, I believe they say, don't they, lost for words. For it is an absolute with me to articulate, yes – give life to any sort of mood, a whiff of shifting, or that sudden and electric spasm in any given situation before, long before, others have sensed so much as even the odour of its coming. And yet, when they told me, when I was told – when at last I had the truth and was holding it tight (stroking it with care, and very lovingly), well then the feeling that overcame me I find (because yes, even now I still find it) quite literally in any sense approaching vivid or real, frankly indescribable. The pleasure . . . all I can say is that the pleasure suffused me – surged up from deep within and ripened quickly before breaking cover: hot little offshoots, each one of them with high hopes of its own, seeking an outlet – a vapour, fusing then into stirringly pervasive crystals within, yes (and now without me).

'Mr . . .? Mr Cage . . .?'

I think the nurse-thing, young child there, may have been dog-gedly jogging me – upping it slightly with maybe just a hint of

1

incipient panic at her continued inability to effect in me any real headway down the road towards arousal; she maybe needed to smile quite kindly, and bring me round. So I must have slept, then. This too: very unlike me, you might as well know now. If I do not consciously will things, they tend not to materialize. Even for others. Especially for others, as a matter of simple fact.

'Mr Cage? It's – your father. Your father – yes? I'm so sorry, Mr . . . but, well – he is at rest.'

'At rest?' I remember saying quite clearly – looking full at her – quick and alive as I could possibly be. 'He is resting? Are you telling me that?'

She looked down, and then away. Poor little beast that she was.

'No . . . I mean he has. I'm so sorry. He has just passed on.'

My eyes, I felt, were as hard as stones, and glittering too.

'Dead,' I said, as I rose to meet her – her, yes, and this thing head-on.

'He's . . . yes. Dead. He's died. I'm really so very sorry.'

And then I got the rush: it just teemed into me. Happiness is far too pretty and foolish a word to even think of using. But flowers were thrusting up and bursting open inside me, each of their gaudy clusters filling me up and making me gay. The delight I felt had my whole body juddering in an involuntary contraction that was briefly though very intensely (I squirm at the memory) quite orgasmic – before it yielded just slightly and set about releasing deep into me rippling chains of richly warm vigour, before they damped themselves down into heavy-limbed subsidence, and then a sort of grateful ease. The hot pins of sweat that I had been startled to feel springing right out of me, erect like stalks, now bubbled down into a general wash, spiking my brow with a slick of just damp, now: and cool.

'Dead,' I said (just looking at her).

Did she – I still sometimes wonder it – nearly sense any small part of this? I doubt. She has seen people, hasn't she, many sorts

2

of people in this once-in-a-lifetime death situation, and each of them reacts, I can only suppose, in their own little way. None, though, I imagine, such as I.

'Do you want to . . . see him?' (And she wasn't looking. Not at me.)

I nodded. A nod, I adjudged, would do very well. For *no* – *no* would have been the answer, had it come straight down from God and not got sidelined into the chicane, shunted down corridors, those boxed-in mazes that made me up (that make me me). *No*. Because I didn't, did I, at all want to see him. When, ever, had I? So no, then – not that. But still I just had to witness the fact. The fact of his rest, his passing. I simply wanted to see the man dead. But Good Christ – I had wanted that, hadn't I? For years and years and years.

And then, very suddenly, it lay before me – this so much coveted thing: a father, my father, who only now had lost the power to reach me (he will not have relinquished it; it will have been dragged and heaved at, and then ripped away). The room had not at all the air of deadness I had anticipated – wanted, I had wanted such an air so that I could have – and maybe not just figuratively – circumscribed it, stepped within and kept it around me . . . and then later, when alone, drawn beneath it a further and final line, and this time firmly to end the whole affair.

Sterile – there had been most certainly sterility, here; but that would be true, I remember having felt, even if the room were empty of all but its rather thin and pitiful curtains (marigolds, I

3

felt reasonably confident – they were marigolds, both orange and golden, that writhed their way around their printed trellis, and yet hung so limply each side of the far more prim and cream venetian blind, imprisoned in a sandwich of thick and dusty glass). The floor, upon which the soles of my shoes were slapping quite wearily as I approached the man lying there, rushed to the edges of the room, but refused to give in – as if wholly intent upon undermining altogether its predetermined boundaries and laying open siege to each blank and governing wall; just one tile on and up, however, the struggle was abandoned.

The strange little nurse-girl had gone from me now ('us' is what she felt she had left intact: 'I'll just leave you two together', is what she had said) – and then she did, she retired, maybe even semi-curtseyed, stepped away backwards and making no noise, to see if she couldn't attend to . . . what? Some other mass of quite broken old stuff, spinning on down to an eternal blackness or else that platinum pinhole of light you've heard of, its brightness beckoning and irresistibly seductive even as it sucked up terrified just one more cargo of weakened and no longer maddened fodder on into its maw. And for my father – this man, here – this end, dark or dazzling, had already come.

Not, actually, that he frankly appeared to be thoroughly dead. I mean – not *well*, fairly naturally (it would be idle to suggest that the cadaver before me was exhibiting anything at all nudging even close to the nature of ruddiness or vigour), but you would not, I think – had you been there yourself, standing alongside of me and maybe even holding my hand – have recoiled or shrunk within or even gasped out loud at so stark and irreconcilable a vision of undeniable worldly presence allied to a deadness that spoke in audible silence of some place elsewhere. Because they say it, don't they? This is the story that goes the rounds. That people newly gone, those just snuffed out, they are meant to somehow collapse from within, to shrivel and fade – pale to the point of translucency. Well, not my father, is all I can say. He looked very much as he always had. Had, anyway, within living memory. Stern, and brooking no challenge. The jutting nose, daring you to even so much as think about it. Had I been moved to enunciate, then, with firmness and clarity – just my voice alone stirring up the placid air in this quite still and, now I look at it, pale green room . . . had I simply said, Look, You Cannot Fool Me, O Father Of Mine – you are not dead: I see right through you. Had I indulged in just such a whimsy (I thought of it – I did: I thought of it twice before deciding on the whole, No, no, I don't think I shall) well then in some very terrible though not at all *strange* way, it would not really have surprised me if he had instantly come back with 'Oh yes I am! What in fact do *you* know about any damn thing at all, Lucas? Christ, it's come to this: more than forty bloody years on this earth, and you can't even tell whether somebody's dead or not when they're lying in front of your bloody eyes.' Yes. And this would have been delivered, I felt, in one of his more middling tones – one from the very large and encompassing central range, the delivery betraying certainly no trace of indulgence (though neither denoting outright scorn) while possessed notwithstanding of a withering dismissiveness, its edges just maybe gingerly dipped into the shallows of disdain, though not so thoroughly coated in it as it could so very easily be (so thick, sometimes, that gobbets – great ladlesful of his own special brand of syrupy contempt – could spatter the floor).

And a twinge, yes – just a passing shadow of the mildest sort of panic brushed against me during that moment like a fearful little breeze before the flutter changed its nature and became a kind of warm, now, and insistent breathing. Maybe why I hadn't (twice) spoken out. I don't know . . . just possibly I felt that after all this time, all these years and years and years of hanging around, it would maybe have been pushing this shade we call Fate just, a smidgen beyond what might be seen to be decorous, at moments

such as these. I approached. I stood by him. I inclined my head –
closer and closer to his, though very ready to spring back and
howl at the merest tic or tremor. And twice (again) I considered
placing my hand on his. I thought of it once more – and then,
before I could grant myself the time to reponder the desirability of
any such gesture, I hurriedly and quite decisively did it – just, at
first, two tentative fingers (each of them poised and prepared,
eager to flee at even the touch of scalding and long before smoke
might hiss and rise up). But no. Nothing like that. Cold, quite cold
– as, of course, he had to be. I passed the back of my hand across
his cheek. Cold, quite cold – and surprisingly taut. He would be
vexed, I found myself observing – not without a small but detect-
able shudder of delight – to know that he needed a shave. Not
much really he can do about it, is there? Nothing at all. He can do
nothing, now, about any single thing. He is finished. Done. And
finally, now, I can begin.

The last, you might call it, proper conversation I had had with my
father – discussion, debate, confrontation, wholesale waste of this
man's time: do please feel, as they say, *free*, won't you, to, select
your own epithet from a fruitful fund close to bursting with
variety, but all, truly, coming down to the selfsame thing (and
you'll maybe have a much better idea about the tenor of this, it
occurs to me now, after you have witnessed if only at second hand
the very singular nature of all of these meetings) . . . so yes, the
last time, as I say, that one of these, oh – *encounters*, shall we call

them? Settle for that, will we for now? An encounter, yes, I should think will do very well for the present (though switch this about, if you deem it right, when all the words are out of the way). Was, um – when? This encounter. Well they blur, you know – they all very much liquefy in my memory and the seams and then substance of each are overrun by a seeping and never quite set jelly from adjacent frames. In some, I am wearing prep school shorts and meekly standing there and pretending very hard to listen or at least seem penitent for whatever crimes I was this time assumed to have perpetrated – crimes so enormous, these (I was left in no doubt), that an empire could crumble, while at dawn the mighty sun would struggle to tinge with gold its ashes. When I was at Oxford, oh good God – so very many encounters then, I recall. I would fix upon the idle plume of iris blue curling away from the tip of his fine cigar (I smoke them now myself – they really are the finest) and interrupt little and with no spirit whatever. And down the years, down all the years, this is how it went . . . I would be summoned to his study (it was never, in fairness, quite put like that, but I remained in no doubt: it was a summons, oh yes, in all but name) and I would stoically bear witness to the rolling catalogue of my eternal folly. Contrary to the conventions of jurisprudence, all my previous convictions would be laid before the court (a select assembly comprising only the hanging judge on high and the wretched accused in his box) – and of course as these endless years unfolded, this took ever longer. Towards the finish I had resigned myself to writing off the thicker end of any given afternoon merely to become reacquainted with ancient misdemeanours, real or imagined, before the latest indictment could even be hinted at. Because that was another thing maybe worth knowing: often, he was so abstruse, his suggestiveness so thoroughly obfuscated by smokescreen and innuendo, that all I could do was rapidly shuffle the pack of recent or likely transgressions, whipped-up slights or wholly illusory mortifications and set about snuffling just at the rim of not at all acknowledging the accuracy or justice of any such alleged incident, and certainly owning to nothing. At other times, he could be quite startlingly direct – and never more so than when he was stormed by the possibility of losing me (and this strangeness must always be built in to any calculation). I do not know now – and I am sure he was frequently near suffocated by a lack of knowing then – whether or not he embraced with joy, sniffed the heady air of liberation, at the scent of any such putative riddance. For what, after all, was I for? All I could ever appear to him was ultimately biddable, a butt for his boundless displeasure. But what – and I think it occurred to us both – if I was no longer there to be summoned?

'The point as I see it,' he had opened – pouring an ample measure of his ancient Hine from the Irish decanter into a straight-sided tumbler (balloons he thought ludicrous: even the word), 'is that you've blurred it, Lucas. Blurred it, see? What we have here is a clear case of shilly-shally. And I don't at all care for it. Hear me? Don't at all care for it. So the reason you are here is a simple one. Perfectly simple. Hear me? Wholly straightforward. You and I are going to work it all out. Get to the bottom.'

How do I remember so precisely his phraseology, you may be moved to wonder. Well I can tell you that: because it was always unforgettable. *Unremarkable*, oh dear God yes – took an eternity to say nothing whatever. But the rhythm, the pace – they've stayed with me for ever. It goes without saying – and I feel sure that this must already be very evident, perfectly clear – that his pomposity, his unflinching sense of his own indomitable rectitude, they were quite unbreachable, while at the same time, I am positive, utterly unconscious. Not a day passes when I fail to most humbly offer up thanks to the Lord, if He be there, that such or similar afflictions have passed me by. To grow up unlike him and without him was, for decades, my closest approach to ambition.

8

His eyes were impassive, though the ubiquitous cigar became just mildly angered as he coolly drew upon it in that studied and so measured manner that came to be, in one way, the mark of the man. He rested the tumbler at his lips, and the very dark brandy instinctively seemed to know what was expected of it: I imagined the oily swirls pulling themselves together and mustering their resources as somehow the liquor made its way into him. Which I quite understood – for to have loitered simply about the mouth would have made this spirit seem callow and unforthcoming in the face of a tacit requirement. (You might, it has just now occurred to me, imagine this scene to be unfurling across a partners' desk, conceivably, in a vast and oak-lined library – hot licks of firelight just out of frame, but splattering anyway glinting pinpoints over the fleshy and puffed-out cheeks of buttoned hide upholstery, touching the spines of standard bound sets so that their tooling was briefly emblazoned. You might further have inferred – maybe due to his manner, possibly to do with the fact that he was sipping a cigar and kissing at cognac while I, without props, was simply marooned on a chair – that here was one of those prep school shorts days, that my mid-term report had been maybe found wanting, and here was no more than pep-talk spiked by the undercurrent of threatened comeuppance. But no. It was morning. We were in the smaller of the glasshouses and I could smell the musty blush of ripening tomatoes. Just two summers ago.)

'This . . . woman, Lucas. Alice, yes?'

I nodded. Alice, yes. That was her name. Of course it was her name. Was he seriously seeking assurance that she had not covertly abandoned it in favour of some other? Something new and fearful he would have to assimilate?

'Well the point is this, Lucas. She works. Hear me? Labours, yes? Toils. At a job. And you don't. It's not right. What I hear, she's practically keeping you.'

I said nothing. It was not true, this – no no. It was my father who was keeping me, wholly and utterly: always had. As his accountants could easily have told him. Alice, well – she was hardly more than chipping in with the odd though strangely welcome treat.

'Your *mother* –'

And he stopped and stared right at me. Always did – always did this, you see, just in that split second after he said these words. It was as if he was desperate to catch me out, here – seek out and identify some fleeting expression that might break for the border – dart across my unsuspecting eyes as the words 'Your Mother' briefly filled the air, before fading back into the quiet. I know he was always disappointed. I had no feelings one way or the other, about my mother. She had been perfectly all right, to the extent of my recollection. Certainly she had done me no harm. When it had been explained to me by Nanny that Mother had had to go to meet God and help him run Paradise, I had nodded my understanding of the facts. She would be good, I thought, helping to run Paradise. I was always impressed with the way she handed to Cook the orders of the day at eleven each morning, in time with the chimes of the grandmother clock, and then went to see to the flowers. For what must Paradise be if not a torrent of scented blossom, a litany of sweet good things? So feelings? No, not in truth. I did not hate her. Any loathing I had was for my father alone – he had the rights, exclusively. And as for love . . . it had yet to touch me.

'Your mother, Lucas . . . would not have wished this for you. She wanted to be proud of you. We tried to give you everything, but maybe we –'

'You will not give me what I want.'

'– *talking*, Lucas. I do believe I was *talking*, yes? You will be kind enough to address your comments to me when, and only when, I have finished –'

'What I want you never give me –'

' – *talking*, Lucas. When I have finished and not before. Clear? And how *can* you – ? How *can* you, Lucas – a grown man, just sit there and whine to your father about not being *given* things? Hey? Why don't you get out into the world and *capture* them? Hey? Hey?'

Well now I was *certainly* not going to respond or, indeed, co-operate in any single way with the man. I do not *whine*. I never *whine*. His use of that word, I thought, was quite unforgivable.

My father sighed. This was usual, whenever he spoke to me: it was only a matter of time. And then his lips were quite suddenly tugged tight to one side and his eyes flickered briefly and quickly closed down. I was afforded a fleeting and mercifully very rare glimpse of his tiny teeth as a hissing sound not far short of a whistle escaped him.

'This poison . . .' he muttered, 'is all over me . . .'

Maybe it is, I remember thinking, but still you walk and breathe.

'Now . . . *Alice*, Lucas – yes? I mean – how long has it been now? A year? Two years? Longer? I mean to say – *what*? Hm? You going to marry the girl? She won't wait around for ever, you know.'

And yes I am aware – I know, I know: I said I wouldn't react, wouldn't dream of taking part in his trumped-up mawkish game – but how could I have prevented the horn of derision that blared down out of my nostrils? *Marry* the girl? Good Christ. Some weeks pass when her very existence fails to cross my mind. And if he is asking how long it is that I have *known* the woman, well . . . I shudder when I realize that it seems as if there was never a time when she wasn't hovering somewhere – behind the bushes, around the corner, across the table (ready to pounce). And he was wrong about another thing too: because she would, Alice – she would wait around for ever.

My father's voice was acid, now – in common, I imagine, with the bile and worse that was eating him away.

'I take that somewhat unseemly snort of yours, Lucas, to be a no. Well what on earth *do* you want, then? Hey?'

'You *know* what I want. I don't know why you don't give it to me. I think you do not give it to me because you know it's what I want.'

'I didn't mean – oh *Christ*, Lucas, I didn't mean a material thing. I was talking about . . .! And *why*, actually? Why, Lucas – now that the bloody thing has arisen yet again – just tell me *why*, for God's sake, you're so passionate about the old bloody Works? Hey? It's just another *building*. We've scores of buildings!'

And here, oh yes the word was right: *passionate*. Oh yes, oh yes – oh *God* yes, yes. It was the old printing works that I wanted, coveted, craved – always had since I first had entered it long before my father acquired it – centuries ago, when I was a boy. That vast and wholly terrifying edifice – a monument to mechanical industry and the sheer blunt honesty of rough brick walls and clanking metal (grinding, grinding). Hell's cathedral, I once had dubbed it. Alice – by nature, it seems, disinclined to understand – had looked at me doubtfully; my father laughingly called me the fool from Bedlam. Which I maybe could be (I do not shrink from the appellation because of course the fool, so often, is the sage of the piece. This is known: there is a well-worn tradition in this). Moreover, if I am, as my father insists, truly the fool from Bedlam, why should I not be in that place? Why am I poor Tom, cast out in the cold on the blasted heath? I should be where I belong. So why can't the bastard father just give me an *asylum*?

And then, there had of course been all the doctors to deal with. Just old Pilfer, initially, before all this hospital business – the permanently ailing old family physician who should, by rights, be long ago dead (instead he would appear to have healed himself, largely with recourse to single malt whisky: 'cured' could very well here be the appropriate word). Pilfer, I always considered, would be the most wonderful name for a lawyer – except, of course, that had a fellow with such a handle ever seriously contemplated the profession, his very surname, conceivably, might well have served to deter him. Is one conditioned by a name? Shakespeare's rose, and so on? I once knew a chap at prep school, finicky sort of a thing called Martin who utterly refused – threw the most terrible tantrums – even for one moment to consider going on to boarding school. His father, I recall, had himself been somewhere or other quite minor (not one of our great public schools – just somewhere or other quite minor) and he was I suppose understandably keen for the boy to follow on. The sole objection seemed to be that the family name was Sow, and the lad was already devastated, quite pre-crushed by the burden of four-odd years of unceasing jokes and taunts on the theme of piggishness – he had tabulated each of the variations, cross-referred and subheaded under such affiliations as Sty and Swill, Trotter and Gammon. And then his defiance changed into attack – he had rounded upon his father: 'You of all people should understand! *You* must have been through it! You must know what it's like!' I remember him shrieking, time and again, in public and private. His father, I recall, made no attempt whatever to in any way evade

13

the challenge. 'Yes,' he had agreed. 'It was murder at first. Piglet, they called me – I was, I suppose, on the smallish and plump side. Pink-cheeked too. But there was a French boy there called Joux. He *really* came in for it, poor old chap. Left after just a couple of terms. You see, Martin, there's always someone worse off than yourself. That's the whole *point* of boarding school, really: you just have to ferret out that person, haul him to the surface and give him merry hell.' Ran into young Sow, oh – years back now. Did you finally, I asked him, go to that boarding school of your father's? Yes, he said. And did they, um . . .? Yes, he said: they called me Piglet. But you, er – survived, quite evidently, I prompted. Yes, he said. Just that. Never saw him again. And no – I don't at all wonder what he's up to now. Weak and rather ineffectual boy. Finicky sort of a thing, as I say.

So I think I may deem it plausible, at least, that the hapless old drunk we call Pilfer – consciously or otherwise – could maybe have selected the medical profession because here there was no very pertinent nominal connection. One of our solicitors was called Bone, it occurs to me now. Could be – how can we ever know? – the same thing at work. One reason, I imagine, why I am maybe more attuned to all this sort of thing than most is that even to this day I do tend to call people (men, at least – people one deals with) by their surname solely. A hangover from Harrow, I can only suppose – where yes of course my father attended too. *His* father, I gather (never ever knew the man), went to somewhere perfectly beastly. Anyway. And yes naturally it has struck me, oh – long before now that my own name is Cage – except that it isn't, you see – no, not really. I am not at all comfortable with it being my name. I view it as my father's name – my father's name wholly. It is my father whom I look upon as the last of the Cages. I, for myself, am beyond all that.

'I have arranged for him a place at The Abbey.' This was Pilfer.

'The Abbey?' Me, now. 'The Abbey – really? A full State funeral and a plot adjacent to the poets? Slightly premature, surely? Or do you mean he is to become a father with a capital F? Taking the cloth, is he? Late in life, I should have said . . .'

'Oh God, Lucas. You know as well as I do what and where The Abbey is. Why can't you ever be – ? I've got him a very nice private room, all mod cons. The medical care there is excellent. Ambulance due any minute. *Costs*, of course, but . . .'

'So what, actually, is wrong with him, do you think?'

Pilfer distorted his face. A preface of heartfelt concern in order to usher in some bumptious evasion cowering beneath the cloak of a well considered prognosis, I adjudged. Drunken old fool.

'Well as I said to you, it seems to me to be some sort of . . . *erosion*, is the only word I can, um . . .'

'Cancer? You mean cancer? He has cancer?'

'It's not quite as . . . I mean *yes*, it is some form, strain of a, er – what is loosely called cancer – but it's not quite like any I've seen. My own tests have not in all truth really been, um . . .'

'You haven't a clue, have you? Not the merest clue.'

And I really might just as well, you know, have added on 'You drunken old fool'. Certainly he picked up on the tone.

'*Christ*, Lucas – you really are the most insufferable – ! Do me just one small favour, will you? If ever you get ill, please don't come to me – all right? Treating you – my heart just wouldn't be in it.'

'*Dear* Doctor Pilfer,' I smiled as I turned away from him. 'Please do pour yourself a drink, while you are waiting for the ambulance.'

I felt him watching me as I ambled towards the door.

'I, er – I already have, actually, Lucas.'

'Yes,' I said, as I left him. 'So I observed.'

Sometimes he was conscious, my father; at other times, not. They were giving him things, they whisperingly informed me: for the pain. The ruination within, the doctor had muttered, was just all over him.

'I *think* . . .!' – and in high contrast, the nurse was very close, now, to screaming, her eyes struck open as wide as those of a made-up marionette, her lips arched way back from her teeth and forming an elastic box; I imagine that the generous intention here was that if my father failed to hear her words (and you would have to be near dead to do so) then there remained the chance that possibly he might just register at least some of her big animation – become on some level aware of her general repleteness in the department of beans (if one cared to be flippant). 'I *think* . . . that we are feeling just a little bit better today!'

My father smiled – so weakly.

'You, my dear . . .' he just about managed (the voice was robust no longer – that voice, at least, had already been vanquished) – ' . . . are looking very well indeed. For my own part . . . I am dying . . .'

'Now now!' admonished this extraordinary, quite unearthly, I suppose little more than a girl. 'What sort of way is that to be talking? Anyway, Mr Cage – look! Your son is here to see you!'

I was standing directly beside the man. Did she, I wondered, imagine him to be blind? It was she, rather, I think, who failed to see. I felt better when she had gone.

'I haven't,' I said, 'brought you grapes.' Don't quite know why I did this.

My father sighed. And with no emotion:

'Don't like grapes . . .'

I nodded. 'Mainly why.'

So things stood, for some considerable while.

'Lucas . . .' he then came out with (trying to sit up, and not nearly making it). 'This could well be the last time we talk. We must . . . talk.'

I said nothing. I had nothing to say. If, however, he wanted to talk, well then by all means let him.

'You are,' he continued, 'my only child. And yet I never knew you . . .'

'I was,' I murmured, 'always there.'

I had, I reflected, little choice.

He turned his head away. His skin was mottled and loose – his eyes were dull, near opaque, and his ears seemed quite enormous. He looked, I remember thinking, not just tired and over, but also perfectly repulsive.

'Everything . . .' he whispered (ah! So unlike the man I remembered), ' . . . is coming to you. You know that? It's all up to you, now . . .'

Well yes: so I had assumed. God alone knows what my father really thought me to be (or if he thought of me, or if) but even had the depths of his loathing known few bounds, he was not, I hardly think, on the verge of bequeathing his wealth to any sort of variation on a cats' home. His lawyers and accountants, to my certain knowledge, had been toiling ceaselessly for years to ensure that the Revenue's share was no more than nugatory. So yes: I assumed. Of course, I understood that had there been anyone else but me, things might well have been different.

'Treat it all,' he went on, 'with *care* – yes, Lucas? With *care* . . .'

'All I want,' I said quite evenly, 'is The Works. You know that. The Works is all I want.'

The noise he made – feral, not remotely nice – I think denoted a familiar exasperation. Well, I reasoned – the man was entitled to one last round of being heartily sick to death of me.

'And . . . Alice . . .?'

Do you know, there might even have been hope in his voice. How very like him: here he was, strung so frailly across the mouth of the darkest abyss of all – truly the very last ditch – suspended only by ribbons of gauze, and still he could from somewhere dredge up this vestigial sliver of hope. With anyone else, I might just have cared. Even, conceivably, have been touched by something approaching pity.

'No,' I said. 'I told you. Alice – she really isn't a part of anything.'

The hope was gone: I watched it die.

'It's not, is it . . .' he somehow wheezed (the voice was difficult, now, to quite make out) ' . . . a *man*? Is it . . .?'

I wondered for how many years he had suppressed this question. The thought quite thrilled me.

'No,' I smiled. 'No.'

Because no, you see – you really must see this: it isn't a man and it isn't a woman – I had not yet been touched by love. What it is (all it is) is . . . well yes: The Works. No matter how it may sound to you, it really is, I can only assure you, quite as simple as that.

'The Works! The Works! The bloody *Works*! Christ Almighty, man – can't you set your mind to anything else? All I've heard from you for days on end is the bloody old bastard printing works.

Christ – it's practically falling down, that place. What on earth's *wrong* with you, Lucas?'

This was Jack Duveen – the big white chief who had for ever presided over my father's tribe of solicitors. He knew just everything concerning all of the man's very varied and lucrative business interests, and so to a degree I was constrained to listen to at least some of what he had to say. There was, however, a limit to how much hectoring I was prepared to tolerate.

'I should prefer it, Mr Duveen, were you not to address me in that manner. If you please.'

He stopped, Duveen, his rifling through papers and stared at me directly.

'What? *What*? What in hell do you mean by that? I've known you, Lucas, you might care to remember, since you were a bloody little schoolboy! Who in Christ's name do you imagine you're talking to?'

'I am talking,' I replied, very quietly, 'to my late father's solicitor. Who will do as I ask as it is now I who am paying his frankly quite extortionate fees. Otherwise . . . there are other firms of solicitors in London, I believe.'

Duveen sat back in his chair, gently wagging his head this way and that as, wide-eyed, he beheld me.

'You really are, Lucas, you know – you really are the bloody limit. How in God's name did Henry stand you?'

'My father is dead, Mr Duveen. All that is in the past.'

'I see. And it's to be "Mr Duveen" now as well, is it Lucas? You're not going to be calling me Jack any more? As you have been doing – Christ! All your bloody life! Jesus.'

I shook my head. 'Apparently not. Now, Mr Duveen – can we please get settled the only matter I am immediately prepared to deal with.'

'But *look*, Lucas – ! There's so much here you have to –'

'The Works, Mr Duveen. The Works. Please may we?'

He dropped his gaze and gave his all to heaving the heaviest of sighs. This was defeat. He might have intended signalling, oh, I don't know – possibly the resigned abandonment of his better judgement in favour of a reluctant indulgence, something of that order – and look, if it helped him get through, I really didn't mind. But I well knew the truth: this was defeat.

'Right, Lucas. OK. The Works. The Works, The Works and nothing but The Works. Yes?'

His voice was both flat and sing-song, now – as if laboriously reiterating for the umpteenth time to some recalcitrant child a fundamental mantra that should long ago have been memorized by rote.

'The position is this, Lucas. All the other buildings Henry owned on that particular stretch of the river – Tobacco Wharf, the old spice importers and that . . . I think it was a fish cannery, or something like that . . . there are others, but I expect you know. All of them now have been converted into either finished condominiums or else just serviced shells. In all cases the freeholds have been retained. Most of the apartments have been sold on ninety-nine-year leases – ground rents, naturally. Three penthouses – one of them's a duplex – are currently under offer. Collectively, they'll fetch around seven, seven-and-a-half million, give or take. The old printing works – the bee in your particular bonnet, Lucas – is the next in line for development. Architect's plans have been submitted and approved. Initial building work – interior demolition, mainly – due to commence, um . . . when is it? Got it written down . . .'

'No,' I said. 'Cancel that. No architects. No demolition.'

This time, I think, his surprise and impatience were wholly genuine. He was becoming rather testy, which could only be enjoyable.

'Cancel it. I see. What – you're going in with a hammer and a paintbrush and you're going to do it all up yourself, are you? Or what – you don't mean to sell as *is*, do you? Plenty of takers, that's for sure – but it would be very unwise, Lucas. I'm bound to tell you, well – for your father's sake, really. Made up into ten, twelve apartments, well – it's worth a bloody fortune. Work schedule's only nine months – not too long to wait. Christ – it isn't as if you need the *money* . . .'

'I'm not selling it, Mr Duveen. It is the only thing I have an interest in keeping. Have it made weatherproof and sound, and that is absolutely all. I hope that is perfectly clear. Absolutely nothing internally must be touched.'

Duveen stared down at his shoes. They appeared to have given him fresh inspiration.

'Lucas. Listen to me. This property, along with all the rest of it, is yours. I understand that. You're perfectly at liberty to do what you want with it. But the place as it *stands* . . . Christ Almighty, it's still got the old presses in place. Half the bloody windows are missing . . .!'

'Three presses, yes. One of them mid-nineteenth century, I believe. American. As to the windows – the frames are all there. I have checked. Obviously the glass has to be replaced in very many cases. This is a part of weatherproofing the building. As, Mr Duveen, I have already said. I further require a new boiler, capable of heating the whole. Radiators. The chimney stacks, I note, are in need of repointing as well as, no doubt, a thorough internal overhaul. New locks on the doors, please, Mr Duveen. And ensure that all fire safety regulations are complied with. And that, I believe, is all.'

'Right – OK, Lucas. Fine. Now indulge me – yes? You've got the building all cosy and dry – six great echoing floors of it and sod all else except a couple of rusty old heaps of machinery. What then? You turn it into a museum?'

'No. I live in it. It's where I need to be.'

21

I really do think that just for that instant Mr Duveen did actually believe that I had lost my mind. I enjoyed it immensely.

'*Live* in it? What in Christ's name do you *mean*, Lucas, *live* in it? It's a bloody great crumbling *printing* works! You've *got* a house – you've got a fabulous house, Lucas, in Cheyne bloody Walk, for Jesus sake! And there's Henry's house too, now. And anyway – !'

'I am selling both. It is in hand.'

'You are selling both. It is in fucking *hand*! Great. Superb. And you don't think that tens of thousands of square metres of ugly great nothingness might be erring just a tad on the *generous* side? Do you plan *parties*? Most of bloody London could come along. You'd be the host with the most. *Jesus*, Lucas – I tell you this sincerely, I really, do think you've lost it. *Look* – look, Lucas, look – no, just let me say this: listen. Just *meet* with the architects, yes? Just have a look at their –'

'I've made it plain, Mr Duveen. I need it to be left as it is. As to the space – of course I realize it is far too much for my personal requirements. Certain people I know or will know shall share it. They will, I believe, be pleased to. Right, then – I think that is all. The other properties are professionally managed, I believe? That arrangement will stand. You'll keep me informed?'

Duveen just nodded, and stood when I did.

'One more thing, Lucas. Just one more thing. I intend immediately putting all of your father's affairs into scrupulous order. I would be grateful if some time very soon you would instruct some other firm to take it all over. You are quite right – there are others in London.'

'How funny,' I said. 'I was just about to request of you the very same thing. So glad we're in agreement at last. Goodbye, Mr Duveen.'

Duveen might easily have been considering whether or not to knock me down. Instead, he settled for this:

'Lucas. You are. Quite detestable. Now Henry is gone, any

pretence need no longer continue. You really are an out-and-out *shit*. Do you know that? Lucas? Do you?'

'*Dear* Mr Duveen . . .' I smiled. 'You will, won't you, prepare your final account?'

And then I just left. I think, as I closed the door, he could still have been speaking. It doesn't matter. Duveen, like Pilfer – they were both my father's men and my father's gone and now so too have they.

Braced, I suppose you could say I was, following this actually fatuous but necessary encounter. But real invigoration was near to me, now – because of course I just had to go *down* there, didn't I? Had to see and touch it.

Very surprisingly and beautifully situated. The Works. Not at all in line with all the major wharves and gentrified warehouses, just downriver from The Tower. There is a sort of inlet – I doubt it's natural: the dog-leg seems too carefully sculpted – and when you turn down there (the path is narrow and verging on rural – tufts of coarse grasses force their way up and through these crude and rusted metal protrusions, which were maybe once to do with mooring) you feel that London is somewhere else. Although it lies in the shadow of clusters of dark and brooding monsters (and seems almost neat in comparison) it is, rather strangely, not at all easy to locate. Just as one assumes one has reached a dead-end (and a very old and seemingly pointless wall there reinforces such a supposition) one glimpses the wink of another sharp turning which leads you along enticingly. My heart, I confess it, did not stop, as hearts at times like these are said to, but certainly for a moment or two I was made far more aware than usual of its vital presence within me, the insistent beat (which seemed to be urging me on). And the first time I laid eyes on the place – years ago, now, just years – I had felt inside me the very same thing.

The building is cuboid (exactly so, I should say – flat-roofed and four-square) and apart from caramel stone transoms spanning the old loading bays, composed entirely of what must be many hundreds of thousands of hand-made red bricks (the walls in places are four feet thick), each one different and riddled with worm-like crannies that scoop up the dark and contrast it sharply with the surface dapplings of sunlight. The mortar between is arid to the point of crumbling, weather-eroded like an old man's gums to near invisibility. (I like it like that. Like that it will remain.) Large, such very large windowframes cover the façade, some with as many as thirty panes apiece; where each of the slender glazing bars intersects, there is bolted a small and protuberant roundel. All these frames are severely pitted with rust, which I find wholly charming. Above the main double doors is a keystone – Coade, I feel sure – and the big sad lion's face there gazes down on me now. I am emotional; truly, here is the only thing my father ever had that I craved. And I knew he would destroy it and I begged him not to. All he said was that I had no understanding whatever for business, and that one day (mark his words) I would be thankful. Well I am thankful – but not to him. I just am brimming with delight that he had no time to reach it. That time for him ran out. And now it is mine. And safe. The lion need no longer look so sad.

Inside, the air is heavy, but oddly sweet. The air, it is – it is actually visible in strong and off-white slanting plumes, even on an overcast morning or at twilight, as it is now. Each step I take on the throbbing floorboards reverberates up and down and all around me as I mark out with paces my territory. I have climbed the creaking stairs and am right at the top: this is the space in which I shall live out the rest of my life. I back myself into a corner, the better to survey it all. The roughened brickwork agitates the skin at my nape, and I squirm back further until I feel it biting, and the harshness warms me. I am emotional. I am beginning to remember how it is to . . . feel. I am not, you see, all I am perceived to be (both good and bad).

It may well be (and I could easily understand it) that still you are, I don't know – to some degree perplexed. Possibly, you could be thinking that Duveen – or even, God, my father – had a point. It is, after all, just some big old building that could be rapidly converted in common with the others and sold on piecemeal for (yes I know) a considerable fortune. But – as Duveen pointed out – it is not as if I need the money: I *have* a considerable fortune. What I need now in addition is altogether different. This building, I have always known – and here and now, as the grimy windows grow ever more dark as night once more descends around me, I hear it whispering, telling me that it is so – it has never required (wished for, if you like) conversion to anything other than what it is. So few things do. I do not, you see, wish to *hector* this building. I do not want to badger and nor to reshape it – it should not be cruelly wrought and cast forever as something it is not. It must be left to its nature. Just as the people who come to live here, I am wholly determined, will be encouraged in their dormant needs to do just what they are best at. Here will be a process of sharing, each man and maybe woman pitting what he or maybe she not just has within, but will soon come to be eager to bestow. Then I shall feel that I have come to fruition: people, then, will need what I have. Even Alice – Alice will be welcome, along with the others. She does not, in truth, need me (not, anyway, in the way that both she and my father so fervently hoped that she might) but the *shelter*: this, I feel, she will welcome. And in differing ways, this is true of so many. For even those who appear to belong, you know

– they can so very often be strays. You will see. Most are in need of the figure of a father (if not of the father himself).

Look here: the oldest and grandest of the presses. Noble, isn't it? And massive too; it should never have been brought to such a state, you see – because it was always intended to be oiled and burnished, sleek and powered. I am shifting gently away from it neat and small piles of silt . . . silt, it seems, and soft still hillocks of granulated decay – the hue, it now foolishly occurs to me (and even, yes, its gritty texture) that of tawny Cornish shale. All this will be swept aside, and the lives of people will be enriched. I imagine them, cramped and crouched within their outer shells, and stymied – stumped and crestfallen, as I and this building have been. This is what happens when your nature is suffocated and all your good intentions stripped away.

It is dark, when I leave – and although the stage is well set for fear and deep misgivings (each long shadow could easily conceal a creeping demon) I feel no more than the mere container of a great white sparkling effusion of hope (a murky stirring of vicious contentment). I cannot make out the face of the big and sad old lion, but I know him to be there. I kiss the building – I touch The Works – and as the tips of my fingers trail and linger, unwilling to finish a final caress, this pang that now invades me is keen and heartfelt, stopping up my breath as I hurry away, and rush on into the night. For now and at last . . . I am touched by love.

I

a beginning . . .

CHAPTER ONE

'Jesus, Jamie – look: it's a *dream*, isn't it?' Caroline had spat at him. 'Can't you see? It's just some stupid bloody spoiled and overgrown kid's half-baked adolescent *dream!*'

Jamie, just gazing upon her, could scarcely believe it. Not the fact that she was pale and stiff, wide-eyed and utterly shocked by rage again – and nor that they had once more (again) tumbled beyond and over the brink, looked like to Jamie, and soon would be going back over the whole of it, no no – here was normal, now: so much was expected. It was just her ripping loose with such frankly wrong and wildly unsuitable *terms*; I mean – this was *Lucas* who was under the microscope, God's sake – Lucas Cage, of all people in the world. Stupid? Adolescent? *Please*, Caroline – get a grip! Think of what you're *saying*: he's the only really intelligent grown-up I *know*. The dreaming bit is maybe OK, though: Lucas is surely a dreamer of dreams so, oh God – so thoroughly alluring – and maybe, just maybe, if Caroline would for Christ's sake and just two seconds cut all the yap and listen to reason she would see that he could also be the founder of all of our futures. And I want one of those, want one badly: I need to know a future is looming. And with Lucas – just to hear him speak (even to watch him silent) was somehow to come so easily to believing in the dream. Yes I know – sounds yuck and cheesy, I know, I know: it's just that you so much wanted to be by his side, his hand in yours. Well *I* did, anyway. Caroline, not. She says I'm weak. She could be right.

'But *listen*. Caroline – just listen for a moment, will you? I mean, look – look around you. This flat. Dump, right? Right? That's what you're always telling me, Caroline. Isn't it? Right from the bloody minute we bought the bloody place. Christ.'

'It *is* a dump, Jamie – of course it's a bloody dump and I told you that, actually, even before you put down the deposit, but – oh Christ do you *have* to keep on smoking like that? You've only just put one out. You're probably killing your own son with passive smoking, do you know that? Do you *care*? And half of that deposit was *mine*.'

'You should know by now, Caroline. Over the years, you should have observed. I'm a chain smoker, aren't I? It's what chain smokers do. And don't keep dragging Benny into everything.'

'You don't have to tell me. Place stinks.'

'Well exactly – place stinks. In every way. That's what you've always been *saying*. And Christ alone knows what the *deposit's* got to do with anything. But never mind all that. Look: here is this offer, handed to us on a plate, and all you can do is – !'

'Oh I see. I *see*, Jamie – I see. We move into some oh-so-fab bloody loft apartment and suddenly the chain smoker quits. And us – we're all fine again. That it? Because, what – you'll touch the hem of fucking Lucas's *garment* and one more miracle will be instantly enacted before our very eyes? Oh get *real*, Jamie, Christ's sake. You're seeing this bloody bloody building of his as the answer to *everything*. It's only a building, Jamie. Lucas is only a *person*. All we would be doing is just carting everything some-where else. We've got *problems*, Jamie – and what in Christ's name do you *mean*, don't drag Benny into everything?! He's our son, you stupid bastard. What are we supposed to do? Leave him out of the calculations? He's one of the *problems*!'

'Caroline. Just listen, will you – ?'

'He, poor sod – he's just one of our real and serious grown-up *problems*, Jamie. And we've got to somehow sit down and bloody work them out. Yes? Not just toss them into a tea chest and lug

30

them on down to, oh Christ – *Wapping*, or wherever this bloody thing is, and – I don't know: *what*, Jamie? Hm? Tell me what. Just what are you *expecting*? I mean – do you think it's going to be like all the *adverts* for places like this? You with a cocktail on a Corbusier lounger in front of the panoramic view of Tower bloody Bridge? It's only a *place*, Jamie. All it is is just somewhere *else*.'

Jamie slumped back. Stubbed out the cigarette, lit up another one. Well yes – yes it *is* another place. And another place is where I need. It's maybe because of here, all this, that we've failed so *badly*. I hate it. It's just so dingy and noisy and I'm so fed up with queueing for buses in the rain . . . and the other thing, of course (and it can't be long now in rising up, can it, and hitting me full in the face), is that even this poky little flat, even this, I can't any longer *afford*. I know! It's just too shaming. But look – when they made me . . . when I lost my *job*, all right? It quickly became a pretty straightforward choice: mortgage repayments, or eating. And of course, being the frightened-to-death middle-class drone I was brought up to be, for months and months it was the mortgage, wasn't it? Mortgage won hands down. And then I thought Oh Christ – hell with this. Live a little, right? I can always catch up with the arrears when I get another job. Well. I think we're all sufficiently adult (seen quite enough of life) to more or less know how the rest of it went. So really (and here is just one of the – I should have said really quite *salient* points that I would so much love to din into Caroline's head) it's not actually a question of *choice*: picking and choosing just doesn't arise. This place is due for repossession. No bones about it. So it is either Lucas's offer of a dreamlike space in practically a wonderland (second floor, just by the old service lift: I've seen it – I love it) or else the streets, plain and simple. Why can't she grasp this? Caroline. Why can't she see what's in front of her face?

Caroline sighed. She closed her eyes and covered them with a hand as the fingers of the other stiffly fluttered for a moment in the air – that funny little gesture, odd little way she had; Jamie had long ago concluded that it was on a par with a flattened wrestler with his face crushed sideways – slapping down hard his palm upon the canvas as the hold became increasingly unbearable, when he could stand no longer to be pinioned beneath just so much weight.

'I'm making tea,' she said then, briskly. 'Do you want?'

'*Please*, Caroline – if you'll only just *think* about it . . .!'

She shook her head.

'Well I'm having some, anyway. Benny'll be back from school, soon.'

Jamie thought he might as well, then, go along for now with this forced and uneasy interval (suck on orange quarters, gargle and spit a bit). Couldn't anyway for the moment think of anything further to usefully say. Can't just go on wheedling and imploring '*pleeeeese* . . .' and '*listen*, can't you?' for the rest of the afternoon. Well can I? Exactly. So I'll sort of go along with it.

'F.A.B.,' he said.

And Caroline stopped – she just stopped dead and immediately at the door to the kitchen.

'*Sorry* . . .!' rushed out Jamie, with a little alarm. Maybe not quite quick enough, though – so better do a few more: 'Sorry sorry sorry, Caroline. Sorry. Just slipped out. OK?'

'It just sums you up. It says just about bloody everything I, oh – so totally *hate* about you, Jamie! Our marriage is *over*. We've nowhere to *live* – !'

'Ah but that's just it! We *do* have somewhere to – !'

'We've got nowhere to *live* – just listen, you bastard – and we've got a little *boy* to think of and still you're just talking like a bloody *cartoon*. You *know* it drives me crazy when you do all that – all your bloody silly *slogans* – and still you just –'

'It was an accident. Christ's sake, Caroline. Told you – just slipped out. I won't again. More a catchphrase than a slogan, I should have said. And it's actually animation, that one, not a cartoon. I think I will, you know, maybe have some tea. Might be nice.'

Caroline turned to glare at him.

Jamie blinked up at her. 'If you're making it.'

She spoke quite slowly, and her eyes were narrowed. You had to be there, Jamie would tell you; if you were there, it could be scary.

'You never will, will you Jamie? You'll never grow up, not ever. You're just stuck in idiothood – a bloody kid for bloody ever.'

'You do use that word rather a lot, you know, Caroline. "Grown-up", "growing up" – all that. And I'm not so sure if it's all that great. I mean look, at the end of the day – where does growing up actually *get* you?'

Well, Jamie conjectured (Caroline was hissing and smacking her thighs as if she truly meant business – and now she had hurled herself back on to the sofa, and fingers were drumming) – the business of growing up has very clearly been kind to, well – *Lucas*, but then he's just a natural. Urbane at birth, I should have said: thoroughly capable from the off. For myself, all I ever remember wanting to be when I grew older was an enfant terrible. Oh dear God. And look at me now.

'Jamie. Listen to me. You go on and on about how I should always be listening to *you* – but get this: news for you, yeah? I *have* been listening. I've been listening for just *years* – ages and ages to all of your balls. And now it's your turn: you're going to listen to *me*.'

'Uh-huh. Which would be some kind of a *first*, would it? Caroline? My listening to you? Jesus Christ Almighty – you never bloody *stop*. What about this tea, then?'

Caroline closed her eyes. She was not to be, mustn't again be diverted – and Jesus knows it's never easy. Every single thing he comes out with – each moronic utterance that falls from his weak and pitiable lips – could so very easily propel her into yet another grotesquely spinning and clamorous avenue of pin-sharp angst, and the need for retribution – but if she were to rise to every single one of them, well then – years could pass and still she'd never get things said. Which was, of course, more or less the root – just exactly what had come to pass (you think I don't know this? Haven't maybe *twigged*, or something?): years *have* passed – all my precious years. And all I've got now is Benny, oh my so sweet boy (and thank you, Lord, for keeping him safe). Benny, yes – and Jamie. And Jamie is going (and surely now he knows it?).

'Jamie,' she began – quite measured, but still with her eyes closed, Jamie could only observe with a flicker of something he had yet to quite pin down (nail in place and put a name to) but he knew full well it was, ooh – a good long way down the road from anything remotely approaching a pleasantly tingly antici-pation or even, if he was honest, so-so complacency. 'Jamie – light a cigarette.'

'Hm? Sorry? Light a – ? But I've got a –'

'Yes I know, but soon it will be finished and then you'll drive me mad – I'll go crazy with you scrabbling around with the packet and that horrid and bloody little lighter and I'll scream at you for doing it and then I'll lose my *thread*. OK? So just –'

'But it's still only halfway, um –'

'Just *do* it. Light it. And listen.'

'Yes, Bwana.'

And her eyelids flickered. She was maybe during just that one split second trying to determine whether or not he had done this on purpose – a forthright and deliberate provocation – or whether it was merely that his sense of place and moment were quite as shot as she'd always believed. Maybe he simply had no control whatever over any single one of his senses. Either way, she would not be deflected: it was time to let him have it.

'OK. Here it is. You lost your job, Jamie –'

'Uh-huh. Uh-huh. Here we bloody go! Oh yes – very nice. Look – last *time*, OK? I didn't lose my – they were restructuring, right, several strata of the workforce more or less on an ad hoc, ground roots basis, and –'

'Don't! Just listen. You lost your *job*. That is, I'm sorry Jamie, but that's the *point*, here. Whatever the cause, that is how it affected us all – OK? And I wish I'd told you before that I was leaving you, Jamie, but –'

'Oh come on, Caroline! You don't want to *leave* me! We're fine – we're fine. And I'm telling you – soon as we –'

'Christ's sake Jamie *listen* to me, will you? I'm only going to do this once. Just shut your mouth and hear what I have to *say*.'

'But all I'm saying is – all I mean is, Caroline, that if we could only, all of us, get out of this miserable little flat, then we'd be –'

'*What*? What would we be, Jamie? Actually? In Cloud Cuckoo Land? Part of some old hippy's communal dream? Ringing bells and wearing *beads*?!'

'Christ's *sake*, Caroline! Communal *dream*! What in Christ's name are you talking about *beads* for . . .?!'

'Just another little pair on Lucas Cage's fucking *ark*. I'm not going, Jamie. Not. I'm not going anywhere with you, Jamie – never, not ever again. And that's what I was saying, that's what I mean – I wanted to tell you ages ago, and then when you lost your job –'

'I *told* you. I didn't –'

'And then when you lost your poxy little *job*, OK? I held off a bit – I maybe shouldn't have, I just don't know. But anyway I *did*, and –'

'Yeah yeah. You didn't want to hurt my feelings. I know, I know. Don't like to kick a man when he's down – that it, Caroline?'

'That's . . . kind of it, yes Jamie. But none of that matters any more. The point I'm making –'

'It matters to me . . .'

'Oh God *please* won't you listen to me, Jamie?!'

'No I bloody won't. I say it matters to *me*, bloody Caroline, because what we're talking about here is *my* job, *my* wife, my bloody home and, Christ – some kind of a *future*. What's so suddenly wrong with *hope*?'

'And Benny? What about Benny? That's typical of you, Jamie – Benny didn't even *feature*, did he, in your catalogue of woe!'

'Don't try and pin that one on to me, Caroline. You know I think the world of –'

'Yeah well you can think what you bloody well like, Jamie, quite frankly – because I tell you this right now: Benny won't be there. Not within a million miles. So don't hit me with this "hope" thing, Jamie, because quite bloody frankly –'

'You can't do that, Caroline.'

'Just you fucking watch me, you bloody selfish pig! I'm not having my son mixed up in some sort of a guru *cult*. What the hell sort of mother do you think I am?'

'*Cult*?! Christ Almighty – it's a *cult* now, is it? I tell you what sort of mother I think you are, Caroline, since you ask me – a fucking bloody *certifiable* one, that's what sort you are. Where in God's name did you get all of this – ?! Oh *Jesus* . . . I mean: Jesus!'

'*I'm* not the certifiable one – it's you, Jamie – you and your sick and fucking loopy little buddy *Lucas*. You're the crazy ones. You're *dangerous*. And him – he's just downright *creepy*.'

'Oh don't be so bloody *stupid*, Caroline. All this is nothing to do with any of that. All this is because after, what – how many years? Most of my bloody awful life just working and working they suddenly made me – I suddenly lost my *job* and now in your eyes I'm just not a *man* any more. That's it, isn't it Caroline? Yes it is. And that's bloody all of it.'

'You're crazy, Jamie. If you think that, you're just crazy . . .'

'And anyway – what about you? Hey? You never even had a

bloody job in the first place. How come you manage to escape any blame here? Why's it all *my* fault?'

'*Benny,* you bastard! Benny's my job. That's what we *agreed*.'

'Yeah well. Maybe we did. But that was before . . . all this.'

'And now it's after. Now it's now. I'm off, Jamie – I mean it. And Benny's coming with me. And don't ask me –'

'Caroline – look . . . *listen* to yourself . . .'

'Fuck off. Just fuck off, OK? I don't know *where* we're going, but we're going. You – you can just do as you like. Which you will. Because you always bloody *do*. Got it?'

Jamie sighed. He sighed again, as Caroline seemed to be joining in. She was up now, and bustling.

'Roger,' he said. 'Roger Wilco. And Out.'

Caroline's lips were white and thin and quite as compressed as ever he'd seen them.

'Could you go now, please Jamie? I don't want you here when . . . I don't want Benny to see us like this. Why don't you go and see Lucas, hm? Get him to help you select your new curtains, or something, yes? Maybe burn some incense.'

Jamie ground out his cigarette and lit up another. Most of the fight had fled from him, now. All that remained was severely weakened.

'It's not,' he sighed, 'as if Benny hasn't heard it before . . . poor little devil.'

'Yeah well . . .' was Caroline's only exhausted rejoinder. 'Enough is enough.'

Jamie softly closed the door behind him. Oh God. *Hoooo* . . . Right, then. Maybe I will – go and see Lucas. Not to pick out curtains, though. He actually told me he wasn't having any of that – nothing at the windows at all, he said (not to be countenanced, were his actual words). Something about spoiling the purity of the line, I think was the general gist of the thing: I really wouldn't know. And nor would I argue. He knows about these sorts of things, Lucas – knows about everything like that. And anyway – it's his, isn't it? The Works. Yes. It is. So it's all up to him.

I think, though, I sort of know what he means – all this purity stuff and conservation. It's not just about curtains, you know – oh Christ no. It's more to do with just everything coming together – it's about it all, I suppose, well – *working*. And Caroline, if I'm honest – she never would've fitted. At least we all of us seem to agree about that. Lucas himself, you know, has expressed the gentlest of doubts. About her. I now feel easier about saying it. Anyway: she's made her choice, hasn't she? You heard her. I think she only would have spoiled things for the others. Not that she's a *bad* person, Caroline – oh my God no, don't get me wrong. Don't go listening to a lot of what I say in the heat of the, you know – moment, and everything (you know how it can be). Christ – compared with my first wife, Caroline's a saint. You won't have met her, Eileen – and nor, my friend, would you ever wish to. We weren't together long. Every night when we went to bed (you may not believe this) she'd have a bloody great kitchen knife stuck under her pillow. Christ, I'm telling you – the tension nearly did for me. Barely slept a wink, first few months. Well face it – one bad dream and it could've been curtains. Every dawn I opened just the one eye gingerly – check to see if the sheets were crimson. Took her to this bloke, one time – Harley Street, just round the corner of. How many sessions and how much wasted money? Basically told me it was all psychological. Yeh? I said. Yeh? Well just you try living with it, mate. The 'logical' part doesn't much enter, I can tell you that much – and here I am dealing with all the psycho end of things. Ah well. I left her one Whitsun in Ashby de la Zouch. So – all in the past now, thank God. Trouble is, this past of mine is fast catching up: it seems to be moving quicker than I do.

So. Might as well get myself over to Lucas's. Maybe get some tea. Check out again my own not-so-little billet up there in The

38

Works. And how am I feeling, you might be wondering, following on from this latest little marital contretemps? *Sad*, I think, deep down (although I may not seem it). Sad and guilty and, yes – ashamed and also, in a funny sort of a way, at base disappointed. That, yes, and also just a little bit peckish. Do with something. Maybe lay in some provisions, shall I? I'm not sure of the system, but I do know that Lucas has just had installed this utterly enormous fridge and freezer: it's more like a vertical mortuary. Yeah: I'll be on my way now – no point in hanging about. Just light up another fag, and I'll be off. Because I am, as I said, a chain smoker, you see; you are maybe unacquainted with the type. Understandable. This day and age, we're a dying breed.

'It's real good of you, Lucas, yeah? I mean – all of us, yeah – we're all real, like, grateful. You know? It'll be just, kinda, till we get it all, you know – sort of got something sorted, yeah?'

From behind his desk, Lucas smiled expansively, and his heavy-lidded eyes momentarily glistened.

'Do you hear that, Alice? From young Theme here? Such politeness.'

Alice had had, at the time, her nose and part of her face quite deeply burrowed into a thick and heady profusion of darkest orange arum lilies densely rammed – and it seemed haphazardly – into a mottled and possibly artfully dented galvanized bucket with both the hue and seeming resilience, Lucas had only recently observed, of a Cold War destroyer. She raised her head now and shook away from her eyes the club-cut chunks of her hair that had not swung back down into place of their own accord – and while two fingers were still teasing no more than four, maybe just half a dozen irksome and persistent strands from the corner of her mouth, she nearly chuckled and said quite equably:

'Well Paul's an *extremely* polite person – aren't you Paul? And an absolute genius when it comes to, you know – with flowers.'

Paul Theme looked down and began in earnest to screw the toe of his black and white basketball sneaker into just the one old and original and deeply gleaming walnut floorboard – keeping his eyes well low and tracking the headlong streaming rush of just this single mighty plank as it soared away into all that distance, only hitting the perimeter of Lucas's vast and sunlit attic regions when it had assumed both the thrust and acuteness of a dagger's tip. He would not look up until the worst of his blood-heat had subsided from his face, though the pulsating red at his temples remained very visible to all. Tubby and Biff – who knew him well (and so they should do, by now) – had independently and within a second of one another applied to their faces two simpering grins of joky indulgence, and seemed eager to punt them across to both Lucas and Alice where they would be met (it was somehow understood) with immediate sympathy and a stealthy affection.

'It's not really nothing, the flowers,' Paul eventually got out, shrugging away the plaudit – one eye up and lively, the other (rather amazingly, it had fleetingly occurred to Alice) darting here and now there to maybe make entirely sure that this unfamiliar coast was as clear as reports were suggesting. 'When you bung them in a you know – glass, like, sort of container, you, er – *vase*, kind of style – you get to see the whole of the arrangement, yeh that's true enough – but this way, the way I done it – put them in something, like, real sort of ordinary, yeah? It helps you get closer to the true, like, original flower silhouette. Yeh. Plus I always get shot of most of the leaves. Same with your tulips. Roses and all.'

'Don't go *on* . . .' whispered Tubby, his mock-conspiratorial whisper very much as warm as the collusion in his eyes.

Alice and Biff laughed lightly at that – quite in tune, as each of them could hardly help but notice. And then, as if on cue, they stopped.

'Sorry . . .' blustered Paul – the crimson seeping back up the throat and suffusing his jaws. 'Didn't mean to, er . . .'

'Not a bit, Theme,' said Lucas, softly. 'Your peerless flower arrangement has already become rather a dazzling part – a *component*, I rather feel – of the entire floor. Any more tips for us, Theme?'

Paul shook his head while he was already speaking:

'Just always to, you know – make sure you got them in a place what makes you happy. Basically. You don't want to go hiding them away in some sort of room what never gets no use, if you take my meaning. Couldn't happen here, course . . .'

'Indeed not,' agreed Lucas – spreading his hands on to the surface before him, and then quite slowly splaying out each of his fingers in a tentative and almost exploratory fashion as if the scheme had only recently been put to him – and although intrigued by just how the business might go, he would nonetheless be taking things slowly (feeling his way). 'A drink for all, I think, Alice. Drink, yes? Let us toast the future success of our newest residents.'

'The only other thing what you got to remember,' hurried on a suddenly emboldened Paul, 'is that you don't never push the stems on down to the bottom of the vase. Or whatever.'

'*Bucket* . . .' smiled Tubby – who wasn't, you know, what you would call fat in any way; no, not at all.

'Yeh,' grinned back Paul. 'Or bucket. Yeh.'

Alice was passing out tall and flaring flutes of champagne. I reckon, thought Biff (who hadn't yet spoken, but that didn't stop him thinking, did it?), they must've had that lot already well opened, or something. Cos I didn't hear this Alice bird make no pop with it, or nothing. And me, when I does it – and if I can, I'll get out of being the one what has to – there's always the most bleeding awful sort of explosion, pretty much. And yeh I do know what I'm doing wrong, as a matter of fact, because it's all been explained to me; it's just that when I gets down to the very last sort of twist, like, I just go all . . . I just get a little bit of a sweat on and just about let go the sodding thing and oh dear oh dear – you get one hell of a mess, you do that: yeh. As I often discovered in the past.

'And for you, Lucas my darling . . .' said Alice, quite softly, as she placed just by his hand a small cylindrical glass of something rather yellowy, alive with an oily swirling: not champagne, thought Biff (that's for bleeding certain).

Lucas sipped it.

'Your very good health, one and all,' he announced. 'Cheers, Theme. And so too to you – Biff and Tubby. Tell me – does neither of you possess something so ordinary as a surname? Or is there some dark secret that none of us should know? I do not, of course, intend to be in any way rude. It just happens to be an interest of mine.'

There was a fair deal of quite good-humoured snuffling and shifting of feet, following that – partly a throaty and stopped-up response to Lucas's toast (glasses quite awkwardly proffered to nothing) and also an easily worn if hard to deal with quasi-embarrassment with this name situation. Biff thought, Well: I suppose we owes him something, this Lucas – whoever he is – after all he promised to, like, do for us.

'Nah nah – we *got* them. Course we *got* them,' Tubby now rushed to assure Lucas and Alice (because Biff and Paul, well – they already knew).

'Yeh,' put in Paul. 'Dracula and Frankenstein!'

Appropriately muted mirth was duly displayed by way of

response to that – a very slight widening of Lucas's eyes denoting his receipt of the message, Alice quite jocularly batting away all of Paul's nonsense with one of her hands, both Biff and Tubby making Yeh Yeh He Would noises ('Trust him', Biff was nearly clucking).

'It's just that,' Tubby went on, 'we don't really sort of remember when it was we last, like, used them, to be honest with you. We *always* been Biff and Tubby – ain't that right, Biff? Not on *forms* and things, course – but we try to avoid them, don't we? When we can.'

Lucas nodded: seemed to understand perfectly. Which was a blessing.

'And why do they call you Biff, Biff?' he enquired, serenely. 'Are you in the habit of, what? Hitting people? Knocking them about? Are you maybe known for this?'

Biff shook his head. Everyone hovered, waiting for more – but that seemed to be all of it, for now. (Except for Paul, of course – he wasn't hovering: he knew Biff too well. And Tubby – he was learning.)

'And you, Tubby? Tell me – did they by any chance call you that at school?'

Tubby sipped champagne and rubbed on a nostril and coughed just a bit.

'No,' he said. 'No. Oddly enough, they um – called me Slim.'

And yes, he could have gone into it, Lucas (delved a smidgen), but he opted instead for addressing Paul:

'And about those *stems*, Theme. Why is that? What is the thinking behind it? Leaving the stems some way from the bottom.'

'*Well*,' went Paul. 'You ram them right down and what you got is rot. Plain and wossname. Simple, innit? They go much faster, see? Another thing what I do is I spray them. Spray them, yeah? The flower heads, I mean. Not the *stems*, obviously, because that

43

would be bleeding stupid. No – the flowers, see? It's like nature. People think – right, bunch of flowers, yeah? Chuck them in a pot, and that's your lot: sorted. But nah – it ain't. You want your morning jew on them, see. And then you're looking at evening mist of a night-time. Plus, you basically want to change your water every single day, if you're talking gospel. Most people, though, they don't need the hassle. But me – I does. I does it always. Never miss.' Paul looked up from the floorboard (he was getting now to recognize every crack and whorl). 'Sorry . . .' he whispered. 'I was going on again, wasn't I? You wanna tell me, Tubs, when I gets to going on, like that . . .'

'Yeh well I try!' scoffed Tubby, with fondness. 'Don't do a lot of good!'

'Alice,' said Lucas. 'Was that someone at the door, do we think?'

Alice was already setting down her barely sipped-at flute. 'I *thought* I heard something . . .' And she narrowed her eyes as she gazed into the distance.

'Yeh – *I* did,' agreed Paul very readily, trying rather like a spaniel to come within the range of Alice's eye as she sidled past him – and soon she had got into her stride.

'I didn't hear it. Heard nothing,' threw out Tubby. 'You, Biff?'

And Biff just hunched up a shoulder, which might have meant anything, including evasion. Paul now threw across to Lucas a quick sort of half-smile, while both Biff and Tubby appeared to have contracted their mate's fascination for the conker-coloured floor . . . and still there remained ahead of her a good way for Alice until the doors at the far end were wholly discernible. Only as she was about to grab with both hands and set herself to heaving at the thick black japanned and heavy hasps and latches did she hear now distinctly a quite urgent and echoing bang-bang – which all those tens of yards ago had come across as only the just about scuffle of maybe some rodent: now it could be thunder.

Jamie nearly tumbled into her as she swung open the doors.

The first thing he focused on, after the winsomely smiling Alice, was this really quite maddening cluster of people all bunched up at the far end, and behind them, somewhere, Lucas. Damn, he thought – oh damn: it never occurred to me he might not be alone. Lucas was gesturing, however, and calling over to him, oh – something or other, probably some all-encompassing greeting, Jamie could only assume (because I'm telling you – the distance, it's so almost comically unreal, I might well be witnessing a mime show, here). And now as he walked the endless walk, Jamie felt acutely aware of just the whole of him burning – his hands were bulbous and awkward hanging down at his sides, and his ears, it seemed, were growing red and ever larger with every step he took. (I can now make out that there are three men here . . . where's Alice gone? I feel quite safe with Alice; I think she must still be behind me . . . and I'm sure I don't at all know who they are. Introductions all round, then, I can only suppose. Dear dear. All I really wanted was a maybe not so quick and intimate word with Lucas.) Who was standing, now – his arm extended by way of warm salutation (that, thought Jamie, might more or less be how Lucas himself would have put it; no – he would have done it, oh – so much better than that).

'My dear *Dear*,' Lucas greeted him. 'Come and meet the family. You have, I take it, *come* . . .? You are *here*?'

Jamie nodded briskly. 'Yes yes. Yes, Lucas, I um . . . yes.'

'So. The inevitability has finally come to pass.'

An inevitability, then – and one that has finally come to pass. And so it was, was it, so very inevitable? So utterly stark and clear to if not just everyone, then certainly to Lucas? That I would come, and alone. That Caroline would so certainly – one day and some time – leave me? Apparently, yes.

'Yes, Lucas, yes. You maybe have known all along.'

But I can't, Lucas, go *into* it – much as I admit I had been

45

yearning to do. I mean, Christ – who *are* all these people? Just standing around and staring at me.

'Well welcome,' said Lucas. 'Alice – a glass for our good friend Dear, here. Now, let us get down to acquainting everyone with everyone else, shall we? Jamie Dear – a printer by trade, I think I am correct in saying? Here we have Mister Paul Theme with his inseparable cohorts, Biff and Tubby. Or, if you prefer, Dracula and Frankenstein. Alice I think you know.'

Hands were extended, together with the odd good-humoured if somewhat clumsy exclamation. Jamie accepted eagerly from Alice the proffered tall and cool flute of champagne.

'From where we all hail, we forbear to enquire,' continued Lucas, rather grandly (just as Tubby's sideways glance fleetingly collided with Biff's: Biff didn't know for sure what it might be Tubby was thinking, like, but what is occurring to *me* now, anyway, is no more than this: Lucas Cage, right? He always talk like this, or what? And if I got this right off of Pauly, he's offering us all, this bloke – no questions asked – a bloody great loft thing in this here very building where we're gonna be left in peace to get on quietly with all we got to do. Well *why*, then? Ay? I mean – what's the thinking behind it? Not in no way *normal*, is it? What's he going to get out of it? Big questions, these, my way of reckoning: put them to Pauly later on, is what I'll do, we ever get out of this room. Been stood here now like a bunch of prawns for bloody ages; it's almost like, I don't know – we're all just waiting to be dismissed, or something. Just like school. On the plus side, this Alice woman is busy coming round with refills of fizz – so stick out the glass and show willing, must be favourite for now, my way of thinking. What's she to him, then, you think? Not wife – no way. Does what he says, don't she? More like some sort of secretary, or something).

'Do you simply adore the flowers, Dear? They are the work of young Theme here, I am very proud to say.'

Jamie's eyes were as wide as those of a culprit, fearful of a rude unmasking. Flowers? There are flowers? Oh yeh – there – there they are, the flowers. Ugly great brownish things, dumped in a bucket.

'Yes. Nice,' he said, quite airily. 'Or they will be, when you've sort of *done* them, anyway. Do you mind if I smoke, Lucas? Can I?'

Most people contented themselves with a low and knowing titter or so. Not Paul, though: Paul didn't.

'Smoking, Dear, is one of the things we must speak of. Do sit, won't you?' Lucas suggested, as he settled himself back behind the surface of his desk (and his hands were flat upon it again, all fingers splayed out). 'Our formal list of, um – conventions to be maintained by us all will be circulated in due course. Alice, I think I am correct in saying, is hard at work upon this very thing almost as we speak. Is that not so, Alice? Quite. But for now I will briefly outline one or two of the more salient points. Now I realize that many people here will be keen to carry on their interests – we have many working artists, I am delighted to say. Dear Alice, for one. And among them not least is Theme, here. Correct, Theme?'

'Well . . .' stumbled out Paul. 'If you can call decor – doing up places, and that – *art* . . . well yeh. Suppose so.'

'A noble art,' Lucas assured him. 'And one that will come into its own very soon, I fancy. We shall all be eager, I feel sure, to be permitted to draw upon your very considerable talents. Young Tubby, here . . . or shall I call you Slim? Remind you of the old school, hey? Anyway – our good friend here is a remarkable cook, I am assured by Theme. And that, Slim, bestows upon you the ranking of one of the most important members of all, in this little community of ours.'

'Yeh . . .?' responded Tubby, genuinely amazed. 'Um – why is that then? I don't quite get . . .'

'Because, dear Slim, you will be catering to us all!'

47

Tubby glanced over at Paul, but there was nothing for him at all, there: complete blank wall.

'Oh . . . yeh? What – sort of, what . . .? You mean we . . .?'

'We all,' supplied Lucas with a flourish, 'dine together, quite so. In the evenings only, of course. During the day everyone is perfectly at liberty to attend to their own domestic arrangements. But I really do believe it to be quite *key*, you know, for us all to congregate around the table for dinner. I am quite convinced that it is what binds a family together. Friend Killery is our current resident chef. Dear Killery. His enthusiasm, I fear, is not quite equalled by his capabilities – as I am sure he would be the very first to own. The heart isn't really *there*, I feel. Alice too has rallied round from time to time – a vast improvement, I have to say – but her duties are various, yes, and simply there are not enough hours in the day. So you see, Slim, we need you. Yes? Comfortable with all of this, are we? Yes?'

'I, um – well, if everybody's . . . yeh, suppose so. Try not to be responsible for a mass outbreak of *poisoning*, anyway . . .'

'Ha! Don't listen to him,' put in Paul. 'He's a right bleeding miracle in the kitchen, old Tubby is. If you'll pardon my wossname . . .'

'I'm sure you're right,' smiled Lucas. 'As very very soon we shall have the privilege of discovering for ourselves. Now – a few more points, very very rapidly. I have been watching with deep sympathy, my dear Dear, the way you have been agitating your left-hand jacket pocket. A packet of twenty and a lighter, if I'm not much mistaken?'

Jamie exhaled in a rush. 'I'm gasping,' he admitted.

'Alas, alas – it cannot be done. Come come, Dear – don't look so crestfallen. Let me explain it to you, yes? This is a rather ancient building, as you are well aware – much wood, as you see. Floors, staircases – even the old lifts. And not so many dividing walls. It would, I feel, be an unacceptable risk for us all – quite apart from the far graver risk to yourself, Dear. Also . . . I confess to finding it a disagreeable habit. But it is a small price to pay, as you will I am sure come to see, for all the glories you will reap in return. Think of it as a means of prolonging your life within a fine environment. Yes?'

All eyes fell upon Jamie, and he felt it acutely. Even the *thought* of not smoking had rendered him practically incoherent. His hands were trembling badly, and his lips were, oh God – simply all over the place.

'I – just don't *know*, Lucas . . .' he quavered. 'I mean I just don't think I can . . . Christ.'

'It is amazing, you know,' said Lucas, quite kindly, 'the extent of our capabilities, our resolve, if the prize is seen to justify the pain. I for myself have the very fullest confidence in you, Dear. Now – to other business.'

'Would you, um – mind very much, Lucas,' rattled out Jamie, 'if I just, er – quickly popped out for a moment? I have to . . . It's just that I've remembered there's something I just must, um . . .'

'Off you go, Dear!' sang out Lucas, really quite gaily. 'Shall we expect you for dinner?'

'I, er – *yes*, Lucas. Yes. Thank you. That would be, um . . . It's just that – sorry, everyone. Alice. Right now I just must –'

'Quite understood. Farewell for now, Dear. So, Slim – that's one more place for this evening. Killery will be here, as usual, along with Oona. Charming people – charming. You, Theme, might well have things in common with Killery. Very consumed with the style and artefacts from the nineteen-forties – is that not right, Alice? The whole of the period, really. Sure you'll get on. Old man Barrington and his current delight, Frankie – they'll be here too. He really is quite irrepressible, Barrington – no idea where he gets such stamina. Along with the others . . . all of them quite delightful, I do assure you. I shall supply you, Slim, with a final tally in very good time, so please do not concern yourself on that particular score. Simply do me the kindness of steering clear of any form of offal, yes? Offal I simply cannot abide. In all other directions, please do feel free to indulge all of your culinary ambitions, yes? To the full. Alice will serve as your exchequer. Excellent. Now, gentlemen – Dear has now left us and is no doubt very busy further torturing his lungs, so Alice – please do advise him later, yes? Of what I now have to say. Now I realize you all have various affairs to attend to, shall we say, but there can be no computers here, I fear. Yes yes – I witness your expressions of, what? If not horror, then certainly surprise – and I confess I antici- pated just such a reaction. But I must be firm. No Internet – nothing of this kind. The Works, you see, must not be – *invaded* by elsewhere. I feel this most strongly. We must be inviolate. Quite separate – standing alone. If you do not see this now, you will come to in time, please believe me.'

'Oh well now look, Lucas . . .' came Paul's rather hesitant objec- tion. 'I mean – I sort of, yeh – get what you're on about, because it is, yeh – well special, this old place. Caught it from the off: *whap*. But see – all my, like, database . . . I just don't see how I can . . .'

'You have a formal company, do you then, Theme?' Lucas enquired quite politely.

'Well . . . I dunno about *formal* – what you quite mean by *formal*, like – but yeh. Got me own business, sort of style. Headed paper, and that. "Theme's Schemes" is what it is. It's the three of us, basically.'

Lucas became thoughtful. 'Mm. "Theme's Schemes", ay? And obviously you considered this a rather *good* choice of name for a company, yes I see. But listen, dear Theme – companies such as yours, interior designers and so forth – Colefax & Fowler is one such eminent example, I believe: I don't know whether you're familiar . . .?'

'Don't think I know the guys. Where they drink?'

'No matter. The point I am making, Theme, is that such concerns existed very well before the advent of technology, and I have no doubt that yours will continue to prosper under similar limitations. It means, of course, that you have to get out and about rather more, but this can surely only be a benefit, no? Meeting the client, face to face? But gentlemen – enough, for now. I am sure we all have duties that must be attended to. Do please feel free to discuss matters between yourselves in your own good time. We shall reconvene at dinner. Slim – Alice, I do assure you, will shortly be in touch. Yes? Good. Excellent. Until then, Theme. Mister Biff. Slim. Farewell, one and all.'

Paul raised a hand, and they all turned to go – Biff busy thinking Well thank bloody Christ *that's* all bloody over: Christ Almighty, he sure can talk, that bloke, that's for bloody sure (thought we'd be stood standing there best part of the night). The chief thing hammering away at Tubby was going like this: Mm, yeh, OK – that's all very well, but look: *I* smoke – I do. Don't have to have one on all the time – nothing like that – but I do, me, enjoy my quiet little fag, time to time, I don't mind saying – as I bloody well intend to go on doing. I mean yeh, OK – this place: godsend, right? Couldn't have come at a better time – just you ask Pauly. Jesus. But still – there's got to be a bleeding limit. I mean – what? This Lucas guy – he catch me with my Bensons: what he gonna do? Bung me in *detention*? Have me writing out *lines*? And what I have to go and mention bloody *'Slim'* for, ay? Stuck with it, now. And Christ – my name's bloody *Tubby*. Got to have a little word with Pauly – get some ground rules sorted, here. See what's what. Looking well thoughtful, Pauly is (do you know what? We been trudging along now, the three of us, seems like half a bloody hour, and only now we've reached the bloody door. Looks like Pauly's got a spot of bother on getting the fucker to open).

How's this handle work, then? That's what Paul was trying to get his mind round. Do I twist the bastard this way, or what do I do? Like a bloody safe. Ah no – hang about – here we go: yeh, that's got it. Turn and wave now, will I? Yeh – be nice. He been nice to us, ain't he? This Lucas weirdo. And Christ – telling you: I hadn't run into him just the other night in that well dodgy old dive (and what he doing there, ay? Dunno yet) – well like I say, we'd be in dead schtuck, we would, the three of us. We just ran out of places to be. I ain't, you know – religious nor nothing, but I'm telling you it straight, mate: it were like a bleeding miracle, Lucas showing up when he did. So we don't want to go rocking no boats: making waves is out of order. As I got to get well into the thick heads of them two, there.

'So, Alice,' said Lucas. 'What do you think to the newest additions to our little flock? Our band of brothers and sisters.'

Alice laughed. 'You sound like the Abbot of some very ancient and venerable *chapter*, Lucas,' she said, while carefully mixing for him another of his drinks – just two fingers of Tanqueray gin, topped up with barely warm oolong tea; half a sugar cube, then, and briskly stirred with a long silver spoon.

'You are getting to know me,' smiled Lucas. 'You were aware that such an image would please me. Are you not having anything, Alice? Nothing for yourself?'

'I've got a drop of champagne here still, darling – and then I really have to get on. I never quite understand why there's always so much to do around here. But there is. I maybe might go on strike.'

Lucas sipped his drink. 'Dear Alice,' he said.

Alice smiled, and bent low to – what? Maybe kiss him. Lucas

did nothing until he felt the imminence of her shadow dulling his face. He swivelled quickly towards the window and spread wide his arms.

'The light! The *light*,' he exclaimed, 'is truly one of the most wondrous features of this extraordinary place. Don't you think so, Alice?'

Alice straightened herself (hastily pulled out of her foolish, stooped position) and softly she agreed with whatever it was this time that Lucas had uttered: aided and abetted this latest prevarication.

'So,' she said. 'Where did you find this new lot? I *think* they're OK . . . it's difficult, isn't it? With just first impressions to go on. Except you don't feel that, do you ever? Doubt. God, that – *Biff*, was it? Don't think he opened his mouth. Paul seems quite nice, I suppose. Ha! I have to say I agree with Jamie about the *flowers*, though: they didn't look done to *me*, either. Do you think he's really capable, Jamie? Giving up smoking?'

'I think . . .' said Lucas, slowly, 'that I understand what maybe drives him, young Theme. A vague and semi-insight into his passions, conceivably. I myself think the flowers look rather wonderful. As I said. And *Dear*, well – love him though I do, we would never seek in that direction, would we, any form of aesthetic *understanding*, I think that is clear. I am surprised, you know, he didn't join us sooner. I expect in some very tedious and bourgeois way he had to justify such a thing to himself. Or, more likely, await the marital expulsion. Caroline doesn't actually hate him, I feel – though I can see how she might well find him unbearable. As to the smoking – he'll do what I say.'

Alice did not immediately respond. And then she did.

'So I suppose the same is true of me, then. Is it?'

'Forgive me, Alice . . . I don't quite, um . . .?'

'Well – about Jamie and the flowers. He thought they were just a load of lilies thrown into a bucket, and so do I. So I suppose that makes me a –'

'Ah I see. Dear Alice. No no.'

'But you *said*, Lucas – you *said*. You said, oh – what did you say? No aesthetic *something*, you said. So that means that you regard *me* as having no sort of . . . *look*, Lucas – !'

'Alice. Calm yourself.'

'Well I *will*, Lucas – I will, I expect – I daresay I soon will, yes, be calm and everything – but just now at this very moment I am feeling very uncalm *indeed*, actually – and I would like you to just tell me this right here and now since we're actually just the two of us talking without all the, oh – *brethren* all over the place . . . just *tell* me, Lucas, if you don't think I'm good enough for you . . . to be here . . . because if you do – if you *do* think that, Lucas, well then I . . . I . . .'

'What, Alice? What? You what, in fact?'

Alice looked full at him, as her eyes clogged up with tears and her neck seemed to sag down under the weight of her head which she shook from side to side – maybe out of despair, or else a lingering hope.

'I . . . I . . . I just simply couldn't *bear* it. If. You thought that.'

Lucas's head was wagging almost in time with hers. A tight smile had compressed his lips into a hard near-whiteness, though a light was glowing dully in his eyes. He stood before her, and Alice looked up into those unfathomable eyes of his, beseechingly. She could not say what it was she quite needed to receive (now, at this moment, yes – or ever) but still she was again, once more, so aware that it was *something* . . .

Lucas lifted up her hand, stared intently at the dappled knuckles and brought down his lips to briefly brush them.

'Alice,' he whispered. 'You *belong* here . . .'

And her eyes, for a moment, were alight. Then they flattened back down again, still wet and opaque, the corners dipping sadly.

54

'Along,' she said woodenly, 'with all the others. Yes?' And then she looked up at him, her eyes wide now with anxiety. 'Does it make you . . .? Lucas? All this. The Works. All your . . . people. It makes you *happy*, does it? You're happy now, are you? I mean I *think* you are – you seem to be, sometimes . . . but what do you *feel*, Lucas? You never ever tell me what you *feel* . . .! I'm not like you, darling – I can't . . . perceive. I need to be *told*.'

'It is solely the fact,' he said – low, and very gravely, 'that I feel at all. You see. That is the wonder.'

And then he was animated, and he so suddenly clutched hold of her hand that she gasped.

'Come. I've got something to show you. Something no one else has ever seen. This – this, Alice, is just for you, I swear it. Come. Come.'

And just these words laid siege to Alice, and she was thrilling to the moment as Lucas propelled her out on to the balcony just beyond that half-glazed jib door, there, to the side of the largest window of all. Alice was laughing like a drunk, now, as her cheeks were slapped by coldness, and she screwed up her eyes in the dazzle of the milky, yes, but fiercely glinting sun, so unnaturally bright. Lucas still was excitedly tugging her behind him as they stumbled along the clanking iron gangway – and Alice was just so very eager to be taken now wherever on earth he cared to lead her. The firm and insistent grasp of his hand made her feel charged and so sure-footed that had Lucas made to leap now out into the glaring open void and still not let go of her hand, then she would in near-ecstasy have hurtled on down with him and eagerly to a crunching spattered death (as if her very life had depended upon it).

Lucas had stopped, now, at the foot of a wooden stairway so narrow and sheer as to be not much more than a near-vertical ladder, as maybe on a ship.

'What is this? Lucas – I've never seen this before. Where does it lead?'

Lucas turned to face her. A sudden icy breeze had lifted up his hair, and this – with the raw agitation all over his face – made him appear to her as something like wild.

'You have to,' he cautioned her slowly, 'from this moment on, be utterly, utterly silent. Understand? No noise whatever.'

Alice was nodding, her eyes caught up in this new contagion of shared excitement, even as she was stuttering at him But *why* Lucas – why? I don't understand – why won't you tell me why?

'Trust me,' he said.

And she did. He led the way up – one thin and bowing tread at a time, each one moaning – and Alice, blanking out the whiff of trepidation, followed on gamely. But her need to discover was tempered now by unignorable qualms – which she knew was foolish, but she felt them anyway. The wind was now buffeting the two of them harshly, and she glanced once upwards to be sure of Lucas, and then just briefly down, to see how far she'd come. A thump of panic struck her throat as she swam in the vision of steep and spinning distance and just those silver spangles of the motley river violently askew and jaggedly interspersed with hard and crude unfamiliar angles. Above her was the deep streaked sky and nothing else at all. Lucas had vanished – gone from her sight completely. She might well then have frozen for ever or just let go, had not a hand thrust out now – it was reaching down for her from within a darkened hutch she had not seen. Lucas's whole arm was circling jerkily and with seeming impatience, urging her to grasp – a tacit underlining of the absolute silence demanded.

Alice gripped his forearm tightly and clambered up the last two steps while huffing with energy from the side of her mouth in a quite useless attempt to rid her eyes and mouth of the frizzed-up snatches of her hair that the squalls of wind had tossed up into a mad abandon. As her face drew level with Lucas's insistent and glittering eyes, she saw them narrow into further warning, as one straight finger he placed on his lips. Alice scrambled up and was hauled the rest of the way into what seemed to be no more than a cramped and blackened loft. She crouched at Lucas's side, waiting and expectant. For what seemed like many long minutes, she stayed down low – her awkwardly bent over ankle and calf threatening more and serious pain, but still she would not shift. She gently tugged at Lucas's sleeve and dared to utter (so muted was her voice, it was barely more than breathing):

'Lucas . . . what is it? I'm a bit frightened . . .'

The gloom was – was it? – gradually dispersing, though she sensed rather than saw Lucas shaking his head. Then he turned and said to her, low and slowly:

'Look. There. Do you see . . .?'

Alice peered into the distance. She was aware now of a musty smell and warmth around her – dry old wood and maybe a low-note of rot, the humming scent of sweet decay. Before her were only colliding shades of greyness, hardly discernible nuances of dark, and she came so close to sobbing with exasperation at her stark and total *stupidity*: why in the name of God can I not *share* this with Lucas? But listen! A faraway movement way down there now made her tauten; there came from out of her now a small and wholly involuntary 'O' of alarm and bad surprise and she clutched at Lucas more tightly as she became aware of just the hint of a lazy shifting, that swiftly died back down into silence again. Her leg was now near breaking beneath her.

'There,' urged Lucas, so gently. 'See it? *There* . . .'

And then she did: two little glinting yellow-white lights within a just guessed-at and formless mass of something barely darker than all that surrounded it – then an almost undulation, that softly settled down.

'What . . . is it?' whispered Alice.

Lucas's breathing was level and low. 'Them,' he said. 'There are two . . .'

And Alice blinked. 'Two? Really? Two . . . what?'

Lucas might have nodded. 'Owls. Barn owls. Just a few hundred breeding pairs in the whole of the kingdom . . .'

Alice said nothing. She could think of nothing to say.

'And these . . .' went on Lucas, so softly, 'these two . . . are ours.'

Alice carefully shifted her leg, stretching it away from her and some way to the side; it was either that or suddenly screaming.

Lucas turned to her and placed his lips so tantalizingly close to one of her ears. All she heard breathed into her was the sound of a hornet, caught in a jar . . . *jizz* . . .

'What?' she whispered. 'What, Lucas? Did you say?'

'*Jizz* . . .' said Lucas again. 'A birder's term. The way certain types behave. In or out of their usual environment.'

She felt his grip on her arm grow tighter. Alice was briefly distracted by a muted sort of scuffling, momentary and distant, and then it faded. And all that way away, those two yellow eyes just hung there, stark and unblinking – and Lucas's too, as Alice could well imagine, were quite as hard and bright. She barely heard him when he spoke to her again, so thickened and deep his voice had become.

'The owls, Alice. The owls now are a part of it too.' And then, with an added intensity: 'They all of them have to be *cared* for, you know.'

CHAPTER TWO

'*Look . . .!*' insisted Paul.

And then he sighed and glanced about him, maybe seeking fresh inspiration; the sigh still whistled – seemed to momentarily reverberate around the deep green walls of this cavernous bathroom. Because Jesus – this had to be about the third time now he'd tried to make bloody old Tubby see the sense of it. Couldn't understand why he was making such a bloody fuss about nothing.

'All I'm saying, yeh, is that we stick our heads round the door and say hi, that's all. Not saying you got to *love* them, am I? And then you get to know all the doo-dah about this cooking lark and we come over as all sort of friendly, like. We don't wanna go looking like we're *hiding*, Tubs: told you. Important, yeh? When you're all, like, open about stuff – people, they don't hardly notice you're alive. It's when you got your head down – ducking and diving. Know what I mean? When you're, like, slamming doors in people's faces – that's when they starts to going Here – what's his game? What's it all about, Alfie? What's them blokes up to, then? Human thing, that is. Well standard.'

'Yeh – I hear what you're saying, Paul. I'm not stupid – I know what you mean. I'm just not happy. Less you say to anyone, the better.'

Tubby shifted himself from his perch at the edge of the huge and cast-iron roll-top bath and deftly flicked his cigarette end into the lavatory bowl. Even before it briefly sizzled, he was hurriedly glancing this way and that (expecting what, exactly?) and with one hand he feebly swiped at any telltale traces of lingering sin. Paul came over from the big chrome heated towel rail (bleeding hell – done a fair old job of barbecuing my bum, that has – you don't notice how hot the bugger is, telling you, till you peels yourself off of it). He placed a fraternal arm as far as he could reach across Tubby's considerable shoulders.

'*Nature*,' he said, while fairly boisterously jostling and hugging him (bringing him round to his way of thinking). 'Only human *nature*, ain't it? Hey? Course it is. Look – all we do is, we knock on the door, OK – we go Wotcha Mister Killery! I'm Paul – this here's Tubby, how's it going? OK? How's the missus? Doing all right? And that's it. You sweet with that, Tubs? *Course* you are, son. Where's the down side, ay? Then we get ourselves back to old Biff – see what he's up to, silly bastard. Plus, let's be honest – you got to know what you're in for, aintcha? Now you're all set to do a Delia.'

'Yeh and that's another thing,' piped up Tubby, all of his grievances back to the fore. 'What you have to go shouting your head off about my bleeding cooking for? Ay? Christ – I ain't *that* good. And how many people are there in this bleeding place anyway? Could be bleeding hundreds of them. Bloody hell . . .'

'Don't you go giving me none of that, Tubby! You're a bloody artist behind that stove, you are, and you bloody well know it. And what you talking about *hundreds*? It's only the one bleeding building, innit? You ain't doing Meals on Wheels.'

'Yeh well it's a bloody *big* building, innit? Any road, I ain't doing nothing fancy . . .' grumbled Tubby. 'Here – I knew a bloke once what done Meals on Wheels. Way he drove – dear oh Lord. Most of it was all over the shop, time he got there. Says to me what he done was, he scoops it all up and shove it them anyway. Never got no complaints.'

'Joking. But see, what it is, Tubs – why I marked your card: I felt

I had to give the man something. See? When he, like, sort of said it to me about the place, I was going Yeh, well nice, I'll have us some of that. But I were getting this sort of feeling that this guy Lucas, all right – he was after knowing what we was gonna sort of put back into it, yeh? So I hit him with all the decor lark, course I did – but you can't be arsing about with furniture and dumping a load of flowers in a bucket for too long, can you? But food, well – that's got to be different, hasn't it? Funny though, weren't it? The way he keep banging on about them lilies. I just bought this bloody great load up the Columbia Road and stuck them in the first thing I claps eyes on. He goes on like it's bleeding Michelangelo, or something.'

'Yeh? Well why were you doing all that about the stems and all the rest of that bollocks then, Paul? You had me going there, you did.'

Paul laughed. 'Yeh. I thought I was pretty fair. Dunno. Reckon I must've read it somewhere, or something. I just reckoned he wanted it. So look – sod all that. What about it, Tubs? Ay? Let's go and meet with this Killery bloke and his wife, bird, whatever. It's only being sociable. You know it makes sense.'

Tubby nodded, slowly. 'Yeh. OK. Suppose you're right. But listen, Paul – listen. This Lucas guy, right? I mean – you must've been thinking this and all. It's a bit bloody funny, innit? How's he get off on it, ay? I mean – what's it all about? And don't go saying "Alfie" like you always bleeding do – gets right up my nose. You reckon he's a nutter? Gotta be, hasn't he? How you meet him anyway? What – he just come up to you in this club then, did he? What he say?'

'Well basically,' shrugged Paul, 'he just says to me – You wanna come and doss in The Works? The Works, I go – what's that, then? And he sort of fills me in – and I gets to thinking, don't I? Thinking, yeh. And I go Yeh, sounds favourite, Lucas – but I got these mates, see. Cuppla mates. Fine, he says – no probs: bring

61

them along and all. I thought he was pissed, maybe. Well out of it. Yeh. Anyways – we're here now, ain't we? And basically that's gotta be what it's all about. Alfie.'

Except that, well, that's not quite all of it – how it had gone down with Lucas that night. Not if I'm standing before my Maker with my hand on my wossname. I mean – I give him the *bones*, Tubby, yeh . . . but I reckon I go the extra mile and it's only gonna mess up his head. Cos I'm not that well sure, if I'm honest, I get it all myself. See, first off – I got this sort of, well – *problem's* going it a bit strong. More a sort of a, what? Question mark, could be. Something I maybe got to go off quiet and sort of work it out on my own, like. Get it sorted. And Biff and Tubby, they don't know nothing about it, right – and I got anything to do with it, that's how it's bloody gonna stay. Because, see, they wouldn't get it – they'd get it all wrong. And yeh, like I say – I don't really get it myself, and that's why it wants looking in to. Come over me quite recent, all of this, if I'm honest. While back, I catch one of my mates going on the way I been going on just lately . . . well, wouldn't give him the time of day, I'm telling you. I know some people what might reckon he'd be in line for a bit of a slap. And Biff and Tubby – they're the same (course they are – why bleeding wouldn't they be? Cos *I'm* like that, basically) – and so what we got us here is a case of total schtum, yeh? Till I, like, get my head round it, one way or the other. Cos I got to be honest – like this I don't like it (you know what I'm saying?).

So this club, right – bloody stupid name like what most of them got: Ragout, they call it (and I couldn't have told you, mate, how you're sort of meant to say it, like, or nothing). I think I maybe must've got a whisper about it from a friend of a friend, sort of style, yeh – and for ages I didn't do nothing about it on account of I was right bleeding petrified, you want me to be straight with you. What, I was going – it's what, exactly, this club? It's not all full of manky nonces, is it? Cos I can't be doing with none of that.

Nah, this bloke's going – it's not nothing like that, that's the whole thing, point: different, see? There's gels there and everything, he goes to me – it's just all a bit blurry, if you know what I'm saying. Dee-jay's magic. Plus they do a proper cask Fuller's, you interested, and the dancing scene, man – it's well wicked, telling you: this ain't no lie. Plus, round the back, they got all-right nosh (you up for it). So yeh – sounded OK, didn't it? Not too bad. Maybe just the job. But I don't know if you, you know, get like what I do – just sort of not doing nothing about it, like, on account of maybe hoping, I don't know – that something's gonna, like, happen, or something, or just that the kind of wanting to, yeh, it maybe sort of goes away. This went on I don't know how long. Then just last week, Sonia, right – Sonia, you got to know, she's my pretty much regular lady, OK, though we never, like, lived together, nor nothing like that – she says she's fucking off up her mother's (some sort of family-type thing going down, I didn't too much listen to her, you want me to be honest with you) and I just went Yeh OK then darling – and I'm thinking Yeh all right then, fair enough – this weekend I check it out, why don't I? Cos come on: what's it gonna cost me? Ay? I don't like it, I just get myself back outside again, yeh? Slip off down the boozer – get well wasted with a couple mates (Biff and Tubby, shouldn't at all wonder – cos what it is now is, well – we're sort of like a band of brothers, if that don't come over too manky; we, like, look out for one another, sort of style – except it's me what does most of the looking, I got to say. Tubs don't sometimes see things the way they are, see – head-on, and real, like; and Biff, well – he's a good old lad, but he ain't no Brain of Britain, if you know what I mean. But we're mates, basically, is what I'm saying – me and Biff and Tubby, yeah: thick as thieves).

So before I got meself down the 'Ragout' (oh dear oh dear) I thought Hang up, son – what am I gonna wear to it then, ay? How I wanna come across? Usual run of it, I don't never have no problems on that front cos I sort of got down a style of my own, if you know what I'm saying. I'm pretty into clothes and that, you want the truth – and yeh, I come in for a fair bit of old stick from the lads (but blimey – Biff, telling you, sometimes you'd swear he got all his gear down the Kentish Town Oxfam in the middle of a bleeding blackout). But me, well – I do punt out a fair old wedge on threads, I'm not denying. Well be fair – it's part of what I am, see. And I'm telling you – you need all the help you can get, cos some of these dozy tossers up West – because I don't talk like what they do . . . because I don't go poncing about going Oh *rarely* how perfectly *gorstly* . . . because I just come out with it, ordinary like – they think I don't got no sense, or something. Think I'm pig-stupid. Well stupid I ain't – but I do, I do really go for nice things, you know? And I'm good at what I do – colour schemes, lighting (flowers and all, apparently – which I did not know). Fact is, I sometimes think I should have stuck to it – not let all the other take over. But you get greedy, don't you? Human thing, that is. Nature. But I was one time pulling down a fair old whack with Theme's Schemes, you know; it weren't nothing fancy, I'm not saying that (weren't big time) – but word was getting about, if you know what I'm saying. But yeh – trouble is, you get a little bit of a tickle out of something what ain't quite kosher and, well – you don't too much mind, do you, the cash in hand, no questions asked. And like I say – I do go big time on quality gear, yeh? And quality gear, as we all know too bloody well: it don't come cheap. Some days, though, if I'm honest, I could jack it all in – just get shot of the pressure, you know? Always that having to be one jump ahead, looking over your shoulder (ducking, yeh, and diving) – wondering who you can talk to, trying to work out when to stay schtum. Yeh well. I reckon it's a bit late now, don't you? Up to my bleeding neck, aren't I? Tell me about it.

So what I go for in the end is a very nice charcoal Armani two-piece, yeh? White silk turtleneck what don't have no label but make no mistake, son – top of the range (word was, some ware-house got done over round Staples Corner and I tell you, mate – I were in like Flynn). Plus I always make sure the shoes are well shiny – ankle boots, they was, with zippers, if we're being wossname: Bally, but I'm not a slave to it. Also, I got a Cartier watch; everyone's got it down as a Sexton, but it ain't – it's proper, that watch is. Got it off of this geezer not too long back as part of a, shall we say, little outstanding debt. Yeh. Else I would've set Biff on him, poor bugger – and it were a laugh, really, cos Biff, yeh? Sometimes he's real in the mood, you know? And this night, yeh, he was well up for having some of that – but nah: bloke saw reason, didn't he? My experience, people do, when their noses are pressed right in it. Well face it – what you want a nice watch for, if your arms is broke? And it's got a crocodile strap (which is tasty).

I nearly didn't go in. Walked past the door got to be twice, didn't it? Cuppla bleeding bouncers, weren't there? So I had to work out good and fast what they was looking for (what they wasn't). Seemed a fair old place, though, apart from the muscle. No sort of neon or nothing – weren't no thumpy music coming out of it. So I works me way back – and yeah: magic – sweet as you like. Geezers nod me in like I'm a regular, or something. Maybe they reckoned I was. So I go down the stairs, like (and I'm still thinking to myself, aren't I? This some poncey dive, then I'm right out of here fast as bleeding lightning). But do you know what? Hey? Tell you: The Ragout, it only turns out to be the nicest bar (club – whatever) I ever been to – real class, it is (you wanna maybe get yourself down there – you might be doing yourself a favour). You got leather – what are they? Along the walls, like, and in the little booths. Bonkits. Something. Buttoned red leather – very choice. And you had these lovely orange lamps all over – set real low and cosy, like. Bar itself was all brown and glossy, like one of them old-fashioned ships, yeh? And the geezer behind it, right – he had on him one of them little wine-coloured bum-

65

freezer jackets with black wossnames and gold buttons on it like what you see in them old movies about Manhattan, and that. Blimey, I was going – I really like it here: this I really like. So I orders a martini (nah – it ain't my usual, course it bleeding ain't. But I thought it'd be nice: it just seemed right, yeh?). And it come in one of them little sort of triangular glasses (well – not like a *triangle*, course not – but I reckon you know what I'm on about) and there was this red and green olive on a stick. I ain't never had one of them before, and I'm telling you – I ain't in no big hurry for another, you know what I'm saying? Next drink I had, I parks the olive in the ashtray there, look.

So I gets to having a shufti. Sort of half full – little one-to-ones going on, nothing heavy. Lot of straights in suits. Or maybe not so straight, who's to say? But you'd never know nothing to look at them. Fact is, he was dead right, this mate of a mate – there was plenty of gels; groups of three and four seemed to be favourite: fair enough. One or two of them was looking over, like – and one or two of the blokes, and all. And I liked it, really, cos I sort of got it. I mean – one guy there, yeh? Really nice clothes – proper manicure, clean sort of thick quite long hair, yeh? Now normally, you don't want to go looking, right? Not unless you're after your neck in a collar and a couple of crutches. But it was OK, here. Here it was kind of natural. So I sips my martini, and I'm thinking Well what do I do? Talk to someone? Not talk to someone? What's the set-up here? How's it meant to go? And that's when I claps eyes on Lucas. Just a couple of stools away, he was – and it's funny, he looked that sort of settled – it was like he'd been sat there staring at me since I first come in and I never ever clocked him up till now. He lifts up his glass. So I thought All right, then – and I lifts up mine, and my lips are sort of going Cheers, mate. Then he come over, don't he? Bleeding hell, is how I'm thinking – what is now occurring? What is going down? I ain't never been in this sort of a position before, so I'm jumpy, just a bit, yeh – but *cool*, you know? I guess what it is is, I'm kinda curious: see how it all shakes out, sort of style.

He's sat up next to me, Lucas is – course, I didn't know he was called Lucas, not then I didn't. And I just thought Yeah – decent-looking bloke, nicely turned out (bob or two, look of that suit). I thought he might've, I don't know – gone something like *Well*: I don't reckon I seen you in here before, have I? Or some other naff old cobblers. But he never. He just got on with his drink – some orangey sort of muck, looked like (never did get to know what). And eventually he says: Well. Well, he says. And I'm thinking: Yeah? Yeah? Well what, then? Hey? Well what? But nah. Well nothing, mate: well sod all. Clammed right up, he did. And I tell you this – I couldn't hardly believe it when I hear myself going: My name's Paul. So he nods. Still ain't saying nothing – just nodding; staring at his glass and nodding away, there. And then he's, like – What's your second name? And I just thought Oh yeah? What's that about, then? Bit out of order, ain't it? Place like this. So I thought I better come up with some sort of fake name, or something, but as it turned out, I never. Dunno why. I just says Theme. Is who I am. Paul Theme. And there he is on the nodding jag again. Then he turns round to me and he goes:

'Well, Theme – delighted to make your acquaintance. Lucas.'

'Lucas. Yeh? What – that's your second name and all, then, is it? That some sort of rule round here?'

'No no. No rule. There are no rules in The Ragout – barring proper decorum, quite naturally. No, I fear it is simply a peccadillo. I thank you for indulging it, Theme. A further martini, perhaps?'

'Yeh. Ta. I don't mind one. They sort of hit the spot, if you know what I'm saying.'

Lucas ordered the martini, and the barman raised his eyebrows enquiringly as he pointedly glanced at Lucas's tall and narrow tumbler. By way of reply, Lucas flattened his fingers across the rim, and briefly closed his eyes.

'Reside in the vicinity, do you Theme?'

'Nah. What – live round here, you mean? Nah. Little bit out of my bracket, mate. Lucas. No – I'm down Willesden way, just for the moment. Dunno for how much longer, though.'

No I bleeding don't. Because I tell you – Wee Davy, right – him what owns the place, yeh? Well he's getting right breezy, Wee Davy is. Pauly – Pauly: when you gonna clear out all this gear?, he's always going. All in good time, Davy – all in good time, I says to the man: can't just offload it overnight, can I? You know that, well as I do. Well I don't know . . ., he starts whining: I don't like it, Pauly – I ain't happy, you hear me? Maybe you be better off with some other gaff, ay? Cos I'm telling you, son – the heat put a finger on me, I'm done for, mate. Ah *can* it, Davy, I goes to him: *paying* you enough, aren't I? Maybe you ain't, he come back: maybe it ain't just about the money no more, Pauly. I go down just one more time and I ain't never gonna see daylight again, son. Yeh well, I go: yeh well. But no come on – leave out all the Sweeney talk: he got a point, Davy has, if I'm being totally honest with you – he got so much previous, well: it's ridiculous, basically. Plus – when people get jumpy like Wee Davy's got jumpy, you don't too much wanna be around them. Not too close. Cos they just might one morning take it into their heads to drop a little word into the wrong ear, see? And my game, you don't take no sort of risks what you don't like kinda have to, if you can get what I'm saying to you, here.

So anyway, Lucas and me – we get to chatting away, like what you do. Well – I *say* chatting. It was only after, I twig! I was doing all the talking (which ain't too much like me, I got to say – but I reckon it were the combination of wossname what got me really going for it: this place, The Ragout . . . and *now* I know how you're meant to say it, on account of Lucas: it's basically 'rag', right, and then you sort of go 'ooh', like, after). Because in this place, like I say, I was feeling real at ease. Plus them martinis – blimey. They warm you up and calm you down and then they let off a bloody Cruise Missile right up your skull. And also, if I'm honest, it was having bleeding Sonia up her mother's – bit of a relief, don't mind telling you. Gets a bit clingy, Sonia does. I mean – nice girl, don't get me wrong or nothing, but blimey – she can't half go on. Telling you – what with her and Wee Davy, just lately, I reckon that a quiet couple of drinks somewhere real nice was just what I was up for. So I'm banging on to Lucas about my doing up of rooms, and that (the bloke I used to be), and then I chucks in a bit about moaning old Davy and Biff and Tubby (not too much – I'm not a mug: said about Tubby's cooking, though, I do remember that much – cos he is, you know: he's a right whizz). Didn't bring up old Sonia, some reason. Sonia, she don't come up.

'So that's sort of about it, Lucas me old mate. You pretty much got the lot there, you have. Life story.'

'And this landlord of yours,' said Lucas. 'Not quite your ideal? I might be in a position to offer something rather more favourable.'

Ay ay, I thought: ay ay – here it is, then. Blimey, I was going – fast worker, ain't he? And telling you – I were just trying to work out in my mind what I was, like – *feeling* about all of this, when bugger me if he don't say something like Oh yeh – and your two friends are also welcome to come along, they fancy it (except he put it, you know – that funny way what he does). Then he fills me in on The Works, he called it – told me where it was, and everything, and then he says So what you reckon? Fancy it, or what? (Well, like I say – what he actually said was all flowery and round-the-houses, like, but that's what it come down to at the end of the day.)

'Well *yeah*, Lucas, but look – I'll be honest with you. I don't at the moment have too much bread, you know? I mean – pretty soon I'm expecting a fair old whack, yeh. But just now, well – boracic ain't in it.'

'Understood,' smiled Lucas. 'I'm not actually asking for money.'

And look – I know it wasn't cool, but I just couldn't help myself: I just laughed right in the geezer's face – straight up, I did.

'Yeh,' I'm going: '*right* . . .!'

'I mean it,' said Lucas. 'No rent would be payable. Food and heating are both supplied. I think you'd like it.'

Paul just eyed him.

'What?' urged Lucas. 'Tell me what it is that's troubling you.'

'Well *look*, um – Lucas. I'm not *saying* nothing, or nothing – right? It's just that, well – you know. Be quite frank with you. This sort of thing . . . it just don't happen, is what I'm saying. People with big and trendy warehouses, or whatever – they don't just go round offering free accommodation to some guy they just met, what, half an hour ago in a . . . I don't know, could be a well dodgy bar, this – what do I know? And then tell him to bring along all his mates all for free and his bleeding sick mother and all.'

'You have a sick mother?'

'No I – *no*, Lucas, I don't. I just –'

'Because if you *do* have a mother who's poorly –'

'No – scrub it, Lucas. I don't. I was just –'

'She'd be entirely welcome, I do assure you.'

'Look – just forget the pigging mother, OK? She don't exist. I'm just – *saying*, that's all. Just *saying* . . .'

'I see,' said Lucas. 'Well look – why don't you and your friends come over one afternoon soon and view the old place? I think you'll be very pleasantly surprised.'

'Yeh but . . . look, Lucas – don't think I'm being . . . I mean, it's well large, all this you're saying, and that . . . but, well – what do you get out of it? What I mean to say is – what do you *want*?'

'Well,' said Lucas. 'Quite simple, really. Anything you are willing to give. Contribute. Interior design – very useful. Your friend's expertise in the kitchen, well – of incalculable value, I do assure you. Maybe a little light sweeping . . .'

Paul turned to look at him, now: really looked full into Lucas's eyes for the very first time. He saw nothing there to shy away from.

'And . . . that's it? You don't want nothing . . . more?'

'I want,' replied Lucas, levelly, 'only what you are eager to give. Nothing further.'

Yeh, Paul was thinking then: yeh. And that's what he was thinking now, and all: because yeh – that's how it had all gone down, all right. But I can't, can I, try and get Tubby's head around that little lot – and as for Biff, oh dear oh dear: please do leave it out. See – *subtleties* would be missed, I try to spell it out. So better I don't cause no confusion. But what I got to do now is get things bleeding *moving*, as per bloody usual.

'So like I say, Tubs – what say you and me go knock him up, ay? This Killery guy, whoever he is. Get it sorted.'

Tubby nodded. 'You say so . . . but listen up, Paul – when we gonna shift some gear, ay? You said we'd do some soon.'

'Oh Gawd don't *you* start! We only just got shot of moaning Wee bloody Davy and now *you're* laying a number on me.'

'It's just that, well – do with a few bob, that's all.'

'Yeh well we all could, Tubs – we all could, all right? You see money coming out of my ears? Do you? *Trust* me, son: working on it, aren't I? Now then – Killery. Yeh?'

'Yeh,' said Tubby. 'Yeh. Here, though – it's a bit of a funny do, all this – ain't it Paul?'

'Yeh,' said Paul. 'Yeh it is. Don't worry. I'll soon have it all sussed. Find out what it's all about . . .'

'Oh don't do it, Paul – beg of you.'

Paul laughed and clapped his old mate across the shoulders and bundled him off down the passage to the foot of the stairs.

'... Alfie,' he went.

They were both still standing outside what Paul had worked out, according to Alice's instructions – unless he'd got the whole bleeding thing all arse over tip, yeh – really did ought to be Killery's door. Should he, what – knock them up again, maybe? Tell you – these apartments, lofts, whatever it was Lucas chose to call them: so bleeding huge, they easily needn't have heard (or maybe one of these here Killerys was still only halfway through the long journey over).

And while they were both still stood there like a couple of lemons, Paul and Tubby (with Tubby, Paul was getting a very strong whiff, going well off the whole bleeding idea – more and more as every second passed: edgy, he was), they were still busy chatting away wossname to the dozen about the girl what they just clapped eyes on – just passed her in the corridor. Blimey, Tubby had gone – just downwind of the still trailing perfume – bleeding hell, Paul ... you clock the buffers on that, or what? Tell you – never reckoned there'd be nothing of that order, here. I somehow thought – I dunno ... I guess I thought everybody'd be some sort of a weirdo or misfit, or something. But Christ – that one, she got all you need: fit in anywhere, that one could. I could well squeeze in meself, Paul, I don't mind telling you, son; legs she got – crack you in half. Yeh, said Paul – yeh, she was all right. And Tubby, he put his eyes through all the fish-faced goggle

72

routine as he chokes out All *right*?! All *right*?! What you bleeding talking about – all *right*?! She was helluva bleeding sight more than all *right*, son – she was mega world-class stonking, that one was. And you see the way she smile at us? That little smile she give us? Yeh? Reckon I could be well in there. She maybe Lucas's little slice of night-time comfort, you reckon? Cos that Alice – bit too much like my old geography teacher, Alice is, but this one, well – different league, ain't she? Tell you what she reminded me of a little bit, Paul – your Sonia. Well, in the face department, leastways – same sort of hair, and that; I mean – don't get me wrong or nothing, Paul, but well – you gotta face it, haven't you son? Nice girl, Sonia, I'm not saying – but she ain't your standard issue pole dancer, is she? Ay? Is all I'm saying to you, mate. I mean . . . well easy on the eye, no danger – but she ain't no centrefold, is she? And Paul said No – no she ain't. And Tubby said Here – talking of Sonia: she dossing down with us here and all is she, or what? And Paul said Nah – nah, Tubby, she ain't. And Tubby said But you told her, right? Like – where you was going to be hanging? And Paul just shook his head and said No I never, matter of fact. And Tubby said But she's gonna be worried, ain't she? She come back from up her mother's and finds you just up sticks and scarpered, she gonna get the hump, ain't she? Can't blame the gel. Reckon you wanna give her a bell, son. And Paul said Look – just leave it, OK Tubs? Ain't nothing to do with you, is it? And Tubby said I were just *saying*, Paul, that's all . . . and Paul, he said Yeah well just don't, all right? (Christ – these people ever gonna answer this bloody door, or what? Reckon we ought to, what? Try the door, will we? See if we get a result.)

Paul leaned down on the lever handle, and gently pushed. The door opened easily and he held it just ajar, awaiting reaction (a voice, a noise – anything, really: been in these situations before, see), and when nothing came, he swung the door wide and was initially confused and just slightly disoriented to be confronted with not yet another wooden-floored flight path, lit like a film set courtesy of these vast bloody windows that seem to be just all over the place, here. Instead, he found himself in what seemed to be a small and rather plain and very brown, well – what would you call it? *Vestibule* wouldn't be too far off the mark; little sort of hall, it was, with a coatrack umbrella-stand sort of thing with a bevelled mirror at its centre and surmounted by a heavy carved pediment which reminded him of that wardrobe at his Nan's. Paul reckoned it was oak, and 1870, 1880 – that sort of time. Thick tweed coats and chocolate-coloured fur-felt trilbies were slung over the hooks with several cane and crook-handled umbrellas clustered beneath, rammed in tightly among a surprising number of walking sticks – one of them ebony, Paul now noticed, topped by a lovely polished silver ball – very much as used by Fred Astaire in, God – just how many of those fabulous films? (Style? Pretty much invented it single-handed, Fred did, if you want my take on the matter.)

'Hallo . . .?' came a voice now, from somewhere distant. 'Someone there? Anyone . . .? Come on through! Come on through!'

Paul was looking for a door. Tubby was just behind him, jostling his shoulders and repeatedly husking into his ear Well whoss going on? Whoss going on? Whoss going on? (on and on), and Paul was not just irked but momentarily flummoxed because, well look – this little hall shouldn't at all by rights even *be* here, OK (it's not that sort of building) but the fact that I'm now stood slap bang in the middle of it, well – it stands to reason that there's got to be some other door somewhere what leads us out of it and into, Christ knows – a parlour, or something: front room of some sort (and Christ Almighty, Tubby – *do* leave it out for just one poxy second, will you? There ain't *nothing* going on, is there? So schtum: I don't need the hassle).

And then he saw a gap. He saw this gap, and was well down

the road to thinking *Funny* . . . and just at that moment he heard the approach of someone quite close – maybe on the other side of, um . . . what *was* this, exactly? It's so bleeding gloomy, here – not at all easy to see. And then he had a hold of it – it was a screen, a flat – a pasteboard dummy sort of wall thing like they maybe have in studios, or something (Pinewood, maybe – or that other one: one of them). And by the time the man came through the gap to greet them – smallish bloke: great big grin under a funny little reddish moustache – Paul had noticed too that they were only about eight or nine feet tall, these screens or whatever they were (because there's lots, I can see them now – all at different angles, and slightly overlapping; God – look at that: they've all got these wheels attached to the bottom). Somewhere, miles above, there's got to be a soaring, vaulted ceiling – like everywhere else in this place. So why can't I see it?

'Hello – hello. Do come in. Sorry – did you knock? We never hear, if anyone knocks. Particularly if the wireless is playing at the time. We don't actually very much go in for knocking and all that sort of thing, here. You're the new ones, is that right? Yes well – it's all quite unbelievably friendly, you know. Very open. You just walk in. That goes for the whole of The Works, actually. You ever want anything – want to see someone, well – all you do is, you just walk in. Sorry, um – to sort of go *on*, and everything. My name's Mike, by the way. Come on in, come on in. And you are?'

'Paul,' said Paul. 'I'm Paul – and this is Tubby. Pleased to meet you.'

'Mutual. Come on through, the two of you. Come and say hello to Oona.'

Paul was happy to do as he was told. There was between the three of them a fair amount of mild collision going on now, with muffled apology, often accompanied by just the one cough of stunted laughter, because this sort of poky little hall affair gave on only to a very narrow corridor – again, it looked like, formed by these funny old screens – and even as Paul was registering this muted ochre floral wallpaper and very glossy treacle-brown wainscotting (all around the base, but just above the castors) and yes, even a picture rail, look, and here was an old chromolithograph of (guess who) Winston Churchill in full-on fuck-you victory mode (framed in beaded walnut and hanging from chains) . . . even as Paul was busy marvelling at all this surprise – and liking it, really liking it – he was also trying to get his head around how and just why it was all so bloody dark in here. And then quite suddenly (and to Tubby's way of thinking, not before time) they found themselves standing, the two of them, close to the centre of a nice and cosy little sitting room, the sort you really don't see any more – fourteen by twelve is all it's got to be, ball park, if Paul was any judge – and there on a small and beige sofa of maybe moquette with definitely Rexine piping was perched quite neatly what one supposes can only be this Oona woman then, yes? And she looked, thank Christ, amazingly normal (because telling you – if she'd been got up in a nightie and a fireman's helmet and cradling a buckler emblazoned with our beloved flag while jabbing at the Hun with a trident, Paul in all honesty would not have been too much knocked back – because no listen: I dunno whether Tubby's clocked it or what, but it's a right little time-warp, this place is; as if you just strolled casual-like into, what – the Dark bloody Ages, or something).

'What a place!' Paul was exclaiming – his voice chock-full of a good deal of the rare and innocent delight that had genuinely overcome him. 'But how come it's so gloomy in here then, Mike? Wotcha, Oona – how you doing, girl? All right?'

'This is Paul,' said Mike to Oona.

Oona laughed and then said Hi, Paul – I'm fine, and you? And Paul was nodding away and saying Yeh yeh to all of that, but he was blessed if he knew what it was that coaxed the fat laugh out of her. Don't matter too much; all right laugh, though – bit dirty, which is well OK.

'And,' Mike continued smilingly, 'here we have Tubby. Tubby – this is my wife, Oona. How nice to have visitors.'

'Why do they call you Tubby?' Oona wanted to know. 'Have you always been called that? Because you're *not*, are you? Tubby.'

'Yeh well . . .' said Tubby. And he thought of ambling down the road to going Well at my *school*, see, funnily enough they actually used to call me . . . but then he decided Oh sod it, why should I? Ay? Where's the bleeding mileage? Ay?

'This place!' Paul was going again – eyes really wide, and drinking it all well down.

'You like?' asked Mike. 'Some people, I know, think it rather, oh – odd. Well it *is*, of course. Odd. It's just how we are. What we like. The light – you were asking about the relative darkness, yes? If you look up above all these little home-made walls of ours, you'll see. See them, yes? They're very effective. Also cut the height.'

And now that Paul's eyes had pretty much adjusted to the soft and really rather comforting half-light, he could, now Mike came to mention it, sort of make out something, yeh – like a bloody great colony of vampire bats all just hanging there, way up high in the rafters about half a mile above them. Mike looked down with modesty (now that the brilliance of his ruse had been rumbled) but his mouth was nonetheless tugged to one side by nothing short of pride, this well overladen with sheer excitement at the thought that in this Paul, just maybe, was someone who might truly and deep down appreciate all he had done, here.

'Blackout curtains . . .' he said quite simply.

Paul was looking up at them again, and then he lowered his gaze to level with Mike.

'*Kidding* me . . .' he said, with caution. '*Black*out curtains? Nah – you're having me on, aren't you?'

'God . . .' Oona sort of half-laughed. 'If you think *that's* weird . . . Christ.'

'It's the real stuff, actually,' said Mike. 'Proper McCoy. You can still get it in great big rolls, if you know where to go. Some of it's gone a bit sort of brown in places, unfortunately. Well – it's over sixty years old, after all.'

'Like most everything else here . . .' said Oona – in a tone of voice that had Paul looking. It was still quite mischievous, still got a bit of a dig to it, this voice of hers, but I don't know . . . she went a bit sad, I thought, when she was talking then.

'Won't you sit, both of you?' Mike offered – pulling out a couple of straight-backed chairs from under a heavy square dining table with candytwist legs and thick crossed stretchers. 'It's something of a . . . mission, I suppose. We just decided that during the War, the world – well, *England*, anyway, was, despite all the dangers and privations, just simply a better place to be. More human. There were *values*, you see. And everyone understood their places in society. There was a sense of *family.*'

'Simple . . .' put in Oona. 'Mike – why don't you make us some tea?'

'Simple, yes,' he agreed. 'Tea. Good idea. Tea, Paul? Tubby? Yes? Excellent. And so I – we – set about, um – recreating it, I suppose. As best we could. I've been collecting all this stuff for, oh – ages and ages, now. Years and years. Decades. You used to be able to pick it up just everywhere, you know. One time. And really cheap.'

'Yeh,' grunted Tubby. 'Not surprised.'

'But it's pretty rare now, some of it, you know,' tacked on Mike, quite defensively.

'Yeh,' agreed Paul. 'Like this chair I'm sitting on as a good for instance. Utility – right? Government approved. Lovely smell of beeswax coming off of it, and all.'

Both Mike and Oona looked amazed, and then at one another.

'*Right*,' said Mike – quite loudly, and more gratified than he could begin to find words for. 'They've all got the original labels on the underneath, if you want to look . . .'

'Magic,' approved Paul. 'Take your word for it. Yeh – I'm in the decorating game myself, as it happens. Read a few books, like. Picked up bits here and there. And yeh – don't neither of you go minding old Tubby, will you? He's a good lad at heart but he wouldn't know a Looey Cans commode from a kicked-in bleeding tea chest, would you Tubs? If you'll pardon my wossname . . .'

Tubby pulled a face and sniffed a bit.

'Chair's a chair, far's I'm concerned. You got a fag round here, Mike, any chance? I'm just out. And yeh – I know it's against the *rules*, and that, but I could really do with a drag right now, I'm honest.'

Mike glanced over nervously to Oona; she held his gaze for no more than a second and then she widened her eyes. Mike was visibly much more relaxed (now that she'd made it all right) and he confided to Tubby, quite conspiratorially:

'We've got some Woodbines, somewhere.'

'Yeh?' said Tubby. 'Didn't know they was still going. Here – they're not bloody wartime and all, are they? Be well gone.'

Both Mike and Oona laughed out loud at such an absurdity.

'No no,' Mike assured him, as he rattled around in the central drawer of a practically black and mock Jacobean sideboard. And then, as he offered them, he added quite apologetically, 'Well – the *packet* is, yes. It's an original packet of maybe 1940 – but the cigarettes inside are fresh. Well – quite. Not that we smoke them ourselves. They're more of a prop, really. Also – we don't like, if I'm being frank . . . breaking any of Lucas's, um, suggestions as to how we all conduct ourselves, here. He's been so very good to us – it seems wrong to, you know – go against him on the little things. When he gives so much.'

'You reckon?' checked Tubby, as he wormed out this bleeding

little cigarette from the bog-green hull-and-slide packet of ten before him – and he got it lit quick before Mike was, Christ Almighty, I don't know – all come over with a vision of Our Lady or Saint Lucas, or something, and offered him up the Woodbines by way of a bleeding sacrifice (tell you – any minute now, he'll be flogging his back).

'Even our blackout curtains, you know – they're quite an indulgence on Lucas's part because he won't have curtains anywhere at all, as a rule. He allows these as a sort of concession because from the outside you don't at all see them, you see. It just looks black, like all the other windowpanes. Lucky, really.'

Tubby nodded. 'Yeh well – that knocks right on the head all my plans for pink and frilly gingham in the boudoir, don't it?'

'Ha! Don't mind him,' laughed Paul. 'Not his fault he's a bleeding ignoramus, is it? That right, Tubs? You can't help it, you don't know nothing about nothing. Tell you what I reckon though, Mike – I reckon what you done here is right on the money, mate. Brilliant. And all these little walls – you, what – do it because they had small rooms in them days, yeh?'

'That's exactly right. Lucas wouldn't countenance any actual constructions, here, and I wholly appreciate that. But the sort of little Thirties semi we were aiming at, well – you could have fitted about six of them into this space he's given us here. Most of it we don't use at all, which is a terrible waste, I suppose, but there it is. And the furnishings now, of course – they're all in scale. Would've been completely lost, otherwise. The *place*, though – the actual *location*,' Mike was ploughing on – the light of real enthusiasm gleaming proudly in each of his wide-open eyes – 'the location of The Works is just absolutely perfect, of course – wholly authentic – because . . . I don't know if you've noticed, but the buildings to either side of us – here and here, yes? – are modern, you know. Very recent. Oh they're in the *style* of, granted – but they were actually put up in the late Eighties. I've been into it.' And here his voice withered, and dampened down into sour. 'Custom-made apartments for all the *yuppies* of the time.' But once this unappetizing morsel had been satisfactorily expelled from the rich good things in the surrounding gumbo, Mike could resume with relish. 'Though the point I'm making here is that the original warehouses at each side of us, right – they sustained direct hits over two successive nights at the height of the Blitz. Spring of forty-one, as far as I can date it. This building, I'm telling you – it knows all about the War, believe you me. Lived *through* it, you see. Came out the other end. We owe it our . . . respect, I think.'

Ay ay, thought Tubby: now where the bugger I put that scourge? Reckon I'll give our chum here a loan of it (tell you straight – this one, he'll end up nailed to a bleeding cross. And liking it). Another thing – I don't know why, Gawd alone knows why Pauly keeps banging on and on about this gaff. Thought he was having a laugh, first off, I did, but he ain't, I can see that now. Means it, the silly plonker. Well look – you tell me: what's so bleeding clever about cutting out all the light with black stuff and living in a shoebox all dickied out in every colour you can think of, all the way from puke right up to shit? What's all that about then, ay? Cos if that's art, you can shove it, cock. Only reason I'm sat here is to get the lowdown on all this bleeding cooking malarkey what Paul has dropped me right into up to my neck. It's not that I don't like a bit of messing about in the kitchen – I'm not saying that cos I do, if I'm honest. And yeh – I get a fair old result, I'm not denying. But all this eating together like one big happy family – well Christ. I mean – it's all a bit like . . . oh bloody hell: it's *school* again, ain't it? Ah well. Least we got a roof over our heads: something. Cos it was right what Paul was saying about Wee Davy, while back – he was getting to be a right liability, that one was. I just hope Paul don't lose sight of why we're here, that's all: we got to get down to a bit of business, and we got to do it soon. Get some bread together. You look at him now – all oohing

81

and aahing over . . . what is they're yapping about now? Oh yeh – a mud-coloured tile fireplace what's all sort of zigzag style; type of rubbish what you and me'd put a sledgehammer through as soon as look at the bleeding thing. It's like I walked into the Antiques bloody Roadshow, or something. And this Oona kid – take one look at her. What can she be? Thirty? Thirty top, I reckon – and she's half tasty, and all: fair pair of jugs, look. What she want to be banged up with a bleeding preacher in the Chamber of fucking Horrors for then, ay? Trouble with this place – it's jam full of nutters. Anyway – I got to cut in, haven't I? Cos they're on to the bleeding *lino* now, God's sake, and I reckon I don't say my bit and get the fuck out of here, I'm telling you straight – I could well fall into a coma.

'Mike,' said Tubby – had to cough a bit, get the bloke's attention – 'fill me in on the kitchen, yeh? I don't even know where it's at.'

Mike broke away with reluctance from his rapturous recreation to Paul of the total bliss that enveloped him that glorious day when he discovered this dingy little quite forgotten back room in a paint shop at the end of a Georgian terrace in Spitalfields, due for refurbishment – and how he had unearthed there the original rolls of wallpaper frieze a full twelve inches deep and in three tones of ginger that you now see about you – all made long before rationing will have firmly knocked all such things on the head.

'Oh yes indeed, Tubby – yes indeed,' said Mike. 'A little dicky-bird told me I was to be relieved of my chef's hat and apron. *God*, I'm pleased. And *so*,' he scoffed in, he adjudged, a suitably avuncular and self-deprecatory manner, 'will everyone else here, I'm very sure of that! My mashed potato, I must be honest with you, very rarely scaled the heights. Not so, Oona?'

'Yeh well . . .' muttered Tubby. 'Like I say – I won't be doing nothing fancy. Humble fare. That's my style.'

'Perfect,' enthused Mike. 'That's just perfect. And did Lucas mention to you about the –?'

'Offal? Yeh. Liver aren't us. Check. Anything else I wanna know?'

'Not really. It's all very straightforward, actually. Tell you what, Tubby – what say I meet you down there at, what? Say – six? Six should be ample. It's in the basement. Walls are as thick as the Tower of London, down there. Lots of deep buttresses. We eat there too. Light it with candles, don't we Oona?'

Oona sighed. 'We do,' she said. 'We surely do.'

'It's perfectly magical,' concluded Mike. 'There are these old pine refectory tables – I think you'll approve, Paul: mid-Victorian, at a guess . . . not, of course, my period. And we sort of sometimes push these all together and then Lucas always says a few words before we, um – break bread, as it were.'

'What?' interjected Tubby. 'Sort of on the lines of how he'd like to buy the World a Coke?'

'*Ha*!' snorted Oona, clearly amused.

'We're not,' retorted Mike, quite stiffly, '*exactly* like that.'

'Well,' allowed Tubby. 'Good to know. Six, then. You coming or what, Paul?'

'Soon – I'll catch you later, Tubs, yeh? I just wanna dekko at them cruets over there. Bakelite, are they? And just look at that,' he marvelled. 'They even come with the little spoon.'

Mike was nodding with unrestrained delight.

'The blue and green mottling is particularly unusual,' he said. 'Brown was more regular. There was this terribly well-known factory near Stoke: these could, I'm fairly positive, hail from there.'

Tubby for some reason glanced across once at Oona – who was staring up blankly at what in a normal house would have been a plastered ceiling, but here was a soaring and shadowy void darkly festooned with these billowing thunderclouds of thin and faded fustian. Then he turned, banged his knee and elbow amid a maze of dung partitions, swore like a madman awoken from a nightmare and fumbled his way back into the twenty-first century.

(Yeh. And I didn't even get no tea.)

CHAPTER THREE

Oh thank the Lord, thought Jamie, as the taxi finally swung into the turning he'd been telling and *telling* him about: at last I can see it – it's there, look – just ahead, yes? The large square brick building, see it? Yes?

'Blimey,' said the taxi-driver. 'That's a turn-up. You know what? All these years, I never even knew it was there, this little turning. Amazing city. Amazing. Innit? London. Ay? Amazing city. Every day you're learning. You know how many years I been in this game?'

'Yes,' replied Jamie, very wearily. 'Twenty-two, come Christmas. You told me. Just pull in as close as you can get, could you? Main doors, there.'

'Twenty-two come Christmas, yeah. Told you, did I? Don't recall. My mind. What – just over here suit you, will it? And I never ever knew it was here, this little turning. Every day, this game, you're learning something.'

Well *why*, thought Jamie quite bitterly, have you been blandly assuring me for the past twenty minutes that you knew *exactly* where it was I was meaning and that I was just to sit back and not worry on account of we'd be there in a couple of shakes? It wouldn't have been so bad if the rest of the journey had gone like a dream, but oh no, oh God no. And it's a total bugger really, isn't it? Because normally, you know, I'm a very great fan of the London cabbie – how the, you know, whole system goes – the works, sort of thing. You hop in, you hop out, and then that's the end of the matter. What could be more efficient? (Caroline – she's always saying what a total waste of money they are, taxis. If you've got so much spare cash just sloshing around, Jamie, she'd go, then you'd be a lot better off, I should have said, investing it in a bigger mortgage so that we could stand some small chance of getting out of this little shit-hole you've forced us all to live in. But oh *no*. Jamie – that would be too *sensible*, wouldn't it Jamie? Much better you go swanning about in cabs while every afternoon I'm left to collect Benny from school on the *bus*. Christ, Jamie – at least if we had a *car* it wouldn't be too bad . . . ! That was Caroline. On and on.) But me, I've always thought they're pretty good value, taxis, because they save you *time*, you see: in the long run, that's what they save you – time. Less relevant these days, I have to admit. Time is pretty much all I seem to have left. Great acres of it. Or at least it *would* be – would be all I had were it not for Lucas. The nearest I get to believing in God, you could say.

So anyway – I was darting out into the street and trying to hail a cab and I had to keep an eye on all my stuff piled up on the pavement and I kept on thinking just two things (well three, I suppose, if you count me going Oh why oh why is it that you can never ever get a cab when you really need one? Three if you want to count that). But mainly I was thinking Christ – my luck, it's going to start to rain, isn't it? And what's that going to do to the rug and my LPs and that loosely trussed-up huddle of paper-backs? Because I didn't have the time, did I, to pack up everything properly; I didn't want Benny to, sort of – see it going on. I thought that might be unsettling for him. Me, it would have ripped into ribbons. So I just sort of scraped together a few bags and a couple of boxes and just more or less basically *went* for it, really. Yes. And that's the second thing I was thinking: pitiful, isn't it? Just look at that sad little heap of not much stuff. Not a lot to show, is it, for ten years of marriage. Or nine. Could be nine. Anyway – a hell of a time to be married.

And the first two taxis I did manage to flag down I had to let go, of course – because they both had this perfectly infuriating little Thank You For Not Fucking Smoking sign stuck smugly in the back (because you see if you're a chain smoker, as I am, you learn always to check for important things like that; it's the same with booking restaurants. Theatres and cinemas, it goes without saying, are a complete and utter no-no. Yes. And don't get me on to you-know-what because I'm trying very hard, quite frankly, to blank it all out. I mean Christ what a bloody position: I'm offered a haven, a bower, a retreat by that dear man Lucas, and then I am denied my one and only comfort – my craving, my vice . . . oh Christ, my *life*, let's face it. What in God's name am I going to *do*? Don't know. Don't know. As I say: I'm trying very hard to blank it out).

Anyway. The third taxi to come along – the one I ended up in and am now and right this minute very gratefully vacating (the amount on the meter, oh God it would blind you – most of it down to the twenty-minute sightseeing tour: that's adventure for you). Oh Christ *anyway*, this cab, this driver – he didn't at all seem to mind what on earth I did or didn't do. Certainly he watched me with studied dispassion as I humped and heaved all this junk into the back; he just sat there, *Evening Standard* open at the racing propped against the wheel, and him just idly paring a thoughtful thumbnail. So anyway, I bundled it all in, in the end – oh, just anyhow, and there was barely enough room left for me – and all I wanted now, oh God yes, was just to *be* there because frankly, what with having just gone another ten rounds with Caroline (not so much a parting shot as the full 1812) I was in no mood, believe me, for . . . and then there had been that interminable wait in the *building* society, oh dear God, yes that. I don't know if it's the same with you (I mean it can't, can it, just be me? That it happens to? Oh Lord *please* don't tell me it's only me) but I'm always stuck behind the woman who wants her entire banking history laid out before her and gorgeously illuminated, and then when she's finally satisfied I've then got to cope with the abstracted teller who won't keep me a minute, sir, it's only that she's got to just quickly key in the entire extent of her latest *novel* – and Jesus, you don't get a look in, matey, till a chapter break, or maybe – I don't know – when the suspicion dawns on her that the subplot is about to break (kick in – make itself felt) and only at this point she might possibly judge it a not too bad moment to be fleetingly torn away from the subtleties of her art and just bloody shove across to me my fifty fucking quid, the boot-faced rancid old *tart*.

And all the way here in the taxi – oh God, this bloody driver! Ern, the bloody man is called. How do I know this? Because he bloody *told* me, didn't he? He told me his age, the number of years he's been driving his passengers to the brink of distraction (twenty-two come Christmas, right? The fact will be with me for ever) and also that his youngest has got his own little car-hire business in a very choice part of Florida and that come next spring he and his good lady Vera are both going out there for an all-expenses-paid three-week holiday of a lifetime, this to include unlimited access to the rides in Disneyland, and all part and parcel of the courtesy of his youngest (who is – oh Christ why do I remember this? – called Stanley). His other boy, Jake, is doing very nicely for himself, thank you, in this big firm up the City – he was always the most studious at school, forever had his nose in a book (don't know where he gets it, but it's sure not from Ern) and shortly he'll be articled, which will be nice for him. They're all booked in – including their Janet, the middle one – to have a slap-up meal on the day the results come through down at Mario's, close by the Old Kent Road, because he's telling you this for free, mate – never mind all those poncey nosh-houses up West, there ain't nowhere'll do you a nice three-course like what Mario will, and what you're looking at is twelve pound fifty a head all in, which has just got to be favourite, doesn't it? Plus, he knows old

Mario – used to know his dad and all, if the truth be told – and so after there's always, oh Jesus – chocolate fucking *mints*, and I want to do myself a favour and get down there and all I've got to do is drop his name to Mario who'll then look after me – and did he mention it, his name? Yes you did – you did: it's *Ern*, it's *Ern*, it's . . . oh Christ help me – your name, it's bloody *Ern*.

And when I made it as plain to him as I could – just short of causing mortal offence (because I couldn't risk, could I, being summarily ejected in the middle of Docklands with all my bags and boxes) – that I really wasn't, if he didn't mind, interested in *conversation*, he just hunched himself forward and started up on this eternal high-pitched and whingeing monologue – and I had to keep on thinking Look, it can't be far now, it can't be long now (but Jesus, though – I'm pretty bloody sure we've been down this street before) and just for God's sake do your best, Jamie, to keep hold of what's left of your composure, light up another fag and just concentrate on sweet good thoughts like my wonderful new space in Lucas's Works (if ever I am destined to see the place again) and how very lovely it would be to just lean forward and stick a bloody fork into the back of Ern's great fat and stupid *neck*.

'Doctors . . .' he was going now. 'What do they know? Hey? Every week, you got conflicting reports. You pick up a paper and you don't know what to think. Alcohol is bad for you . . . alcohol *isn't* bad for you . . . sugar is bad for you . . . sugar *isn't* bad for you . . . eggs, and that: dairy. *Dairy's* bad for you . . . dairy *isn't* bad for you . . . then they say beef is bad for you . . . and lamb *isn't* bad for you . . .'

And then I just *knew* we'd passed this bloody pink block of flats, there – maybe even twice. And by this time I was so completely maddened that I found myself shrieking. 'Here! It's just around the thing! The junction. Take the lext at the right lefts!'

The taxi didn't even hesitate; it just blithely sailed on past.

'We can maybe hang a U, in just a bit,' the man assured me.

'Yeh. And then they turn round and say lamb *is* bad for you . . . and white bread – that's meant to be bad for you . . . now they say it *isn't* bad for you . . . well I mean, what I mean to say is, what are you supposed to think? I mean – be honest: all this crap – it could drive you nuts, couldn't it? Round the twist. Can't do a left here, guvnor. Used to be able to. Then they closed it off, didn't they? Road planners . . . what do they know? Hey? They make a road a one-way . . . next time you come they made it a *two*-way . . . you get a nice little ring road . . . next thing you know they shut it *down* . . . They wanna try driving a cab for a day, they do, road planners. They don't know nothing about it, road planners don't. Same with this bloody *government* . . .'

'Oh God. Oh *God* . . .'

'They say they're going to pump more money into the NHS . . . and then they *don't*. My Vera's been waiting for part of her stomach since Easter before last. Then they say they're going to give more money for education . . . and then they *don't* . . . next thing you read is they're all saying how they're going to put all this money into public transport . . . and then they *don't* . . . which is why people are taking cabs more, you ask me: you don't get the hassle.'

The taxi, now, had come to a stop. The man just sat there, shrouded in an aura of concentrated indifference that tottered at the very brink of downright impressive. Jamie was crouching down low, the better to unload his stuff (while still managing to give his head a hell of a crack, though – and, as he was still half blind and groggy from the zap of pain and then the seeping ache of it, bloody well managing to somehow crack it again).

'All these bits of stupid paper money . . .' moaned the cabbie, though still with heavy disdain, as Jamie passed across to him the thicker end of that morning's hard-won building society withdrawal. 'I mean – joke, isn't it? In the higher scheme of things. When it comes to *war*, though – oh yes: always find the funding for *that*, won't they? Look at them, what are they – smart missiles what the Americans got. Daresay we got them too . . .'

Jamie, now, had unloaded the last of it – and God, he was feeling just so, oh – *piningly* keen to be shot of this damn man Ern for ever and ever and safe, then, deep within his womb. Still hung about for some change, though (stupid paper money or no). And while he used the time to carry out a rapid mental tally of his various bags and boxes and as he was awaiting the arrival of whatever small amounts of change the cabbie would see fit to tip him, Jamie was suddenly aware of this square and largeish quite prominent sign on the wall of The Works, fairly high up and to the left of the doors. 'Trespassers Will Be Prosecuted' is how it went (that was the sum total) – rather smartly engraved into a good thick slab of what could very easily be slate of some sort, Jamie conjectured. No nasty little stick-on letters or ready-mades for Lucas. But it was odd because despite all the times Jamie had loitered longingly in the shadows of the building, he had never before noticed it; it could, he supposed, be new. And God, you know – they used to be all over, signs like that. Jamie remembered them well from his childhood. They had thoroughly established themselves as one of the few sure-fire dependables: if ever one happened upon the sort of place that stoked a young boy's spirit (boiled his blood) – the frighteningly alluring verges of the darkest and glossy green and then so quickly thick and coal-black forest, say, or maybe the diesel-sweet tangle of railway sidings, harsh and clanking – there, always, would stand the sign, a symbol of denial with an outstretched arm, the palm towards you. Jamie, then, had thought that he could more or less understand the meaning of 'trespasser' because it came up, didn't it, in some old prayer or other; roughly translated, it could be seen to mean some lucky and certainly adult person who did as he bloody well pleased. 'Prosecuted', though – and it's funny, this: God alone knows where he got the idea (where, as a child, does one?) – but

91

he was quite convinced that here was the inevitable consequence of something to do with electrocution. He had never, therefore, in the whole of his boyhood thought to trespass one single inch beyond the clearly delineated ambit and boundaries of such a sign, earnestly believing that if ever, in madness, he could summon up the throat-clamping courage to even dream of doing such a thing . . . well then his very next step would surely guarantee the crack and then sizzle of a hot and blinding lightning flash, and all that would be left of Jamie to mark this first and last act of trespass on earth would be an idly smoking, charred and conical heap of cinders.

All just so much childish nonsense, quite naturally – but Jamie nonetheless admitted to this sign here making him just slightly uneasy even if it failed to, as it surely would have done in those old and distant days, bring him up short (soon to go pale, and quiver).

'Half a mill apiece? Them smart missiles? Shouldn't wonder. Now hang on – you give me, what – thirty, right?'

And then Jamie became aware of a little knot of people, half in the shadows of the big double doors, one of which was thrown wide open. And of course they were *looking*, weren't they? Of course they were.

'A mill . . . ? Two mill . . . ? Shouldn't wonder. Right, then – so that's two I got to give you – or shall we call it evens, ay? *Three* mill . . . ? *Five* mill . . . ? I mean – who's counting? Cos I'm telling you, mate – with them smart missiles, the sky's the limit.'

Jamie just brushed aside everything. He'd wholly lost track now of what, if any, money might or might not be due to him – so go on then, bloody Ern: pocket the five mill or whatever you were on about – and now please do coax this black and purring cab of yours into very deftly executing one of its tight and fabled U-turns and then you must promise me you'll drive away swiftly, and straight into hell.

'Goodness me!' Jamie heard a woman say, as he bumbled over – very awkwardly, yes, because he was carrying far too much for just the one journey and he immediately regretted having strained his aching red and white fingers just that little bit further so as to just about manage that other big bag, there. People, he thought, when they were carrying lots of things (Christmas shopping, airports – Christ, stressful enough at the best of times) they always looked to Jamie somehow . . . stupid. The way he saw it: people who bustle appear not just agitated but menial – and people piled up with so much bulky ballast look just plain dumb. And so – knowing this – Jamie was very displeased indeed with himself for being all these things (bustling, menial, hampered, dumb – wholly inexplicable in this particular instance because he'd known, hadn't he, that there was this knot of people, hanging around and *looking*). Three of them, he now could see – ought to be enough, don't you think? A man, the woman who had spoken and just to the side, there, this other one – woman, girl. Christ – knockout, actually: absolute bloody knockout, to Jamie's way of thinking. And don't ask him just yet how the woman who had spoken was looking (and oh damn – she's speaking again, now – saying something else: have to soon give her just a bit of attention) because if you want him to be honest he had been wholly trans-fixed by this other one, you see – woman, girl – who was smiling at him now so, oh – *brilliantly* and her hair was long and shining and it was not often in broad daylight, you know, that you saw such very high-heeled and pointy and very, um – moving shoes. Not in this day and age. Not in Jamie's life, anyway. Not recently. Oh Jesus – not *ever*, you want the God's honest truth. The very few women Jamie had known – wives, largely – had tended to the homey side; homey, yes – and sometimes mad.

'Yet *another* new arrival – what a day we're all having,' mar-velled the woman – not the heartstopper, no: the other one, the first one. Who, Jamie now saw as he simply let drop all his rubbish just inside the door and had it keel over and slither where it would (I don't know why I bothered with the half of it, tell you the truth – it's mostly junk, not much more than junk), was not at all bad on the looks front either, in a bit of a gypsy and maybe arty bohemian sort of a way (it was possibly just the hair and earrings) . . . but face it, she wasn't in the league of the other one, the second one, who was still just standing there with her legs, and everything – and smiling, yes: smiling too, and right at him, seemed like.

'Hallo,' said Jamie – taking a fair crack at making it an all-encompassing sort of a greeting, while still sensing it bend in the air and then home in like something smart, intent upon Miss Universe.

'I'm Judy,' said the other one. 'Welcome to the sanctuary. You'll love it. We all do. This is Teddy – my, um – what *are* you, Teddy? My partner, are you? Boyfriend? Lover? What would you like to be?'

Teddy scratched at the underside of this fairly copious beard of his (which seemed to Jamie to have all sorts of hues and tones appearing in it here and there and from time to time: black, sort of rusty brownish, whitey-grey – even the odd little tuft of blonde, it sure looked like, unless the gleaming and milky winter sun was up to its usual tricks).

'All of those, I hope,' he smiled. And then he extended his hand to Jamie, and looking him squarely in the eye, he said to him very seriously: 'Lillicrap.'

Jamie blinked. 'Really?' he said. (Because I'm not quite sure I, um . . . but whatever he said – it wasn't, was it? – 'really' wasn't really the answer.)

Judy laughed. 'It's his name. He's got a thing about it. He's called Teddy Lillicrap, aren't you darling? Now our new friend here knows, so you can wrap it up cosily again and put it back in its box.'

'I'm Jamie,' said Jamie. 'Jamie Dear. Hello Judy. Hello Teddy.' And now he had at least a pretty good excuse, didn't he, for training the whole of his attention on (oh yes – you bet) the other one, the second one.

'I don't . . .' said Teddy, 'have a *thing* about it, Judy . . . it's just I think it's best got out of the way at the outset, that's all. Clears the air – and then we can all sort of get down to things. I don't actually quite mean that – but anyway.'

'I'm Frankie,' said the vision. Sweet voice – quite deepish, very sweet.

'Don't listen to him!' joshed Judy. 'He's got a *thing* about it. Teddy – why don't you help Jamie with all his bits and bobs?'

'Hallo, Frankie,' said Jamie, reverentially. 'And what – you live here too, do you?'

'Oh yes,' she answered happily. 'I'm a part of our merry little band. I'm with John – you must meet him. He should be here any moment, actually. He's just popped across to get the car. You'll *adore* him – everyone does.'

Jamie nodded with energy – almost as if she had conveyed to him really the most fabulously interesting and life-altering information (which, in one sense, she had, of course: she lives here – yippee! And then there was John. But there would have to be, wouldn't there? There was, face it, always a John. And, in Jamie's experience, very often a John whom everyone adored).

'I expect,' said Teddy, 'that you're the – the second floor back, yes? The very last slot, you've got there. We're only just down the way from you. East side – down a couple of steps. Anything you ever need, or anything –'

'Oh *yes*,' rushed in Judy. 'Anything at all – just come right on in and ask. Promise? We mean it. Never ever think that you don't want to, oh – you know how people are – barge *in*, or anything, because honestly, I don't know how it *sounds* – what it sort of makes us all *seem* like but we're not, are we Teddy? Frankie? We're just not *like* that, here. We're all, well – in it together, really. And you'll be just the same, you'll see. It's Lucas, really – he just makes it all . . . work.'

Teddy smiled. 'All for one . . . that's the style. Anyway – come on, Jamie. I expect you want to get sorted, yes? Just tell me what I can carry.'

'Oh here he is!' piped up Frankie. 'Here's John.'

Jamie turned as he heard the crumble of the car's approach – and oh! Oh my goodness, what a . . . oh my God, just look at that. Beautiful. Superb. A blue that's nearly black – and Christ, so sleek. Jamie didn't actually *have* a car (as Caroline rarely ceased to remind him) but he had had once – a third-hand BMW, which had been perfectly fine (got sod all when I sold it, though) – but ever since boyhood he had dreamed of, yearned for – even felt quite lusty over the gloating thought of one day owning a car like this. Just to touch and . . . inhale it. Oh God just *look* at this bloody car, will you? Good Christ – it's even more gorgeous than Frankie.

'That is just . . . stunning,' whispered Jamie. 'Bentley, is it? No it's *not* a Bentley, is it? Bristol? Is it a Bristol? It's . . . excellent.'

'Lovely, isn't it?' enthused Frankie. 'John's pride and joy. Loves it more than me, I sometimes think.'

And Jamie was nodding at that – because yes, he could see – at times it could be a very close-run thing: torn between two beauties. But John didn't have to worry, did he? No, John did not. Because John had them both. Didn't he? Oh God: I do hope I'm going to get on with this John, whoever he is.

'It's actually,' rattled on Frankie, as she tottered across on those amazing shoes, 'an Alvis. Nineteen fifty-something, not quite sure. Come and meet John – but you must promise, Jamie. Promise you won't go on *too* much about the car or I'm telling you – we'll be here all night.'

Jamie followed her over (God, and what a shape) and then his eyes were sweeping the length of the luscious flanks of this lean and deep blue lovely thing (God, and what a shape). Didn't want too much to focus on the driver, but would have to, really, sooner or later.

'John,' gabbled Frankie delightedly, as she skipped over on the cobbles to the other side of the car and opened the door. 'This is Jamie. New arrival. He absolutely *adores* the car – but you're to promise to *please* not talk about it. That beastly beggar's not round the corner again, is he?'

John laughed, and extended a hand through the window.

'Didn't see him, Frankie. Don't think so. John Barrington, by the way. Charmed. Frankie gets a bit upset, don't you Frankie, about this beggar chap who tends to hang around here, time to time. Seems harmless enough to me. Not a pretty sight, though, I have to say.'

Frankie made a big show of shivering.

'He's creepy. He's disgusting.'

'The odd thing is,' put in Judy, 'he never actually, does he – ask for any money. I give him a bit, sometimes. Feel quite sorry for him.'

'Urgh!' went Frankie. 'I wouldn't ever give him anything. The way he just *looks* at me . . .'

'Yes, well, anyway,' John now smilingly concluded. 'Excuse my not getting out, will you Jamie old man? It's just that we're running a teensy bit late this afternoon. It would help if I could leave the old bus here, but Lucas won't have it. Anyway – welcome to the club. We'll have a jaw over dinner, maybe – yes?' John slid his hands up and down the steering wheel. 'She is a beauty, isn't she?'

Jamie glanced over very briefly at Frankie – short skirt well hoiked up as she slid in next to John – and said Yes. And then he dropped his gaze to the long and low snout of the perfect Alvis and *Yes*, he said: yes, oh yes. And then, quite suddenly, the car moved off and was manoeuvred with care into that tight little turning that that bloody man Ern had never ever known was even there – and he, Jamie groaned to recall, in this game for twenty-two years, come Christmas (would you believe it?).

Jamie was aware, now, of Judy by his side.

'That,' she said, 'was John. Were you surprised?'

'I, um – what do you mean? You mean about his . . . ?'

'Age, yes. Surprised? Were you? I was – weren't we, Teddy? When they both first came here. No one's quite sure how old he is *exactly* – I reckon he can't be much short of seventy, although I have to admit he hasn't got much in the way of *lines* . . .'

'Oh *no* . . .' put in Teddy. 'Oh no no no – I don't think he's that old. I'm sure not. Mid-sixties, I'd say. He's a very good man, John is. A very big man, too. We couldn't do without him, that's for sure. Not without John, we couldn't.'

'Oh God I *know* that, Teddy – of course I do. I'm not saying anything *against* him. I love him dearly – we all do. It's just – well . . . you know. Frankie's only about twenty, I think. Pretty little thing, in many ways. I'm not saying it's *unheard* of, or anything. Still – lucky old John, I suppose.'

'He deserves it,' said Teddy. 'And poor old you – you're stuck with me.'

'*Darling* Teddy,' laughed Judy. And she kissed him on the cheek. 'John, you see Jamie, is really most terribly *rich*. Not as rich as Lucas, of course – but still most awfully well off. He doesn't *work*, or anything – he's just got money, some reason. And Frankie, of course – did you love her? Isn't she lovely? I mean a lovely *person*? She doesn't work either. Fairly naturally. We, alas, have to, don't we Teddy?'

'She has *got* a, um – profession,' qualified Teddy. 'She's an actress, isn't she? I thought someone said.'

'Well,' said Judy. '*Dancer*, anyway. God knows what sort. I imagine something tending towards the erotic, wouldn't you

98

think? Teddy's an actor, by the way. A very brilliant one. And what do you do, Jamie? Anything exciting?'

Jamie laughed. 'Not a lot of anything, frankly,' he said rather ruefully. (And Christ, you know: it's true.)

'Well . . .' put in Teddy. '*Actor* . . . pretty much only the odd little voiceover, these days. Commercial radio. Bit of voice training, time to time. Neither the National nor the BBC are driving me *mad* – let's put it that way.'

'Oh don't be so *silly*, Teddy – you're a perfectly *wonderful* actor, and well you know it. It's just that, Jamie – the right *part*, you see, hasn't come along in a little while. But soon – mark, my words: name in lights, where it belongs. Anyway – here, you see, we all put in what we're good at. I expect you know that. Teddy sometimes does these most marvellous readings after dinner – don't you, Teddy? Could listen to him for ever. And he's getting up a play at Christmas – highlight of the year. What's it going to be this time, Teddy? Have you decided?'

'Not quite sure. Might do an Agatha Christie. Could go down well. Or maybe a bit of Shaw . . . ?'

'Shaw would be nice. But not *Pygmalion* – sick to death of all that *My Fair Lady* stuff. And when he's not doing that sort of thing, Teddy makes his own wine – we all get through absolute *gallons* of the stuff, don't we my sweet? Except for Lucas, of course. Not him at all. He drinks gin and some sort of funny tea, you know. In the same glass. That's Lucas.'

'Well,' said Teddy, 'of *course* not Lucas: it's not *meant* for Lucas.'

'No. It is a bit . . . *ordinary*,' Judy supposed. 'Lucas maybe thinks it quite filthy. Well – I suppose it is *quite* filthy, isn't it Teddy?'

'Oh yes,' responded Teddy, very jovially. 'Perfectly vile. Cheap, though. To make, you know. And Judy's rarely idle – are you my love? It's a bit, um – tricky to quite define what it is that Judy does . . .'

'Not tricky at *all*,' she reproved him. 'I'm a sex therapist, Jamie.

Perfectly straightforward. It's just that I haven't got very much of a client base, just at the moment – so I just do a bit of work for the Samaritans, now. Which can be very *draining*, you know. And if anyone in The Works has got a *problem*, of course . . .'

'Some evenings,' said Teddy, 'she's completely exhausted.'

'It can be like that . . . A lot of my patients fell away completely, you see, when I was out of action for a while. We travelled, didn't we, quite a bit, Teddy? And then I contracted this, oh – raging dysentery . . . had it for months. Doctors were quite worried, at one point.'

'My God,' said Jamie. 'Where on earth did you get that?'

'Hm? Well in my *bottom*, silly! Where on earth do you think? Anyway – come on, Teddy: let's get Jamie here all unpacked and settled in. And then at dinner you can meet the whole gang. We've got a new cook tonight, apparently – which can only be a good thing. Poor old Mike just kept on doing these hideously dreary stewy things with those great big heaps of perfectly dreadful mash – wasn't it awful, Teddy? The mash? Have you met Mike, Jamie? Oh no of *course* you haven't – you've only just arrived. Well he's a lovely man – isn't he Teddy? And Oona. Lovely couple. It's just that he's a perfectly dreadful *cook*, that's all.'

'I met his replacement, very briefly,' said Jamie. 'He's called Tubby.'

'*Really*?' Judy exclaimed. 'Tubby! How wonderful. And *is* he – ?'

Jamie shook his head. 'No,' he said. 'He isn't. Lucas has taken to calling him Slim.'

'Oh isn't that just so like *Lucas*!' Judy laughed. And then she was wistful. 'Dear Lucas,' she said. 'Dear, dear Lucas.'

The three of them walked the few steps back to the doors of The Works, and each was now busy saddling themselves up with Jamie's bags and boxes.

'And John . . .' said Jamie. 'When you said you couldn't do

without him – what does he, um – contribute to the, um – community?' (And what in Christ's name, he was thinking, will I?)

'Oh well,' sniffed Judy, 'I would have thought that was perfectly obvious: money. As I said, he's got piles and piles of it. People with money put it in, you see – Kimmy, she's another one – but poor folk like us don't have to. Well – not much. But you should see their floor – John and Frankie's space. Perfectly gorgeous. Yes – it just goes to show. Quite amazing what you can achieve with just a team of top designers, a gang of navvies and a fucking fortune.'

'*Judy* . . .' cautioned Teddy.

'Well it's *true* . . . but I don't at all begrudge it. I expect he deserves it. Frankie does, certainly. I must admit I was just *slightly* pleased, though, when Lucas said no to the curtains. John had had, oh dozens of the things made up at God knows where – Harrods or somewhere, I expect – for all his great big socking windows, but Lucas wouldn't budge. He had to dump the lot, didn't he Teddy? Poor old John. Anyway – is that everything, Jamie? Yes? OK, then – let's show you the way to your brand-new dream home. Um – *Jamie*, my dear – now we're all friends . . . don't think I'm, um – you know, making any sort of a *point* here, but . . .'

'Yes?' queried Jamie. 'What?'

'Well it's just that while we've been standing here having this perfectly delightful little chat . . . you've actually smoked about three of those rather stinky cigarettes of yours. Did not Lucas . . . ?'

Jamie nodded in misery. 'Oh yes. He did. I'm quite up to speed on that score, Judy. Four, actually. I've just got through four. I'm a chain smoker, you see. It's going to be . . . difficult. Still – on the plus side, I'm perfectly easy about the no curtains side of things: haven't got any curtains. Haven't actually got any *furniture*, if I'm being honest.'

'Don't worry. Everyone will rally round. They always do. And as to the smoking . . . maybe I could give you some therapy. Yes? You'd maybe like to try? All part of the neighbourly service.'

'I thought, um . . .' demurred Jamie. 'I thought you did – sex.'

'Well I *do* – I *do*. But well – sex . . . smoking . . . there's bound to be some sort of a *link* there, don't you think?'

Jamie dropped to the ground the fag end of his last for, ooh – quite some time, I suppose. Christ. The only reason I've been hanging around out here for so bloody long, if I'm being totally honest with myself. Once I go through that door, it's over.

'I've never really thought about it. A link,' he replied. I mean: let me consider this for just one moment. Sex without a cigarette afterwards is of course wholly unthinkable . . . but then how on earth can I judge if that's what normal people would regard as a link? I mean, for me, anything – just *anything* without a cigarette before, after and about twenty bloody more throughout the middle is just so completely out of the *question* as to be . . . Oh God. Oh Lordy Lordy . . .

'Don't worry, Jamie,' Teddy said, kindly. 'There's always some rule here not everyone's wild about. John with his curtains and the parking thing – your smoking . . . Speaking for myself, I mean – I'm not too crazy about Lucas's way with surnames, but there you go. But look – we'll help. Help you. You'll really love living here, you know. Just love it. We all do.'

Jamie nodded. 'I know. I know I will. I love it already. OK you two: point me in the direction. And Judy, here – here's my bloody Gauloises. Take the lot and hide them and don't tell me where.'

Judy laughed and pocketed the packet. 'Don't worry, Jamie – I'll bury them. No I won't – I'll tell you what I'll do : I'll tie them to a stone and drop them into the river. But you do see what I mean about *Teddy*, don't you? Telling you – he's got a *thing* about it. I mean, Godsake – it's only a *name*.'

They were, Judy kept telling him, nearly there now (not too far) – but Jamie very surely didn't remember all this endless trudging the first time; maybe Judy, like that bloody little erstwhile cabbie of mine, whose memory I seem destined to carry close for ever-more – is imagining I might appreciate the scenic route. She might have saved it for a time when they weren't, the three of them, packed up like mules – progress fairly regularly arrested by someone, usually Jamie, having to retrieve some or other bit of embarrassing detritus that clattered out of one of these now very frankly vexing ill-slung-together boxes and bags. (Telling you – next journey I make, it'll be all the way back down again to upend the lot of it straight into the bins. Which are where, exactly, I wonder? All sorts of little details of that order to be sorted out, which is a bit more frightening than exciting, just at the moment.) God, you know – it's so very long since I was somewhere new that I have practically forgotten as to how it all *goes*. So that's one thought, yes. But it's not nearly a *big* enough thought, is it? No, not by a mile – to even come close to masking, smothering, ruth-lessly kicking and battering to the ground and then stamping on the face of the enormous thought, the huge and shapeless, quite breathtaking *craving* that was already all over him – he felt each tendril as if it were a thorn. I wonder, was Jamie's next and fevered, desperate hope, whether if I suddenly came over all helpless (no great stretch) and maybe even somewhat pathetic (pushover, all this) – whether then Judy might just possibly forget about all that nonsense that I gabbled to her about the Gauloises and just maybe slide that soft pack back into my hand? What do you think? Those stubby white cylinders of scented delight: I do so need the reassurance of the harshly sexy dreadful scraping at the back of my throat as I haul on down to the soles of my feet a good half-fagsworth of yearned-for poison. (Christ, I feel so craven.)

But by now they really were, Jamie was sensing, very nearly at journey's end (he recognized, he was sure, that tall and unusually narrow window, just there, still with its old opaque and greenish wired glass panes, and that lovely row of big iron hooks, each holding up a slightly battered but still bright red metal bucket with the word 'Fire' stencilled boldly across it in black; they all contained water – none of it sullied, Jamie just had to observe, by the usual scum of flattened cigarette ends). Of course, he conjectured, such features could be everywhere: I've yet to explore.

And then there were people, all in a huddle and just to the right of a very short staircase leading down into blackness. Girls, it seemed – no more than a couple of girls, it looked like from the back . . . and next to one of them, I now can see, a *real* girl, little girl, schoolgirl type of thing – couldn't be more than, oh . . . I don't really know, if I'm honest, what she couldn't be more than – no good at all with ages, particularly when they're this young . . . but going on the scale of Benny, then I suppose she could be, what – ten? More? Not much more. *Maybe* much more, don't know – but she is quite small. And you know, that's rather a funny thing – seeing a child here (a real one, I mean – as opposed to all the rest of us); hadn't at all figured on that, in Lucas's great scheme of things.

'Aha!' declared Judy, as they all plodded onwards, doggedly heaving their ludicrous burden – and one of the girls (and in the flurry of her turning, Jamie was aware of no more than a rather pert and tidy ponytail, which you don't see too much, do you, these days) seemed to spin around in some sort of alarm and maybe even eager to bundle behind her some little thing as she did it.

'A veritable coven!' cried Judy, it seemed with affection and her customary large and hostessy aplomb – and she and Teddy and Jamie with huge and mutual relief let go now of all these bloody boxes and slippery bags.

The anxious face of the ponytailed girl was smoothed into an easy relaxation at the sight of Judy (so yes, then, Jamie thought: she had been taut before).

'Oh it's you, Jude – hi baby: how you doing? OK guys? Teddy?'

And as Jamie was dutifully registering the unmistakably nasal Americanness of this (and rather liking it) the girl was bringing back into the open the little red phone which she had instinctively palmed.

'Aren't mobiles allowed here either?' Jamie asked, as affably as he could muster (more new people: all these people – I feel quite dizzy).

Judy twisted up her nose and eyes: it was as if the vote was cast and now lay quite perfectly balanced, leaving Judy poised on the very edge of plumping this way or that.

'Mobiles are frankly just a teeny bit of a grey area . . .' was her slowly delivered verdict. 'Isn't that right, Kimmy? Now look, everyone – this is Jamie. Our new boy. Kimmy – and Dorothy' – the second girl briefly and maybe with reluctance bobbed up into view – 'and we mustn't of course forget little Mary-Ann, must we, hm? Mary-Ann – say hello to Jamie.'

The little girl had been staring at him long enough, Jamie was well aware of that much. Seems a pretty little thing; wouldn't mind her looking somewhere else, though. (Oh *Christ* I need a fag . . .)

'Do you,' piped up Mary-Ann, 'have any children, Jamie? For me to play with?'

Jamie smirked, passed the back of his hand across his lower lip, shuffled his feet and blushed a bit – all the standard reactions when a wide-eyed child very simply sets before you an utterly reasonable question.

'Well, er – no, not really. No. Fraid not. Well I do actually *have* a, you know – little boy. Mary-Ann. He's called Benny, yes. But he's not, um – here, as it were. So no.'

Mary-Ann closed her eyes and nodded quite sagely, as if she had been expecting nothing less.

'I see,' she said. 'Another broken home.'

'Oh God*sake*, Mary-Ann!' Dorothy mock-scolded her. 'Don't listen to her, um – Jamie, is it?'

And then her whole face just suddenly collapsed from within – her eyes were lost to sight and both cheeks were shrunken. And as Kimmy's hand had swiftly and instinctively flown to her shoulder, and now was rubbing into it some much-needed comfort, Judy too stepped forward at once as if to form a shield and, if she had to, take the bullet.

'Oh Dorothy . . . oh Dorothy . . .' she cooed so gently. 'Don't get upset again. Please. Hush. There's no harm. See? No harm . . .'

'C'mon, Doe,' said Kimmy, more brightly. 'We're outta here, guys. But that thing with the mobile, yeh Jamie? It's like Judy says – it ain't exactly, you know – Owe Ewe Tee, yeh? It's just that, well – you don't wanna be doing it if Lucas is about. Is all, I guess. It's not like he's gonna, like – you know, *do* anything or, you know – say anything . . . it's just . . . well, you kinda get to know what he does and doesn't go for, yeah, and, well – he's the last guy you wanna go upsetting any which way, right?'

And Judy, Teddy and Jamie solemnly nodded in unison to that. Mary-Ann was still staring up at Jamie's face – so fully, but without expression – and Dorothy (who is, is she, the mother then? It would seem so, yes) was making pretty fair headway in the rallying round department – energetically chewing on her lips

106

as she gently pressed the flat of a finger to each of her eyelids in turn.

'I'm sorry . . .' she whispered. 'It's just sometimes – the things she just comes out with . . . God, it's hard enough . . .'

'Hey, Doe – we're gone. Catch you guys at dinner. Good to know you, Jamie. Don't be a stranger.'

And Jamie admitted to some considerable relief, what with just everything, as the trio moved off, Kimmy with a hold on both of Dorothy's shoulders, now, and piloting her along as if she were lost or blind – with little Mary-Ann very nobly taking up the rear and trailing behind her the distinction of one whose honoured duty it was to bear up on high some glittering train in a right royal procession.

'Oh hey hi, you guys!' Kimmy was practically hollering, as she ambled through the wide open door of their huge apartment. 'Was just trying to call you. Didn't reckon on you two still being around. Hey, Mary-Ann – what say you fix us some coffee? That good? Doe – you wanna go lie down, or what?'

'We're just leaving,' smiled a small and strikingly pretty Japanese girl, as Dorothy shook her head and just stood there. 'The cube's on the side there, Kimmy, and three of the paintings are done. Rest next week. Bye, Kimmy. Bye, Dorothy. Come on Larry – shift yourself.'

A tall and very bony young man was happily uncoiling himself from the cross-legged position he had taken up on the floor and gradually click-clacked his way back up to the perpendicular, the angularity of his movements recalling to Kimmy something of the manner of one of those old and foldaway wood and brass carpenter's rules, a pair of which she had one time had framed and then sold on for five thousand dollars as one of her occasional series of conceptual pieces.

'Oh great – that's great, Lin. I'll get the gallery to come by real quick. So no coffee? OK. See you Tuesday, yeh?'

'Tuesday, sure. Bout ten, that's OK?'

'Great. Cool. So yeah – thanks Larry, kay?' said Kimmy, as she waved them both away, keeping one amused eye on the endless fun of little Lin's neat but rather flat bottom as it shrugged up and down within the skin-tight constraints of those black-as-night and patent-leather jeans of hers – which Kimmy had one time just sworn to Dorothy that Larry, he must do, every morning stitches her into while she stops breathing (or maybe, I don't know – it's just that she never takes them off). Lin sure did have that typical Japanese lady-gait: it looked kinda sore, you know? Like for a long time she'd been astride something wild and bucking.

'C'mon, Doe,' said Kimmy, pulling to the door, but not quite closing it. 'Come sit by me and chill, huh? I'll get the fire going real good.' And then louder, and into the distance: 'Hey Mary-Ann, my little lemon cupcake – how's that coffee coming along?'

'Sorry about earlier . . .' said Dorothy miserably as she slumped herself down into the deep and very long cream calico-covered sofa – which on how many evenings had huggingly swallowed up the three of them, and sometimes Mike and Oona too.

Kimmy was down on her haunches and twisting up torn-out pages from old glossy magazines – or maybe they're new ones, I can't too much be bothered to take a look, and so what the hell anyway? – and now she dropped them lightly into the mouth of a large black cast-iron pot-bellied stove, four-square and grinning on its big fat and widely spread out lion's-paw feet.

'Hey, Doe – it's me, remember? Not ever you got to say sorry.'

'Oh . . . I just always feel – *hooo* . . . such a bloody fool, times like that. Specially with strangers. Will I ever – will I? Kimmy? Do you think I'll ever get over that bloody man? Wouldn't it be good – it'd be really good, wouldn't it, this, if you could just reach inside your head and pluck out all the pain and worrying and nagging and, oh – *pain* . . . and just put it somewhere else, in a box, or something, and then bloody well get on with the *rest* of your life. Because it's a good life, really – yes, I know it is, you don't have to tell me. If it wasn't for him. It's just so *heavy* – dragging it around all the time. If he's – if he's *gone*, well then why can't he just *go*, then?'

'I told you, Doe: just don't let it bug you. It's not – he's just not worth it. And hey – which one of them is?'

Dorothy sort of laughed (and sort of bravely) as she absentmindedly fingered the corner of one of the three new paintings on the table beside her.

'The cube's looking good,' she said, glancing across at the orange perspex box there – jammed to the brim with tightly coiled-up feathers. 'Are they chicken, the feathers?'

'No idea,' said Kimmy. 'Goose, I think she said. I didn't ask.'

'She's awfully pretty, Lin, isn't she?' Dorothy then said, quite airily. 'I've always thought she was, anyway.'

Kimmy had the fire lit now, and within just seconds the bright hot crackling filled the void – it was as if the monster's huge and toothy mouth had gobbled up whole a glimmering pumpkin.

'She doesn't think that,' said Kimmy, falling back into the sofa – half on to Dorothy, whose hair she now idly was teasing. 'She said to me once that she sometimes real, like – hated the way she looked, you know? She reckons she looks like someone just hit her hard in the face with a frypan. Me, I think she's kinda cute. Guys sure go for that type.'

'*Hah*!' snorted out Dorothy. 'Guys! They go for *any* bloody type, don't they? At the beginning. Guys. Huh! Maybe I should –

yeh, I *will*, actually,' she resolved quite suddenly, hauling herself up and then smoothing herself down. 'I'll go and help Mary-Ann – she can only carry in one mug at a time, little thing. I'll go and put it all on a tray. You want biscuits?'

'Sure . . .' agreed a now slightly preoccupied Kimmy, as she squinted critically at the three new paintings. 'Biscuits. Cool. Yeh sure . . .'

Behind a half-wall and down two steps was the endless, beamed and high-vaulted space they called the kitchen. In pride of place there stood a large four-oven steel industrial cooker with a gleaming conical matching canopy – it came from Kimmy's old house in Fulham, and no one had ever used it. The tall American fridge, though – they depended on that (that was a lifeline) due to the constant grazing of Kimmy and Dorothy, and of course for Mary-Ann's flavoured ice cubes which she seemed to have these days with just everything – even her teatime Corn Flakes (and especially she loved them with chocolate milk). Dorothy was pleased that she had arrived just as the electric kettle was grumbling loudly and threatening to launch itself just prior to switch-off – because little Mary-Ann, she *could* manage it (she had done it before) but still Dorothy was never altogether happy – found it hard to hold back when Mary-Ann was bravely and with great care lifting it down, her eyebrows knitted into total concentration.

'Here, sweetheart – let Mummy do it. Let me finish off, yes?'

Mary-Ann simply shrugged, and let her get on with it.

'What did you think of the man,' she stated (because it wasn't a question – it was a statement, this). 'The new person. Jamie. And there are others too, Oona was telling me. Three other men, and one of them's a cook.'

'Thank Christ,' said Dorothy, flipping out on to a large square plate a selection of sweet and sugary biscuits that Mary-Ann does quite go for, I'm fairly sure, but Kimmy just can't get enough of.

'One more of those terrible stews . . . ! It was getting hard to stay polite about them. Poor old Mike.'

'I feel funny,' said Mary-Ann gravely, 'when there are new people. I like it with just the people we've got.'

'Well I know what you *mean*, darling,' sympathized Dorothy (yes darling I do, because I feel it myself). 'But you have to remember that we – we were new people once, weren't we? Not too long ago. And you remember also how terribly kind everyone was to us? And how we all got on? Well that's how we have to be too, isn't it? Otherwise, you see – well otherwise, none of it *works*. And also – they're all chosen by Lucas, aren't they? That's the important thing.'

And Mary-Ann visibly brightened at that.

'Yes,' she nodded – much more positively and pretty much happy by now, it seemed (and isn't it funny, Dorothy marvelled: the ups and downs of children's minds?). 'Yes. And if Lucas chose them, they *must* be good people, mustn't they Mummy? Lucas never ever makes mistakes. I wish everyone could be like Lucas. Wouldn't that be wonderful?'

'Well . . .' demurred Dorothy. 'Yes. Yes – I suppose it would. But we've got the *real* Lucas, haven't we? And that's more than enough for all of us. Just one Lucas is all anyone needs.'

Mary-Ann nodded quite fiercely.

'He's . . . *great*,' she said, with finality. And looking up at Dorothy, she added firmly: 'I just love him.'

'He is,' agreed Dorothy. 'And so do we all. Come on, my sweet – I've got the tray here, so you just follow me in with the biscuits, yes? Whoo – oh *careful*, sweetheart . . . don't tug at Mummy like that – I nearly dropped the lot. What is it now, Mary-Ann?'

And her eyes, oh her eyes – when Mary-Ann's eyes were trained on her again: so full and round and not far this side of the tears that Dorothy knew would just instantly trigger off her own . . . it was then that she came so very close to loathing that bloody bloody husband of hers, the distant father of this fragile thing. Close, yes – but never, oh damn, ever close enough. If only she could slash herself free of every tattered vestige of tender caring and spin over the brink and into the abyss and wallow and splatter in a red-hot cascade of pure and evil barb-tipped hatred – could she maybe be healed by such terrible searing? But no. Didn't happen. She seemed doomed to an exhausting weakness and the gnawing memory of all she had loved in him, and wanted back so very much.

'Lucas . . .' said Mary-Ann, slowly – unsure, maybe, if what she was about to voice was not (even whispered, and just to her Mummy) somehow stained and sinful. 'He won't, will he Mummy? Ever leave us?'

And at least now Dorothy could give free and full-throated vent to decrying so wild and unspeakable a notion as that.

'*Lucas*? Oh my *God*, Mary-Ann – what are you *saying*? We're all of us here because of Lucas, aren't we? Hm? Lucas *is* us, isn't he darling? How could he ever leave?'

'I know . . . I know that, Mummy, of course I do. It's just that sometimes . . . some people do. That's all. I meant.'

'I know, my pet. I know. Look come on – grab the biscuits, yes? There's a good girl. Poor Kimmy – she'll be desperate by now.'

Which proved about right.

'Jeez!' exhaled Kimmy, when the two of them emerged. 'I got to thinking you two had crashed for the night. Come gimme a Fig Newton – I need to keep my sugar up. Two Fig Newtons. Hey, Doe – what think about the pictures? They good as the last batch? Better? What you say, Mary-Ann? This one I like. I like the ones with loadsa red in.'

Dorothy set down the tray. The three of them nibbled on biscuits as they surveyed these latest canvases, now lined up and leaning against the wall.

'I think they're fine,' concluded Dorothy. 'The gallery'll love them. They're the most commercial, the striped ones, aren't they?'

'*Commercial*!' hooted Kimmy. 'You kidding me? These are presold before they even hit. I'm on a real high. Telling you – these babies, they're selling so quick I just don't know if I'll get together enough of anything for an exhibition. Still – meantime, fifteen grand a bang, I sure ain't complaining. Coffee's kinda cold . . .'

'Is it? Sorry. We were talking. What's the cube thing, Kimmy? Are you – is there going to be a series?'

'I reckon there could be. See how it goes, yeh?'

'What I don't . . . understand,' said Mary-Ann. 'I mean – Mummy tried to explain it to me once, but I still don't quite get. I mean – if Lin and Larry *do* all this stuff, then how come – ?'

'Ha!' laughed Kimmy. 'How come I get to put my name on them, yeh? Baby – you ain't the first. See, honey – art, the whole thing of art, yeh? It's all shook up, now – all changed, big time. What it all is now is, like – the *concept*? The idea? You know what I'm saying? So the cube, yeah? I thought – hey: perspex box with feathers. Anyone done that? The BritArt guys? Anyone? I don't believe so. So what the hay – and who knows? It goes down big, we do a series: red, green, blue – you get it, honey? Maybe we fool with the feathers, some. Then we got a icon on our hands. We sell for, what? Say only eight, nine grand, the first of them – checking it out. My dealer – Marty, yeah? He takes maybe three on account of he's a greedy little pimp and a rip-off merchant – but hey: I love the guy to bits, what can I tell you? Larry – him we give a couple hundred, Lin gets five, six hundred say, for, like, bringing it all together . . . and the rest, sweet things, comes right home to momma. Us. Four grand, maybe. How cool is that? So the way I figure: *concept*, baby. Way to go! So, like – Rembrandt? Van *Go*? Hey guys – eat your heart out. You know what I'm saying?'

CHAPTER FOUR

Amid the ochre half-light in Mike and Oona Killery's home-made and boxed-off little bedroom, there hovered a pall of sweet and sickening warmth, and they loved it, now – had maybe, even, come to need it. It was only when friends and neighbours put their heads around the door – Teddy and Judy, say, or Dorothy maybe (and little Mary-Ann, she really did hate it, little thing) – that anyone would remark upon the blue and lazy, thick licking flame at the base of their reconditioned Aladdin Pink Paraffin heater. For themselves (and in particular when winter was looming) Mike and Oona were very content to give themselves up to the mildly heady indolence that descended like a shawl (and they drew it around them for comfort, as well as to keep bad things at bay). Don't you find it makes you feel ill, ever? someone might ask them, concerned. And Mike would say No. Or give you the most awful sort of throbbing headache? And Mike would smilingly raise an eyebrow and lean across to Oona – and Oona, she'd smile too with languor and say No.

But no one would be calling, just now. Not at least, this far to the rear of their intricately crafted little warren of rooms and dog-legged passages. Because oh yes – Mike was quite sure that someone or other could well be pottering about in the sitting room right at this very moment as we speak (they often did, if the truth be known, because despite how everyone went on about it all, it was really quite surprising the number of people around here who were truly rather fascinated by this precious little chunk

114

of Blighty, held in amber). Teddy, I know, finds it all very homely – wishes, he says, that his place could be like it. And John, old John – John with that flapper of his, Frankie – yes? Well – transfixed, really, wouldn't be too strong a word, where John is concerned. Not at first, no – but you should see him now. And it's a mutual thing, really, because I honestly have come lately to hang on his every word – because listen: he actually did, you know, John – he really did live through the whole of the show. I mean admittedly, when War broke out he could only have been about, what . . . ? Well nobody quite seems to know exactly how old the fellow is (and you're not going to *ask*, are you? Not if people don't volunteer, you're not) but say for the sake of argument he's sixty-five, yes? Which seems to be pretty much the average sort of guess. Well right, then – take sixty-five from, um – what are we in, now? Two thousand and, uh . . . well look, what it all more or less boils down to is that he was a child, a schoolboy, of maybe just eight or nine by the time we finally brought the Jerries to their knees (and that's not much less than Mary-Ann's age, I'm fairly sure – and just one year more than our little Jeremy would have been, you know. By now. Yes. Yes. Seventh birthday on the twenty-third of next month. Never even saw his second, little Jeremy. Well. That's it. Can't dwell). The point I'm making here is not that, though, no – nothing at all to do with any little part of that. What I'm saying is, well – *you* have memories of when you were eight, don't you? Childhood memories? And seven. Far back as three, some people go, I'm told. But I for myself could never claim that. Things are fairly vivid in my mind from, ooh – about when I was six-ish or thereabouts, reasonably sure. Bay City Rollers, Gary Glitter, Queen's Silver Jubilee – all that sort of horror. So goodness – just think what *John* has to look back on, with the bombs raining down, and everything (and don't think for one moment that I haven't asked him. God, these days – and Frankie, she could kill me – I never let the poor man alone). And here's something funny about memory: listen to this. At first, John, he said to me No sorry, Mike – I'd love to help out, believe me – flesh out a few things – but I'm a complete bloody blank, I very much regret to have to tell you. Down the years, all my brain cells have been pickled in Scotch: no use to you at all, old man (is how he was going). Ah but then – then he came and saw all the *stuff*, didn't he? And just one glance at these old Crosse & Blackwell tins I've got – rhubarb, one of them is, and I've also got beans – all with just these tiny crudely printed labels (all this down to the paper shortage – I'll tell you all about it, some time) . . . and then when he saw the box of powdered egg, there – and next to it the cloudy bottle of cod liver oil, oh my goodness – the memories came out of him almost in the form of a staggered series of stylized retches and gaggings – a delayed reaction, as he put it (because he's a real true gentleman, John is), to the *difficult* times, yes – and then the warm smiles of memory were wreathing him too – lovely to look at – and suddenly he was recalling the bright summer sun on the new-mown lawn and the jawbreaking blackjacks bought for a farthing with his mother's precious coupons – and Spam and no bananas and the old 'Dig For Victory' poster (which was plastered up just everywhere, he told me, one time: I've had to make do with a Sixties reproduction) and then the whistling and booming scary broadcasts as they all of them would cluster after tea around the wireless. He's unstoppable sometimes, is John, which is – oh, I can't tell you how great that is for me. Suddenly, though, he can come over just a bit sad, you know? Gets a bit sort of blue. And he goes Oh Christ I tell you, Mike – I feel so bloody *old* . . . and that's usually when Frankie steps in and kisses his shiny pink head and says Oh come on John, for God's sake – why don't we get out of this fusty old museum (no offence, Mike – didn't mean anything, Oona) and let's get the car and go and have us some *fun*, yeh? And her age, how can you blame her? But it's odd, though, isn't it? (I think so, anyway.) You know – what some people go for in life. And the things that leave others quite cold.

Goodness. Where did all that lot come from? I didn't actually intend to go into any little bit of that. Because it wasn't John and the War I was meaning to talk about – no, it was Oona, my Oona. All I meant was (oh yes – I remember how we got into all this, now) that there's often someone or other wandering around in various bits of the house (I call it a house) because, well, I expect it's clear by now – that's just how it is here: you're passing, you drop in. That's the way it works. And it's very nice. So special. But obviously there are times, aren't there, when you want a bit of privacy (only natural) and this is where our house has the edge over all the other unconverted spaces, see. Tell you what we do, will I? All we do is, we hang this little enamel sign over the handle of the bedroom door: I found it in the Portobello Road. It's a kind of primrose colour, and it says in blue: 'Sorry, We're Closed – Even For The Sale Of Lyons Tea. We Open At . . .' And then underneath that, you see, there's a little sort of clockface affair and all you do is you twiddle the hands around to whatever time you want. Beautifully simple (unlike nowadays). It could actually be just post-war that sign (1950, the man I bought it off reckoned – maybe late Forties) but still it's a little gem, don't you think? We love it. Anyway – people know now, you see, to keep a little distance when the Lyons Tea sign is up. Oh you get all the jokes *afterwards*, of course you do: Enjoy your *tea*, did you? Refreshing *cuppa*, was it . . . ? All that sort of thing (Judy's the worst). But you take it in the spirit, don't you? You have to face it: that's what getting on with people is basically all about.

So anyway. The only down side of the paraffin heater (the trusty old Aladdin – which is where we came in) is . . . well, in honesty there are two things, really. The first is that it only really seems to heat the air around your head – the floor it wants nothing to do with. So although the area of the bedroom remains pretty snug in itself, all told – only twelve by nine, after all (standard at the time) – there's no denying, you can't get away from the fact that it is surrounded, on three sides anyway, by an awful lot of bare and lofty space, and despite the blackouts and everything, the draughts that whistle in beneath the partitions can cut your ankles to ribbons, I'm telling you here and now; and particularly when you're in a general sort of clothes-removing situation, if you take my meaning. When your first bare foot touches down on that linoleum, you surely do know about it. So that's one thing. The other thing is, before we got the heater we used to make a concerted dive for under the bedcovers and snuggle up eagerly, Oona and me, both sets of our teeth c-c-clattering away like a chorus of castanets, they were (it was funny and yet somehow erotic, in a maybe slightly childish way), and this was as well so very *authentic*, you see: like I say – quite exciting, all on its own. Because during the War, you know, a man and wife retiring early to enjoy the pleasures of the marital bed was truly one of the very few temptations on offer, in the darkest days – the blackouts enclosed you (so no one was going to be bawling up at the window 'Ere you – Put That Light Out!') and of course it was *free*, wasn't it? Didn't even involve any coupons. So a huddling together for mutual warmth in the creaking wood and metal bedframe piled high with a make-do-and-mend half-assembled quilt, possibly a rag rug made up of shredded blankets and maybe even a greatcoat or two is pretty much exactly how people went about things. But the trouble is, you see, the old Aladdin heater again; telling you, you just *roast* under that lot, when it's doing the business, and so in no time at all you start in on chucking off all the covers, and . . . I don't know, that just doesn't seem right: not authentic, somehow (goes against the spirit of conservation). So what we've taken to doing now is turning down the Aladdin to the very lowest level so that in truth all you're getting out of it is the basic and fairly crucial stench of the thing . . . and then we just light candles. The plain cream utility ones, it goes without saying, with maybe the odd nightlight thrown in. You can still buy them in bales in lots of street markets – the sorts of stalls that still sell traditional scullery ware such as those segregated galvanized buckets with a cupped and slatted drain on the one side in which to grind down and twist on the sopping old cloth mop-head, prior to giving the whole of the floor a damn good rinse after so much soap and swabbing. We've got one of those, as a matter of fact; we keep it in a little storage cupboard I once knocked up from a few old scaffolding boards. Also in there is a 1934 Ewbank sweeper, a green tin dustpan and brush (proper bristle) and cut-up combinations that we use for dusters. Oona tells me they all work very well – as, of course, they had to, didn't they? For a whole generation not so fortunate as ourselves. She does say too, in fairness, that it's crazy to go to these government surplus stores to buy these old sets of combinations just to take the pinking shears to them so as to make dusters (because I don't go that far – I don't actually wear them: you have to keep a sense of proportion in all things, you know. I'm not a nutter. I'm a Y-Front man myself, for choice) – and yes, I admit, she has a fair point, there . . . but look, they cost next to nothing and they really do add to the whole that small but all-important touch. Look – this sort of maybe pernickety detail, it either matters to you or it doesn't: I think you know where I stand. Ooh yes – and by the way: in that little store cupboard of ours, yes? I've also got a fuse box with those big cream porcelain sort of piano-key things that you pull out and then wind around the terminals the appropriate thickness of wire (you get three sorts on a card) and an enormous bile-green enamelled gas meter with all these dials like the control room in a submarine. Takes old pennies. Neither of these is actually connected up to anything, I have to say – all the services are centrally provided here, courtesy of our noble benefactor – but I'm telling you: you creak open that cupboard and you see all that stuff and then you inhale the mingled aromas of paraffin and mothballs and candle wax and DDT and I'm telling you – it takes you right back in time: whisks you away. It's really rather funny, sometimes, because of course the War years aren't for me a memory, of course not – and yet little moments such as that, it's more like reliving one's own long-gone past than anything else I can think of (and certainly more so than anything that actually *does* pertain to my earlier days, because nothing at all from the nineteen-seventies stands out to me in any way whatever. It didn't then, and it doesn't now).

Sorry. Sidetracked again. It's just that everything here rather neatly links up, you see – it all has its natural place in the logical order of things, just as it did in the old days. When things just fell into place, and every step of life did not need to be plotted and then *understood*.

One thing about those candles. It's suddenly come back to me. I think the memory has been jogged by a fleeting glimpse of Oona, now, wearing that lovely hand-smocked nightie with the little pink bow at the Peter Pan collar – sprinting for the bed, as the chill begins to bite. Once, quite early on – very soon after I hit upon the candle idea, as a matter of fact – I came into the bedroom, I don't know . . . maybe sooner than I might have been expected, and, well . . . (and goodness, you know – I really don't know why I'm telling you all this, I honestly don't . . . it just must be some sort of natural extension to the almost obsessive spirit of openness, here – here, yes, and all around us) . . . well anyway – Oona was already under the bedclothes, you see, with her face turned away from me and towards the wall – and there was much, um . . . agitation, shall we say, of the coverlet: the rose and lupin counter-pane was in danger of leaping away and rippling to the floor. The rhythmic wheezes of sheer disbelief that were coming from the bedframe very quickly found a partner in my own. At first I thought I'd maybe leave it. And then I thought No – no no: here, this place, Oona and me: it's all about togetherness, isn't it? So what I mustn't be, then, is left out in the cold. So I gently lifted back all of the bedcovers (she didn't yet know I was there, you know – which was, in the circumstances, wholly understandable: she, most certainly, was well down the road to somewhere else entirely) and there I saw her rucked-up flannelette nightshirt and clutched so tightly in all her tensed fingers was one of our hitherto white and innocent, utterly blameless utility candles. Had I maybe sounded over-censorious as I intoned quite coldly Oh Please, Oona – You Mustn't Let Me *Interrupt* You (?). She jerked and started like an electrified rabbit – I assumed, maybe wrongly, at the sound of my voice – and then she coolly proceeded to take me at my word: a good three minutes I was standing there, shivering like a lemon in my lime-green pyjamas and feeling rather surplus to requirements – while meanwhile things had got completely out of hand, and only very gradually began to subside.

We laughed about it, later. Well all right, then: *Oona* laughed about it later (came damn close during, if the truth be known). I simply suggested to her – because at times you just have to go right out on a limb, you know, and try for understanding – that this was maybe not the intention that the old and venerable English firm of Price & Co had possibly had in their collective minds when they all were slaving night and day at the height of the Blitz in order to ensure that every single one of their countrymen – whether maybe as an aid to chortling over Jane in the *Daily Mirror* or else could be making their way to the shelters – had recourse to basic illumination. She wasn't even a bit repentant. Well – even Oona isn't perfect (although she's a good deal more manageable these days, I have to say: being here with me seems over time to have calmed her). She said to never mind basic, she had found it all very illuminating indeed. She even started telling me that such a thing was anyway *authentic*, if you please. Said she had read in the November 1941 issue of the *Lady's Home Journal* (because yes – I buy up all the old magazines, whenever I see them) that to take a candle up to bed was both an economical and practical thing to do in these times of stress, and was guaranteed to impart a warm and rosy glow! Yes that's as *maybe*, I was going – but all they meant was for you to *light* it, Oona! (What, dare I ask, had got into her?) Another time I had to draw the line most firmly was when I got to the bedroom one day soon after tea (put up the Lyons sign) for a prearranged session (albeit, as I had explained, a brief one – I had the whole of my Vera Lynns to recatalogue later that evening, as I recall) and there she was sprawled out on the bed and strapped on to her head was one of our gas-masks! *Oona*, I said – *Oona*, I was going (and hopping from foot to foot as I did it – because I'm telling you, your toes and soles can freeze to that lino) – what in God's name do you think you are *doing*? And she honked out something or other, I assume by way of reply (and maybe God above could have told you what she was saying – sounded to me for all the world like a calving elephant). But I could see by her gestures that she was in earnest about this and I thought Oh well look – I'm no *prude*, for God's sake, so if it'll *please* the woman . . . but oh my God, I tell you this as I told it to her afterwards: never again! Hear me? I mean – *No*, all right, Oona? A gas-mask is a safety precaution, a serious piece of protective equipment and not, it should be fully understood, here, any sort of recreational *tool*. My main objection, if I'm honest, was not based upon some latent fear of enclosure or fetishism per se, no – it was just that every time she moved her head the great long hard and sticking-out muzzle-type bit would up and clonk me bang in the face – and when I did my best to duck down out of the way of it, well then blow me if she wouldn't swing her head right back the other way and I'd get the full force of it slammed into the side of my nose. And all the time I'm jigging up and down! *Look*, I told her squarely, after: *listen*,

122

Oona – now hear this: if this is rapture, well then I'm sorry but my name's Joseph Chamberlain!

Anyway. She's beyond all these nonsenses now, I am very pleased to say. She does still have her G. I. Joe of course, he still lingers on . . . tell you about him, will I? Well I suppose it's harmless enough. On the rare occasion that she smokes a Camel . . . oh hang on: I just have to tell you about the Camels, first – cigarettes, yes? Not, you know – *actual* camels, or anything (of course not). Well you see in this country you can't get the untipped type any more (the originals) so what I do is I buy a regular flip-topped pack of twenty and slice off all the tips with a razor-blade (Gillette – you carefully unfold it from this little blue envelope as the man himself gazes back at you) and then I transfer all the cigarettes to a wartime soft-pack that came as an unexpected bonus with a job lot of, as it turned out, very stale Hershey bars and old *Saturday Evening Posts* from someone who said they'd got them decades earlier when RAF Northolt were having a clearout: just about plausible, you have to suppose. There was also some Wrigley's in unspeakable condition. Anyway. So. She taps out a Camel from the soft-pack, fools with the gunmetal Zippo (more often than not, not actually going so far as to light the thing because at base she's not all that keen, if she's honest) and then she smooths on a brand-new pair (though actually the very same one each time – there's a strong element of playacting to all of this, as you might now be coming to quite understand) of seamed and dark mink-coloured nylons and she whisperingly confides in me how her secret handsome G. I. boyfriend had nuzzled her neck and slipped her a packet in the back of a Willys jeep, not too long after all the jitterbugging was done. 'That's my Joe,' she'd go. And I remonstrated with her about the 'Joe' part, I have to be honest. Well – if I'm *really* honest, I wasn't too keen on any little part of this pungent little fantasy, but this 'Joe' thing I really couldn't let go.

'But why does he have to be *Joe*, Oona? Hm? I mean of all names – *Joe*? Very unoriginal, isn't it?'

Oona just shrugged and drawled her answer back at me in a sort of an American accent, I had to charitably suppose, while drawing deep upon her unlit Camel.

'It's the guy's name. He's called *Joe*. OK? What can I tell you? Hey Mike – you wanna hit the hay now, or what? Lover boy.'

Dear oh dear: so much *masquerade*. It's extraordinary, isn't it? How some people feel compelled to retreat into a world of their own manufacture. Maybe – and who could ever know? – when we *did* make love, and she was in this sort of mood . . . maybe, it was 'Joe' she could be thinking about? Who can tell what goes on in the adult mind when primal urges are the order of the day? For myself, at moments of such intimacy, I give myself up utterly to Oona, body and mind. I'm not saying that sometimes the Andrews Sisters don't somehow manage to winkle their way under the tarpaulin (I think it's just a uniform thing) but that I do assure you is the extent of it: there have to be circumscribed limits, you know – otherwise you can lose all track and perspective.

I am on the whole, I think, a considerate lover. Foreplay – what they these days are pleased to call foreplay – had, of course, not yet been invented during Britain's Darkest Hour, and I can't begin to tell you just what a blessing that is. Not that I wholly neglect the, you know – niceties of the prologue: I always clean my teeth with Euthymol Dental Cream (totally fresh – you can still get it in Boots with nearly the original lettering); the real badger brush is a bit of a pain, if I'm honest, and I'm seriously thinking of replacing it with a blatant anachronism (it's just that you spend such ages picking all the little bits out). But as to the actual, you know – *act*, yes? The nitty-gritty business end of actual sexual intercourse – well once again, our wartime ancestors had it all sorted out: cut and dried. Look: it's basically a male release we're talking about here, isn't it? That, I think, must be obvious to everyone. So all this nonsense about a woman sucking in her cheeks and straining to have an orgasm while the man is busy gritting his teeth and bloody well killing himself in his red-faced efforts *not* to . . . well: completely unnatural, to my way of thinking. Oona now, I think, sees this, so in our case things never take too long: over in a jiffy, more often than not. Which frees you, doesn't it, for other things. While Oona runs a bath, I quite often fill the time by going to the lavatory. Which does, of course, have to involve the dreaded Bronco, I'm afraid – but look, I won't be the first or last, will I, to observe that sometimes these things just have to be done; sometimes one must suffer for one's art.

Mike left Oona sitting on the beige moquette and Rexine sofa with her legs tucked up beside her, and strumming through a yellowed *Woman's Realm*. She seemed content enough, smiling from time to time at the occasional thoroughly familiar quip from an old ITMA tape, and the muffled gales of mirth that inevitably followed; a permissible aberration, Mike had eventually adjudged – the cassette recorder concealed behind a fretwork grille within the bulbous and showy cabinetwork of a long-defunct but once proud Ekco wireless (you just can't get the valves). Those old tapes, in fact – and no listen, Mike won't keep you long on this, he promises – they used to be a fair little source of income, one time. Mike devoted days and weeks to scouring the most arcane sources imaginable for any forgotten or quirky wartime broadcasts, and then he got them very cheaply copied (he met a bloke who did this) and dickied them up nicely for resale. Because it was amazing, he'll have you know, just how many amateur but pretty much full-time nostalgics there were out there: his Roneoed catalogue went out to more than three hundred addresses, at its zenith (the Nottingham area, for some reason, being a particularly rich and lucrative market). And then there were the reprints of old wartime recipe books – how the harassed housewife somehow managed to eke out a handful of not much at all in order to feed and nourish a family of four (and keep them smiling through). They all went down extremely well, oh yes they did – until the big boys moved in. Suddenly, the feeling was all around you that in the past was where just everyone and his uncle should have at least one foot firmly planted. The BBC seemed to have discovered its own unrivalled archives pretty much overnight, it seemed to Mike, and the market was flooded with cassettes and CDs of just anything that had survived half a century of neglect (failing its outright destruction). Reissues of Marguerite Patten cookbooks became quite the thing for a time, not too long ago – and Mike could be wrong about this but he's fairly sure that someone somewhere even went to the extent of reprinting a little pamphlet by Gert and Daisy, humorously devoted to the vexing question of just how those precious rations might be cajoled into going just that little bit further. And all this in the booming 1990s! (Who would have believed it?) For himself, Mike was torn: he revelled in being able to finally acquire so many good things (because even the most dedicated purist did, you know, tire of hearing and rehearing the same few Churchill speeches and the odd song featuring bluebirds or a nightingale, time and time again). But on the other hand, it did severely knock on the head his own little pirate operation. But there – isn't it so often the way? You receive a kiss, and then they cuff you: why complain?

Mike had tugged on a sleeveless Fair Isle V-neck over his collarless blue and white striped shirt (dead men's clothes, Lucas once had called them, but as ever, there had been in his voice neither malice nor mockery – none to Mike's ears – and anyway the observation was no less than accurate: the Croydon branch of Help The Aged, Mike always found, was a peerless source of hitherto mothballed fifty-shilling chalk-stripes, gaberdine raincoats and fur-felt trilbies, once the property of the freshly deceased). What would you do, though, Oona had put it to him one time, if Lucas had told you he was banning them, the period clothes we're always wearing? Well he *wouldn't*, Mike had instantly answered her; but if he did . . . oh no question: I'd bin the lot. No I wouldn't – I'd give them back to the charities they came from. Oona had nodded at that, quite slowly (she was sipping Bournville Cocoa at the time, as Mike recalled – we've got the china mug with a handle like an ear), and then she said OK, all right then – what if Lucas told you that he merely disliked them? That our presence in these clothes he found just mildly offensive? Oh that's easy, Mike had responded in barely an instant: I'd bin the lot. Anyway: so much was hypothesis. Lucas didn't ever interfere in that sort of thing. Quite the reverse: individuality was encouraged. Well – just as well on the whole, don't you think? If you look around you.

'So OK then, Oona – you'll be all right for a while, then, on your own, will you?'

'Of course,' smiled Oona. 'I've got caramels here, look – and if I get lonely, Joe can come over for half an hour – maybe fix me a Bud, and then we can boogie.'

'Yes well,' said Mike. 'Not too many caramels, Oona. New cook tonight, remember – we want to do him justice. I'm off there right now, as it happens. Show him the ropes. Oh God – it's nearly six. I'd better be going.'

'Well I'm sure he won't be as good as you were, Mike.'

'Oh no – that's nonsense. He will be – of course he will be. Most people would, let's face it. I damn well hope so, anyway. Tell you the truth, Oona, I was getting pretty damn sick of eating all those stews myself. I'll tell you, will I, what I think it was that let them down? Thrift. They fell victim to economy. I mean – you know how Lucas gave me a totally free hand? I could have gone to market and ordered, oh – just absolutely anything and he wouldn't have batted an eyelid. But I used to get so taken with the wartime *spirit*, you know? It became quite mad, really, because I'd be scouring the stalls and offering them crazy money to please set aside for me all the muck they pretty much chuck out, these days. Chittlings, brains, brawn . . . hooves, tails – whole great bags of stuff that dripped . . . oh God, I won't go on: you'll be sick on the spot. And Christ – the Bovril I went through . . . ! No,' Mike concluded with a rare magnanimity, 'it's time we had new blood.'

And it was in this spirit of generous concession that Mike now thunked and clanked himself shut into the deeply silent oak-planked service lift, bracketed in iron, that juddered and whined as usual when he jabbed with force at the lowest button, and then with a palpably strained reluctance (as if all its resistance had come to naught, and now it just had to give in to this terrible pressure) those thick and tightly twisted hawsers moaned and barely perceptibly, the cage was lowered. Mike looked up at the open square access vent set into the ceiling and just as ever, as the grumbling of the cables seemed to both deepen and yet somehow whip itself up into near-screaming as each successive floor sank past him, he thought of nothing but how very safe he felt, as the last of the evening light was winking briefly, and then dulled down into the blackness above.

Mike was still half a corridor from the kitchen proper – most of the serious pots and pans, the ones you needed help with, were ranked up in order of size in the adjoining passage, the very largest of them suspended from a bank of red iron corbels, each one of which, according to Lucas, had once supported a brass and jangling bell on a thin curl of steel, in form not too unlike that of a double clef: a simple means of gaining the exclusive attention of just anyone anywhere, in the days when the old printing presses thumped and hissingly rolled (a simple means, Lucas added with a sigh, alas now lost to us: we shall possibly investigate avenues that might ensure its restoration).

And now Mike was nearer – and yes, there could no longer be any mistaking the buzz and clatter: here was industry, plain and simple. Because he had, he supposed, been expecting if anything no more than the hang-around bulk of a dragooned pretender, waiting to be told. But no – not a bit of it: well just stick your head around the door and have a look, then, if you don't believe me. See? There's Tubby: just watch him go. So that was surprise enough; what Mike had not even distantly bargained for, however, were all the teeming other people who seemed to be, oh – just all over the place: Teddy and Judy (what are they doing here?) and my new friend Paul (a very sensitive young man, to my mind) and that other one – what was he called? Never seen the old kitchens so busy. Which was broadly the drift of Tubby's way of thinking – still was, as he rapidly peeled yet another potato (second nature, if you wanna know, mate: how much practice I had doing all this sort of caper, ay? Down all the bleeding years) and lobbed it with aplomb into a large dented copper and brass-handled cauldron, where it plopped into the water and bobbed about palely with seemingly dozens of others. Because look: I *told* Paul, didn't I? Didn't need no bleeding escort – I have done this before, you know: I am capable of turning on the gas all by my bleeding self, Paul – I ain't no stranger to a box of bleeding Vestas. And oh bloody hell no, Biff – you ain't tagging along and all, are you? What's this, then? A fun day out in the fucking country? What's the matter with you anyway, Biff? Why can't you settle? Ay? Put your mind to something. Why don't you hang up your clothes in that bleeding cupboard over there? Ay? Or . . . I don't know – what can he do, Pauly? Must be some bloody thing he can do!

'Here here here, Tubby old mate – be cool, ay?' Paul was laughing. 'Keep the lid on. No good getting all fuck-faced about it, is there? Ay? Biff and me – kindness of our hearts, mind – we was just coming along to, like, help you get sorted. Ain't that right, Biff? What mates are for.'

'*Told* you,' hooted Tubby. 'Don't need no bleeding help, do I? And another thing, Paul – when was you any sort of good at all in a kitchen then, ay? Couldn't boil water, you couldn't.'

'Well that's just where you're wrong, mister bleeding gourmet chef, yeh? Blimey, Biff – I reckon all what I said to friend Lucas about our Tubby's wossname, er – thing, what is it? – *prowess*, that it? Nah – no good asking you, Biff, is it? Anyway – whatever's the art of sodding about in a kitchen, yeh? Reckon it's gone to his head. Suddenly he's Mister Wonderful, and he don't need no help from no one – even his best mates, what's looking out for him. Only marking your *card*, son.'

'Oh don't go giving me none of that cobblers. Paul! You know bleeding well what I'm on about. I'm best on my own – always was. Proved that to you, didn't I? Ay? Showed you. That last job we done. And what you *mean*? Ay? You trying to tell me you're a little bit tasty at cooking or something, Paul? Cos that's a new one on me, I'm telling you. You ever got a whiff of that, Biff? Ay? When's last time you ever knock us up anything at all then, Paul? Don't never remember you even going down the Chinese. You don't even do us a *brew*, you don't.'

Paul was laughing, now: really enjoying hisself.

'Wrong – all wrong, Tubby mate, as it so happens. Many's the time I been watching a egg in a saucepan of, what? Water. Yeh. And all the bubbles, right?'

'Oh leave it out, Paul. You're just dicking about.'

'No straight – listen. Got my eye on this egg, OK? Just poncing around in the water, yeh? And I says to it – know what I says to it, Biff?'

Biff thought about that for a moment.

'No,' he said.

'No – right then: well I'll tell you.'

'Look, Paul . . .' said Tubby, quite wearily. 'I got to get down there, yeh?'

'I'll *tell* you what I said. I said OK, Mister Egg – reckon you got one on me, do you? Well come on out then, if you think you're *hard* enough!'

Tubby sighed. 'Oh Christ . . .'

Biff looked very serious and then he jabbed a finger directly at Paul, right between the eyes.

'That,' he said, 'was *funny*. Yeh?'

'Look, Paul,' broke in Tubby (Jesus – they get like this, telling you: go on all bleeding night). 'I'm off, OK? You wanna come along, well then fine. OK. Can't bleeding stop you, can I?'

Paul leant over and chucked him on the cheek.

'No, my petal,' he smirked, 'you can't. Oh and another thing, Tubby, while we're talking. Don't you ever go on about a job in the same way as messing about in a kitchen, OK? On a job, yeh – I agree with you, mate. You're best there is, when you got a bit of space. Respect. Mean it, son. But bloody hell, Tubs – we're only talking meat and two veg, ain't we? Ay? Not like it's wossname surgery, nor nothing, is it?'

'Brain . . .' said Biff. And they both of them looked at him, briefly.

'Ych,' nodded Paul. 'Quite right, Biff old mate. Not *brain* surgery we're talking here – is it. Tubs? More the merrier, ay? You know it makes sense. All of us mucking in like what we do – yeh Biff? It's what it's all about.'

'Oh *Christ* . . .' moaned Tubby. 'Here it comes . . .'

'Innit? Ay?' insisted Paul. 'Yeh it is. Alfie. Now come on – what you thinking about, Tubs? You don't get yourself down there in double quick time, mate, you're gonna be late. Entcha?'

So that's how it all went down: Paul got his own way, course he bleeding did (well when didn't he? Paul? Ay?), and so the three of them found their way down to the basement – no problem: just straight into this well rickety old lift and *shooom*! All the way down, no messing, sweet as you like. And when he clapped eyes on it, Tubby was impressed, he wouldn't mind telling you. This was a kitchen proper, mate – not at all like what I'm used to. *Clean*, for a bleeding start. Bloody great range, there – looks like it come straight out of a crematorium. Lots of surfaces (what you need) and out back a freezer the like of what you would not believe: feed an army, stuff in there. Plus, in the fridge (you could walk right in, but I wouldn't fancy it) there was just all sorts. So I pulls out all this really lovely-looking meat – got to be fillet, ennit? We are talking prime, my son. And then I gets to nosing about, getting my bearings, sort of style – opening and shutting this cupboard and that, and that – generally getting down the feel of the place, know what I mean?

'You know what?' said Paul – yeh, he only *said* it, but I'm telling you: sounded more like a yodel, down here. Reckon it could be something to do with this sort of arched and curvy ceiling way up there, look, and maybe the tiles we got on the floor.

'No need to shout, is there?' came back Tubby. 'And what you got there, Paul? Don't go messing things about.'

Paul had his hand stuck well inside a big glass jar – but he held it stock-still, now, as his eyes went as wide and stricken as they could run to, he was that affronted.

'Messing *about*? Messing *about*? What you mean, son – messing *about*? I'm *sampling*, ain't I? All your best cooks are well into that, you know, Tubby. Thought you would've been well up to speed on that one, son. Always having a taste, they are. These is . . . what you reckon, Biff, get your laughing gear round one of these, mate.'

Paul rammed something soft and brownish between Biff's lips, and Biff now was concentrating hard as he dutifully chewed it. Paul was energetically champing down on a couple more himself.

'So – what you think then, Biff?'

'Look Paul . . .' said Tubby. 'If you're gonna help then bleeding *help*, OK? Get the lid on that jar and give me a hand with these pots here, all right?'

'Yeh yeh – all in good time, Tubs. All in good time. So what you reckon we got here then, Biff?'

Biff was still chewing it, whatever it was. He seemed confused.

'I dunno . . .' he said.

'You know what I reckon?' said Paul – getting his lot down and stuffing in another. 'I reckon what we got here is your dried peaches, or something in that sort of line. Yeh Biff? Peach, you reckon?'

Biff was still chewing it, whatever it was. He seemed confused.

'I dunno . . .' he said.

'More like . . .' said Tubby, grudgingly (and I'd better just haul out all these bleeding pots myself then, hadn't I? I can see just what sort of a help these two is going to be – why'd they have to bleeding *come*?). 'More like apricot, if it's that sort of taste. Probably that.'

Paul put another one in his mouth and closed his eyes as he clucked his palate (like a bleeding duck, looked like to Tubby).

'Apricot, ay?' went Paul. 'Yeh – see what you mean. Could well be your apricot is what we got here. What you think Biff? Apricot?'

Biff had swallowed it now, whatever it was. He seemed confused.

'I dunno . . .' he said.

'Oh dear oh dear!' Paul was guffawing (and telling you – if Tubby hadn't been heaving over an armful of steel pans with lids on and I think an aluminium steamer, this one is, he would have clapped both his hands to the sides of his face, the ruckus was that

133

bleeding bad – seemed to bang off of all the bleeding walls and come right back and slam you right in the kisser). 'You don't know too much of nothing, do you Biff old mate? Never mind. I loves ya still!'

Paul messed up Biff's hair at the front and pinched his cheek and Biff just stood there, blushing under the weight of it.

And Tubby was right this bleeding second on the verge of putting his foot down. I mean, come on now: be fair. I got to get my head around this, yeah? Cos it's down to me. I got to do three courses for, dunno – about fifteen people, I reckon (that Alice said fifteen for definite but to see there's plenty on account of she wasn't quite sure if the Hitlers was coming down: I swear that's what she said), and the clock ain't standing still on me, is it? Nah – cos clocks, they ain't in the business of doing that, are they? On and on, is what clocks go: that's the nature of it, as well we all know: tick bleeding tock. So what I mean is – I can *do* this, OK? I know I can *do* this, right? It don't bother me. But what I do not need is a couple of jokers sodding about and getting all in the bleeding *way*. So I'm just going to tell them to sling their hook . . . I'm just going to turn round and say Look Paul – Look Biff . . . and here just wait a minute! Hang about . . . what's all *this* now, ay? Oh *no*! Oh Christ preserve us – I do not Adam and *Eve* it! It's only bleeding *more* people what've come banging on in through the door, innit? Oh well that's only bleeding *marvellous*, ay? I mean – what? I brung my banjo down, I could give them all a little *tune*! Gawd – I'm telling you: it ain't easy, this. Face it – nothing is, when there's people about. All they do is fuck you up.

'Hello hello *hello*!' cried Judy excitedly, as she hopped, skipped and jumped her way into the kitchen – one hand trailing behind her and scything the air in a blind attempt to catch a hold of Teddy, who was lagging. In her other hand she was clutching what looked like to Tubby a socking great big bunch of flowers, only with the actual flower bits not sort of there at the ends of all the doings.

'You must be Mister Tubby then, yes?' she greeted him – coming up really close so that all this greenery was tickling the end of his nose. 'So many new faces! My name is Judy, everyone – and this bronzed demigod behind me is my partner, soulmate, lover – anyway, Teddy. All the wine in the cupboards behind you is Teddy's – isn't it, Teddy? Makes it all himself, and it is totally *delicious*. These, Mister Tubby, are herbs.'

'I was wondering,' said Paul, 'where all the booze was. Who's this Herb then, Judy love? My name's Paul. This is Biff. Say hallo to the lady, Biff. And yeh – Mister Tubby you already met.'

'Hm . . . ?' checked Judy, a little perplexed. 'Oh no no no no *no*, you silly boy! Not *Herb* – *herbs*! See? These. There's fresh thyme here, Mister Tubby – see this, yes? And flat leaf parsley – that's mint, that's spearmint. And Basil.'

'Who's this Basil then, Judy love?' laughed Paul. 'Nah – just kidding you. Well I reckon that's right good on you, all these herbs – ain't that good on her, Mister Tubby?'

'Oh Christ's sake Paul leave it *out*,' growled Tubby. 'My name's *Tubby*, missus – um, Judy. Just Tubby. You don't have to go bothering with no "mister", OK? And yeh – ta for the herbs. I go for fresh herbs, I do. Make a big difference.'

'*Essential*,' avowed Judy, with large emphasis. 'I grow them all on our balcony, you know. Great big bushes of them. The sun we get up there is really extraordinary – even in winter. I can't tell you how nice it is to meet you all! Welcome – welcome. What *fun* we're all going to have. Yes? *Great* fun. Come and say hello to everyone, Teddy! Don't *skulk* . . .'

Teddy stepped forward and muttered to the floor that he had, actually, just earlier, kind of given a little wave to everyone generally because, well, Judy was, you know – talking, and he didn't want to sort of interrupt.

'Anyway,' he tacked on. 'Lillicrap. Now, Tubby – I think you just might be running a bit low on what I flatter myself in calling, um – burgundy. I do several types – chardonnay, and then a sweeter white and what on an awfully bad day could just about pass for a good ordinary claret. I'll bring some more down a bit later.'

'Sounds favourite,' approved Paul. 'What say we all of us have a little bit of a taster of Château Teddy right now then, ay?'

'Oh *yes*,' agreed Judy. 'Let's all toast the newcomers, yes?'

'Um – *look*,' put in Tubby. 'I don't want to, you know – like kind of put a spoke in, or nothing, but . . . could we maybe sort of leave all that out till later, like? It's just I –'

'Oh but of *course*,' understood Judy immediately. 'Whatever was I thinking of? Mister Tubby's got a *meal* to be getting on with, and here we all are just getting in the *way*. Plenty of time for drinkies later, boys! Come on, Teddy – off we go. Oh – hello Mike! How lovely to see you. Look everyone – it's Mike. Didn't expect to see you, Mike – caught sight of the Lyons Tea sign, didn't I? Goodness – you're getting quicker and quicker! Anyway – welcome, welcome. Quite a little party!'

Yeh, thought Tubby – it is and all, ain't it? Maybe the Coldstream sodding Guards might happen along, give it a minute. Then we can all line up and troop the bleeding colour.

'Oh – don't mind me!' laughed Mike. 'I just dropped by to see that, um – Tubby here had, you know – found the place all right – but I can see he's well stuck in. Hey, Tubby? Well stuck in, yes? Hallo again, Paul. I've dug out those Eighth Army medals I was talking about, if you're still interested at all?'

Paul's eyes were already alight. 'Yeh? Oh *yeh*, Mike – great. I'll have some of that right now, if that's OK with you.'

'Oh yes – I'm not doing anything at all until dinner. I must say, Tubby – it's a tremendous *relief* to me that you're now doing, er – all of this.'

'Yeh well . . .' went Tubby. (Oh blimey – I got to be polite, haven't I? I just got to be polite. I mean – all I wanna do is just slosh them all in the face and scream at them to get the fuck *out* of here, but I *can't*, can I? I just got to be polite . . .) 'It'd be good, you know . . . to sort of start getting going, like . . .'

'Yeh yeh,' laughed Paul. 'Hint taken, Tubs me old lad – we're out of here, OK? Come on then, Mike. And your Oona sweet with it, is she?'

Mike nodded eagerly. 'Oh *Lord* yes – utterly tickety-boo. Oh yes and *Paul* – you recall you were rather interested in that tea service? The black and white one?'

'What – the Shelley?' checked Paul. 'Oh yeh – triffic, that was.'

'Well – I've also got – hold on to your hat, now! I've also actually got one or two pieces of Clarice Cliff . . . !'

Paul's whole face was shining. 'Nah! You're having me on! What – kosher Clarice Cliff? Bizarre Ware, is it? The orange and blue caper?'

Mike was nodding as if desperate to once and for all rid his head of the whole idea.

'Absa-*lootly*. Let's go, shall we? Well look – very best of luck, um – Tubby. I'm sure everyone here is just so terribly happy that *I'm* not cooking any more – they'll just fall on anything you do like ravenous lions! Oh . . . not that I mean that what you do won't be, um . . . well – you know, I expect.'

'Oh *nonsense*, Mike,' deplored Judy, batting at him one get-away-with-you hand. 'That thing you did just the other night – Sunday, wasn't it? That gorgeous creamy chickeny sort of cas-serole-type thing, yes? Totally *delicious*. We all thought so. Everyone did.'

'Oh well *thank* you, Judy – thank you. You're very kind. You coming then, Paul? Yes? OK then, all – see you at dinner.'

Paul and Mike were on the point of leaving when Mike turned back and with what seemed like extreme reluctance – it was almost as if the burden of guilt had of a sudden become just too much for him to bear – he added on flatly:

'Actually, um, Judy – it was *fish*, that thing. On Sunday. Not chicken. Fish.'

'Really?' Judy came back brightly, not in the slightest bit fazed. 'Well it was totally *delicious*. We all thought so. Everyone did. Now come along, Teddy – let's go and fetch down the plonk for Mister Tubby. Actually, children – I say that in jest: it's totally *delicious*. We all think so. Everyone does.'

Mike and Paul were gone now, and Judy and Teddy were not too far behind them. Tubby (and Jesus – it took a while) could finally begin to relax.

'Well what you waiting for, Biff? Ay? Go on then – out of it. Why don't you – Christ, I don't know – go and hang up your clothes in that cupboard we got there, yeh? Look – do what you like, right, just not around here – OK Biff? Blimey – you near emptied that whole jar of wossnames, you have – apricots, or whatever they was. You got a taste for them now, have you? Decided you like them?'

Biff had now swallowed the last of them, whatever they were. He seemed confused.

'I dunno . . .' he said.

Tubby just chucked up his eyes to heaven and waved him away and at long bleeding last just started to get *on* with it. Because I'm telling you: it ain't easy, this. Face it – nothing is, when there's people about. All they do is fuck you up.

Teddy jammed a freshly-washed bottle up tight to the neck of the narrow spigot, twisted the flange once and firmly anticlockwise and his lips now were moving in steady time as he counted up to seven, and then shut off the tap. He knew, now, to the absolute moment, just how long a standard bottle took to fill to within a cork's depth of the lip. It had become now, really, something of a way of life, he supposed, all this winemaking business. He had started off – oh, like so many optimists before him, he imagined: a simple shop-bought kit, the one glass flagon. Initial mixing was soon giving way to a peculiarly varied succession of many evil smells and the odd outright and always terrifying explosion before the great day would finally dawn when the very first sample could be drawn off with care. This was then quickly poured back and soon, with equal care, repoured through muslin (because it's not, is it, meant to look like that? Is it, Judy? All sort of thick and cloudy and pretty much bloody-looking with all those funny little flaky bits not just floating, but sinking too?); and then it was solemnly tasted by both of them. A mouthful was held (the idea, Teddy later reflected, of going the whole hog and actually getting the stuff down you, seeming at the time just that one step too far into the arms of commitment) and then an over-postponed enquiring eye was passed across to Judy. Who looked as if she had all night been gorging on limes. Or else was maybe stiffening the sinews prior to planting one hell of a smacker upon the pustular snout of a slack-tongued mutt of indeterminate breed. 'Not, um – *great*, is it?' Teddy had ventured. 'Well . . .' came Judy's gasped-out suggestion (because she had, you know – she'd swallowed it) ' . . . it does seem to lack a certain, um . . . maybe if we added a little bit of sugar?' So they did that. And of course it didn't melt, so the next very tentative swiglet was not just swinishly sour, but crunchy to boot. Well this batch, possibly, we could use for, I don't know – cooking, maybe . . . ? Offer it to the kitchens, should we, for something on the lines of coq au vin? It would be better, countered Teddy (well look: one has to face such initial setbacks head-on, you know; else where is the scope for improvement, you see? If you are not ready to acknowledge your shortcomings) . . . if it's usable at all, I would suggest it would be better just sprinkled sparingly over a bagful of chips. And yes they tried that, and no it didn't work (the chips appeared to rot, before their eyes) – so that first batch, it turned out, proved to be just ideal for tipping down the old Belfast sink in the farthest corner, there (and Judy would later swear in whispers, when Teddy was out of earshot, that the porcelain glaze of the surface has never really wholly got over it – pink, look, and roughish).

Yes well. All that was a long time ago, he was pleased to be able to report. These days, what we had ourselves here was a well-honed and slick operation, even if Teddy did say so himself – and on a pretty fair scale as well, now. A whole great double bank of vast glass amphorae we have here, look – three quarters of which are at any given time doing all the business – fermenting away with the best of them – and just across here, do you see, are these four very large old sherry casks that Mike (bless him) had alerted Teddy to, oh – many moons ago, now. There was this old pub, wine bar, in Clerkenwell, think it was, that had failed in its much-publicized bid to escape the wrecker's ball, and Mike had been grubbing around in the cellars because he had been reliably informed that all the old point-of-sale stuff had been arbitrarily dumped down there for decades. He got some very nice little bar-shelf striplights advertising Mackeson Stout and Schweppes, a whole unopened box of thick and heavy 1930s beer mugs and then (Oh! Treasure of treasures! Even now, Mike can still thrill to the moment, the frisson, when he slid out this one folded sheet of printed paper from its original protective envelope) – a 1942 'Careless Talk Costs Lives' poster by Fougasse, never ever used! Framed, now, and standing on the tallboy just by the horribly caved-in ARP helmet and the still virgin bale of landgirls' thorn-proof stockings (and, according to Miller's, worth a pretty penny). But the point of all this from Teddy's point of view was the fact that these lovely old oak casks were going begging – all he had to do was go and get them. Trouble was, God – they were quite unbelievably heavy, even empty, and they anyway seemed to be welded into their positions. At first he had felt quite daunted. And then he did what he should of course have done in the first instance (just as Mike and Judy had told him to): he went to Lucas. Explained the situation – how important they were to him, and what an enormous difference it would make if the wine could rest in barrel for, oh – even a couple of months, you know: you'd be amazed the difference it will make. Lucas, as ever, listened in silence (and what was going on behind those quite impassive eyes of his? Teddy could never have told you; talked it over with Mike, who was also in the dark) and then Lucas quietly requested the address of the (as he put it) hostelry in question. The very next morning a van turned up at The Works, and these three strong blokes had the barrels up in the lift and stacked in a row and fitted securely to these very sturdy X-frame trestles (which Lucas had overnight acquired from God knows where): we were up and running – never looked back. And later that very same evening, Teddy found a finely wrapped and beribboned package placed outside his door. Inside there was a proper maroon-coloured vintner's apron (embroidered with the words 'Teddy: Winemaker'), a silver sommelier's tasting cup on a chain in the form of a scallop shell, and also a bottle of 1961 Château Latour. On the card, Lucas had inscribed quite simply 'Drink Me: I am your role model'. Teddy had felt – oh God, how can he tell you? How can he begin to express his emotions when even back then all he could feel was choked and loved? And Judy had held him, and rocked him gently, he was sobbing and laughing so much, and later even howling with delight. They had not opened the Latour: it is there for a very special occasion indeed. The card he had framed, and it hung now just above the barrels and alongside the pinned-up and spread-out apron: 'Teddy', it says: 'Winemaker'. (I can only thank God that Lucas did not see fit to plump for the 'Lillicrap' option.)

'I should have checked, shouldn't I, how much burgundy they had down there,' Teddy now threw over his shoulder to Judy, who is somewhere, and busy doing, um – what now, exactly? Ah yes – assessing the weight of one of her mottled and ample pink and naked breasts in one cupped hand and then, more gingerly, hefting up the other and then holding them both steady for no more than a beat before changing the whole tempo and switching to jiggling them up and then down alternately, in mean syncopation.

'I should think,' she thought, 'a couple of cases should do it, for now. There's certainly heaps of chardonnay – I saw it in the fridge. The claret's had one hell of a bashing lately, though. I think people saw it was the only way possible to get down all those endless casseroley things. Was it *really* fish, do you think, in that awful goo on Sunday? I only said *chicken* to be nice . . . Tasted more like rodent, caught in an eruption. I think I've got a lump.'

'Two cases it is, then,' said Teddy. 'Oh Judy – you always think you've got a lump, don't you? I don't recall a single time when you haven't been wholly convinced that at least a good half of your entire body isn't, oh – running *over* with lumps. Anyway – lumps are a part of us. Love me, love my lumps. You get a bit older, so you get a bit lumpier – goes with the territory. Remember that lump I had on my neck? Turned out to be nothing at all, didn't it?'

'That lump on your neck,' said Judy, 'turned out to be your *head*. It's just that we'd simply never noticed it before. All covered in hair and beard. No but *seriously*, Teddy – listen to me: this *is* a lump, this time. I can feel it. It's round and hard and that's what lumps are, isn't it? Round and hard.'

'You're meant to be doing the corking . . .' is all Teddy had to add, this time (I think I can maybe see what could well be looming, here, and it might behove me to be quickly elsewhere). 'And *do* pick up all those clothes and papers, Judy love – I really do wish you could learn to be tidy.'

Judy slumped back into a chair. Her absorption with her breasts (like the breasts themselves) seemed to have altogether deflated, and she contented herself now with the odd wry and squint-eyed glance down there, and just an occasional tweak on a nipple.

'I'll pick them up later. You're obsessive. It's only, oh – *stuff*, Teddy – it won't kill you, will it? And you do the corks – there's a love. You know I'm always useless when I've done a stint of Samaritans. God, it really does exhaust me. Hey – what did you think of our kitchenful of cockneys? I think they're almost certainly all crooks, don't you? Underworld types. I thought they were all *lovely* – particularly that Paul one. A cheeky chappy if ever there was. I do hope they don't turn out to be anything really beastly, though, like murderers, and so on. Jack the Ripper used to prowl round here, you know. Mike was saying. Maybe they're his long-lost sons. I must say I do think it's just awful that you're not even the weeniest bit interested in my *lump*, Teddy, you know. You *ought* to be interested – they're your breasts too, if only you wanted them . . . That *Jamie*, earlier – oh I did terribly take to that one. And you know I'm sure – I really do think I would be able to stop him smoking. I really do think I could. It's simply just a question of getting him to *believe* again. Therapy is therapy, really, when all's said and done. Because I'm absolutely sure it's *wife* that's the trouble there, you know. Did you see how little he had with him? Sad. I can just imagine it – it must have come to the point when he just said Oh *God*, whatever-the-name-of-his-wife-is – have everything! Take anything you want because all I need to be is *out* of here!'

'Soaps,' said Teddy. 'You watch too many soaps.'

'One of my pleasures. Where are you going?'

'Where do you think I'm going? Got to get the wine down, haven't I? When *I* have done the corks. Now come on, Judy – don't – *jostle* me like this. Just move aside, can't you? Pick up all this rubbish all over the floor, if you're looking for something to do.'

Judy was standing squarely before him, and her eyes had within them the light of challenge.

'Feel. My. Lump,' she said.

Teddy touched his beard and looked away.

'You haven't got a lump.'

'Feel it anyway.'

'Judy . . . the wine, yes? Got to. Can't, um . . .'

And he nearly said 'let people down', which would not, he adjudged, have been good. Instead, he touched her cheek and kissed it and whispered to her gently:

'You know I love you. You know I always will. Yes, Judy?'

Judy blushed and smiled and tapped the end of Teddy's nose with the pad of her outstretched finger.

'Silly,' she said softly, looking down. 'Of course. Of course . . .'

She picked up – what was it? Oh yes – that fuchsia and cornflower cardigan affair – housecoat sort of a thing (but shorter) and bundled it around her.

'Come on then, Teddy,' in the voice she used for rallying the troops. 'Let's get the corks in, shall we?'

It wasn't until all the bottles were stoppered and in boxes that Teddy spoke again.

'Why . . . *do* you, Judy? This Samaritan thing . . . ?'

'Oh please, Teddy – not again. I keep on *telling* you why. Hm? Don't I?'

'Yes but . . . some of these – *men* you speak to. They've taken to asking for you personally. I checked. I'm sorry, but I did. I mean – why would they do that, Judy? Ask for you personally. I mean – the whole thing's meant to be about anonymity, isn't it? Isn't that the whole thing about the Samaritans? So why do you – ? Why would they – ?'

'Continuity, I expect,' said Judy dismissively. 'Remembering where you left off.'

Teddy probed his beard at the tip of the chin with just one finger, as if he was trying to locate in there something small and insistent.

'But – it's *sex*, isn't it? They only ever want to talk to you about sex. I've heard it. You never get suicides or debtors or drunks or junkies or knocked-about women or any of that, do you? Never get women at *all* . . .'

'Look, Teddy. It helps them. I've told you.'

'But . . . but have you ever thought what they may be up to? You know – I mean, *doing*? At the other end . . . ?'

His hand was like a claw, now – agitating the beard up and down the whole of one cheek, maybe just prior to tearing it out at the root.

Judy held his forearms, and looked at him earnestly.

'Listen, Teddy – listen. Watch my lips. It *helps* them. Yes? That's why I do it. It *helps* them.'

Teddy nodded. It was not a nod of satisfaction, or even under-standing. They had been here before, you see (oh yes: many times) and so here was merely the acknowledgement that once again they had arrived at the wall, beyond which it seemed just impossible to penetrate.

He now had all the bottles loaded on to the trolley, and he stooped to tie up the straps.

'Right, then,' he said. 'Just get this lot down there . . . shouldn't be too long. Good Lord – look at the time . . .'

'Off you go then, Teddy,' Judy sang quite gaily. 'See you soon. And if you run into Jamie, give him my love, won't you?'

Only when the door shut behind him did Judy appear more thoughtful. It would be so much easier for me, doing what I do

(God – sometimes I could do with a cigarette myself), if only he could just *understand* – just get past whatever it was that troubled him so. And it was the same, you know, with my sex therapy practice – just as it is now with the Samaritans. I say it and say it: I do it because it *helps* them – how many times? It helps them, yes. And mmm – it helps me too.

And Jamie, rather oddly (and Teddy hadn't at all been thinking about Jamie), was indeed the very first person he did in fact run right into – quite literally, as it happened: nearly had the trolley over.

'Hey steady on, Jamie! You nearly had the trolley over, there!'

'Oh God I'm most terribly . . . !' stuttered Jamie, righting himself from a near-headlong and could have been awful fall, and rubbing his knee at the point of collision. 'I wasn't looking where I was . . . most awfully, um – you know, *sorry*, and everything, um . . . oh God look – this is perfectly hideously embarrassing, but I seem to have actually forgotten, er – your, um –'

'Teddy,' said Teddy. 'It's Teddy. Where are you rushing off to?'

'*Teddy* – of course it's – oh God of *course* it's Teddy – I knew that, of course I did. Teddy, yes – it's Teddy.'

'I know,' smiled Teddy. 'So what's the big hurry then, Jamie?'

'Hm? Oh well that's just it, you see – I've got all the *times* wrong, and everything. I seem to have thought it was long past seven and in fact it's only, um . . .'

'Six. Sixish now, must be, I should have thought. So, what – you were under the impression it was dinner-time, hey? No no – quite

146

a wait yet, I'm afraid. I've got some Fruit Gums here though, look, if you're desperate.'

'Yes – that's *exactly* what I was – you see, I actually went to see Lucas, but –'

'Not at this time,' said Teddy with authority, bringing down his eyelids and shaking his head. 'Never get to see Lucas at this time of day.'

'Well yes – that's what Alice said. I didn't know. I mean she said it as if I *ought* to have known – almost as if I was mad, or something, *not* to have known but . . . well, I didn't. Do now. But I didn't then.'

'Oh yes. Known fact, that. Never get him at this time. One of his special times, this – always keeps to himself. Also ten till eleven in the morning, and just after lunch for an hour. It's as well you know now, really. Save any future, um . . .'

'Well quite. Thanks. Do you know – I didn't even know Fruit Gums were actually still *going*. Used to love them.'

'Fruit Gums? Oh Lord yes. Couldn't live without them. I'm a two pack a day man, myself. Want one?' offered Teddy, holding out the half-done tube.

'Well oh Christ – I've got to stick *something* in my mouth or I'll just go completely *crazy*. What I was going to see Lucas about, actually. See if he'd maybe relax the rule about, um . . .'

'Smoking? He never will. Quite firm on that one. Finding it hard then, are you? Expect it must be. Here – have a Fruit Gum. Black one's next up, look.'

Suddenly Jamie appeared wild and hunted.

'*Hard*?' he let out, in a barely stifled scream. 'Oh Jesus *Christ*, Terry – *Teddy*. Hard isn't even bloody *close* to what I – ! It's been just, oh – *hours*, now, and I think I'm near to losing my *mind*. I'm ill. I feel so *ill* . . .'

'But still, Jamie old chap – if you've already managed *hours*, well – it's a pretty good start, isn't it? Hey?'

Jamie looked nervously to the left and right of him, as if to make doubly sure that no eavesdroppers were skulking, who might drink in this next bit:

'Well . . . I did, oh God – I did have just *one*, actually. Blew it out the window. Nearly fell off the ladder. Could have killed myself. And then I felt, oh – pretty disgusted, if you want the truth – because look, I expect I'm just like the rest of you . . . I don't want to go round doing things that Lucas has expressly, you know – *forbidden* . . . why I went to ask him, you see. And then when Alice said . . . oh Jesus – I just went right back and lit up another. It's hopeless. *Did* fall off the ladder, this time: could have killed myself. So I thought: *food* – food'll maybe help me. Glass of your wine or two, yes? See – I did remember *that* much, anyway. Oh Christ. Yeh OK – I'll have a Fruit Gum. Jesus. I tell you, Teddy – I'm just not going to be able to *do* this.'

'Well Judy's offer of therapy is still very much open, if you want to give it a try. She said to pass on all her love, by the way.'

Jamie gnashed down with a violent energy – gave those Fruit Gums a right bloody savaging (the black one, yes, and also the green and amber ones beneath it: compulsive, you see? Why have one when more are going?).

'Really . . . ?' he managed. 'Oh that's very . . . very kind. Everyone here is just so . . .'

Teddy shrugged, as if it was obvious. 'It's just how it is here. It's how it all works. Look – why don't you zip up and have a quick word with her? Hm? I've got to get this lot down to the kitchens and then I'll pop back up later. Have a talk with her, Jamie – she's very good, you know. She really is. Very positive. Nothing to lose, is there? Hm? But hey – I've just had a thought: didn't you give her your cigarettes earlier? You did, didn't you? So how – ?'

'Oh *God*, Teddy. You obviously have no idea at all what an addict is *like*. Devious, Teddy – devious, yes, and desperately, just totally *dependent*. You don't really think I would've given them *all* away, do you? No no – I had more. Loads more. Most of the bags you were carrying were jammed bloody solid with them, if I'm honest . . . oh God, Teddy – just *talking* about them – ! I need – I *need*, Teddy: I *need* . . . !'

Teddy touched his shoulder.

'Go and see Judy. And think of Lucas.'

Jamie shuddered and closed his eyes tight and made a huge effort to just, oh Christ – pull himself *together* – just to pack in raking back his shivery fingers through this sticky and frenzied hair of his: even that would be a beginning of sorts.

'You're . . . right, Teddy. Of course you are. My first day here and already I'm placing myself in, oh – such *danger*. Which I – so don't want to do. I will. I'll go and see Judy. Maybe she'll help me . . . *Thank* you, Teddy . . .'

Teddy tapped Jamie's back in a show of encouragement, and then set to trundling away his clinking cargo of very nearly burgundy.

'Mark my words,' he called back over his shoulder. 'One day soon – you'll be laughing over this. We all will. See you later, Jamie old chap. Chin up!'

Jamie passed a not-at-all-sure hand across his cold and always sweating forehead (Christ I'm just dripping with it). Ych? he thought. *Yeh*? Well maybe. I hope so. I really do hope so. Because I'm sure as hell not laughing now.

'Now you're really really really sure you like it, Judy, do you? You're not just being nice, or anything? Just saying it?'

'*Lord*, Frankie my little petal,' John was sighing (though there was plenty of indulgence there, for anyone to see), 'she's *told* you, hasn't she? Hm? She loves it – don't you, Judy? Yes she does. She said so. We all love it. It looks perfectly divine on you.'

Frankie ceased her pirouetting in the middle of the room and spread out wide the full draped skirt of this rather sumptuous silk velvet dress that clung to her and then rippled – deep plum, and bound in a darker satin. It seemed for a moment as if she was maybe on the point of dropping down into a curtsey – but no: she was simply gazing, quite lost in the dress (and there was love in her eyes).

'It *is* gorgeous, isn't it?' she giggled with mischief. 'Well it *should* be, shouldn't it Johnny? God, Judy – I can't tell you how expensive it was!'

Judy smiled. 'I can well imagine,' she said. 'More chardonnay for you two lovebirds? You'll go just a teeny bit more, won't you John?'

'I don't mind a top-up,' said John – leaning forward with his glass. 'It is actually astounding what these shops get away with charging, these days. I mean to say – lovely thing, oh yes of course. But my God – when all's said and done, it is only a *dress*, isn't it? Still. Look how it makes my Frankie even more beautiful than ever.'

'Oh *sweet*, Johnny!' laughed Frankie, bending low and kissing him briefly.

'What else did you get on this little spree of yours?' asked Judy – pouring more chardonnay into her own glass, now – registering that then there was barely an inch remaining in the bottle, and tipping in that bit too. 'Well . . .' she qualified, '*not* so little spree, by the looks of it. All these clothes . . .'

'Oh – not too much more,' said John. '*Plant*, of course – our monthly areca palm. I don't know what it is about the plants I buy. I've tried watering them, not watering them. Feeding them –

starving the buggers. In the sun, out of the sun – I think I've covered the waterfront. But no. I sometimes feel like I'm running some sort of a botanical hospice, or something. I nurse the swine with love, and then they die.'

'Ha!' laughed Judy. 'Could it be that the pots just aren't big enough?' And then she was suddenly alert. 'Did you children *hear* something, just then? Anything? Sort of tapping sort of thing?'

John and Frankie blankly gazed at one another for no more than an instant – and then they did, the two of them, catch just maybe a hint of something like that. Judy was up and striding to the door – which opened a crack, just before she got there.

'Um – hello . . .' said Jamie, rather tentatively. 'I wasn't quite sure whether I should, er . . .'

'Oh God come *in*, Jamie – come in. Look, everyone – it's Jamie. You remember Jamie, don't you? Come on, Jamie – don't be shy. I was just going to open another bottle of chardonnay – you've timed things very well indeed. We don't really tend to *knock*, you know, here. The sound of knocking – quite amazed me.'

'Oh, well, right.' smirked Jamie, feeling like, oh – two things, really, as he shuffled the length of another vast and wood-floored space. *One*: a shambling fool – and *two*: a fucking fag. And then he saw Frankie, and Christ – all he felt then was an instant rush of pure white lust. God oh God, she was absolutely bloody perfect, I'm telling you, this woman. And look at that fabulous dress! The ideal thing to latch on to with two fevered hands and rip off her body in shrieking and opulent shards before breathlessly getting down to all the warm and lacy cinched-in ripeness she was bound to be sheltering within. Because I'm like that, you know – the hit is instant and quite frighteningly powerful or else, for me, there's just nothing at all. A bit like with John's dark blue and gleaming Alvis, out there (oh and John's here too – hi John!). I could have licked it all over, that car, you know. Were I to have squirmed myself on to the leather upholstery . . . well I tell you quite frankly, soon I would have become heated, and not too far away from the brink of orgasm. It's really rather weird. I don't try to work it *out*, or anything, not any more. The way I am. I simply acknowledge that these are the things that go on within me: like it or not, there it is. Yes. But *Frankie* – oh my God, this Frankie! A class apart. And what I want to do – what I really want to do is not get to *know* her, no – not ask her out to dinner and then maybe plan a picnic or a trip to the theatre, no no: none of that, nothing like that at all. What I want is to fuck her on the floor. Right now. This hot instant. And it would be nice, of course, if her boyfriend John and Judy, dear Judy here, could maybe see fit to absent themselves with all due haste and discretion – but if not, not. Watch, if you will: watch, by all means. Applaud, if you'd like to – if you feel the urge. Christ Almighty you can set up a booth and sell *tickets* and whoop and catcall and stamp and cheer for all I bloody care. Just so long as I'm down there on the floor being deep in and dirty with this wondrously fabulous woman. Yes. Indeed. But failing that . . . *hooo*, yes, I'll have a little glass of chardonnay, will I? Yes – a vat or so of chardonnay might go some way to effecting a stranglehold on my searing craving for the beast of nicotine while I pack away my agape and still dripping lust for the night and send it straight up to bed – alone and unfed – because we are not tonight at home to Mister *Pushy*. And Christ – this knee, you know – it's giving me a hell of a time, now: really aching. Didn't think I'd bashed it all that badly.

'What's wrong with your knee, Jamie?' asked Judy, solicitously. 'Here, Jamie – Teddy's best chardonnay. Cheers. You keep on rubbing it. Old war wound, is it? Be careful – Mike Killery will add it to his collection.'

'Ha!' scoffed Jamie (he's emptied the glass and now he was holding it out to Judy – caught her before she even had time to turn; who the fuck's Mike Killery?). 'No I, er – sort of ran into a lorryload of Teddy's very best, um – something else, I'm afraid. Red.'

'Ah,' understood Judy. 'The burgundy express.'

'*Knees*,' said John, with force. 'They can be unforgiving bastards, knees, you know. You give them a clonk, think nothing at all about it, and years – oh God, years and years later they come back and trip you up. Literally, in my case. First things to go. Memories like elephants, knees. Mind you. I'm dropping apart *generally*, so not too much to go on, really . . .'

'Oh don't be so *silly*!' rushed in Frankie (it was as if a scowling tabby had been circling her new-hatched chicks: someone had to be there to *protect*). 'You're in beautiful condition, Johnny!'

John laughed at that – and Jamie, he had to grin along as well because look: he *wasn't*, was he? In much of a state at all. Old Johnny, as she calls him. I mean Jesus – he's got to be nearly twice my age, hasn't he? This man. And look what he's bloody well got! He's got Frankie. *Why* . . . ? Money. And he's got the Alvis. *Why* . . . ? Money. *Christ* . . .

'Like the Alvis . . .' Jamie heard himself saying. 'I mean, you know – beautiful condition.'

John was smiling his contentment at the verdict – but soon was distracted by Frankie who was holding her nose with one hand, while the other was flapping up and down as if in an urgent attempt to flag down a cruising taxi – or maybe she just suddenly needed to go to the lavatory.

'I've just *remembered*,' she fizzed. 'About *knees*, yes? When you were talking about *knees* – it reminded me of something just so totally silly from when I was a little girl. Oh God – isn't it *crazy*, the things you remember? I was running around one day – you know, the way children do, and I – well, I suppose I – I don't know, I must've hit something, or something, and I went off crying to my mother – My *knee*! My *knee*! (I was going). Mummy mummy I've hurt my *knee*! And do you know what she said?

You'll never guess what she said to me. She said *Well*, Frankie – that'll teach you, won't it? That'll teach you to stop running around all the time without your *shoes* on! Isn't that funny? Without your *shoes* on . . . Isn't it just amazing she should have said that to me?'

'Mothers can be odd . . .' said Judy.

'And how simply *mad*, though,' babbled on Frankie, 'that I should even *remember* all that! I mean, God – it was just *years* ago, that.'

'Well yes,' smiled Judy. 'We all sort of assumed . . .'

'And *Alvis*!' went on Frankie – really keyed up and very excited by the now seemingly unstoppable momentum of her own train of thought. 'Whenever anyone says *Alvis* – because it's such an odd sort of funny sort of word, isn't it really? Alvis. Anyway – it always makes me think of, you know – *Elvis*, right? And I read the most amazing thing. You want to hear it? Quite amazing.'

'Is this,' checked John, 'about the Alvis? Or is this Elvis, now?'

'Alvis,' said Frankie. 'No – *Elvis*. Oh honestly, Johnny – you're confusing me, now. Just let me tell the story, OK? So – Elvis, yes? The – you know: singer guy. Well apparently – and I know all these figures are right because I purposely memorized them because I just thought it was all so *amazing*. In 1977, OK – God, before I was even *born*! – in 1977 there were a hundred and fifty Elvis Presley impersonators, apparently, in the world. Kay? Hundred and fifty. Whole world. But by the year two thousand, yes? There were – guess how many. Tell you: eighty-five thousand. Eighty-five *thousand* – can you believe it?'

'It's extraordinary,' mused Judy, 'what people get up to . . .'

'No but *listen*,' rushed on Frankie – both her hands, now, lost in a flurry of quite frantic semaphore. 'The thing is this. There's this expert, OK, and he says that if the rate of growth continues, um – there's a word, can't remember – if it sort of goes on at the same sort of rate, thing – well then by two thousand and thirteen, which

154

isn't really, is it, all that far away now? Well by two thousand and thirteen, a third of the world's population will be Elvises! I mean – quite *amazing*. And it was an expert who said it, so you've got to think, haven't you?'

John was standing now, and laughing like the uncle it was that maybe Frankie adored so much (Jamie could only surmise).

'Well,' he said, 'let us enjoy the moment before that grim day befalls us, is all I can say. Come Frankie – we've been indulged by these good people for quite long enough. Let's go and get changed for dinner, hm? Or are you wearing that?'

'Mmmm . . .' deliberated Frankie. 'Not sure. I might wear the gold sort of long one. Do you know the one I mean, Johnny?'

'Well – not offhand, but I'm sure you'll refresh my memory. Thank you so much for the wine, dear Judy. And do pass on all congrats to Teddy, yes? It's really one of his very best efforts.'

'I'll tell him. He'll be pleased.'

Frankie was gathering together the fruits of her shopping trip.

'God, Judy – did I say? That beastly beggar was there again, when we came back. Urrrgh . . . do you know – Johnny had just parked the car – you know: where he does. And this horrid dirty man actually came *up* to him. Stood right in front of him, didn't he Johnny?'

'Mm,' agreed John. 'Told me he was ill and poor. Gave him a few bob. Felt rather bad.'

'You shouldn't have,' came back Frankie, with petulance. 'He could have hit you! He could have beaten you up!'

'Whereupon,' laughed John, 'I daresay I would've felt a good deal *worse*! But there – he didn't. Come Frankie. Let's away.'

Frankie nodded – and then, as if on an impulse, she let all her carrier bags drop to the floor and walked straight over to Jamie and knelt before him. Can Jamie, um – sorry but, er – could Jamie maybe just run this past you one more time? This is Frankie, OK? Drops bags. Comes over to Jamie. *And kneels on the floor before him*! And then. She slipped up the leg of his trousers and placed her lips on his knee.

'There . . .' she said softly as she raised up her eyes. 'All better now . . .'

Jamie was entranced – entranced, yes, and wholly aroused. He glanced in fever over to John, who looked so very benign and easy and was smiling like a pontiff on Easter morning.

'The kiss divine,' was all he said.

And later, when John and Frankie had finally gone and Judy was behind him somewhere, massaging his temples, Jamie got to thinking seriously about, oh – this whole damn thing. Was there maybe, here, something in the water? Could it be that? Some unknown chemical that bestowed tranquillity – made everyone so giving, so kind – so totally free of all the greeds and fears and turmoil that, Christ – in London, you get to thinking is all anyone *comprises*. No – not a chemical. Lucas. It's no trick. It's Lucas. Even when he's not around, he *is*, you see. He hovers. He's everywhere. Just like the air.

Look at Judy: gently and firmly soothing away the confusion. Earlier, when he had attempted to convey to her in a gabbled and very likely largely incomprehensible rush, the terrible pain of withdrawal that was eating him alive, she had calmly fashioned a small white tube from a piece of card and had urged him to suck on its end. He looked at her, of course, quite wildly – and also as if she were thoroughly deranged. I mean, what – wasn't she going to pack it tight with poisons and light the bloody thing? Well no – apparently not. So he did – he sucked it. Sucked it hard, and then he began to chew. She wrested it from him when, mad-eyed, he was on the point of swallowing whole the entire now sodden and masticated mess – and she said quite coolly OK, then: the surrogate doesn't seem to be working too well . . . and then we got into the massage which I think, I really do think, might be sort of helping, slowly. And listen. Even though Judy is a damned attractive woman (wonderful breasts – I occasionally feel the brush of one or the other at the back of my neck) I don't at all, you know, feel I want to be doing bad things with her on the floor. And . . . I think now I might even be feeling the same about Frankie. Both these women have touched me . . . but it doesn't have to, oh – *be* like that. Does it? All the time. And who anyway could dream of coming between so close a couple as that? For Christ's sake: Frankie and Johnny were *lovers* . . .

And God. It wouldn't be as if leaving a girl alone (and, face it, where she was perfectly happy to be) was anything approaching a *new* thing for Jamie. (Mmm – mmm . . . that insistent pressure, deep inside my head – I just feel nothing but bliss . . .) No no. Not a *new* thing, would it be? How many times have I looked at a girl and thought Yeeesss . . . maybe – just maybe if I get up and this time do something about it – now, right now: do something *now*, for Christ's sake, before she can move away – then maybe, oh God just maybe tonight she could end up in my bed. But no. Never happened. It was always as if they sensed something. All they ever ended up in, this endless succession of drifting visions, was the distance. And then they faded from sight.

I lie here spent and useless, in a swoon of such contentment. I don't ever want the feeling to end: I am at one – and that is a good thing. What is better, though – much – is that I am now poised; poised, yes, and on the verge of fusion.

CHAPTER FIVE

'I'll tell you, shall I?' said Mary-Ann – as Dorothy piloted her into the dining room with Kimmy close behind, all of them waving at the hail of greetings and such jocular exclamation: Mike, he's flapping his napkin at us, look – and Oona, she's raised her glass (her usual red-lipped and somehow secret half-smile). Teddy's pouring wine and Judy's absolutely killing herself over something or other with that new person, I think it's Jamie, who's looking pretty pleased with himself (she loves jokes, Judy). Frankie and John I don't think can be here yet, are they? No – they're not yet down. 'Will I tell you the bit I really do love most about dinner?' Mary-Ann continued.

'What is it, angel?' smiled Dorothy. 'What's the bit you like best?'

'Yeh,' chimed in Kimmy. 'I mean, what – it can't, like, be the *food*, right? Tonight, maybe, we got better with the new guy.'

Mary-Ann shook her head for quite a long while – teasing out the time until she just couldn't bear withholding her news from them a single moment longer; and then in a delighted and wide-eyed rush she just, oh – *told* them:

'It's the dressing up! I love it when we decide about our dresses and everything, Mummy, and especially when we match, like now.'

And Dorothy, yes – she knew what Mary-Ann meant. Because these days, mm – she rather liked it too. It was Lucas, of course, who had so very subtly directed the way things had gone. In the

158

old days, Dorothy had come down, oh – just anyhow, really, wearing anything at all that came to hand: whatever she'd been wearing all day long, more often than not. One or two others were the same, at first. Teddy, rather memorably – not the world's most elegantly dressed man at the best of times, it has to be said (Judy was forever going on at him). Mike and Oona – oh they were always quite perfect, of course. He in one of his seemingly bottomless collection of eerily similar hardish serge and boxy demob suits (and sometimes even a stiff and shiny collar on his shirt, the brass stud just visibly gleaming above the tie knot – although he did admit it made chewing and swallowing rather painful; when he had started doing the cooking, though, he settled for just a muffler). Oona looked marvellous, as ever: the hair in a chignon and sometimes wearing a two-piece costume in maybe a very dark emerald or anthracite (or the Christmassy richness of a luscious port – she had that too) – or at other times a very flattering and glittery cocktail dress (nipped-in waist) with maybe platform sandals (ankle straps tight around her minky seamed stockings), the hair this time perhaps tucked under and rolled lushly into a perfect pageboy – and always the bright red sticky lipstick. Even her handbags and compacts were always in keeping; she had gathered together all of this stuff, she had once passingly mentioned to Dorothy, ages and ages before any of it became even just fleetingly fashionable; the general craze died back down again, of course, and now has shouldered its way forward into full-time and ageless 'austerity chic'.

Yes: that's Oona for you. I, in contrast, for a long time took to wearing trousers with one of Anthony's business shirts. Or a pullover. The unlaundered variety – this is what has to be grasped, here: those few that still bore the essence of him. Anthony is, was – yes, well: I expect it's reasonably obvious, just who Anthony is. Was. But I'm not going to go on and on about this, so please don't concern yourself. But briefly. He is Mary-

Ann's father. My husband. The man I married on our wedding day and that funny little priest with the big red pimple on the side of his nose ('I thought I was going to *dissolve* . . . !' Anthony had roared to me later, in Venice. Our legs entwined in the wreck of a bed in our perfect suite, overlooking the Grand Canal. 'I didn't dare even *peek* at you!' I had delightedly shrieked back at him – a coughed-up and chirruping hysteria that was, oh – just miles beyond laughter – forcing its way it seemed like just always up into my throat and right out of my mouth: an endless torrent of unstoppable happiness). Yes. And the priest, the funny little priest, yes? He had said Do you take this woman? And Anthony had said I do. He said I do. I *do* take this woman, yes I do, I do. And I was his. Because he'd *taken* me, you see. And he was mine. And now he isn't. Because there is this other, um – person who has him now. He is still, of course (of course), Mary-Ann's father. But no longer is he my man. You see. This is how it is. Kimmy says to get over it: get over it, she says, or it'll kill you. And every day I try – and it does, it eases. I stopped wearing the shirts and pullovers when all they smelled of was me. Lucas . . . he said nothing, nothing to me directly, you know . . . ? But somehow I became aware – as if by the merest thought and gesture on his part he was in some way conveying to me, right deep inside, the seed of an unspoken idea – not a command, no no, but the gentlest suggestion as to what might go far towards pleasing him, and help me too. And it was then, at dinner one evening, that I suppose I looked about me properly for could it *really* be the very first time (really properly) and I saw then, of course, how just everyone else had put into it all this *effort*. The tables always quite perfectly laid (Lucas's cloths and cutlery, china and glasses – fine, so very fine) and a beautiful abundance of flowers . . . and also beautiful, sometimes quite heartbreakingly beautiful, was the dancing glow from the rivers of candles that made everyone seem to be warm, and peachy. Teddy's lovely wine in a succession of carafes – and poor Mike's food, but so lovingly prepared. And me? I felt disgust – self-loathing. All I ever did was just shamble in looking sloppy in one of that man's shirts and just *take*. It took me a while to see how very bad I was. So I changed all that. I wear my prettiest dresses, now (but not the ones I wore at the very beginning: the ones I took to Venice), and Mary-Ann, she does too. And you can see how much she likes it: she's just this minute told us. So Lucas, you see, was right all along, just as he always is – and yet throughout he had said to me nothing. Nothing at all: not even so much as a word. But on that first evening I came down – dressed like a woman again, and trying so hard to be positive and caring – there was all around me the gift of warmth and I felt uplifted, and just so happy to *be* here. He smiled, Lucas. Just once (I shan't forget it) – he glanced across at me once, and smiled. I wonder, sometimes, what it would be like to, well – what it would be like to be Alice, I suppose is what I mean. You know – to actually be with Lucas (God – to be with *Lucas*, of all people on earth: just think) on a different, a singular – well anyway *another* level.

If, of course, she is. Alice. It is hard to know. No one quite seems to. From Lucas, of course, you get nothing at all on the subject (and no naturally – you wouldn't expect it) and Alice herself, she's, well, very – not *secretive*, no, that wouldn't be it, that's not quite right – but she surely is something of a puzzle. To me. I mean apart from sort of running all the awful and boring side of The Works (and it's funny – despite its name, it's the one part of here I want nothing to do with: don't even like to think of its being managed and financed, just like some ugly business venture. I view it, I suppose, as just an eternally and shyly emerging flower – flourishing, and quite as natural as that: I don't want to know about the works). But Alice – this is what I was saying – it's difficult to quite see what she does with her time (which I know, yes, is very rich, isn't it? Coming from me). There is Lucas, of course. To look after. Whatever form that daily takes. Oh yes and then – I'd forgotten – there are her pictures, aren't there? The watercolours, yes. She paints these . . . I suppose rather decorative little things, smallish and bright. Local buildings, the river, vases of flowers, dogs, fruit – oh and The Works, of course. Lucas has several of these in an honoured position up against the lovely old brickwork, there, just by the largest of the printing presses. He said to us, once, that he thought them the finest paintings he had seen, and that he loved them. Alice – she was there – Alice, well – she could have just *melted* with pleasure when Lucas said that (and God, can you blame her? Had it been me – me to whom such praise had been directed by Lucas, I think I might well have exploded and died). Of course I think it is the subject matter of the pictures, rather than their execution, that Lucas must love so very much. Not that Alice is in any way a *bad* painter, or anything; John was telling me one time that her control of the medium and sense of colour are quite remarkable, and I have not the slightest reason to doubt him. They're just not particularly, you know – to my personal taste, sort of thing. I actually prefer those funny and rather garish wartime posters that Mike and Oona have got stuck up all over the place, though I couldn't tell you *why,* or anything. Never used to care for anything at all, like that: very traditional, I've always been. Or was. When I was with – well, you know: then. I just wish, if I'm honest, that Alice could have more success with them, the pictures. They don't, you know – *sell,* or anything, she laughingly assures us, quite often. Well, I don't suppose they do. Not, is it, what people really go for, these days (like Kimmy says – art, now, it's all shook up). I mean – yes *Judy's* bought one or two of them, I know that, but then Judy's just such a good soul that she'd happily put out money for an accidental spillage of emulsion caused by an overactive chimp (if only she thought it would boost and nourish the chimp's self-esteem). But the rather wonderful thing about

Alice, you know – it has often made me wonder – is that although she's perfectly aware of Kimmy's very easy and lucrative set-up with her dealer (Alice doesn't have a dealer) and the fact that Kimmy is really no more than a, well – sort of art director, I suppose (I don't think she'd argue with that) – yes yes, despite all this, not once has Alice demonstrated anything but outright pleasure at Kimmy's increasingly evident success. No hint of rancour. Which could be one reason, I can only imagine, partly why Lucas could maybe have selected her. To be with him. If with him she truly is. It is hard to know. No one quite seems to.

OK. Quite enough of that. Yes all *right*, Mary-Ann – I *know*, darling, you're hungry, I am too . . . just don't *tug* at Mummy like that, all right? You know I can't bear it. So OK, then – where shall we sit? Kimmy? Any preferences? Because that's another thing – just one more little thing about being here, all of us, for dinner every evening: there aren't set places. Lucas, of course: he always sits on the same big chair right at the centre of us – so the seat to the left of him is always the first to be filled (Alice takes the right). It was he who encouraged us all to chop and change – and of course at first I didn't like it. It's a British thing, that, isn't it? Think so. We do so like our own little spot – like in restaurants, yes – very much so, there. If you're shown to a central table – one with no wall at all to cover your back – well, I don't know if you're anything at all like me, but quite frankly it's enough to put me off the whole idea of eating altogether. Can't bear the exposure. Not that it really arises any more, now – all of that. Can't in truth remember the last time I was even in a restaurant – you quickly get out of the way of wanting to do anything at all like that. It's like visitors – you know: people from outside. It happens, early on . . . and then, by some sort of mutual and tacit acquiescence, it all just falls away. But *here*, of course – wherever you go, wherever you sit, whoever you're next to (wall or no wall) it's perfectly *safe*, you see. Mary-Ann didn't at all take to the system in the early

days, either: she became terribly clingy, you know, after her, um –
when we all . . . after things changed. But God – you should see
her now! I mean it. She just loves to be in a different place every
single evening – well look at now! There, you see? Did you see
her? She's just shot off, look (never mind about her poor old
Mum!) . . . and where's she gone, now? Who's she making for
. . . ? Ah – Oona. She's decided it's Oona she's going to be prat-
tling to, tonight (best of luck, Oona!). Kimmy, now – she's started
talking to John and Frankie, who've just this minute come in (and
God, you know – that Frankie: I'd die for legs like that. I mean –
long, is what I mean. Mine are quite shapely, thighs not too bad,
good ankles – not many complaints . . . but just to have her *height*,
that would be a wonderful thing. She certainly does know how to
carry off all these fabulous new clothes that John seems never
to tire of buying her. Well there: I wish them both well. Don't
actually know them at all intimately, or anything, but they both
seem terribly nice). It's not, actually . . . sorry – sorry about this,
but it's just occurred to me – it's just that I got thinking about legs
there, a minute back – Frankie's yards of thigh – but in truth I'm
not actually remotely bothered, you know, about the state of my
legs or bottom or breasts or anything like that. I'll tell you what
does really bug me, though – sounds stupid, I know, but it's always
been a thing with me: my arms. My arms above the elbow. Can't
bear even so much as to look at them. When I was still with –
when there used to be quite a few business-related parties I had to
go to, I could never wear anything off the shoulder: couldn't even
have dreamed of it. Because I wouldn't have wanted to, you know
– let him down, or anything. With all the other wives around. Yes.
Anyway.

So what's the situation now, then? Lucas will be arriving quite
soon (I know that because Alice is here now, and Lucas always
comes in just a few minutes after: don't worry, you'll get to learn

all the quirks when you've been with us all just a little while longer). Well look – there's two new faces: I'll go there (why not?).

'Hello, you two – mind if I just . . . ? I'm Dorothy – I'm with Kimmy over there, do you see by the door? American – terribly lovely. My best chum. And that's my little girl, there – rabbiting on to Mike and Oona. Mary-Ann, she's called.'

'Oh *yeh*,' Paul Theme was approving – eyes alight and his arms spread wide. 'What a right lovely little thing she is and all. I was just – wasn't I, Biff? I was just this second saying to my mate Biff here: Biff, I were going – who do you reckon that pretty little kid belongs to then, ay? Straight up. Weren't I, Biff? I'm Paul, Dorothy – pleased to meet you. Make your acquaintance. And this here's Biff, like I say.'

And Dorothy slipped into her seat right next to this highly attentive young man ('You all right there, love? Yeh? You got plenty of elbow room for when the nosh come down? Cos I can squidge myself well over here, no danger at all – and old Biff, we can chuck him out the window, he's any bother. Right, Biff?').

Biff, for his part, was tracing the pattern in the deep rose damask tablecloth with the tines of his silver fork, and in his mind he was going Dear oh dear what the bleeding hell is Paul bleeding on about this time then – ay? Tell you straight – I can't work out what he's about, since we come here. You talk about all the business, he says to you schtum – which ain't no fucking use to me, mate, I tell you now. All I know is the business. Christ – it's what we bleeding *are*, which is what he seems to have bloody forgot. Plus he's going on earlier about all the bleeding plates and candles and all the rest of the bleeding pantomime we got here, and all I'm going is Yeh, Paul, yeh: it's a plate – whoopy-fucking-doo, you know? And candles – what? They ain't connected up to the mains down here, then? And he goes: Trouble with you, Biff – you wanna know the trouble with you, then? And I come back No, Paul – no I bleeding don't, mate. Cos there ain't nothing wrong

165

with me – no, hear me out: it's you, son. It's you what's gone all doolally. I come here with Paul Theme, my mate, and my other mate Tubby: business partners (Three Musketeers, I go: Stooges, more like, he come back). Last time I seen Tubby he was down the kitchen there in one of them stupid bloody great chef hats (I ain't kidding you) and banging on about whether he put too much wotsit – vanilla or some bloody poncey thing, whether he over-done it in the ice cream or the whipping cream or some other sort of fucking cream, what do I know? Nice. So that's one of them a couple platters short of a jukebox. And Paul, now – he's yacking on to this new bird here about her snot-nosed sprog and I'm just stuck here thinking how's it come about, then – both my mates have lost it? Yeh. So all right then – come on: which one of them you want, ay? Cos I got two of the sods on offer in this here bargain basement Santa's Grotto: I can do you Mrs Bridges in the bleeding kitchen, faffing about with his wooden spoons, or (that don't tickle your fancy) I can knock you down for next to nothing little Mary Poppins here – who at any minute now is gonna up and feed the fucking *birds*. Dear oh dear. All I can say is, if Tubby don't come up with some ace nosh pronto, I'll have him, so help me – ram his bleeding head in the blender: cream that, Tubs.

Ay ay: what's this now? Everyone gone all quiet. Lights just got even lower (how they do that with candles then, ay?) and now just what is occurring? Oh yeh – someone just come in. Standing in front of his chair. Strike me dead if it ain't St Francis of Assisi – you reckon we're gonna kneel down now, or what? Oh no – I tell a lie: it's *Lucas*, isn't it? It was only Lucas, all the time. Dear oh dear . . . seems a long while now, I'm telling you, since I heard old Pauly sort of laugh out loud at anything what I tell him. What I get now is, he just give me a look – and the face on him, I mean it: like a horse's arse. Not like, what – just a couple days back when I go to him 'Here, Paul – bend your ear round this lot: I remember one tosser, one time, OK, and I says to him: Your ears must be burning, mate. Oh yeh, he goes – why's that then? Cos I just set fire to your *hair*, you dozy cunt!' Laugh? Paul was pissing hisself: lovely to look at. Yeh . . . good days, them.

'Friends . . .' said Lucas – it was barely a murmur, and very very soft – while he spread out the palms of his hands as if to make clear that there was nothing concealed (and no reason, here, why ever there should be).

Paul didn't mind telling you he was well impressed with the whistle: black velvet and dark red revers – beautiful cut; I could, you know, be doing with a few new duds: well sick of my lot, if I'm honest. And here's something – just take one look at all the faces: all, like, looking up at him, they are. What this man has got going here is large respect, son, and no messing about. And I only just twig, don't I, why we're all looking up at him – all sort of gaping, like. It's on account of he's still just stood there with a sort of smile on him and his hands sort of stuck out like that and what it is he's doing is he's looking right into the faces of each of us in turn. Like when I was a kid in church of a Sunday, this is a bit – when we was all lined up waiting for your man to stick the old host in your gob: expectant, that's what this is. See! He just done me, then – and I don't know: come over all wobbly there, just for the minute. Had me going, you know? Yeh but look over there. Clocked it? Over by the kitchen door (and dear oh Lord, talking of kitchens – I dunno what sort of a muck sweat old Tubby must've worked hisself up to by this time – waiting for the off – but for myself I don't got no doubts on that score: he'll come up Trojan, Tubs will – you mark my words). No but look – over there, like I say. Funny little couple I don't know – ain't even spotted before, if I'm honest: knocking on a bit, I reckon. Yeh but anyway – *they* ain't looking up. They ain't looking at Lucas, no way. And they ain't busy eyeballing each other neither – nah, they're both just looking down at the table like they don't know what it is, or something: bit funny.

'Here . . .' whispered Paul to Dorothy. 'What's with them two over there then, ay?'

Dorothy's eyelids fluttered as she glanced about her nervously. This was not right – talking, when Lucas was among them, and looking. She knew, though, exactly the people that Paul had meant: she didn't need to follow his gaze.

She said very low and hurriedly: 'Oh – you don't have to worry about them . . . that's just the Hitlers. Sh, now – Lucas is about to speak.'

Paul just blinked at her once.

'Do *what*, love . . . ?'

'Hitlers. Sh. *Lucas* . . . !' Dorothy hissed back at him, her eyes wide with the urgency to convey to him immediately that what we all had to be now was just *silent*.

'This evening . . .' said Lucas. 'Tonight. Is something of a red-letter occasion for us all, I have to say. Some of you might already have encountered one another. But for those of you who have not – we have among us many new friends. Theme, here, sitting next to the ever-delightful Dorothy – charming dress you're wearing, Dorothy: colours quite perfect for you – is a master of design, among, I am sure, many other things – and he urges you all to call upon his very considerable talents. Mister Biff, I have divined, is strong and silent, rather in the manner of the vibrant undertow of a deep dark river: his might, I feel, will be vital. And in the galleys – soon, I trust, to emerge – is Slim, our new chef: Mister Tubby. A miracle, I have no doubt. Ladies and gentlemen – at this point, allow me if you will to propose a very generous toast to the great man Killery, here – our culinary alumnus.'

'Hear hear!' went Teddy – and a general rumble of loving and laudatory assent was flowing now over a gorgeously embarrassed Mike Killery, his face as red as that rather memorably awful coq au vin for which he had only the other evening apologized both profusely and repeatedly, prior to binning the larger part. Oona

168

reached across and kissed his hand. Mike just grinned, his chin near skimming the table as his eyes peeped up shyly, maybe to ascertain if it was safe to come out yet. Dorothy felt so very pleased for him – and still she was thrilling within: my dress is charming – *charming*, it is (the colours quite perfect for me).

'New to us also,' continued Lucas, 'is my dear friend Dear, here. For those of you who have yet to have the pleasure of meeting him, Dear is seated just here, being extremely well looked after, I have no doubt, by not just the eternally effervescent Judy – a very good evening to you, Judy. Your hair in the candlelight is tonight an especial pleasure, I have to say. Not just Judy, then, but also friend Lillicrap. Aren't you, Dear? Yes. Indeed.'

Lucas glanced about him – nodding again briefly at each face in turn. His features then settled down into something rather more grave.

'Friends,' he said, so softly. 'Touch, if you will . . .'

All hands, now, were linked around the tables. Jamie had joined up with Judy and Teddy completely instinctively; Paul Theme had thought the idea a right good lark, and laughingly went for it. Biff briefly hesitated, but not for too long: a show of strength is clearly called for (and what: you deaf? You *heard* the man, didn't you? My might is vital).

'Let us,' Lucas was now gently intoning, 'offer up our thanks. Thanks be to whatever force it is that has demonstrated such benignity and wisdom as to have gathered us all together. We are humbled. We are as one.'

He then sat down abruptly, and almost immediately a delighted and easy hubbub fluttered through the room as napkins were unfolded, glasses of wine tinklingly poured, and the laughter of kinship as well as, thought Jamie, a rather heady exhilaration, filled the room right up to the brim, as it curled around him, lovingly.

'That prayer,' he said to Judy. 'It was almost, wasn't it, a prayer to himself, in many ways. No Judy – listen: I'm not at all saying that is a *wrong* thing. I think it's perfect. It's something to believe in. Um – Judy . . . who's that couple over there? They didn't join hands, I noticed. Who are they?'

'Are the patches working?' smiled Judy. 'Oh by the way, Teddy – John said to tell you that the chardonnay is simply perfect. Drank two gallons.'

'I'm glad,' said Teddy. And by God he looked it.

'Yes, they – I *think* they're working,' qualified Jamie. 'Mind you, I've got so damn many of them plastered all over me, they couldn't really fail to, could they really? Every time I breathe I'm getting zapped by a pack of Gitanes.'

'Oh *look*!' exclaimed Judy, her hands clapped together. '*Food*. I do believe. Yes yes: here comes Mister Tubby!'

Amid the onrush of unsimulated oohing and lowing and out-breaks of sporadic applause that greeted Tubby as he wheeled in an enormous and steaming tureen – and trailing behind him great hot wafts of big and tasty things to come – amid all the cheering, now, that had Tubby's shiny kitchen face split by pleasure, his eyes lost to sight – amid all this, Teddy leaned over to Jamie and muttered to him conspiratorially that No – no they didn't ever, the Hitlers, join hands or talk or do anything at all that the rest of us did. No one knew why. They seemed to work against the, um – what did Judy say it was, once? The *ethic*, pretty sure: work against the *ethic* of the place, yes. We just let them get on with it. Oh look – mm mm! Soup, is what we have here, if I'm not very much mistaken. Smells rather wonderful . . .

Tubby was ladling out generous bowlsful of a darkish brown and thickly creamy soup, orangey lumps of heaven knew what plopping down too, from time to time. Kimmy seemed to be in charge, tonight, of passing them round.

'I do hope . . .' Tubby said, quite bashfully. But the aspiration failed to get around to any sort of closure.

'But,' checked Jamie, 'that's not their – I mean, is it meant to be some sort of a *joke*, or something? That? I mean – that can't be their *real* name, surely?'

Teddy raised his eyebrows (a bit wished it was Judy, doing all this).

'Who knows? Shouldn't have thought so. Most people with that name – they rushed to change it, I'm pretty sure I'm right in saying. Mike's the man to tell you all about that side of things, I should have thought. Well. When's my soup coming, then? Judy's got hers, look – so where's mine, then? Is it good, Judy? The soup? Good, is it? God I do hope so.'

Judy was lowering her spoon back into the bowl.

'It is actually . . .' she said – and she seemed to be genuinely amazed – 'quite *astonishingly* good. Truly. The layers of flavours are really quite –'

'Ah!' cried Teddy with approval. 'Here's mine! And one for you too, Jamie, look. Excellent. No – like I say, we were introduced to the two of them right at the very beginning. Dave Hitler, Alice said he was called. And Mrs Hitler. Don't think we got a name at all, for the wife. So there you are. Completely in the dark. Oh my gosh this *is* good, isn't it? Very rich stock . . . cream . . . lardons, croutons. So *smooth* . . .'

Jamie nodded. 'Delicious,' he said. 'Delicious.'

'Mind you . . .' mused Teddy. 'I'm not really the person, am I, to talk about surnames, really. I winced, you know. I don't know if you, um – noticed, or anything, Jamie – but when he, you know . . . Lucas, yes? When he *called* me that . . . oh God. I do it every time. Always will, I expect. I mean to say – no one *else* here reacts, or anything. I get no sort of teasing. It's me. It's just me.'

'That soup,' declared Judy, dabbing at her lips with her napkin, while still she managed to go on smacking them, 'was absolutely bloody historic. I *told* you, Jamie – he's got a thing about it. Haven't you, darling?'

'Well wouldn't *you*?' retorted Teddy, quite het up; and then he calmed. 'It was – quite, quite delicious, I really must say.'

'No,' said Judy, with firmness. 'I wouldn't. Better than Hitler, anyway.'

Teddy looked miserable. 'Maybe,' he said. 'Maybe . . .'

Judy shrugged back a heavy coil of hair from the tip of her shoulder.

'Does it really . . . ?' she coyly enquired of either one of them. 'Look especially good tonight? My hair? Candles do *help*, of course, but . . .'

'Perfect,' smiled Teddy. 'Wondrous. Isn't that so, Jamie?'

Jamie beamed with many sorts of pleasure (I just simply love all this).

'*Yes*,' he said. 'Oh yes, Judy. It's . . . beautiful.'

Judy kissed Teddy at the rim of his beard and set to patting Jamie's hand, as she concluded her simper.

'You're both so *sweet*,' she cooed. 'Ooh. Ooh! Look: more food! Oh yum. What's next, I wonder. I would say I could eat a *horse* – but it's always been a bit of a bad joke that, really, because with Mike, well . . . you never really *knew*, did you . . . ?'

And Tubby, as he both proudly and shyly wheeled in all the mains (and here – I'll let you in on something, will I? It weren't the cooking what began to sort of get to me a while back there, nah nah – it weren't nothing like that, nah. It were, like, how the fuck am I gonna bang all these bleeding meals on the table at the same bleeding time? But I tell you what: I done it) – yeh, as he wheeled in all the mains, he was really flying, Tubby was. He got to talking one time down the pub to some sort of luvvie, right – bit of a ponce, you want the truth . . . but we was just on opening time so there was sod all people about so I goes ah fuck it: no one's gonna clock us. Ain't none of my mates about who's gonna start to thinking *ay ay* – old Tubs gone well bent on us, look. So any road – this geezer, right: bit-part actor, is what he was telling

172

me. Yeh right – that's what *I* thought, and all: oh yeh? And, like, what bit when, mate? Cos I never saw him on the telly, nor nothing. Don't matter. All I wanna say is, he was on about how when you're, like, on the stage, in the wossname – theatre, like (think he were doing panto: might have been the back end of an arse) – you're on this bloody great high what even no charlie can't never get close to. Then for just like for ever you got to deal with coming down out of it before you're, like, on again and right back up there. And at the time I just says to him Yeh yeh, whatever (he were getting a bit too pally: anyone walk in the door and I'm well gone, son). But right now – this is what I'm, like, trying to say to you – right here and now this minute, yeh? I reckon I twig what he was on about. Cos they bleeding loved that soup, you know. Bleeding loved it. Fair lapped it up. It's nearly like I don't even got to wash out the bowl – that's how much they bleeding loved it. And the pot, what is it . . . ? Tureen, I think (could be wrong. Funny old word. Makes me think back to Maureen, that time: well tasty shag, but blimey she could talk) – anyway: tureen, right? Wiped clean, it is. Yeh. So I was thinking to myself, wasn't I, just a while back there, like I says – Yeh OK, son, fair do's: you done good on the soup front, no argument – and I reckon these steaks and all the doings (and I marinaded them, see, is what I done: that's the trick of it, you wanna know. You dunk them in all sorts and slosh them about a bit and they come up smelling of roses) . . . so yeh, I reckon these steaks are truly the business – lovely marbling, dark sort of scuzzy colour on them, see (you only got to look). Yeh but what I'm dealing with here is, what? Fifteen, sixteen of the buggers, aren't I? Ay? So I was thinking well look, this is it: either the half of them's gonna be as cold as a mother superior's twat, or else what we're looking at is, like, relays. But nah – didn't turn out nothing like that, as it happened. This kitchen, I ain't kidding you – it's like it come straight out of some fancy hotel up West. You got surfaces like what you could play football on, yeh? And all these gizmos I discover what keep all your gubbins well piping for as long as you want, son – and it don't go all dried out on you, neither. So what I do is, I get me spuds well creamed, don't I? One touch of the button on this fucking cement mixer, looks like, and we are talking *silky*, my son. Then I unloads in all the butter and the slashed about cabbage and the garlic and a couple great handfuls of your fresh ripped-up herbs, look (I got basil, I got parsley, I got thyme, I got the red sod, what's he – paprika, yeh, on the button: tell you, mate – I got all sorts in here). The peas, right (and I like peas, big time: your pea, to my mind, is as sweet as a nut) – well, they're taking care of theirselves, if I'm honest, so what I'm really sweating over now, right, is my gravy. Now I don't know, do I, if you're anything like what I am, but I reckon at the end of the day that whatever you done, it stands or falls by your gravy. And this great pot of the stuff I got here . . . what's that you say? Tell you what's in it? Do *what*? You are extracting the Michael, entcha? Get out of it, mate! Trade secret, that is – been handed down, that has: between me and my maker, cross my heart, I do – and slit my throat if a single word should pass my thing (I also do a wicked liquor for your eels – maybe tomorrow, eh?). Lips. If one word passes my lips. Yeh, so listen, like I say – this great pot of gravy is come up just lovely. Real good smells it got, you know? And glossy, like a Derby winner's bum.

So what it is now is – I doled them all out, right, the plates (and I thought of getting old Paul or Biff to give us a hand here, yeh? And then I thought nah, sod it – this is me, ain't it? This is mine). So I got them all out, OK, and I'm sitting down meself, now – I'm next to this Yank bird, aren't I, and some old posh bloke, look – and I'm telling you (I ain't making this up) they're all hanging their faces well over the doings and *ooooh*, they're going . . . *mmmmm*, is all I'm hearing. And they ain't even tasted it yet. So all in all, I reckon I'm on a little bit of a winner here, say it myself.

And here – hang about: posh geezer and Yankee Doodle, here – they now got their chops well around a forkful, ain't they? And if they was someone like Biff (now look – he's a good bloke, Biff, I ain't saying – salt of the wossname – but he ain't got what you'd call real *class*, has he? Ay? I mean be honest: we ain't talking no pukka gent, nor nothing – you wouldn't want to bring him round the Queen's gaff, would you?) – so yeh, some common old fucker like Biff, he's already gonna be telling you it straight, ain't he? Ay? His face all stuffed full of food, right, and him spluttering all through it, and his mouth hanging well open like he's a bleeding cow, or summing. But what we got next to us here is a good few slices more *genteel*, if you know what I'm saying. And yeh OK – I'm already hearing a fair old number of whoops and yellings out and all the rest of the caper from down the table a piece – one bloke, that Mike geezer, yeh? Mister Blitz? He just come over, he did, and he slaps me round the shoulders and he says to me I'm a genius, he says: what he says is I am one fucking genius, son! Yeah. (Except he didn't do the fucking.) Mm. So *nice*, yeh? But I reckon I'll just hang about a bit and see what these two here got to say. What is going down now is they got it well necked, haven't they? So what with one thing and the other I don't think I got too long to hang about.

'Oh *man*!' was Kimmy's initial exclamation – soon to be followed by a good few more: 'I mean, like – oh *man*, you know? This is, like, *toadally* to die for! Last time, Tubs, let me tell ya, I had a steak like this I was in this, like – *diner* on the Upper East Side? And I was like I am *so-o-o* sad about leaving New York on account of never, right, in England am I gonna get to eat a steak like this one. So like I mean oh *man*, you know? I'm just like blown away.'

'I must say,' chimed in John, with enthusiasm, 'it really is most remarkably good.'

Well, thought Tubby: I am well liking this, aren't I? Hey?

He said, quite softly, as the fingers of his left hand aimlessly but compulsively were crumbling French bread:

'There's a herb butter there and all, look, you want it . . . Shouldn't need it, by rights like, what with the gravy and all. But if you like sort of want it, kind of style – well, it's there, is all I'm saying to you.'

Mike Killery was standing now, and people were clapping before he'd even uttered. He pinged the bowl of his wineglass with a spoon.

'Friends! Friends! Just give me a moment, please! If you will. A toast . . . is almost too small a gesture here, I think we must all be in agreement – but a toast anyway is what I propose – to Tubby! Quiet, please . . . ! Just one more moment . . . To Tubby, everyone – the man is a genius! Not just that – but you good people are now free of all my kitchen horrors – no no, thank you, thank you – you're all very kind, but I know only too well. I had to eat it as well, you know! So. To Tubby. The chef!'

The room was full of cheering (the drumming of knuckles and the clinking of glasses) and no one was yelling more loudly than Paul (See! See! What I *tell* you? Ay? Come up Trojan, my boy did).

As Tubby did his best to cope with this new and sudden and wholly involuntary transformation of his into a radiant convector heater, Mike sat down amid a welter of acclaim and was kissed by Oona as Mary-Ann leaned across with knit-browed urgency and whisperingly informed him that she was really really glad that Mike had found his own cooking so completely horrid because she had thought it completely horrid too but she had never liked to *say* so, see – but now it was all right to say so, wasn't it Mike? Because you, Mike, didn't you? You thought it was completely horrid too? Yes? Thought so. (She only ceased her gabbling as the rumble of general amusement rippled its way over to her and she realized, little Mary-Ann, with a rush of blood-hot embarrassment that hers was the only voice, now, to be heard.) This she saw immediately was due to Lucas. Lucas was standing, and all faces were upon him – no one wishing to miss out on his glance to each of them in turn.

'I can,' he said, 'add little to that fine encomium. I am obliged to you, Killery. Just to thank Lillicrap, I think, for supplying all this most excellent wine to accompany such excellent food.'

As applause rang around him, his expression grew grave, and breaths were caught. The room was held in expectation – but the well of affection very palpably and even near visibly overflowed as Lucas's features mellowed into warmth:

'Which . . . we must not allow to get cold! Bon appétit, mes amis!'

The laughter was rich, as Lucas resumed his seat. Paul glanced quickly at Biff, who was grinning like a madman; a flicker crossed his face as he realized he had been rumbled, but the grin stayed well in place. Dorothy, next to them – her head leaning lightly, now, just on Paul's shoulder – was smiling over to Mary-Ann who was waving at her delightedly, and Dorothy wept quite openly as the laughter came out of her in ill-controlled gulps. Frankie was pouting quite provocatively, the heel of her hand wedged under her chin as she launched out a series of smoochily audible kisses, blown over the runway of her long and straight white fingers in scattergun fashion to whoever might care to field them. Jamie was devouring with unfeigned gusto his steak and potatoes, as he scratched at a few of the more accessible of his patches: he in so many ways, now, felt quite close to bursting. Judy had somehow managed to link one of her elbows with his, and awkwardly but with much girlish giggling, glugged back more of Teddy's claret. Oona threw into the air a succession of single peas, and caught in between her lips each one effortlessly. John was dabbing at his mouth with a napkin – arching high his eyebrows, and with a thumb and forefinger joined into the circle of just-so excellence, he energetically signalled to Tubby his unqualified approval. Lucas –

sipping intermittently at a small gin and oolong – placidly surveyed the scene before him. Alice felt a part of whatever he was feeling, and looked over to him often, ever more deeply. Dave and Mrs Hitler stared down at the table, the fawning ochre candlelight chasing the hollows of their eyes while caressing the planes of chin and cheekbone.

Tubby was back in the kitchen, readying the unveiling of the third and final act of this smash-hit play what he apparently wrote. 'Way to go!' is what that American bint Kimmy had whooped at him, as he scraped back his chair and mumbled to her and John that time, it don't hang around for no man. 'Way to go!', yeh, is what she was up and yelping. I mean Christ alone knows what it *means*, that (Way to go? What – she's pointing me in the right direction, is she? Don't go walking into the wall, look – use the bleeding door, why don't you?). But yeh, I reckon she meant it encouraging, like – cheering me on, sort of style, like what they all done, really. And seeing as how she was such a big fan of my gravy, and all, I give her the old eye one or two times back there, I did – cos she's well usable, I don't mind telling you (bit of comfort). But nah. Weren't nothing there what I could see. No hint at all of Come on then, mate: what you waiting for? Which just goes to show you, really – most what you hear and read about all this what women is after, and stuff: load of old bollocks, ain't it? Ay? I mean what I mean is they're always banging on about how women look up to a geezer what has proved hisself well able to handle whatever, yeh? Whatever is, like, thrown his way. Well not this one – not a bleeding dicky bird. She may go big on my gravy, but she don't want none of my sauce. Maybe it's she just ain't into blokes. Could well be, you know, shacked up like she is with that other one, what's-her-face . . . the one with the little girl, there: Dorothy, pretty sure. Cos they're both of them in beautiful condition, you know: barely run in. And more and more now in London you can't hardly help but get to noticing: women is keeping theirselves to theirselves, if you take my meaning – and your so-called men, they ain't no better: bleeding queers, left right and centre. This rate, human race'll fizzle out in no time, yeh – and I don't reckon I'll be too done in on that score, mate, I tell you in all truth. Cos what is it? Ay? When all's said and done. Life, and that. You're just ducking and diving, aren't you? Trying to get a crust. Ducking and diving, that's all it is – day in, day bleeding out. Except that tonight, if I'm honest, I don't feel none of that at all. Tonight I sort of do see, really, what people is on about when they say they're kind of, you know – looking forward. I'm looking forward. I am. And I ain't never done that. Do you know – tomorrow, I might just do them my cottage pie. Ain't done it for yonks. Go down prime, that would. Though I ain't forgotten neither the old eels and mash: I could go down that road. Either way, I reckon the apple and blackcurrant crumble's got to be favourite for afters. But for this evening, laydeez an jellmen, let's see how they reckon my chocolate pudding with vanilla cream then, ay? Soon know, son, cos I'm wheeling in the bugger right now this minute, aren't I? And I tell you this: I'm looking *forward*.

'Oh my *Gaaaad*!' is how Kimmy was greeting the sight of the trolley – a good few people were reacting in a similar manner, but she was the most audible, by far. 'Oh my *Gaaaad*, John – *chaw*clet! Oh man – how dreamy is that?'

'*Mm*!' John was laughing. 'And hot too, looks like. We'd better make sure we get some before my Frankie sees it, or if I know her, she'll scoff the lot. Her and chocolate! Love of her life.'

'And look at, John, how Tubs has, like, done it all? I think maybe he used, what – Jell-O moulds? Something like that. You know, John – it's real neat, this thing you got going with Frankie. I think I maybe should've hooked up with a guy like you.'

'Old, you mean,' smiled John. 'And rich. Mm – the formula has been known to work.'

'Old-*er*,' qualified Kimmy. 'As to big bucks, well – I do OK. But sure – rich is good. Rich is always good. But I don't know I ever told you, John – me, I was married once. Yes I was. For a real short time. Jeez, what a klutz. I mean *me* – I was the klutz for doing it. But the guy . . . his name was *Aaron*? He was pretty much a klutz too, you know what I'm saying? I used to call him Elvis, time to time, and then I discover he really hated that big time – so then, me calling him Elvis, it became, like, *permanent*? Oh hey, Tubs! Over here, baby! Little girl starving for *chaw*clet, here!'

'How long were you together?' asked John.

'Huh? Me and the klutz? Oh – couple munce. Hundred years. Whatever. I think it's this dinner, you know – kinda brought it all back. Full-time job working out what the guy would *eat*, you know? He didn't do dairy, he didn't do wheat – meat was a no-no, along with just most everything else. I tell you – hell, I can barely believe I did this for the schmuck – I used to knock myself out with all the veggie cooking, you know? I read, like, Martha Stewart from cover to cover on account of my ma, she says you gotta make a real nice home for your man, you know? Else he's gonna fly. Oh boy – couple weeks in, I woulddda bought him the airline ticket: first class, one way, baby!'

Suddenly the air was heavy with the hot and idle droning of a thousand lazy honey bees, as the warm chocolate pudding and light cool cream slid between lips and slithered over palates.

'Very, very fine,' pronounced John. 'Such a *comfort* . . .'

'It is *toadally* better than sex,' yapped Kimmy. 'I guess you don't feel that, huh? Well lucky John. But see – I really *tried* with that guy, you know? I'd be tearing the fresh herbs over my hand-rolled pasta – scatter them all over my home-made ragout. And what does he do? My husband, the klutz. His face – it like shrivels into near kinda *repulsion*, you know? And he sets to picking out with his eeny-weeny little itsy-bitsy fingers all the what he called this, like – "green muck"? Go figure. Martha Stewart, she says to make a guy a real romantic meal, time to time: cut all the food into heart shapes, she's going. And you know I think *neat* – I'll do that, yeah. Fast forward a month and I'd be, like – I'll cut his *throat* into a heart shape, you know? But I was still trying to *make* something here, yeah? And then I remembered the food I had that night was, like, soup, spaghetti and zabaglione so it was, like: hell with that idea.'

Spoons were being banged on tables – Teddy was shouting out Author! Author! And Tubby quite literally took a bow, and then another.

'Is there any more?' piped up Frankie. And Jamie thought God, she looks right now so very heartbreakingly young – little older than Mary-Ann. Tubby said Yeah – there's plenty: heaps. And Frankie, look at her: just radiant, she is – like a schoolgirl at a birthday party. 'Great!' she exclaimed. 'Don't look, John – but me and Mary-Ann are having seconds. I won't fit my new dress!'

'Yeh!' laughed Kimmy. 'That's how I was, after I dump the guy. I'm like on this eat-any-damn-thing-you-damn-well-please kinda diet? Plus I drink for America. So no time I get to looking like the Michelin guy? Can you *imagine*? I was kinda like breaking up, I guess. Hadn't been for my ma, I don't know I come out of it, you know? She says to me – Take a vacation, Kimmy: go someplace. So I went to, like – *Paris*? I guess you know Paris real well, huh John? Me, I never been. I, like, toadally *loved* it? Where I met Doe – Dorothy, yeah?'

'Ah,' understood John. 'That's where.'

Tubby was on his feet again, beaming like a compère.

'Thanks – thanks all. Thanks. Now listen – there's a beautiful little whole wossname of Stilton I got, anyone's up for it?'

Several male voices were rumbling their eager assent, while a roughly similar number of female ones were fluttering out their protestations: after two large portions of chocolate pudding and *cream*? They couldn't, simply couldn't even dream of it; well – maybe just a *taste* . . .

'And then,' sighed Kimmy, 'into my life there came *cheeses* . . .'

John looked up. 'Really? Oh. And how did they, um . . . ?'

'They? *He. He.* Cheeses *Christ*, right? I suddenly, like – saw the light?'

'Right,' said John. 'Oh right – I see.'

I must say, he was thinking, I do rather love the way she talks – it's so unlike anything I'm used to, this accent of hers. Like when she was talking about Paris just a while back, yes? The way she said it, it came out as Peeris. Peeris. Just like penis, give or take a wrong 'un.

'But Cheeses,' concluded Kimmy, 'he didn't hang around too long. It was like – in and out, you know? Kinda like the klutz, Aaron? After that, I got to exploring my seck-shallidy. This I guess I'm still doing. Plus my art. Which I am, like, toadally into. But still, John – you're real lucky. With Frankie.'

'I am,' he readily agreed. 'There's nothing that really seems to bother her, you know. Can't think of a thing, offhand. Except for our resident tramp, of course. Hates him. She's got me driving the long way round, now. I don't know what it is with her, but there you have it.'

'He is *gross*, that guy. Real creepy. Oh man – this is Stilton, huh? I heard about it, but I never had it. Is it, like – real strong? Do you eat the blue bits?'

'They're the best bits,' smiled John. 'Oh and look – perfection, perfection. Here comes Judy with that heart-thumping coffee of hers.'

'Extra big one for you, John,' said Judy, placing a teacup and saucer before him. The aroma's hit took no time in coming. 'I'll be back with yours in just a minute, Kimmy – all right?'

Judy squeezed her way past the backs of chairs and continued to busy herself at the large chromed coffee-maker (it was half the size of a wardrobe) that Lucas had acquired from . . . the BBC, I think is what Alice was telling me, one time. The whole Corporation went over to prepacked sachets, or something – but this great beast, this is the real McCoy, all right: ground up the beans (dark Continental, full roast – Lucas's specification) and then brewed it up into a spectacularly rich and powerful, scented jolt. Got through packs of it.

'What are you two boys nattering about now?' she asked over her shoulder of Teddy and Jamie, as the scalding coffee hissed and plopped its way down into an ushered succession of thin white porcelain cups.

'Oh . . .' threw away Teddy, 'I was merely and no doubt very boringly bringing Jamie up to speed on my rather less than illustrious career as an actor. Last one I did was for, um – *toothpaste*, Jamie. For my sins. Capital Radio, or one of those. "You can actually *feel* the bright white taste!" That was my bit. "You can actually *feel* the bright white taste!" Yes. About sixty times they had me saying that. At first it was "You can actually feel the bright white *taste*!" but then the writer – I know: unbelievable, isn't it? But the *writer*, all right – Mister Charles Dickens – then decided that no – the emphasis should after all be on the *"feel"*. So we did it all again. And again. Ho hum. And modelling, if you can call it that. Oh yes – I do that too. For these – you know, these funny little mail order catalogues that keep falling out of newspapers and then you chuck them in the bin. I do those zip-up cardigans that seem to be worn exclusively by people who work for the Post Office. Half a day, I was once, with a battery-operated nose-hair clipper jammed up my left nostril – I'm telling you, I could barely breathe. "Smile," they said. "Look happy."'

'It's only for *now*,' admonished Judy, with near parental fondness. 'Don't listen to him, Jamie. One day soon – mark my words: name in lights.'

'Not sure I even really want it any more . . .' Teddy was muttering, tracing random patterns in the breadcrumbs on the table with the pad of one forefinger. 'I mean – Teddy Lillicrap. Christ . . .'

'Why didn't you, um . . . ?' Jamie trod quite carefully. 'I mean, Teddy – what I mean is, if you really do hate this name of yours so very much, why have you never – ?'

'Well that's just what *I* keep saying,' said Judy. 'God knows enough people in the acting profession *do*, for God's sake.'

Teddy nodded. 'I know. It's true. It's just that I always thought that that would be somehow, I don't know – a bit *easy*, you know? Not quite straight. Totally mad, I know – but there it is.'

'Born cussed,' was Judy's affectionate dismissal of that little lot. 'Not only does he have a thing about it – he *likes* having a thing about it. What a man. What *will* I do with him?'

'Love me for ever!' laughed Teddy. 'Anyway, dear people – I rather think the time has come for a bit of a sing-song, don't you?'

'Oh *lovely*, Teddy,' Judy enthused. 'Just let me dole out the rest of these coffees, yes? And Lucas said to pass round the Calvados tonight – the really old one. This is quite a day!'

And Jamie could really only nod. Because it was, it was: this really was one hell of a day. The hardest part is believing that this time last evening I was . . . well what? Arguing the toss with Caroline, was I still? Or had we by now each of us slunk back aggrieved into our murky corners, to wallow in the stew of our own resentment? Was I still that much concerned about Benny? Or had the essential nature of my own survival become the only real true issue here? Couldn't say. It blurs. Certainly I did not project anything at all beyond simply getting here – getting here, yes, and talking to Lucas. How could I know that within, oh – it's only been hours, I could feel just so much a *part* of the place – so terribly together with everyone here? Already the thought of tomorrow elsewhere and without them is not only wholly unthinkable, but there is there the jagged form of the sort of cruel suggestion that could tear at you viciously, if you even thought to lightly touch its dagger tips; it has become one of those things that you simply cannot in sanity consider, because even the first shadows of such a void, lurking, could stop your heart with fear and rob you of the will to draw another breath. Like Judy was telling me earlier. The world – the big world, the real world (the outside world), it has changed so very much in recent years. What once was secure no longer feels so. We tried to shoo away all the bad things, but they never would go. And we – our lives too have shifted, over the years, but somehow we have all found our way here, to be together. We huddle for comfort, explore the possibilities and freely impart all of our talents. What we have here, Judy had said – and she held Jamie's hand as she spoke to him – what we have here is our *own* world, you see. Lucas's world, really, where we feel so pleased to be. So, Jamie, she concluded (and she did – she had such a kind smile), in the words of the song, welcome to our world: won't you come on in? And *yes*, I had said – *yes*, oh yes: I will, I have done. I am a *part*.

Look at the scene. Just glance all about you. Because I can barely, frankly, take it in. The candles are wide and misshapen, now, like wilted mushrooms, their fat and idly writhing flames splicing all the faces into a flicker-book of warmth and animation. The glasses and silver – black and white stripey – are impossibly bright, and now, quite suddenly, I cannot hear . . . all these people are carousing in silence, though their lips still move and their eyes are continuing the dance. Teddy is standing, and waving a chopstick, or maybe a golden wand – and with a gently graduating insistence, now, as arms are linked around the tables – the sound of first whispers and then more boldness is seeping back, an undulating rhythm and hum spiked by laughter and then the odd brief happy shriek. And now through the glaze of my eyes I see it so clearly, and the fug in my ears is dispelled. A rousing chorus, now, breaks over everyone as arms and glasses are raised and brandished.

'Those were the *days*, my friend . . . ! We thought they'd *never* end . . . ! We'd sing and dance for ever and a *day* . . . !'

Yes, oh yes – but here can be no demonstration of fond and mutual remembrance: this is a big and bursting, joyous celebration of the glorious *now* – the fevered embrace of a desperate thanksgiving for all that must never be lost, or even diminished (and never can such things be thought of).

Lucas has risen. He smiles the smile of an adulated general finally come to liberate a strife-torn land from its harsh and mad despotic invader. He bats down his hands as all but the Hitlers make to rise for him, but none of them abandons the gesture: they all see it through. And accompanied by Alice, Lucas takes his leave. There is a lull of sorts, and then a rallying cry as the children resume their play. With a freedom that I so seldom felt throughout my boyhood, when really I should have. My father . . . I really must tell you just this one small incident, among so many. One unnaturally bright and icy autumn's day, he had me in the garden, picking up leaves. By hand. The Lord Jesus, he said, would give me a penny for every single leaf I gathered. I toiled. All morning and afternoon I bent down and picked up leaves. Thousands, I gathered, in big brown paper carrier bags. Many, many thousands. And all the time I hoped, I prayed – oh God: to *God*, I suppose – that when it was all over, when every single leaf had been garnered, I would have enough pennies to go, leave home, get out for ever from under him. I carried the dozens of bags of leaves up the two flights of stairs to my bedroom, and there I waited all night for the Lord Jesus to come to me (because it is at night that magic happens). I awoke with a jerking start maybe just after dawn – and even before my eyes were fully open, the rustle as I stirred and the now quite sickening stench of wet and rotting matter were all I needed to know that the leaves were still clustered about me. I said to him at breakfast, my father, this man: 'The Lord Jesus – he never came.' *Really*? he went – the arch of his eyebrow, the roguish wink sent spinning across to his unsmiling wife, this woman – both coming nowhere near to masking the zeal of malice that tugged at the corners of his mouth. *Really*? he said again: the Lord Jesus didn't *come*, you say? Well well. He rose from his chair and ruffled my hair. 'Dear oh dear. Well it just goes to show you, doesn't it lad? You really can't trust *anyone*, these days.'

And now I watch the retreating form of Lucas, until the sight of him is lost to me. We all need a father, I suppose is what it is: a person to be there for us. But some, the few, really do need to be that person. Is all I can think. To have people close who will feed upon their need of him. I think that's maybe true.

Time, you know, has passed . . . but I tell you this: for my part, for as long as I continue to live, I shall never ever forget even the slightest detail of that very first night in The Works – each fleeting vision, the soft and oozy candlelight that caressed each one of our faces, the flavour of every single mouthful of Tubby's ambrosia, the endless mellow river of Teddy's heady wine: all these touches, burnished anyway, are bright in my memory and locked up tight within me for all the times I need them. Because of anything that came before or after, that was the day . . . oh yes: that *was* the day . . .

II

a middle . . .

CHAPTER SIX

It gets dark, these days, so very early in the afternoon. Before we know it, Christmas will have come (lots to do, lots to do). And it's cold: I feel the cold – more than most, it seems to me. And yet despite all that, is how Alice was thinking – knowing how the winds just go right through me, still he has me, Lucas, climbing that frozen iron stepladder, morning and evening, and delivering into the blackness, laying before the invisible and faintly unsettling presence of the barn owls, a succession of fresh-killed rodents. Mostly rats. I try not to dwell, too much. They are delivered in a box by one of the many faceless men who silently deliver to Lucas whatever it is in the world he desires. They used to be alive, in the early days, the rats, but I had to draw a line. But the owls, Lucas had countered – it is natural for them, dear Alice, he said, to swoop down from high above, their talons and then gullets wildly eager for living prey. Maybe, is all I think I said: oh yes very *possibly*, Lucas – you are the expert, and I bow to your knowledge on the matter. But I refuse to be the agent of death: conceivably this is one area you might like to take care of yourself? He seemed lost in thought. He sipped his gin and tea, and studied the black of a windowpane. And then he assured me that from now on the packages of assorted vermin will have been, um – seen to (not what he said, but that's what he meant). Fine, I said: that's fine, Lucas. Because I sometimes feel I have to, you know – take some form of a stand with him (just sometimes) or I might otherwise lose altogether whatever parts of me could still, just possibly, be mine. My instinct, of course (and he knows it: he knows it well), is to automatically lift from him all humdrum cares and everyday nuisances – and further, to cater to his inclinations before he yet realizes he is even beginning to lean in a particular direction (is this vain of me? To think it?). But he has to know – well don't you think this is right? – that there is a limit. Here somewhere. And with the rats, we reached it (I did it twice, and that was enough). Although I know deep down (and does he? Does Lucas? Deep down know it? He must do; deep down, Lucas – he seems to know just everything) . . . but I understand well that had Lucas *absolutely* insisted on the business of my continuing to deliver these vile little animals, still living, to the – in my view – equally vile and shadowy owls (I have not said this to Lucas) . . . then I should somehow have steeled myself and just *done* it, you know. As I do. But I am glad, on reflection, that I stood up for myself in this, I suppose, small way. And I did so love it, loved him for it, when he quickly conceded. Little things like that bind us closer, I feel. Always closer. Long way further to travel, of course. But you really have to understand (not a single word of this must go any further) that even so mild a form of contradiction always must take place very much behind closed doors. It would not do for the family, as Lucas has taken to calling us, now, to hear of anything but harmony. The whole place thrives on the thrum of harmony, though I think it is due in no small part to my constant tuning that the melody and topnotes forever ring proud, here: in short, simply making sure that everything just *works*. And it really does seem to. This whole place, now – it maybe even surpasses Lucas's most optimistic projection . . . or maybe he always did know, just as he repeatedly said to me, that everything would easily just fall into place, quite as always he had wished it. From the day he met me, he rarely talked of anything else. I remember the day. Well of *course* I remember the day: how could I not? When someone such as Lucas walks into your life, you know that change, big change, is no more than a beat away. (Actually – it's mad, that: to say 'someone such as Lucas', the way I did just there. Yes well – I expect you've guessed what it is I am bound to say next: that there can't ever, anywhere, at any time in the past or future be anyone at all even remotely such as Lucas. And you're right: that is exactly the point that I have to make clear; otherwise, really, there can be no understanding of how it is with me – how it is with all of us.)

I was working in a members' club – long white apron over a smart black trouser suit – very Lautrec, and rather chic. Most of the staff there (and it was a nice club, actually – low lights day and night, big squashy sofas . . . arty crowd, generally, which thinking about it, I suppose, only made Lucas stand out all the more). And so as I say, I think, yes, that it would be fair to conclude that most of the staff there were actors, stymied for now in their quest for a part and in the meantime pouring drinks with brio, always alert and ready with the eyes and teeth for whenever it was that Mister Spielberg would chance to amble through the door, waving about him a fistful of contracts. I maybe rang the changes, though only somewhat, by being . . . oh, I suppose I can use the word this once: an *artist*, OK? Who couldn't sell a painting. Oh God: don't get me on to my paintings. I just find the whole thing so terribly perplexing, if you want the truth. I mean – I *can* paint, I know I can paint; everyone tells me how very painterly all my pictures are. Even a dealer told me that, one time. In Cork Street – there are a few of them down there. So you like them? You'll take me on? (God – how young I was: how foolish.) He didn't actually laugh in my face and tear them all to pieces, but by the look in his eyes, he really might as well have. Dorothy squints at them from time to time, my pictures, and pronounces them 'sweet'. Well in all honesty I don't actually altogether object to 'sweet' – 'sweet' is quite nice, quite like 'sweet'. But that's not *all* they are, surely? Sweet? I mean – I really do *feel*, you know, when I'm actually doing them. A passion, of sorts (that's a bit strong, maybe). Judy, of course – dear Judy – she actually said to me, oh – ages back. Said she wanted to buy one. And then she said, lovely woman that she is: '*Two*. I want to buy *two*, Alice – they're really quite lovely.' Oh *Judy*, I went – you don't really. You can't do. Nobody does. But she said Oh but I *do*, Alice – I really really do. So I sold her one (the parrots) for, oh – I think I only charged her a tenner, or something. Less than the cost of the paint and paper. And the other one (the petunias) I just gave to her. Present. Even had it framed. Lucas, of course . . . he says terribly nice things about them. In public. Which is nice. It is not, however, until I painted The Works that he actually hung one. So I did another – different view, from the river side of things. And he hung that too. I think if I want him to complete the hat-trick I shall have to charter a helicopter, or something, to help me capture the aerial view. That and the foundations are all I haven't done. I did think, at first, when Dorothy said – you know: '*sweet*', like she did. I did for the moment wonder whether this couldn't be out of some sort of loyalty to Kimmy, or something. But no. She really does like whatever Kimmy does (or what Kimmy gets others to do for her, anyway. Which is all right. I do believe that there can be art, true art, in a concept: you just have to think of Lucas). But my stuff, no: it's just 'sweet'. Ah well. Better than rancid, I suppose (well it's how you have to think, really, isn't it? You take what you can get).

But now I'm, oh – I'm completely sidetracked now (because I told you, didn't I? I told you not to get me on to my paintings). The *club*, yes? And Lucas. He was sitting just next to this absolutely enormous and very frondy sort of palm tree kind of thing they had there in the corner – on his own, of course (he is one of nature's solitaries, Lucas, I was soon to discover), and somehow he made it quite clear that he was not at all waiting for anyone to join him. He seemed to me . . . interesting. It's hopeless, actually, to call him that. To say that's how he seemed. I mean he *is*, obviously – interesting. He's totally quite utterly *fascinating*. I think – and I'm far from alone, as I imagine you know. Well have you seen? You must have noticed the way everyone here just gazes up at him, rapt? Yes you have – so you do know, don't you? All about it. Anyway, I've thought and thought about that evening since, and I can't really, you know, get any closer than 'interesting', I'm afraid. What I suppose I am meaning by so, well – it's rather *nebulous*, isn't it? Interesting. Is that I wasn't at one fell swoop *impaled* by him, or anything – but I did most certainly find him immediately, well – *interesting*, is all I can really say. And what he did next made him more so, yes. He asked me for a daiquiri (not that interesting per se, yes I know – but listen. Just wait). So I got Philip, head barman, to make up the daiquiri – and he'd won prizes, you know, Philip, for his, um – *mixology*, they call it now, believe it or not . . . so yes, as I say, I can only assume that the daiquiri was excellent (wouldn't know – don't drink much). I placed before Lucas (although I didn't yet know it was Lucas he was called; I'd already looked him up, though – Cage, it said in the roll of members: L. Cage) – I set before him this little paper doily – we always had to do that with every single drink, big club rule – and then put the squat and golden daiquiri squarely on top of it. He thanked me, and then he raised the glass and tipped the whole of the daiquiri into the base of the palm tree. He didn't look up.

'Was it, um – no good?' I asked (thinking it was all quite amusing, really: he hadn't even tasted it – not even given it so much as a sniff).

'I've no idea,' he more or less drawled. And then he smiled. Lovely smile: warm. Truly lovely. 'I haven't even tasted it. Don't go. I should like another drink.'

'OK,' I said. 'OK, fine. What would you like this time?'

'Oh,' he said – his hand raised up now into this quick and

darting throwaway sort of gesture (he does it all the time). 'A daiquiri. Please.'

And I tried to hold his gaze. I tried to make him look into my eyes and read there that Yes, OK – I had caught on to whatever this game was he thought he was playing with me, but that if he imagined I was to be the butt of his so-called humour . . . well then I wasn't amused. But he wouldn't. Look up. So I just thought Well – he's the member, he's the one who's paying: he wants another daiquiri, I'll give him another daiquiri. It's nothing to me. Philip, he said: Blimey – that was quick. Another one, ay? He'll have to watch it.

The second daiquiri, with barely a glance from Lucas, swiftly went the way of the first.

'Don't go,' he said. 'I should like another drink. Please.'

'Uh-huh,' I went. 'Another drink. Fine. *Daiquiri*, by any chance, Mister Cage?'

And then he looked at me, oh – just *radiantly*, and so full on (that was the moment: that was the moment).

'Oh no,' he said, quite blithely. 'Tanqueray gin, please – large – and a very small pot of warm oolong tea. I shall mix them myself. I don't . . .' he practically sighed, as his eyes engulfed me, ' . . . actually *like* daiquiris. Lucas. Not Mister Cage. Lucas.'

Cheap and easy trick? Do you think? A well-honed routine for impressing a certain sort of woman, and used a thousand times before? Maybe. I thought not. I was, oh – *captivated*, and he saw that clearly. And later, quite a long time later, when we were, I suppose – well, *together*, you might say (as together, anyway, as Lucas and I will ever become) – he told me that he had ordered the drinks, those daiquiris (the first time in his life he had even dreamed of doing so) wholly upon an unexplained but driving impulse. He felt, he said, motivated. He just had to, he said, make me see him. Well. He did. I do. All the time.

He asked me to dinner – not there and then, although I had

196

hoped he might. The next morning, the girl on reception handed me a heavy cream envelope, with just my name on it. Inside was a handwritten note which I still quite often get out and glance at, oddly. I mean – I'm *here* now, aren't I? So why would I look at this note? Don't know. Anyway – I do, is all I am simply saying (it sort of marks the beginning of the beginning of the woman I became). It had been written, the note, I now know, during the very hour he met me, with his broad-nibbed Montblanc Meisterstuck (the one that looks like a plutocrat's black and glossy pocket zeppelin) and stated, really rather formally, that he would be pleased to see me for dinner at the Connaught that very evening, at eight o'clock prompt. I won't tell you about all the problems I had switching around all these work shifts – promising to anyone extra free hours of any sort of labour they cared to name, if only they'd take from me this evening's workload. Because it did not occur to me, you know, to suggest to Lucas that some other evening – maybe tomorrow? – would actually be rather more convenient; and nor, of course, did it so much as cross my mind to decline. I got there early, but he was already seated. I hoped to God in heaven that this damn dress was all right. It was kingfisher blue, a sort of shantung. I don't wear it any more, not now – but naturally I keep it: keep it safe. My hair still smelled of warmth and an alien lacquer (I had practically bribed them to give me a slot). Lucas did not once acknowledge the presence of anyone in the restaurant, though I felt he was known there. I might, on reflection, be wrong about that; certainly – to my knowledge, at least – he has never been back there. Not, anyway, with me.

'Are you,' he asked quite casually – at some point, I think, quite close to the pudding, 'as they say these days – "seeing" someone, currently? Alice? An *arrangement* of sorts, so to speak?'

'I, um – I sort of am, yes,' is how I responded.

Because, um – I sort of was, yes, is how the whole nonsense had suddenly struck me: the suppers and fruitless sex I had for some time apparently been sharing with Adrian. I say 'apparently' because to me, it didn't ever really feel like what I had been led to believe sex should be, if I'm honest with you, here. Not sex as in films, and so on. Books. Because it was never something I really felt like doing – and when I did, I cannot say I was ever, well – moved. *He* had sex – Adrian did, he had it, yes – and there I was, a witness to the act: just that one small dark and cowering part of me undeniably engaged in the mechanics of coupling, while leaving me strangely detached. Washing, afterwards, and putting myself back together again (fluffing up the hair, touch of lipstick – one notch tighter, maybe, on the broad black patent belt: I used to strap me back into myself) – here was the nearest I got to tingling.

'Well . . .' said Lucas, slowly. His finger ends were touching – forming a pale and bony steeple. I felt as if he might well be about to pronounce a sentence of death, or else maybe be poised on the brink of an extravagant gesture (possibly the granting of mercy). 'Well you see it's rather like this, Alice: you really *mustn't*, you know.'

'No,' I agreed immediately. 'I know. I mustn't. I won't.'

And that's exactly the way I was feeling. I really *mustn't* go on doing just any of this with Adrian (being there while he does). And I won't. No I won't. And I told him so the very next day:

'I don't actually *know*, Adrian, whether he is "right" for me, as you rather oddly put it, or whether he isn't. All I know is that I shan't be seeing you again. Oh God – don't *look* like that, Adrian. It was you anyway, wasn't it? Who kept telling me that I shouldn't go on hanging around for some mythical Mr Right? Well I'm not. Any more. Maybe he is simply Mr Right For Now. Don't know. Who can say?'

'Yeh but *me*!' came back Adrian – really rather aggrieved (ruffling his hair, for some strange reason – just a touch of spittle, look, at the corner there of his wet and reddened lips: not nice – not nice at all). 'I mean it was meant to be *me* you settled for – not go off with someone *else* you're not sure of. *I'm* the one who's wrong for you, Alice – you must see that. If it's not Mr Right, then it should bloody be *me*, shouldn't it, you dozy old cow!'

Mm. Yes. Well, as you might understand, this rather non-conversation I swiftly curtailed, right there and then. So that was Adrian. And this is Lucas. Sometimes it really is as simple as that. Not that life with Lucas may be seen from the outside (as I well understand) to be simple – but rather strangely, I really do find it so, you know. I instinctively know just what it is that is expected of me, and then I, well – merely supply. In the quite early days – when Lucas's father was still alive, still a force – I sometimes wondered whether we might some day be married. He wanted it – Lucas's father, I mean: we got on rather well (he maybe slightly loved me). But I always knew not. Deep down. It troubled me at first (Why? Why not? Why should I not be Mrs Lucas Cage? Am I not good enough? All those usual things) . . . and then it simply ceased to. Trouble me at all. Because we are together, aren't we? As together, anyway, as Lucas and I will ever become. Well then: isn't that enough?

I remember too the night he died, Lucas's father. When Lucas came to tell me, there was about him this air of fevered excitement, only barely reined in (his eyes were bright and he seemed so hot). You look, I said, almost as if you have come directly from killing him yourself, the crime still fresh on you. Because I well knew, of course I did, just how much he loathed his father: I knew the fact, yes, but never the reason. Lucas said simply: he is dead – that is all that is required. Do you find that cold? Well he can be, Lucas: he can be. Cold, yes, and often highly demanding – but of course so terribly warm as well. Warm, yes, and (I think we all know this) so very giving, so unquestioningly generous to all around him.

Demanding. When I said 'demanding', back there just a moment ago – that's not actually, um – quite right. With the exception of the handful of rules pertaining to The Works (which seem to afford him an endless fund of amusement) Lucas . . . he does not lay down the law – no no, that's not at all his style, his way of doing things. He simply somehow makes his preferences felt – often by means of no words at all – and from the moment of divination it simply becomes quite natural for this latest inclination to be indulged. An example (and I suppose it is not at all surprising, really, that this one should occur to me) arose very soon after I joined him at The Works. We were, in those days, the only ones here – but all he could talk of was the day (can't you just *see* it, Alice!) when the building would be filled to the rafters with all, as he put it, all the 'right people'. What are they, Lucas, I had asked him. Who? In what way will they be 'right', these people? Oh – you will know them, he grandly assured me: when you see each one, you will know it immediately. People, Alice, who *need* to be here. Just that. And they – they will know it too: you'll see. As I say, he talked of little else. I cannot really tell you, now, quite how I felt on the matter. Because now – now that Lucas's dream has come into being, and everything here is just running like clockwork – now, it seems difficult to even recall a time when all this was not so. I sometimes did – yes I did feel reluctant to share (although I know I am the one who has all to herself the very best of him) and at other times, I maybe didn't even really believe that it truly would happen. I mean to say – what, exactly? Are we talking about here? A Battersea Dogs' Home, but this one for people? We'll see, I thought: we'll see what occurs. But this is not the example I mean – the example I was ready to set before you. One day, as I say, when it was just us here amid so much vast and dark and echoing space (not even so much as an owl), Lucas glanced across at me – we had a lovely fire that night, I recall: just the crackling branches and pine cones making us warm and alive (we glowed for one another) – and he said Do you know, Alice, I sometimes do believe you could seem even more beautiful to me?

I said nothing. And then I said: sleep and shampoo – sleep and shampoo. These, I believe, are the greatest cosmetics. And then he said nothing, in turn. Well of course I just had to, then, didn't I? Somehow get out of him what exactly he was meaning. I needn't have troubled. He languidly indicated these beautifully got-up packages just by the table (which of course I had noticed; had been, in truth – and just like a child – for some time anticipating). Inside them was an array of the sort of underclothes he now likes me to wear daily. They are very constricting, but they do very much flatter me, even I can see that. When those high and shiny shoes are on – the stockings, and so on. He likes me to serve his 10.30 a.m. gin and oolong, wearing just this. And once more at six in the evening. And then, following each of these little ceremonies, he goes out. And then he comes back. That is what happens. Yes. And anyway, as I say . . . this is just one example: an explanation of sorts.

It is very unlike me, you know, to be this frank with, oh – anyone at all. Just not me. Even with Judy, I could never be intimate. But people here, they speculate, I suppose – they must do – on the . . . well, sexual side of our relationship. What goes on between Lucas and myself. And perfectly understandably, they must wonder as to its nature. Well yes: I know I do.

'So what you reckon? Ay? Bout here, you think then?'

Jamie didn't immediately respond. He extended a foot, angled his neck so that his eyes were practically vertical, and then he kissed his raised and thoughtful finger. Paul Theme, though, seemed happy to await whatever considered verdict might eventually be coming – it didn't seem to bother him in the slightest that he wasn't really, Jamie wouldn't have said, all that securely positioned at the top of a very tall and steeply pitched stepladder. Teetering would be going it a bit, but his torso was quite achingly arched, it looked like to Jamie – both arms twisted around and stretched out as far as they would reach, clutching a large unframed canvas while pinioning it close to the wall with fingers white from pressure (ready then to shift it, this way or that).

'I *think* . . .' said Jamie, rather ponderously . . . because look: I don't in any way wish to overtry Paul's seemingly endless patience (God – he's been up here helping out for just hours) but at the same time I've got to get this thing dead square – well haven't I? Hm? Because it's me, after all, who's going to have to be living with it, isn't it? And if it's even slightly crooked or just the merest fraction too high or low – well, I just know then it's going to drive me completely crazy . . . and at first, oh yes, I'll only try to ignore it, won't I? Oh come *on*, I'll be going to myself: what on earth does an inch or two one way or the other actually bloody well *matter*, Jamie? Hey? When set against the great, you know – *scheme* of things? Godsake let it *lie*, why don't you? Yes yes – but eventually, I just simply won't be able to, will I? Every time I walk into the room I'll focus on nothing else at all, and bit by bit it'll wear me down until I am hovering on near-demented with the obsession of the whole sheer *wrongness* of this bloody Goddam picture (because I was just like this with Caroline – ask her: she'll tell you) and then I'll just have to get Paul back up here to redo it, won't I? Because you'll never in a million years catch *me* going up those steps, I tell you that much for free. I just don't know how he does it, quite frankly, Paul; he's about twelve feet from the ground, looks like, and he's as casual as you like – just look at him. For all the world like he's taking a stroll in the park, or something. Me – I'd be three, four steps up and bang: that's *it*, matey, I'm telling you. That's your lot. Start feeling queasy – and my feet, they tremble beneath me. Always been like that. Heights – bridges, planes, you name it (planes – they're the worst: even thinking of them now, it's making me swoon). Alice, you know – just the other evening I ran into Alice on that long sort of balcony thing not that far from Lucas's place. He's not in, she said to me: you should know that by this time, Jamie, shouldn't you? You've had ages to learn: this is one of his not-in times, isn't it? Yes, I said – I did know that, Alice – wasn't actually after Lucas, as a matter of fact. I was just, um . . . taking in a little bit of air. Yes, I said that. The truth was, this sort of cantilevered walkway effort is the only place one can get outside of The Works – under the stars, sort of thing – without actually leaving the building altogether, and to be perfectly frank with you, although I've come on, oh – leaps and bounds, really, I still do feel the occasional tug at the back of my throat when just nothing – not Judy's head massage and therapy (which, you know, really does work, amazingly) nor another load of Fruit Gums and no patch on earth: not one or all of them would ease the craving. Nothing would do it except for just the one (one, mind) of those little white cool and slinky columns of delight. And every time I do it (rarely, OK? You have to know this and believe me: it's very rare, I do this) I still feel like I am slashing at Caesar in a horribly Brutus-like fashion, but look – once or twice, where's the harm? So it wasn't so much a little bit of *air* I had been taking in as a carefully balanced and shredded, sweetly pungent concoction of various delectable chemicals and poisons – and yes, I must say I did feel braced, and all the better for it. Anyway, that's not the point. The cigarette is not what I'm actually driving at here, no. The cigarette is merely the reason why I happened to be there at the time, on the walkway, you see. So Alice, right? She says to me, Do you want to give me a hand, nourishing beastly owls? And I went – *owls*, Alice? Sorry – not quite with you. And then – rather mischievously, it seemed to me (and you don't, do you? Really associate Alice with any sort of mischief), she lifted the lid on this wooden sort of box thing she had there and oh well – *yuk*, is all I can say about it, really. All laid out in there were, I don't know – dead and furry, that's more than I needed to see, quite frankly (only just come from talking to Tubby about dinner – pot roast, he was doing, and a perfectly heavenly-looking raspberry trifle: I tell you, old Tubby – he just gets better and better). So look – I was already well down the road to declining her generous invitation, right? But when she slapped at the rungs of this sheer and clanging great ladder affair bolted on to the outside wall that she seriously intended to *climb* (the top of it, I'm telling you – it was lost to the blackness above) I at first felt sure she was joking. And when she solemnly assured me she was not (which of course I should have twigged because you don't, do you? Really associate Alice with any sort of joking) – well then I could only charitably assume that she was momentarily deranged, or something. *Me*? Up that ladder? Oh dear dear Alice – there's so much about me you still have to learn (ask Caroline, if you want the ins and outs of it: she's written the book. But I warn you now – it's a very dull one). Paul – he's the person she should have talked to. God – just you take one look at him. Shimmied up there like a monkey hell-bent on a coconut, he did – and he seems in no hurry at all to come back down again. Mind you – there is a limit. Got to focus. The time is well overdue for me to tell him what I think.

'I *think* . . .' said Jamie, rather ponderously, 'just maybe slightly down on the left just a little bit, maybe. A tad. Bit. Not too much. There. There. No – too much. Whooo no – all wrong, now. No no no. Back up a bit. Up – up. No – other side. To your right. Other side. Yup. There. Yes. And now just that top left-hand edge, yes . . . ? Left edge. Just *ease* that square, and – *yes*. Yes yes. That's it. Got it. Perfect. Great, Paul. Marvellous. Spot-on. Terrific.'

'Sure, yeh?' went Paul. 'Come back down then, can I?'

'Yep. Absolutely. Got it, Paul. Thanks so much. Wonderful.'

'Right then, Jamie. We got a fair old fix in the wall there, mate, but what I reckon I'll do . . .' said Paul – coming down from that ladder in what looked like to Jamie just the one single action, swoopingly fluid, as if it were a well-greased chute, or something. 'What I reckon I'll do, Jamie, yeh? Is come again later, right, and get a couple mirror plates sorted out down the bottom there, OK? Be like the Bank of England then, I'm telling you. Rock bleeding solid. And it's a fair old picture you got there and all, me old mate. Love all the red and pink doo-dahs all over it, I do. Right little Picasso, entcha? Ay? You knock out a few more of these, son, and I reckon Theme's Schemes could be well interested. Know what I'm saying?'

And Jamie actually felt himself beginning to blush. Yet one more long-forgotten sensation, newly rekindled. Because before The Works, the only time I would instantly redden was either just after one more ferocious and chest-heaving round of bronchial eruption (generally following the first and best fag of the day) or else merely as a result of sheer and untamed fury – usually down to Caroline, one way or another. But look *thanks*, Paul, for what you just said about the painting – I'm pretty damned pleased with it myself, if you want to hear the truth. Can't wait to get started on another – so yeh: as many as you like. But not, I think, *Picasso*, exactly, Paul – hm? Got our cultural references just a wee bit skew-whiff there, I think. Pollock. That's our man. What we have here is a very fair tribute to the venerated father of action painting – Jack the Dripper himself. And I'll tell you how it happened: how it all came about. And still, you know, I can hardly believe it. I mean, what? Me? Paint a picture? *Me*? Got to be joking. But no. I did. I did *this*. I and I alone. Well – Lucas's inspiration, fairly naturally . . . and I'll tell you how it happened: how it all came about.

I'd been up with Lucas, you see (well I told you that he was the motivation, didn't I? The driving force, the man with the ideas:

that's what he is and that's what he does). Oh – and did I mention? I'm restoring the old presses for him – did you know? Oh yes, been at it for weeks, now. You should just see his face as each huge or tiny part begins to glow again, as the ratchets begin to turn, the gleaming brass wheels spinning freely (he expresses no delight per se, Lucas: there is merely about him the aura of satisfaction). He didn't ask me to do it. But somehow it sort of became plain to me that nothing I could do would give him greater pleasure (though quite how he managed to convey this to me without actually putting into words even so much as an approach to anything of the kind, I cannot at all imagine) and so of course because I am, after all, a printer by trade . . . though mainly, I think, because the thought of actually doing something, any small thing for Lucas himself in paltry return for all that he has given me, well . . . it made me feel so very very good deep down inside of me. So of course, as I say, I offered to undertake their total restoration. Not that these grand old beauties are anything like the massive and high-specification machinery I have been used to. Glorified computers, these days, presses are. But these – they're more like, I don't know . . . steam engines, or something. Something fine and lavish and beautifully made and practically extinct despite the fact that they were built to run for ever. Like old cars. Like old John's Alvis, as a good for instance – that was a complete and utter rebuild, you know – told me that at dinner, John did, one time. Bought the basic shell, chassis and so on for just about a thousand, or something – and then came, oh God – the real money. Stacks of it. Just everything was stripped and totally rebuilt – engine dismantled, retuned, all moving parts either restored or replaced . . . fourteen coats of paint, he told me – fourteen! – and a completely bespoke red Connolly leather interior. He couldn't sell it for more than half what he paid out to get it into this quite peerless condition – but so what, is how he put it. He's not *going* to sell it, is he? Doesn't want to. Couldn't part with her. And it gives him (and Frankie, I bet) a huge amount of pleasure: what money is *for*, no? Yes. Yes indeed. Investment in what you love and believe in. Just ask Lucas: he knows all about it.

So yes – Lucas, as I say. I got all these specialist books from an antiquarian dealer – Lucas happened to let slip the bookseller's name (murmured he might be useful) – and I really am making great headway, you know. It's all actually very logical and quite straightforward once you get going and really sort of, you know – hit your stride, kind of thing. One of them – the smallest, a Wilkinson of about, um – 1860 or thereabouts, I think I'm right in saying (nearest I can get) – she's up and running: purring like a big contented cat. The day I finally got her in perfect working order – do you know what I did? I printed off menus for Tubby's dinner, that very evening. Everyone was thrilled. Well – happy, anyway: everyone seemed to love them. Me – I was thrilled. Totally. And Lucas, yes: I think he was too. Paul – he seemed quite extraordinarily interested. Still is. Was even going on about it again, just now – how we just have to get together on the printing side of things – even when he was a mile off the ground at the top of that ladder (and how he concentrates on just anything at all when he's so far up, well I tell you – it's just beyond me). Yes. So anyway. That's largely what I've been busy with, past few weeks (bring you up to speed) – my, as it were, contribution, if you like – because Judy was quite right about that, you know, that first day when I arrived. Apparently everyone, all of us, when first we came here, we all felt we had nothing at all to give – no ability or feature even remotely appealing, let alone useful, or anything. Life, you see, had done this to us. But *no*: the low self-esteem – it just melts away beneath all the warmth here, and then things begin to emerge from under the swaddled layers of disillusion. Low self-esteem, that little thing – oh yes. It can be an outright and total bugger, you know: wipes you out completely. One sad old loser I used to know, one time (me, in point of fact), pretty much epitomized the grey and awful debilitating force of it. Example: out with your friends, right? And into the bar comes a gaggle of girls. Well straight away and wholly automatically you latch on to the least attractive and dullest – not to say the outright dog – among them for the simple reason that, oh – in the end it just saves so much *time*, doesn't it? That thing one has so much of. Yes. Anyway. So you see, what I'm saying is, because of *here*, we all come to give something we were unaware that we even possessed. Except maybe John, of course. That's different. He knew, didn't he, that he had pots of money, of course he did – and he well knew too that it always goes down a treat, money does. But even John – he's much more than that, you know. Oh no. Not just money. *Such* a nice bloke – take anyone anywhere, John will, in that bloody gorgeous car of his. And *hee* – I shouldn't really maybe be mentioning this just yet because it hasn't actually – you know, it hasn't actually – he hasn't actually confirmed it yet, or anything . . . but he did say to me once that one day, maybe, he'd let me, oh God – take her for a *spin*! A spin! Can you imagine? Something that no one, apart from himself, has ever done. Well. That would really be something. Indeed. So: fingers crossed. Anyway. Not talking about the car, just now. All I'm really saying is that I'm just so very happy to actually be able to put something back *in*. Thrilled, is what I am.

And. When I was with Lucas – declogging cogs and tinkering away with various fonts and faces – I jokily suggested to him that when we finally had the largest of the presses in action again (and God – it's a monster, the biggest one is) I could maybe get Kimmy to get one of her people to design us some gigantic posters – run off an edition. Or, I then quickly put in, *Alice* – we could maybe ask Alice? And Lucas said nothing, as usual – though not at all from uninterest, I'm always sure about that. And then I went on to say that the only reason I would want them, these posters, is that although the old brickwork in my great space is just wonderful . . . well, it's just that there's so terribly *much* of it, if you understand what I'm saying. And I've nothing at all to put on the walls. Well. The very next day, someone delivered to my door (silent and unseen) the most enormous great bound-up package – and when I stripped off all the wrappings, inside were six of the largest canvases I have ever clapped eyes on. All wood-framed and ready-stretched, it said on the sticker there, look. The only thing was (and could this, do we think, be a mistake? Clerical error? Oversight by someone? *Joke* of some sort, could it conceivably be?) . . . well, each of them was perfectly blank, you see. Just white and nubbly. Bloody hell, I thought: bloody hell – blank. And then the next morning . . . the paint arrived. Cans and cans of it, and lots of tubes as well – every colour of the rainbow, and a box of brushes. And yes I did see, of course I did, that the suggestion was being made that I put two and two together. Well yes OK – fine in theory, I grant you – but Christ, I'm no *painter*, am I? Christ – I'd butter a canvas and have it with my tea, sooner than – what? *Paint* the bloody thing. So what was I to do? Hm? Well. You *know* what I did, don't you? Yes you do. Because there it is, for all to see – high above the fireplace, catching the light and in just the right spot (to my eye, anyway). Thanks to the mountain goat they call Paul, here. But the painting itself – tell you how it happened: I'll tell you how it all came about.

The canvases, OK? At first I sort of propped one up at a funny kind of an angle over by the biggest of the windows, there – and God, it seemed even huger, now. I know I've been banging on a bit about how bloody vast these canvases are, but truly, I'm telling you – you really have no *idea*. I mean, I haven't actually measured them up, or anything, but we've just got to be looking at, what – eight feet, maybe? Seven? Certainly no less than seven, they've got to be – they tower above me. I mean – really *big*. And maybe four-and-a-half, five across. So you see I'm not kidding when I say that these canvases – God, they're mighty. So anyway. Got the thing sort of propped up, like I say – and now what? Well I just stood there and stared at it, quite frankly. Touch of nerves – little bit of panic. I mean – totally new to me, all this, you know. Never even dreamed of doing anything at all artistic in the whole of my life – not even at school. Never played an instrument, never wrote a poem – can't even begin to imagine the impulse. And God – when it comes to even the notion of something like, oh – I don't know . . . *book* writing, say: Christ. I mean I'm not very much of a reader, if I'm honest – take the usual great brick of a thing along with me on holiday (I buy whatever it is that Smiths at Heathrow tell me to buy – Read Of The Week, Book Of A Lifetime, whatever) and sometimes I manage to wade through the half of it. But how on earth – this is what I'm getting at – how on earth can anyone even think of just plonking themselves down and starting to write one of these fiction type things: novel. Chapter one – page one: Christ. And more to the point – *finishing* the bloody thing. Must take years. I think actually that of all the arty-farty types, they just have to be the weirdest, if I'm honest, writers. It's not natural to want to do something like that. Locking yourself away. I met one once, a writer, at some printing trade do, one Christmas. *He* was a novelist, pretty sure he said – little guy, beardy, long hair, the whole bit: and I'm telling you – *weird*. Anyway – sod him. The point is, with this canvas I was getting just the same feeling, the fear about *scale*. How does anyone manage to cover such a thing? And with what, actually? And further, of course – if you add in the factor of my total inability to draw (even my handwriting – God, you should see it! Looks like the work of a man in the grip of a seizure), not to say no conception in hell of what I wanted to depict here anyway . . . ! Well – panic was growing (didn't like the feeling). I think I would've chucked the idea right there and then, if I'm honest – just walked away from the deal: return the canvases with a polite note of thanks, pass the paints over to Alice or somebody and forget the whole caper completely. But it had somehow wormed its way deep inside my head, rightly or wrongly, that here was a kind of . . . not *instruction*, exactly – not even a challenge – but more a request of some sort, maybe. From Lucas. Although, of course, he hadn't said to me a single word on the matter, I somehow felt that something was *due*, you know? And I knew too that if I did nothing, just put it all away, not even so much as a murmur of remonstration would be coming my way . . . but there would hang in the air like atoms of dust in a shaft of sunlight, the shadow of a void. Of unfulfilment. Disappointment all round. I would somehow have reneged upon my (unspoken) word to an ally.

So I got hold of the thing, the canvas, and with a pencil I found in one of the boxes of debris I carted along here, I made some wholly arbitrary line – more of a squiggle than anything – across the whole of the middle section and then suddenly, oh – I don't really quite know how it happened, actually, but I must have maybe lost my balance or my grip or something, because the whole great thing sort of buckled in and swung over and before I could save it, it had crashed down on to the floor. And I just thought well bugger it, then – I'm not heaving that thing up again: it can bloody well stay down there. And that's when I got the idea: *ping*! it went, the idea, like a cartoon light bulb in the space above my head: *ping*! I had the lids off the cans of paint in no time flat: red – love red (Caroline – she hated primaries: said they were childish – said they were vulgar) – and then another, a darker sort of red (wineish), and then a shocking pink and a yolky yellow and this lovely sort of mauvey indigo colour – and yes, quite a few more after that. Mixed up an orange, at some point during the fever – used a slotted spoon in place of a stirrer. And then God – I was off. Strolling all over the thing, I was – dripping the paint from a fistful of brushes – swooshing it this way and that, crossing over myself and then doubling back over the last of the strokes –

flicking it with my fingers, which made a sort of a spray – bouncing the bristles up and down on the thing as if it were a trampoline: winging it, basically, and loving every bloody minute. And I stopped at the point it pleased me. And then I took stock. I was sweating – I was gasping (and not for a fag – hadn't even given them a single thought: and do you know what? I'd even forgotten to put on a patch! There's a lesson there to be learnt, you know). My shoes were ruined, oh yes totally (well, they were only cheap) and the trousers too, they'd come in for it. My hands, well – it's still all there, you know, under my finger-nails: a miniature version of my first work of art. I was excited. I was physically aroused. I had never in all my life felt so thoroughly *involved* in anything – every single part of me, body, mind, spirit and soul (and I was in love with the paint – high as a kite on the smell of the muck). I heaved up the canvas – and it seemed to me a lightweight, now – and some of the more recent slashes of colour began to run, and the effect of that, it pleased me even more. And now – now it's actually up on the wall (Paul and me, we're still just standing around, looking at the thing) I am close once more to nearly bursting with pride and crying out loud. This has never happened to me before. Nothing like it. Never in my life.

'Yeh,' said Paul again. 'Really go for it, I do. Real touch of class, you got there Jamie mate. So look listen: you all OK now then, are you? Set, yeh? Cos if you're sweet, I'll get meself off out of it, you don't mind. Mike was wanting me to come up with some sort of a display board wotsit for his medals. Got a lovely collection.'

'What would we all do without you, Paul? We'd be lost.'

'*Nah*! Anyway – it ain't just me, is it Jamie? Ay? I mean – that's the whole wossname here, ain't it? All pitch in, like. And like I say, I'm after this little bit of help, like, on the old printer. Tomorrow suit you, would it? Take a dekko? Kick it around?'

'Yes sure, Paul – any time you say. You coming up to Teddy's later? Pre-dinner drink?'

'No I tell you – what's happening tonight is, Kimmy and Dorothy, yeh? They're like coming down our gaff, bit of a snifter. Little Mary-Ann.'

'Oh right. Well look – thanks again, OK Paul? You've been great.'

'Nothing, son. Tell you what – why don't you come down and all? Ay? That Dorothy, you know – bit sweet on you, Jamie old mate. Says awful nice things about you.'

Jamie was amazed. '*Really*?' he said.

'Kosher,' smiled Paul. 'Reckon you're well in there, mate, you want it.'

Or, thought Paul – not. Truth was – it were me, weren't it, she'd taken to hanging about. Give me stuff like Oh Paul Oh Paul – you're *so* good with Mary-Ann, she reckons the sun it shines right out your wossname. Well look, son – hear me out: I don't need the grief. Know what I mean? Fingering my hair, she was, other night there. Says it's great how it like kind of curls up or curls under or curls some bleeding way or another, wasn't hardly giving her no mind. See, thing is – I grown a bit chary of them, nowadays, you wanna know. Women, like. I mean, they got nice bits and bobs, I'm not denying, but at the end of the day, I reckon, you're better off sticking with one of your mates. A bloke what you can, like, talk to – know what I mean? Like say take Lucas, right? Now Alice, she's a nice enough bit of skirt, I'm not saying – but a man like that, a man like Lucas, he don't like *need* her, do he? Not like at the end of the day. What I mean is, I can see how she's useful, this way and that (though not so much of the other, wouldn't have said – not to look at her) – but he wants to *talk*, right – he wants, like, real *understanding*, kind of style, well – he's gonna go to a geezer, ain't he? Every time. And I reckon the both of us feels a bit like that. Well – how we come to meet in that dodgy old dive, ain't

213

it? Else why was he there? Plus also, why was I? Know what I'm saying? Yeh well you *kinda* do, yeh – cos I'll be frank with you, come clean OK? I only *kinda* do meself: what it is is, all of this, is a little bit sort of like, confusing. Yeh. So anyways – what I do, right, when Dorothy come on to me like she do, is I tells her (and I dunno why I done it – weren't planned or nothing, I just comes out with it) that she wants to be sniffing around old Jamie, she got any sense. Jamie? she goes. Why Jamie? And I says to her *because*, darling, he's right sweet on you, Jamie is. Ain't you never seen it? In his eyes, like? No, she goes: I ain't. Well, I says, that's cos you ain't been looking, have ya? You have a gander, gel, next time you gets the chance. Telling you – you're well in there, you want it.

'Dorothy . . . ?' Jamie was musing. 'You sure, Paul? Never sort of *noticed* anything . . .'

'Nah well – you ain't been looking, have ya? You have a gander, mate, next time you gets the chance. Telling you – you're well in there, you want it.'

Mm, thought Jamie, when Paul had gone (he had to, he said, love him and leave him). Well I might – I might take a gander, as he puts it, next time I get the chance, and then again I might not. Because I'll let you in on something rather strange, shall I? You know how I was totally poleaxed by the fabulous Frankie? When I first set eyes on her? Well, in one sense I still am, of course, because I am telling you, matey, what we are talking about here is pure *Playboy* centrefold, and no messing about. So if I had my pick, then Frankie would still be the one – true of any man, I should have said. Now Dorothy, I must say – I mean *attractive* woman, oh yes very . . . but I've never really thought about her in that sort of a *way*, if you know what I mean. Maybe it's something to do with Mary-Ann? Could it be? The fact that she's a mother? But here is close, you know, to how I am thinking. You see, Frankie – well, she's *John's*, isn't she? Yes she is. That's not just how it is, but frankly how it should be. It's fitting: they belong. End of story. And you see, the way I've been feeling recently – and you'll think I'm mad, you'll think I'm crazy, I just know that's what you'll think – is that where I belong . . . no, not that: not *where* I belong, no, because it is here, it is here I belong, I know that, I always knew that: knew that from the start. But for all our ups and downs (yes I know, I know – putting it mildly isn't in it) the person I really belong with (see it coming?) – well it's Caroline, isn't it? My wife, after all. And Benny. My son, my only son. Who I last saw, oh – could be a fortnight ago now, lost all track. And that isn't, is it? Can't be, can it? *Right*, is what I mean. So what I've decided to do – I have the confidence, now: before I just couldn't have dreamed of it – what it is I'm going to do is just ask her over here. Invite her – just to see it. With Benny, of course. Because she might, you know – she might just get it. When she sees it. She might sense what it is we all have here. Well – mightn't she? Anything's possible – that's what The Works has taught me. Either way, I think it's worth a try. Because I really do believe, you know, that everything ought to be in the place it *belongs*. So I am. I'm going to try it.

This picture of mine, you know: I'm looking at it again, now (well – haven't in truth taken my eyes off it once) and do you know what? It's breaking my heart. Just the very sight of it . . . it's breaking my heart.

'So what my people are saying to me, OK,' Kimmy was explaining, 'is that on account of it's near Christmas, right? Everyone's into red. Go figure. What do I care? They want red, they got red. How's the mints coming, Mary-Ann my little munchkin?'

'Still got lots to do,' Mary-Ann replied, as she continued to do lots more. What she was actually engaged in, Dorothy – when she breezed in later – could hardly believe (thought she'd gone mad). There was a large square polythene dust sheet spread out all over the floor, and piled very high at its centre were thousands upon thousands of . . . God, what are they, exactly? Teeth? No – not teeth, thank heavens. Sweets then, are they? I think they must be sweets – or mints, are they mints? They are, aren't they, Mary-Ann my angel? They're those, what are they? Polo things. Polo mints. And Mary-Ann was busy cracking them into bits with a heavy claw-hammer. Not normal, is it? Not the sort of thing you expect to see. But when it becomes clear that of course *Kimmy* is involved, well . . . you get used to just all sorts of things, in time, if you live with a conceptual artist.

'So what's, um – the theme, um, Kimmy?' tried Dorothy.

'I guess if I'm truthful, there ain't one. But hey – we can work on it. Maybe it's like they're all these little lifebelts, yeh? Keeping us afloat? Except for now they, like – can't, OK? On account of they're all broke up. So then I fill up these red kinda see-through cubes here, OK? And we got a containment of shattered hopes and dreams, you wanna see it that way. Or maybe all you got is smashed-up candy. Either way, baby, my dealer, he says he can move an edition of twelve, no problem: ten grand a pop. So like the man says, Mary-Ann – get cracking, huh? That's maybe like a kinda joke. Mary-Ann, she was telling me she could use a few bucks for, like, the holidays? So I figured why pay some other guy to break 'em up? Keep it in the family, yeh? Where you been, Doe?'

'Mm? Oh – Judy's. Talking things over. She helps me a lot. I do feel better about . . . you know.'

'She means,' said Kimmy to Mary-Ann, 'your pops, honey-bunch. She's talking Daddy again, sweetheart.'

'I know,' Mary-Ann said, solemnly – bringing down the hammer hard on a newly unrolled column of Polos (the smithereens set to scurrying away from her).

'She says, Judy, that I've come as far as I'm going to without a new man – someone else, you know. In my life. I just couldn't, I don't think. No one would understand.'

'Sure they would – if they were family,' said Kimmy. 'How we doing on the peppermint front, Mary-Ann? I should maybe send out for like another batch? What I hear, Doe, that Jamie guy is kinda sweet on you. Maybe it's he got the hots for you and you alone.'

'Did Paul tell you that? Mm – he mentioned it to me as well. I think Paul is really awfully nice. I ought to hate the – the, you know – the way he talks, and everything, but I don't. I've really got to love that accent of his. It's so, well – musical, really.'

'We don't seem to be talking Jamie here, Doe. You got to focus.'

'Jamie's nice. He's a nice man, Jamie,' said Dorothy, quite carelessly.

'I like him,' Mary-Ann put in.

'Yes,' Dorothy was quick to assure her. 'I like him too. It's just that I've never really, you know – I've never . . . I don't really think of him in that sort of *way*, if you know what I mean.'

'She means,' clarified Kimmy, 'she don't wanna screw him.'

'Mm,' mused Mary-Ann. 'I assumed.'

'Oh God's *sake* . . .' moaned Dorothy.

'Well *what*? That is what you mean, isn't it? And don't go bothering your head about Little Miss Innocence, here. Kid lives with me, she grows up fast.'

'I suppose . . . I suppose, yes, that *is* what I mean. But then I don't really feel that way about anyone, really. Not really.'

'Not even . . . ?'

'No, rather oddly. Not even . . . him.'

'And Paul?'

'Oh *Jesus*, Kimmy – you really are awful.'

'You ain't answered me, honey.'

'Hush. Leave it. Let me smash some mints.'

'That's *my* job,' pouted Mary-Ann.

'Here, Doe,' offered Kimmy. 'Start in on filling me up a cube.'

'OK. What – just any old how, is it? Just dump them in?'

'You got it. Just dump the babies in.'

'What made you, um – think of mints, actually, Kimmy?'

'Who knows? What can I tell you about the creative mind? Last time it was feathers. Why feathers? On account of no smart-ass yet did feathers. So I figured great – we'll do feathers, where's the down side? And now it's mints. Ain't art just *wonderful*?'

'What're you going to do next?' wondered Mary-Ann, idly. 'We've only got six boxes left now, Kimmy. Will that be enough, do you think?'

'Next up, dear heart, is titties. The guy at the wholesalers, yeh? He says all I gotta do is call and he brings over as much I want. Mints he got plenty.'

'*What* did you say, Kimmy?' checked Dorothy.

'Huh? I said – guy from the wholesalers, yeh? He –'

'No no. Before that. When you were talking about –'

'Oh yeh – right. Titties. Yes sir. They're gonna be big.'

'What – *breasts*, you mean?'

'Sure do. Guys, they like them. Big time. They're a, like – natural?'

'How,' enquired Mary-Ann, 'are you going to get them into the perspex boxes? And whose, actually?'

'Wise guy . . .' smiled Kimmy. 'No, this time around, we put away the boxes. I'm thinking breast *paintings*. Been on my mind.'

'Uh-huh,' went Dorothy. 'And who will, um – paint them, actually?'

'We'll maybe get Alice!' hooted Kimmy. 'No no – it ain't gonna be like that. I'm not, like, thinking paintings *of* breasts, no – what these are gonna be is paintings *with* breasts, see? The breast is, like – the *instrument*? Neat, huh?'

'Mm. I see . . . so, um – what, exactly? Persons unknown dip their . . . ?'

'Pretty much,' shrugged Kimmy. 'Paint up their titties, and I slam the gals face-first on to a canvas. Splat bang and you got it, mam. What you think? Publicity'll go through the roof.'

'Anyone in mind?' returned Dorothy. 'A model?'

'You offering? Nah. I mean, like – no offence, Doe, huh? But for this one I need real giants, you know? Russ Meyers. Watermelons. Knock-your-eye-out knockers is what I got to have, here. But hey – it's no big. Students, they do anything. Twenty quid, they *drink* the goddam paint, I tell them to. So that's what I'm gonna do, come New Year. New Year we're like, Tits R Us. But meanwhile, honeys, it's mint time! Listen up: it's like I always say – ain't art just *wonderful*?'

I must say, I really must say, John was busy thinking (and not for the first time), that it truly is quite remarkable, you know, just what Mike and Oona have between them achieved here with this extraordinary recreation of theirs. I confess to being rather mixed up now, you know – bit confused – as to what little I actually do genuinely recall as a child of the War, and how much seems recognizable to me now solely as a result of Mike's overwhelmingly informed and fascinating banter, and the growing familiarity of all these things I see around me. One small example is that Ovaltine enamel sign, look – the one hung just adjacent to what really is a most convincing facsimile of the sort of bedroom I would try very hard to escape from. I mean to say, I felt absolutely sure that I well remembered that one from our own little local branch of the United Dairies, but Mike assures me that that particular piece of advertising predates me by a good ten years, and maybe even more. Well – nice to know that something around here, apart from the bricks and lintels, is actually older than I am. But then of course I got to thinking that yes, you know – I could very easily and quite accurately recall that very little sign because in those days, you see, bits and pieces, they tended to hang around, you know. Not like now – when something is weeks, days old it is redundant, obsolete, totally surplus to requirements. Those days, God – some manufacturer gives a corner shop a, um . . . I don't know – clock, say; tin sign, that sort of thing. Well goodness, the shopkeeper – he'd die with it still in his possession; pass it down to the next generation, in all probability. Could well account for the fact that so much of this memorabilia still seems to be around, ready to be squirrelled away by enthusiasts such as Mike and Oona, here. Odd, you know, that . . . when you come to think about it . . . I mean, the War, well – the one time dear old London was being battered to bits by Jerry on a virtually nightly basis, and yet more of this stuff seems to have conspicuously survived than from all the other eras put together. It can't *actually* be true, I don't suppose (it barely, does it, stand up to reason?), but that most surely is how it appears to me.

John continued to sip at his whisky. 'Have you any *idea*,' Mike had excitedly put to him, even as he poured it, 'what a bottle of this stuff would have set you back on the black market of 1942?' And no, John hadn't – and yes, Mike told him. Can't quite recall it now, the figure he mentioned. I rather think it was on the lines of forty or fifty pounds, could he have said, in today's terms. Which

I suppose, yes, is rather a lot. I really have no idea, to be perfectly frank with you, about quite what these days is seen to constitute 'value'. I just pay out whatever it is that is asked of me – which seems not just polite, but also it does render one rather freer, I think, to concentrate upon the pleasure that a purchase, this expenditure, has given me – or more usually, Frankie (but yes of course: it pleases me too) – rather than dwelling upon how deep or gaping a hole it has made.

Look at Frankie, now. She seems, thought John, to be in one of her periodically fairly *interested* moods – wafting around Mike and Oona's space, fingering that and gazing at this, Mike sometimes waiting for her to enquire of him some detail or other, but much more often quick off the mark to supplying it anyway. On other occasions in the past, though, as John well knew, Frankie could, in Mike and Oona's place, become the nearest she could ever get to being, well – *sullen* sounds terribly mopey and spiteful and awful and she's not that at all, no not ever. But there are times when she just more or less sits there, you know, twiddling with a glass, and John knows that afterwards she'll ask him again just why it is they have to spend so much time in this weird *museum*? But at the moment, as I say, she seems quite happy.

'I sort of go for this outfit,' she was saying now – tapping the glass of a sturdy box frame with one long tapered, buffed and perfectly varnished fingernail. 'Think I'd look nice in this outfit, Johnny? What do you think, Oona?'

'Oh well now that's very interesting you should ask about that, Frankie,' started up Mike immediately. '*Because* –'

'No,' cut in Oona. 'Not you at all, I shouldn't have really said, Frankie. It'd cover all your legs.'

'Yes but no listen!' went on Mike, with considerable urgency. 'That "outfit", as you put it –'

'Well,' pouted Frankie, 'I do *sometimes* wear trousers, don't I Johnny? Tight though, admittedly. But yeh – I do like skirts and heels and things a whole lot more. Why's there all this crumbled-up brown muck down at the bottom of the frame then, Mike? Who is the old boy anyway? He your dad, or something?'

And even Mike was temporarily silenced (John was chuckling, quietly).

'That . . . !' came back Mike, the moment he could. 'That "old boy" is *Churchill*, Frankie. Winston *Churchill*. You must surely know what he . . . ?'

'Oh *right*,' Frankie understood. 'Churchill, right. Well don't *glare* at me, Mike! I have *heard* of him, you know. I know he was in the War, and everything. He's dead now though, isn't he?'

'In . . . the . . . *War* . . . ?' was all Mike could stutter.

Oona was laughing. 'Oh leave it, Mike. Some people do actually prefer living in the here and now, you know. *I'll* tell you what outfit would suit you, Frankie. *I* think that you would look absolutely divine and thoroughly sexy – even *more* sexy, if that's humanly possible –'

'Oh God *honestly*, Oona!' cackled Frankie, quite delightedly. 'Don't go *on*, heaven's sake.' And then, when Oona didn't: 'How? What would I? Look whatever it was you said? Divine.'

'Oh – as an *Andrews* Sister. Don't you think so, Mike?'

Mike was nodding with energy.

'Oh *God* yes: perfect. Absolutely perfect. US military. But, um – this outfit of Churchill's – yes Frankie? I'm glad you're interested because –'

'I'm not *that* interested . . .' qualified Frankie. 'Is there any more wine or anything, Oona?'

'Oh God *sorry*, Frankie,' apologized Oona. 'I'll just get another of – what shall we have? Teddy's chardonnay? Won't be cold, though, because –'

'I know,' jumped in Frankie. 'No fridge, right? God – I couldn't live like you two, you know. Couldn't do it.'

'Well actually . . . there is a possibility . . .' Mike now ventured with caution; and then animation took over: 'Haven't yet said to you, Oona, but you know that person I got the big Bush wireless from that time? Brick Lane? Well he was telling me just recently that he might soon be getting his hands on a genuine Kelvinator in cream and white. That's a *refrigerator*, Frankie. I told him to bear me in mind. It's gas, of course.'

Frankie laughed. And then she looked about her.

'What . . . ? I mean – that was a *joke*, wasn't it? Wasn't it? I mean there can't really be gas *fridges*, can there? Johnny? Can there? Gas has got *flames*, and things.'

'They exist,' smiled Oona, as she came up with another bottle. 'Oh yes – they do exist.'

'No but listen,' stepped in Mike. 'We've rather sort of strayed away from the *point* a bit, here. *Churchill* – yes? That's a picture of him in his specially tailored all-in-one velvet jump suit. So he could get dressed quickly, you see, after one of his catnaps down in the bunker. Designed it himself – had it made up by . . . well, John – you, I am sure – you and Lucas will be very well acquainted with the firm in question: still going strong. Turnbull & Asser. Jermyn Street. They made him quite a few.'

'I do – I know them well,' agreed John. 'Although I must say I am much more of a Hilditch & Key man myself. True of Lucas too, I think I am right in saying. Except that he – it must have been Alice who told me this – he has them bespoke, of course, from the Paris branch. I content myself with off-the-peg. Frankie, my sweet – one more glass, yes? And then I think we really must be off.'

'Oh yes and the *muck*, Frankie,' tacked on Mike. 'The brown stuff at the bottom of the frame? Yes – it has rather fallen to bits, that one, over the years. But what it *purports* to be . . . and I don't in all frankness believe this for a minute – but it was, well – pretty cheap, so I thought well why not? But it's meant to be the end of one of the great man's cigars – as smoked and discarded in the War Room, no less. Hard to prove, of course, that type of thing . . .'

And then Mike's eyes were ablaze, and scanning the room for reciprocal fire. 'But just think – if it actually *were* . . . ! Hm? I mean . . .' he added on, softly (really quite overcome). 'Just *imagine* . . . !'

Oona was glugging far-from-cellar-cool chardonnay into her and Frankie's glass.

'You started in on anything festive yet, Frankie? Jingling bells? Don't go *on*, Mike . . .'

'Ooh *yes*,' responded Frankie immediately. 'Oodles and oodles. I'll have something different to wear for every single night! Oh . . . and I've bought stuff for other people too, of course . . . But it's funny, you know, Oona – I find . . . I'm finding lately – are you like this? Oh well yes I expect you are because all the shops you two would like to go to must all have been flattened in the Blitz, I suppose. But what I mean is, well – you all know how much I just *adore* to go shopping? OK – yes yes: I know I'm awful, I know . . . but just lately, well – and Johnny, he'll tell you this – I don't really any more like to go out so much. I mean – one or two shops I really know well, you know – that's OK, because they sort of make you feel all comfortable, and things. But – well it's maybe because these days you can never park exactly where you want to be, can you? And Johnny – he hates leaving the car just anywhere.'

'Never keen on the idea . . .' put in John.

'No. And I don't know – streets, people, all that. I just feel so much better when I'm – well, *here*, basically. Right here.'

'Yes . . .' said Mike. 'I think we all know what you mean.'

'Mm,' agreed Frankie. 'Do lots of mail order now. It's better.'

'Any idea,' wondered John, 'what we're all getting for Lucas this year?'

'It's difficult . . .' mused Oona. 'Gets harder every time. But I expect Judy, old Judy – she'll have it all well in hand. She's usually got lots of ideas. Judy has. Except, of course, if we're all expected to chip in –'

'Well we *are*,' said Mike, quite firmly. 'Of course we are. We always are. That's how it *works*.'

'Well yes I *know* that,' countered Oona, quite testily. 'I do think I *know* that, Mike. That's just what I'm saying – because we've all got to, you know – be a part of it, well: not much time, is there? That's all I mean.'

And John was nodding too. It was certainly something of a problem, this: not a chore, not a bind – in no way anything approaching any sort of a nuisance, no no. But it was important, and it needed careful consideration. You see I suppose what has made our big Christmas get-together even more key than it otherwise would be (and it would be – it would be very key, oh yes, you may depend on that – because Christmas, well, it really must be seen to be the culmination, mustn't it, of all we do here: all we mean). But you see it was decided between us, quite early on (not sure exactly how it all came about, but Alice was very instrumental, unsurprisingly – I do recall that. And Judy, she picked up the idea with her customary good humour and gusto and ran with it: been running with it, really, ever since). No, as I say – quite early on it became part of the canon (the lore, if you like) for all of us here at The Works for Christmas – you know, the actual day – to also be classed as Lucas's birthday, and celebrated accordingly. His official birthday. Yes I know – rather like the Queen. Except *not* like the Queen, as it happens, because I think I am right in saying that no one here has even the faintest idea of the actual date of his real birthday (maybe Alice does; conceivably Alice does, though I somehow doubt it). Frankie, she said to me once – when it was the first she had heard of the matter – that it wasn't that no one *knew*, it wasn't that he was keeping it in the dark, Lucas, no no: all it was was that he simply didn't actually *have* one, a birthday. Uh-huh, I was going – as I do. No birthday, mm – interesting. How exactly did you come to arrive at that rather singular conclusion then, Frankie my love? Oh – it's not a *conclusion*, she said: I haven't *thought* about it, or anything. It's just that it seems so impossible, doesn't it? You must admit it, Johnny. Lucas being born. Being, you know – *young*, and everything. With Lucas, none of that seems to *apply*. And for the millionth time, I suppose, I laughed so softly – laughing with her, and so much enjoying the indulgence. And yet somehow, in some very odd and wholly intangible way, one does of course see her meaning.

So you do understand, it's rather more than just a common or garden Christmas present that we have under discussion, here. And further, true to the spirit of the place – as Oona was just there reminding us – the gift must bear the handprint of us all. In my case, all very easy, of course; Judy will have decided whatever is the part we can actually go out and buy for him, and I shall simply supply the money. Everyone else, though, has to put a bit more thought into it. But it's always a triumph; whatever we come up with, it's just always a triumph because what we are really doing, I suppose, is exulting in the *occasion*. The offering itself is, well – I suppose you might call it symbolic.

'I know,' continued Oona, 'that Judy and Paul have already got going on the decorating side of things. I do know that.'

'He's wonderful, Paul is,' Mike approved readily. 'I mean at first I thought he was just, you know – keen on collecting and arranging, and so on. But it's his practical side that quite frankly bowls me over. I mean look, John – do you see up there? The medals, yes? Had them knocking about in a box for, oh – just ages, and Paul, he rigged up that display thing in just next to no time. Couldn't have done that in years.'

'Come along, Frankie – we're off,' said John. 'Yes – he is good, Paul. I saw some sort of great swag efforts he's working on – for the supper room, I'm assuming. Very jolly. Lots of berries, and all the rest of it. Huge great swags.'

'Hmmm . . .' went Oona. 'Yes well I'll be dragging out our usual old decorations fairly soon, I expect. What there is of them.'

'One or two,' put in Mike, 'are really quite rare.'

'Yes,' agreed Oona, 'oh yes – rare, maybe, they are. But not – they're not, are they Mike, what you could actually call *festive*, are they? They don't really *give* much, do they? They don't exactly light up the *room* . . . ?'

'No well,' said Mike, defensively. 'They didn't have too much time and money, did they? During the War. To chuck around on all that sort of thing. Make do and mend – any bit of silver paper or scrap of red rag or cardboard was pressed into service. That's the way it was.'

'Yes except that *now*,' pursued Oona, 'they've all gone the colour of fag ash. Do you know, John – we had one of the very first synthetic trees, once. We did. Before it fell to pieces. And even before that happened it looked just like a bog brush. Only smaller.'

'Never mind!' laughed John. 'Judy and Paul will do us all very proud, I've no doubts on that score. Ready, Frankie? You fit? Yes? See you good people. À bientôt.'

And outside, Frankie said Gosh you know, Johnny, after all this time I still get so confused in all these little passages and things they've got there. And then she said *Hee* – I've just had a thought, Johnny: listen. What do you suppose Mike and Oona can make of the *Hitlers*? Do you think? Because Hitler – you know, the real one – he was in the War too, but on the other side. I think they're creepy, the Hitlers. Not as creepy as the sick old tramp, oh yuck, but pretty jolly creepy all the same.

And inside, Oona said, Mike, I think it's time for us both to take shelter. Mike's eyes were bright; he licked at the dryness of his lower lip and looked about him. He seemed to be drying the palms of his hands on the front of his trousers.

'Really?' he said, quite hoarsely. '*Really*? What – now? Now, you mean?'

Oona smiled, and took him by the hand.

'Why not now? Now is good.'

She hung the Lyons Tea sign on the handle of the bedroom door and Mike, when she tugged him, he followed her in there. And then he took up his position to the right-hand side of the mighty oak wardrobe, and as he dragged, Oona on the other side, she set to pushing. And even though they had deliberately never actually put anything into the wardrobe for just this very reason, it was nevertheless still, as Oona now was grunting out again, an out-and-out bugger to shift. Then she crawled on all fours into the newly revealed low and tunnel-shaped hole there, Mike stooping to scoop aside the blackout curtains, inching in himself and letting them drop back down as he grovelled close beside her. Now they were snug, Mike and Oona – snug and tight within the corrugated arch of a first issue Anderson Shelter – maybe, in truth, the thing in the world that Mike all his life had most passionately longed for. And when he finally secured it (he stroked and inhaled the cold metal ridges) he had smuggled it up in the lift in sections, because for some reason or other he was resolved in his urgent need for just no one, no one but Oona, to ever know of this wonder, because this wonder – it was for them. (Sharing was one thing – but this, this just had to be private.)

'Comfy?' checked Oona – pulling up the thin grey emergency blankets tight to both their chins. 'Shall I start it now?'

Mike was breathing hard.

'Start it,' he said.

The click of a knob nearly echoed in the gloom, quickly followed by a sort of a faintly menacing rattling hiss, this soon settling down into a rapid and regular rhythmic clatter. The flickering and speckled black and white fast and jerky images were suddenly splattered over the hunched back wall, so close to their faces as they swooped across and around the curving sides – very nearly meeting in the space above their heads. A short and kohl-eyed woman with a tight and glossy shingle and extraordinarily beefy thighs (well they *are*, Oona had insisted the last time, when you compare them with her calves, or those tiny little tits) was looming large over the two of them now, her astonishingly long and pointed, slick-wet tongue darting in and out of her black and shiny beestung lips with both the speed and precision of a rotary piston. The frenzied blur of both her hands was jiggling up and down her naked breasts as if she was trying her hardest to be rid of them for good – and then her eyes opened wide into great white pools of total and dumbstruck surprise as a sleepy man with a droopy moustache was ramming hard into her from some-where behind. And while he did it (while he went about his business) Oona was snaking a long-fingered hand down deep beneath the blanket, and now it wormed its way just slightly into the fly of Mike's charcoal houndstooth flannels, and then in a deft and very practised manner it would ferret around for each little button in turn. Mike was slumped over and half across her shoulder, now, feeling his way gradually into and under each layer of Oona's primrose twin-set, steadily closing in – pressing ahead with single-minded determination to the goal of the mighty and multiple hooks and eyes securely welded to the Playtex flesh-toned one-piece brassière and girdle (and he went calmly with care and by touch alone, as might Raffles, or someone versed in bomb disposal). He gasped at once as Oona's hand became more lively – and now he felt the weight of breast number one falling forward and into his moistly eager palm. The man with the mous-tache now threatened to engulf them as the plucky woman's shingle was over his groin and bobbing with purpose like an untamed riveter, or possibly a famished crow (and all the hair there, it didn't seem to worry her at all). And then Mike said Ah! *Ah!* said Mike – and Oona, yes Oona, she went Ooh. *Ooh*, went

229

Oona, as she started to tremble and Mike's whole body went tight and rigid and he screwed down his eyes (so that the vision was lost to him of the man with the moustache, his mouth wide open and silently screaming out his could be pain or pleasure) and through her heavy rapid breathing Oona whispered to him *Andrews* Sisters, *Andrews* Sisters – oh God Mike, do it – *think* of it now, *think* of her now – *Andrews* Sisters *Andrews* Sisters *Andrews* Sisters – aaaaah . . . ! is how she ended, softly, just as Mike said Christ and squirmed beneath her and then pressed up hard to the insistent scurrying of Oona's fingers. He came as she shuddered – though not quite in time with the woman with the shingle and the man with the moustache who had things done and dusted and were now quite openly, and with worrying speed, wiping all their parts. The woman, then – still quite naked – fell into a blinkingly rapid series of very pretty curtseys as beside her, her man was often and with energy bowing up and down like a demented ambassador, hell-bent on protocol. The clatter of the projector accelerated hard, and the racket of it now could have possibly concerned someone wholly unfamiliar with the machinery's quirks and peccadilloes – but Mike and Oona, they were both old hands at not just this game. Then, quite suddenly, the noise and light now cut off dead, and Mike and Oona were once more close in the silence and the dark. She kissed his nose. And then she whispered excitedly:

'Did you? Did you *do* it, Mike? Did you? Do it? Think of her? Did you?'

A low and rasping, drawn-out exhalation came from deep inside him.

'I did . . .' she barely heard. 'I did. I did. I did it.'

Jamie from time to time glanced up and over to Teddy at the table, there, tapping away on that great old typewriter, seemingly oblivious to whatever it might be that Jamie and Judy were nattering about. At first, Jamie hadn't in all honesty been so keen on Teddy even sitting there at all – but then he thought No, that's just plain silly. Isn't it? And wrong. I mean – I do, yes I do talk to Judy about, well – pretty intimate sorts of things, really, but so what if Teddy is a part of it, actually? We're *all* a part of it, aren't we? Every single one of us. Yes. The whole point. Mm – think that's right. And anyway, like I say – just look at him, won't you: tip-tapping away there at whatever it is he's doing. Couldn't care two hoots about anything we're saying; I doubt he's even hearing a single word.

'Well *I* think,' said Judy, lowering her teacup, 'that that's a perfectly *wonderful* idea, Jamie. Don't you, Teddy? Think it's wonderful?'

'Wonderful,' agreed Teddy, straight away and peremptorily.

Automatic reaction? Just another kneejerk return in the midst of the endless rally of a couple's private ping-pong? Or was he somehow typing and listening as well? Could be done, I suppose. I don't at all mind either way; feel rather more conscious now that this chat of mine with Judy might be detracting from Teddy's concentration. Although looking at him, that too seemed perfectly intact.

'I mean,' continued Judy, 'particularly for the little *boy's* sake, yes Jamie? Benny. Little Benny. *Sweet* . . . And do please bring her,

231

if she – you know, wants to. If your wife would like to meet me, at all . . . ?'

'Well of *course* she'd want to meet you,' Jamie rushed to assure her. 'That's if she comes. As I said – when I called, she was out. Wasn't there. Well – wasn't picking up, anyway. When she heard my voice. I left a message, which was maybe, I don't know – it was probably a stupid thing to do, that, I think, because it'll all be full of, you know – ers and ums and stuttering and so on – because I'm still not used to it, rather crazily – all this talking to machines. Christ – I *should* be bloody used to it. Can't even remember the last time I called anyone at all and actually got to talk to a *human*.'

'I'm sure she'll respond, Jamie. Of course she will.'

'Yeh well. Give it a day or two, and then I'll ring again.'

'Is it nice?' asked Judy. 'Being a Daddy? I always wonder quite how it must be. Parenting.'

'Well it's . . . I can't honestly quite *remember* what it's like, if I'm frank with you, Judy. It's been a while. And I didn't really do very much of it, parenting – is that a word, then? Is it? Oh. When I was around. But actually, you know Judy – now you happen to, you know – now you bring it up, sort of thing, I'm really quite surprised that you and Teddy, you know – that you and Teddy aren't, um – didn't ever –'

'Ah no,' smiled Judy, looking quite determinedly happy as she did it. 'We couldn't, alas. Or *I* couldn't, I should say. Could I, Teddy?'

'No,' said Teddy. 'Couldn't. Has "submission" got two B's? Hasn't, has it?'

'One B, isn't it? Jamie? One B?'

'One, yeh. Pretty sure. Two S's.'

'Mm,' thought Teddy. 'Yes – the S's I've got. Right then – one B it is.'

'But *Teddy's* all right,' continued Judy. 'It was me who couldn't. But you're all right, aren't you Teddy?'

'I'm all right,' said Teddy.

'And gosh, you know,' laughed Judy, 'it really couldn't have come at a much worse time. You know – finding out. Being told. Teddy was already most awfully depressed because, well – he was finding it just the teeniest bit difficult to land a, you know – really meaty part, and my practice was –'

'Couldn't,' put in Teddy, 'get *any* part. No part at all, meaty or otherwise. This ribbon, you know . . . it's printing awfully faintly. I wonder if Mike's got another one . . . ? Replacement. This isn't the only old machine he's got down there, pretty sure. So he might have . . .'

'Anyway,' Judy carried on. 'My practice too was going through one of its rather – well, it was all a bit *fallow*, if you follow . . .'

'No one came at all,' said Teddy. 'No one.'

'Oh Teddy – must you always be so – ?'

'Well it's true. That's what you were saying, wasn't it? That we couldn't have learned all this about children and pregnancy and so on at a lower point in our lives because *I* wasn't earning and *you* weren't earning and what little there was I was pouring down my throat.'

'Yes . . .' agreed Judy. 'There was that problem too. Teddy's an alcoholic, Jamie. I don't know if you knew.'

Jamie looked at Judy. And then he looked at Teddy.

'Really? No no – I didn't know. Had no idea. So what, then, um – Teddy? You, er – got over it, did you?'

'Ha!' went Teddy. 'No no – it's quite true, you know, what they say – you never get over it. Never. Once an alcoholic . . .'

'Yeh but,' protested Jamie, 'your *wine*, Teddy . . . all your wine . . .'

'Ah yes,' agreed Judy, 'but he doesn't *drink* it, do you Teddy? Have you never noticed, Jamie? He never ever drinks it, Teddy.

Makes it, yes – offers it around. But nary a drop, as they say. It's beautiful, really. I'm very proud of him. Did you hear me, Teddy? I say I'm very proud of you.'

'Good,' said Teddy. 'Pleased. Where's the . . . where's the bloody question mark gone . . . ?'

'Oh God it was just *awful* in those days, though,' Judy deplored. 'He was really pretty chronic.'

'Ah *there* it is, the bugger . . . Oh I *was*,' agreed Teddy then, with gusto. 'Absolute and total lush. And very boring too, I shouldn't wonder. God – I remember all those dreadful nights in all those clubs and bars, surrounded by a slumped assortment of smashed and stupid people. People who could barely talk but were always laughing. Or crying. Or suddenly being seized by a panic and screaming out at anyone around something like My *Bag*! Oh God – my *bag*! Where's my *bag*?! And then someone just slightly less wasted would slur at him *There* – it's *there*, your bag. What's *wrong* with you? It's right there, look, at your feet, where it's always been, you silly old sod. And then the half-blinded idiot would fall back into his coma, once more pacified. I *know* all this, dear Jamie, because the declaiming looney was more often than not none other than myself. My greatest role. I was a complete and utter natural – wasn't I? Judy?'

'Mm,' nodded Judy. 'I'm rather afraid you were. But then it all changed. Everything changed.'

'How, exactly?' Jamie wanted to know.

'Well how on earth do you *think*?' Judy was hooting. 'Lucas. *Lucas*, of course. What else? Teddy met Lucas in a drinking club, didn't you, Teddy dear?'

'Did indeed. Blue Angel. White Angel. Some bloody Angel. And he saw, you know – saw my problem immediately, and offered to help. Never ever met the man, and here he was offering to help me. And God did we need it. I'd been promised this part in some TV miniseries –'

234

'Ha!' interjected Judy. 'That word! It always makes me laugh, that word now, because for just ages I was always pronouncing it completely *wrong*. Wasn't I, Teddy? Whenever I saw it in print, you know – because they never ever hyphenate it or anything, do they? Miniseries? So I always said it like "miseries" only with the acronym for Northern Ireland chucked into the mix. As if it wasn't depressing enough already . . .'

'Have you quite finished?' asked Teddy, with mock admonition. 'You have? Oh joy. So – as I was saying, yes Jamie? Lucas came up to me in this Angel place, wherever it was . . . oh yes, the *series*, the TV series, that's what I was – yes. So I thought I had this part, you see – been promised – and then suddenly my agent calls me and tells me sorry, but it turns out you haven't. Got it. The part. I shouldn't have been in the least bit surprised, really – but I probably didn't even see it at the time. That I was always so permanently pissed that I couldn't even have carried off a bloody toothpaste voiceover, let alone a proper acting role – with a script to learn, and so on. Yes. And very soon after, I didn't have an agent either. And the landlord – he was making noises, wasn't he Judy?'

'Horrible man . . .' whispered Judy. 'Duper, his name was. Horrible man.'

'Mm – nasty bit of work, Duper was,' Teddy agreed. 'But then again – hardly *blame* him, can you? Hadn't had any rent out of us for weeks. Anyway – Lucas, he said to me . . . well, you know what he said to me, Jamie, because he said it to you too, didn't he? Come and join me in The Works. That's what he said. And do you know? I kissed him. Right then and there, I actually kissed him. Don't know what it was got into me. Well I *do* know, of course – about eighteen large gins, on a typical night. God Almighty. Anyway. We were saved. Just like that.'

'Greatest day of our lives,' said Judy, with reverence.

'Mine too,' Jamie fervently agreed. 'I was in a bar too. I think

235

that's the sort of place he must always be looking, Lucas. For lost souls. It's not a bad place to start, really, when you think about it, is it? It was at the Grosvenor Hotel, I'll never forget it – not the Park Lane one, the posh one, no. The one in Victoria, just next to the station. Know it? Anyway. I was filling in time – waiting for my train to, ooh – Liverpool, I think it might have been. Was delayed. Do they go there from there? Victoria? To Liverpool? Don't know. Anyway – doesn't matter. Somewhere up north, it was. Doesn't matter. Some boring trade do, or other. And he put it to me, Lucas – I think, maybe, I actually thought he must be a little bit cracked, or something, at the time – but he laid it all before me: just how my life could be, well – damn near perfect, really. The way he put it.'

'How did you react?' asked Judy. 'What did you say to him?'

'Hm? Well – not much of anything, really. To speak of. Took his card. Thanked him politely. As I say – I think I thought he must be just some well-meaning sort of nutter, or something.'

'Well-meaning, most certainly . . .' Judy was musing.

'But no nutter,' supplied Teddy. 'Definitely not.'

'Well yes I know that *now*, don't I?' Jamie defended himself. 'But then – well then, he seemed just . . . well, you know: it's just not the sort of thing that *happens* to you, is it?'

'We're the lucky ones,' said Judy, gleefully.

'We are,' said Jamie. 'We are indeed. So anyway – even on the train, when I was still on the train to – I think it *was*, you know, Liverpool, now I sort of think of it. While I was just sitting there, swigging a Carlsberg, smoking myself to death, I began to see my whole life, well – differently. How it was, and what, you know – all it could be. It sounds . . . oh God look – I can tell you and Judy, of course I can, because you understand, you two, I know you do – but anyone else would think I'm . . . well anyway, what I really did honestly feel was that I had, you know – witnessed some sort of a *vision*, or something. A revelation. It really was as strong as that. And I sort of – I sort of watched all the countryside whizzing away past the window, and it was sort of like my – *past*, really. I think I thought. The man I *used* to be. You know? Because now I was different. Felt it. Completely different person. Mm ... I changed. I changed at Crewe. Not trains. No. Identities.' Jamie drifted into thought. 'I wish ... I wish *I* had. Kissed him ...'

Judy gazed at him.

'I think,' she said, 'I think, Jamie, you told that quite beautifully. I really do. And I think you're right, you know, about Lucas and bars and clubs and things. Paul was the same – some club or other. And Alice – even Alice. She was waiting at tables, she told me one time, somewhere terribly smart – terribly upmarket sort of place. And Lucas, he said to her – don't you, you know, want something better for yourself, sort of thing. And Alice, she said to him – apparently she said to him: "Aha! Don't you be fooled by appearances! True, today I am waiting tables in this private members' club – but tomorrow! Tomorrow – who *knows* where I'll be waiting tables!" Ha ha. Quite funny. Which is odd, really, isn't it? Coming from Alice ...'

'Right!' barked Teddy, zipping out a sheet of paper from the typewriter's roller. 'That's it. Finished. The End. Full stop.'

'Oh Teddy I *am* pleased! Can I read it?'

'Just as soon as I get it all copied. Paul was telling me he knows someone who does all this sort of thing. Then I've got to get some more wine down to Tubby ... Isn't he a marvel, old Tubby? It's hotpot, tonight. Adore his hotpot. Best I've ever had.'

'What've you been working on, Teddy?' asked Jamie. 'Yeh – I love the hotpot.'

'Oh!' exclaimed Judy. 'Don't you *know*? Oh well no I suppose you wouldn't, really, would you? Teddy never ever talks to anyone about how terribly terribly brilliant he is, do you Teddy, my sweet?'

'It's only a play,' deflected Teddy. 'Just a little play ...'

'What you wrote!' laughed Judy, delightedly. 'It's for *Christmas*, Jamie. He got so fed up, you know – abridging and chopping about other people's plays that he decided to sit down and write one of his own. Just like that. Can't wait to read it – and I hope, Teddy, you've written me a jolly good part.'

'Good parts all round. Well face it – only way I'm going to get one, isn't it?' Teddy responded, ruefully. 'Great part for you here, Jamie.'

'Me!' hooted Jamie. 'Oh God no – not *me*, Teddy, oh no. No way. I'm no *actor*, God's sake! Oh God no – not me.'

'You weren't a painter either . . .' said Judy shrewdly, nodding at him slowly, and narrowing her eyes.

Jamie looked down. And when he looked up, he was radiant.

'That's . . . *true*, isn't it Judy? OK then, Teddy – *fine*. Look out Olivier, or whoever it is nowadays: here I come!'

Judy clapped her hands.

'That's the spirit! Good old Jamie!'

'OK then, you two – I'll get this thing copied up and then I'll . . . actually, I might as well sort out the burgundy and the rest of it right now, hadn't I? Save a journey. Oh and *yes*, Jamie – I forgot to say. Knowing my problem, and everything, guess who suggested when we first, you know – got here, and everything, that I take care of all the booze side of things?'

'Lucas?'

'In a word. Lucas. Correct. It would teach me . . . what did he say, Judy? That it would teach me . . . ?'

'Responsibility,' said Judy. 'In all such matters. Were his words. And with just a *leeedle* bit of help from me . . . ?'

'Oh God *yes*,' agreed Teddy wholeheartedly. '*Christ* yes – couldn't have ever even contemplated it without Judy, here . . .'

' . . . in no time at all, he was off the booze. Weren't you, Teddy my love?'

'Indeed. Not touched a drop, as they say, for, er – seven

hundred and twenty-one days, now. Twenty-two, if you count today.'

'Let's drink to that!' laughed Jamie.

'*You* can!' responded Teddy, quick as a flame. '*You*, Jamie are welcome to sample the entire cellar. Me – I have to be off.'

'It's like your smoking, Jamie,' smiled Judy. 'Same thing. Magic.'

'Well . . .' doubted Jamie. '*Nearly*, anyway. Still need the patches . . .'

'*And* the cigarettes!' cried Judy. 'Oh yes – no good denying it because I know you do, I know it. But *soon*, Jamie, honestly. You're really very close to it now, you know.'

'Well,' said Jamie, 'thanks to you I am. Yes.'

Judy patted his knee.

'Ooh and what's it *called*, Teddy?' she now wanted to know. 'The play. What've you called it?'

'Ah yes . . . I think you might quite like the title actually, Judy. Think everyone will, actually. Really rather proud of it. It's called – *The Works*. Actually.'

Judy and Jamie both looked up at him.

'Oh *Teddy* . . . !' said Judy, admiringly. 'Inspired. Brilliant title. Amazing no one's ever thought of it before. And is it . . . ? I mean – it's about *here*, then, is it?'

'Not really,' admitted Teddy. 'Not as such. It's more of a throwback thing, really. Sort of an *Upstairs Downstairs* type of thing it is, I suppose. How, you know – in the old days, everyone knew exactly where they stood. What precisely was expected of them. And the wheels – the wheels then, you see, were set into perpetual motion. The *works*, you see: how it all worked. So to that extent, I suppose, it's kind of a bit like here . . . the fact that, you know, we all do our bit and . . . it *works*. Yes. Because do you know what?' added on Teddy, as he fingered the doorpost. 'In the days when I was always in my *cups*, as they so delicately put it, I just felt so lousy every single day – and at night, oh God – the terrible shattered nights, tossing in sweat –'

'I remember . . .' said Judy, quite softly, and shivering slightly.

'Well yes. You would. Who could forget them? And the *dreams* – oh my God. Such fearful, dreadful dreams I had. And that is what I mean, really: what I want to say. My only consolation, in those days, was that like the drink . . . eventually, at some time, the dreams wore off. Receded. Left me alone, yes? But now, this dream – our dream. It doesn't. It's for ever. And I don't ever – never, Judy, do I want this one to ever wear off. Recede. Never do I want it to leave me alone. Yes?'

CHAPTER SEVEN

As Biff was helping Tubby heave out all of those bags and boxes from the boot of the car – across the passageway, he had to go then, and down to the kitchens in the lift – he was at the same time thinking aloud.

'I thought he'd never,' is how the idea was going, so far. 'I never thought he'd go for it. No I never . . .'

Biff got these trussed-up bales of cabbages well under his arm, and then he glanced over at Tubby, maybe in pique.

'Here you! Oy – Tubs. *Talking*, aren't I? You taking this in, or what? Only bleeding *talking*, aren't I?'

'Oh yeh?' said Tubby (I reckon – what I reckon is, I just go these two more bags here, and we're looking at no more than the one last trip, seems like to me). 'Thought you was just thinking aloud, like.'

'Well I *were*,' allowed Biff, quite grandly. 'Not saying I weren't. But you still want someone to bleeding *listen* to you, don't you?'

'What you on about, Biff? Here – you know what I reckon? I reckon we go these two more bags here, and we're looking at no more than the one last trip, seems like to me . . .'

'The *car* is what I'm on about, Tubs old mate. The *limo*, yeh? I were just saying – when word come down that John-John was cool with running us up Smithfield, and that, I didn't think nothing of it, did I? Then when I clocks the motor, I thought no *way*, son: he don't twig what it is we're about, old John-John don't. When he gets wind of we're buying great bloody lumps of meat and all the veg with them bits of farmyard hanging off of them, there ain't no how on earth, mate – no way on God's earth that bloke gonna let us within a mile of this here limo he got. But nah. Sweet with it, weren't he Tubs? Ay? Right from the off.'

Yeh well – bleeding Tubby, he still ain't bleeding *listening* or nothing, is he? Tell that a mile off. So I'll just get down to humping all the bags for him, will I, and go on talking to meself. But I tell you – I was right knocked back, I was, when John-John he says *Yeah*, mate – sure: I'll take you wherever you wanna go – hang about, like, so's I don't get no ticket nor no clamping nor all the rest of the bleeding caper, and then you get what you like, son, into that boot there, look, and it's back to The Works we all bleeding well go. And give him his due – he been true to his word. Don't complain, nor nothing. I reckon he's a bit of a diamond, John-John is – that's what I reckon, tell you God's truth. Pleased with meself, now, for what I done the very first night for him. Blimey – seems years back, now: ain't, though. No – that very first night, yeh? When Tubs was getting sorted in the kitchen, right? Oh yeh – and talking Tubs, OK? Tell you, man – *respect*, yeh? Respect is called for: well due. I mean, what I mean is – I well knew, didn't I, that he was up to your bacon and eggs, fry a bit of steak, sort of style – but blimey! I don't think I never ate so good as this in all my bleeding life. Which is why I don't mind, you know what I'm saying? Why I don't mind, like, helping him out, these early morning little outings of ours. And he's said to me. Tubs has – he's said to me I'm well chuffed with you doing this, Biff: owe you one, yeh? On account of doing it all on me tod, like – be one hell of hassle. I says to him Oh do leave it out, Tubs – what I do, it ain't nothing, is it? Ain't nothing like what *you* do, is it? Yeh. So anyways. We got into a nice little sort of a routine, we have, these days. What it is – I'm always first up of a morning, right? I mean, first up – not just out of the three of us, like, but out of the whole schemozzle, you know? The whole of The Works, like. Yeh. Mind you, up old Lucas's neck of the woods, well – I hear noises going on up there all hours, son. Don't reckon he never gets his head down, that one. He ain't like you and me, Lucas ain't – out there right on his own, he is. Yeh so anyways, like what I was saying – I get meself up, yeh, and I get the old electric polisher going all down the corridors, and that (vacuum down the stairs). Got this long-handled sort of glorified duster wotsit for reaching high up to all them windows. Couple hours, I'm done. The polisher – I come to love it, I'm honest, that old polisher. It don't make much noise, or nothing, and the floors, I'm telling you – come up lovely, they do. Just sails away with you, that old polisher does – like you's an ice skater, or something. So look, right – I'm done with the cleaning side of things, OK, but it's still bleeding early, innit? So what goes down then is, old Tubs – he heaves hisself out of his pit, right, and he do me a very tasty little bit of breakfast. Just for me, he do this – which has got to be major, ain't it? Couple nice sausages, sort of style – bit of crispy bacon (I can go for that heavy, ain't making no bones) and sometimes I have a egg, yeh? A egg just broke all over it. Telling you: sets you up, no messing. Then we comes down, and there's old John-John, regular as wossname – looking like, I dunno – looks like one of them old-style film stars, or something, John-John does – something from the days when people got theirselves up in, like, suits and ties and shiny shoes, and that – and John-John's shoes, dear oh dear: see your face in them, you can (you want to). My gear, it's all got stripes and words on – don't even seem to be made of cloth, the half of it. Dunno why I stuck with it, basically; it's just what blokes is wearing now, innit? So you goes along. Anyway – John-John, right? He ain't into nothing like that. Well – not surprising, really, when you sit down and think about it: got to be a bleeding hundred, hasn't he? But I'm not *saying* nothing, nor nothing. Like I says: right diamond, John-John is, old or not. So yeh – there he is next to this very tasty motor what he got (telling you – I'm sat in the back there, I feel like I'm, I dunno – Prince Charles, one of them) and we all goes off to New Covent Garden, Smithfield – sometimes we go up the Columbia Road for, blimey – half a parkload of flowers, some sort. We heaves them back, and then Pauly – he dumps them in a bucket and then Lucas, right, he says Pauly's a bleeding genius. Got to laugh about it, really. Entcha?

What I just want to get said here, though – get it sort of known, like: on the record, sort of style. Is. That first night, yeh? And there I was going Oh dear oh dear, I was going, weren't I? I do not reckon this for a game of soldiers, I tell you here and now. That's how I were thinking. Thought my mates had gone soft on me, didn't I? Paul with his bleeding flowers and Tubby banging on about his sodding gravy, or whatever it was he was on about. Hadn't got a hold on it, is what I'm saying. Now I sort of do, I reckon. I'm not all the way, mind – but I reckon I know where they're all, like, sort of coming from, if you get my meaning. I'm still on at Pauly, though: I don't let it lie. What *about* it, Pauly, I'm going: when we gonna do a bit of business? And you know what he come back with? He says to me Yeh, Biff – yeh yeh: we will be, quite soon, OK? But in the meantime, Biff, he goes – ask yourself this: why we do the business in the first place, ay? And I says to him Here – what you on about, Paul? You winding me up, or what? What you bleeding *mean* why we do the business? We do the business, son, on account of it's mother's milk and bread and butter and sometimes, yeh, we get a nice tickle, then what we got is *jam* on it. Don't do it to keep us all *healthy*, do we Paul? What got into you? I went *down* didn't I, on account of the business. Near on three bleeding years. You forgot that, Pauly, have you? Slipped your mind, did it? Cos I tell you this much, son – it ain't slipped fucking *mine* that's for bleeding sure. And Paul, he says *Yeh*, Biff, yeh: exactly what I'm on about. Look around you, son. Take a gander at where we end up. This is Easy Street with a capital E, my son: we do our bit – whatever – and all the rest of it's well laid on, ain't it? What I'm saying to you, Biff, is this: *yeh* we'll do some business – might have a little bit in hand with Jamie, as it happens (not that he knows a dicky bird, or nothing) – but only, like, to keep our *hand* in. Only for a bit of practice, like. Cos for the first time ever, Biff – what, you can't see this, can't you? For the first time in our lives, Biff, we don't *need* it. We got what we want. And I'm telling you, mate – I don't know about you, but me, Biff: I likes it. This has just got to be *prime*. Is what Paul says to me. And yeh – I do see that, course I do (well of *course* I bleeding do: not *stupid*, am I?). So I let it lie, time being.

No but hear me out – I still ain't got round to *saying*, have I? Ay? About the first night, yeh? Down the nosh room. After we all done, I goes up to John-John, don't I? And I says to him, er – scuse me, mate, but I reckon you must've dropped this here, some point. And John-John, he looks down at his wallet in my hand, like, and right away he's off with all of his Oh I am so *indebted* to you my very dear chap, sort of stuff (you know how he goes on), and I says to him Nah, mate – do it for anyone, wouldn't I? Truth was, I never had so easy a dip in my life. Blimey, I thought – we'll be all right here: place is fair crawling with marks. Yeh. But then later on, like – when, like I say, we was done with all the grub, and that . . . well, I dunno, really. Ain't never done nothing like it before, I'm telling you. But it didn't seem *right* – you know what I mean? So I gives it him back. And I did think too – got to be honest – I go changing my mind on this one, it's gonna be no sort of trouble, is it, get it back off of him again: telling you, baby's candy don't even enter. But I never. No. I never. Pauly – he was well pleased. Saw the lot, didn't he? Always did do. Clocked the dip. Said nothing. Clocked me give it him back. I'm glad, he said, you done that, Biff. Cos if you hadn't, son, I'd of broke your arm for you. Nice. Ain't it? From a mate. But yeh – I knew what he was

on about, if I'm honest. Why I give it back, weren't it? So yeh. Like
I say: all turned out lovely in the end. Basically.

'Oh hello!' said Dorothy, really quite brightly – and feeling, to be
frank with you, rather good, not at all bad about herself, for
having simply come out with it, just like that. I mean yes, OK – all
I've said is *hello*, God's sake, but the point here is that it came to
me spontaneously: I am not (I can't be) so totally depressed and
fearful any more that I don't even notice the people around me –
people, you know, who have no obvious, um – well, no particular
relevance – let alone *greet* them, or anything. Nor am I compelled
to rapidly sum up or assimilate any given situation before I feel
secure in coming down on one side or the other – whether so
simple a thing as a 'hello' is expedient in the circumstances, say
(even advisable), or might, maybe, for some reason or another
(and face it – what reason on earth could *that* be?) become in some
way misconstrued. You see. And these complications (neuroses,
Kimmy says) I've been living through endlessly: all foolish, I
know they are now – and every single one of them causing me
grief. Just like Kimmy has been constantly telling me. God. Poor
Kimmy – how does she put up with me? *Why* does she put up
with me, actually? I sometimes forget, now, that at some seemingly rather distant and very low point (soon after he'd gone:
there – said it) she took me on as an assistant. Why? It was very
horribly apparent, I should have said, that I could assist no one –
couldn't even support my own day-to-day existence, let alone
attend to the needs of Mary-Ann – who these days seems much

calmer, thank the Lord. I mean – people have maybe only seen Mary-Ann as thoughtful and tranquil and in control, yes I do know that; but it's recent, that – largely down to Kimmy and *Judy*, I have to admit (we all need Judy), and of course to us all just *being* here. Safe. Under Lucas's wide umbrella.

But God – it chills me, you know, to wonder what on earth might have become of little Mary-Ann if it had all been up to me and me alone. Her school work, you know, had gone to pieces, quite frankly – but now she's doing marvellously (or so I'm *told*, anyway: I blank out a bit on things like that). Maybe . . . I'm just thinking that maybe all this – all my hopelessness – is *precisely* why Kimmy should have taken me on (because she's a good sort, Kimmy; can be a bit loud, a bit forward – well, she is *American*, after all – but at base, she really is a good and kind soul. And she'd hate it – utterly loathe it, if she heard me telling you that. Or, I don't know: maybe not). Sometimes, people not just sense when help is needed, but act upon the impulse straight away. And straight away is vital, you know – totally key. People who are only mildly inconvenienced by one or two of life's recurrent blips or hitches might vaguely promise you a pencilled-in window, some time or other in the not too (too) distant future. They do not understand the nature of desperation: people who need, say, money right *now*, or else they'll be closed down (or, worse, badly damaged). People who are starving; not peckish, no no. Not, on balance, being ready to go a bite of something, no: but *ravenous*. Aching with hunger, and near to being closed down (or, worse, badly damaged). Kimmy – she saw it in me. Lucas, well . . . Lucas, he saw it in all of us (didn't he?).

So just to say hello, yes? Without thinking. Small thing to you, maybe – invisible, wholly conceivably. But to me, well – I don't want to labour the point, or anything, but it's really something of a minor breakthrough. And I didn't even pause to consider that it was Jamie I was saying it to, this breezy hello of mine. Because

247

he's the one, I can't forget (because you don't, do you? If someone intimates that, well, you know, someone else is, um . . . what should we say? How do you put it? *Keen* on you, sort of thing – *likes* you, or whatever. Well you never would forget that. No one would). I'm looking at him maybe a bit quizzically now, am I? Which need not be great. I think it would be good if I said something more . . . Does he *really*, do you think? Like me, especially? He seems the reverse of in a hurry to talk to me, certainly. Gives no sign. Can he be shy, do you suppose? As some men are said to be. Never struck me as unduly shy. I think it would be good if I said something more . . . But me: what do I feel? Well if I'm perfectly honest I still feel exactly the same way as I did when I talked it all over with Kimmy, that time. *Nice* man, he very probably is, Jamie – but I've never, you know, really seen him as very much more. Although now I come to . . . you know: *look* at him, I can see, I do see that he is, yes, rather attractive in a bit of a homely and tousled sort of a way. Which can be quite nice. Yes. But. I think it would be good if I said something more . . .

'What're you hanging round here for, Jamie? Have you had breakfast? Terribly early.'

'I, um – yes. No, that is. Haven't had any, um . . . had a cup of tea. No it *is* early, though – I know that. Looks like it might be quite a fine day. Got the makings . . . No I'm, um – expecting someone, actually. Dorothy. Expecting some people. Heard a bit of, you know – bustle and so on, so I came down – but it's just Tubby and Biff. John too, somewhere, I expect.'

She's looking, thought Jamie, at me rather oddly. Is she? Looking at me oddly? Don't know. Hard to say. But if it's true – you know: what Paul was on about. If she really does fancy me (and Christ – why would she? I wouldn't fancy me, tell you) then I suppose she would, then, wouldn't she? Look at me. And maybe not oddly: maybe it isn't.

'Oh *hi*, you two!' sang out a new voice from just behind them.

'My Johnny not back yet? His breakfast's nearly done. I'm doing his favourite.'

Jamie said Oh *morning morning* to Frankie, just more or less at the same time as Dorothy (much to her own satisfaction) chipped in with a bright enough and lightish hello of her own.

'Sometimes,' went on Frankie, 'he has to go miles to park the car. I *do* wish Lucas would let him leave it here. I mean – I understand what he means *generally*, but God – it's such a beautiful car, isn't it? You think so, don't you Jamie?'

'I do,' he agreed, looking at her. 'Beautiful.'

'So it's not as if it would mess the place up, or anything. Johnny says just to forget it. He says that rules are rules. Like the curtain thing. Suppose he's right.'

It was the mention of rules. It must, Jamie later reflected, have been just that one glancing allusion to the, let's face it, pitifully few hard and fast rules, around here (the bulk of our collaborations being not just instinctive, now, but wholly devotional). It's just that I thought . . . yes well *OK*: I told you I wasn't yet over it – I said it to Judy, didn't I? Came quite clean. And now was just one of those moments when nothing, but nothing else in the world would *do*. Which is a bugger, actually – a total and utter bugger because I'm already wearing three, or is it four of these bloody patches and at twelve I'm due to see Judy for a bit more talk and the rubbing of the head and I haven't lit up now for more than four days (Christ – it's nearly five). So *damn*, is all I can think, at the moment. But it's that *feeling*, you know? Explained it. When nothing else will *do*. But. I can't. Quit my post. Because I'm waiting, aren't I? Yes I am: I'm waiting, and it's important. Because finally she did, you know, Caroline – respond to my endless calls and messages. She wrote a note. Sent it second class. Said she'd come once – just to witness for herself this ghastly place I've ended up in (her way of putting it, needless to say) if only just to shut me up. And Benny, I insisted (another bloody telephone message: she just won't pick up, you know – she simply won't do it. Either that or she's just never there; and if not there – where, then?). You *must* bring Benny. No, she said (surprise). Maybe another time. Not this time. So I rang up again. And I said firmly to her machine No *this* time, *this* time: this time is *good*. I'll cut it all short for you, will I? Or we'll be here all morning. Eventually I got her to say yes (if only, I suppose, just to shut me up).

And this – here and now – is the appointed hour. In fact she's late (surprise). So I'm probably not being the best of company here, in the meantime. And it's amazing, you know, because this bit of The Works – just inside the entrance – this time of the day it's just always deserted; today it's like I sent out invitations. And although I don't wish to be in any way rude to Dorothy (particularly in the, you know: circumstances. Taking into account her feelings, and all the rest of it) and it is always a pleasure to rest the eyes on the ever quite ravishing form of Frankie (ah me . . . another day, another lifetime – who knows what might have been?) it is nonetheless and fairly understandably *Caroline* who is uppermost, now, in my mind. And Benny. My son. Both of whom . . . hang on . . . wait just a minute . . . oh God it *is*, isn't it? Oh God oh God it *is* (wish Judy were here). Yes . . . both of them, now, are looming, and if I have to be honest, well – their arriving just at the moment when Dorothy is hanging about (has she nothing to do? No – I suppose she hasn't) and Frankie is idling, here (and she will be, won't she? Till John comes back because she adores him, lucky lucky man that he is), and I'm here meanwhile, as easy as a fidget and sweating and palsied, now, in my need for a nicotine hit . . . so no, I wouldn't have set it up like this, not if I'm honest. On the whole, I'd have things different. This is not how I would have designed it.

Jamie, now, was waggling his hand high over his head, eyes and mouth stupidly wide in their insistence to be noticed. But he knew he had already been spotted: Benny, look – he's broken into a run now, and he's making right for me. When we collide – when his eager young face deep-nuzzles and winds me as I ruffle the boy's hair and clasp him close, he will maybe feel secure or less so, happy or sad, and me – I'll feel just strange. I have glanced over twice, now, to Dorothy and Frankie – jerked a thumb in the direction of the fast-approaching Caroline. Two blokes, you know, would have made themselves scarce by this time. See you later, they would have said – and then they'd be off. But then two blokes – well look, they wouldn't have hung about in the first place, would they? But Dorothy and Frankie, face it – they weren't going anywhere. Look at them: eager and curious (we won't say nosy, will we?) and not about to give a single inch.

'Jamie,' said Caroline, quite flatly. 'This place is a bugger to find. It's like the lost world, round here. Leave your father alone Benny, can't you?'

'It's OK,' said Jamie. 'It's OK, Benny, isn't it?' he whispered down to him (as I ruffle the boy's hair, and clasp him close).

Caroline looked at Dorothy and Frankie, quite as Jamie could have predicted she would: as if she had just now detected on the wind an odour, far from pleasant.

'Dorothy . . .' said Jamie, with deep reluctance (introductions were not yet meant to be a part of all this; anything of that order was, God willing, to come much later). 'And Frankie. This is Caroline. And Benny. Say hello, Benny. Benny is my son. My boy. Aren't you, Benny?'

Benny blushed a bit, and then tossed up and over an almost half-smile – while stopping short of responding to his father's anyway pretty dumb question.

'Hello, Benny!' Dorothy hailed him, with considerable enthusiasm (the more of them you do, you know, the easier it all is to handle). 'I know someone who would just adore to meet you,

you know. Do you know that? Would you like to come with me, Benny? Is that all right, Jamie? We can explore.'

And at first, he'd have to admit it, he was bloody well irritated. I mean, Jesus: how long has it taken me just to get Benny to be here (on my own turf)? And now this woman wants to take him away. But in the last half of the second which was all it took him to swallow down hard on that lot, Jamie ripped up the thought and settled in favour of quite the opposite viewpoint. I wanted Benny here, yes I did (because I think he'll love it – he'll love it here, Benny: I just know he will), but it was never really going to be easy, was it, to get to grips (chew the fat) with Caroline here. No – not easy at all. Because each and every time he would poke at the fringes of the things he most needed to say, Caroline would – oh God, she'd be bound to – she'd glance just once and pointedly in Benny's direction and hiss over to Jamie that she really didn't think that this was quite the *time* (did he?). But it had to be – it just had to be the time, didn't it? She had to see that. Because believe him – Jamie well knew that if here and now was not to be the time, well . . . there might never be another.

'I think that's a *brilliant* idea, Dorothy,' Jamie approved quite hurriedly, and maybe more loudly than it needed to be (because Caroline's mouth, look – it was well ajar now, and just on the verge of coming out with something. So let's quickly muscle in on this one, shall we? And get it all wrapped up). 'Yes – you go off with Dorothy now, Benny, and then we'll all meet up later and have a jolly good, um – chat about everything. Yes? Dorothy'll show you all the exciting things here – won't you, Dorothy?'

'Absolutely,' agreed Dorothy, taking Benny by the hand. 'I promise you, Benny – you have never seen anywhere on earth like this. Let's go hunting. Do you like cranberry juice? Yes? You do? Oh good.'

Jamie was nodding like a maniac, full of only earnest intentions: to just get Benny and Dorothy out of here, fast (because Caroline,

Christ – she had that look, that look in her eye), and to expunge from his own skull all the cackling goblins energetically flexing their Rosa Klebb dagger-shoes: they had left him pricked and aquiver, these ceaselessly furious demands for a hit.

'That's it, Dorothy,' he managed to stutter (as he revolved the pair of them and propelled them forwards). 'Give him the works, ay? No pun, um . . .'

'Oh God *here* he is!' cried Frankie. 'At long *last*, Johnny! Where've you *been*? Oh look *bye*, everyone, OK? Lovely to meet you, um. It's just that I'm doing Johnny's favourite, OK?'

And Frankie and John, in a blur were gone. Dorothy and Benny gave Jamie a wave, and then they turned the corner and were lost to the gloom.

Jamie swivelled a foot and blew out his cheeks.

'*So* . . .' he said. And then: 'Ha ha.'

'We going to stand here all day, then?'

'Hm? Oh – no no. Quite the reverse. Let's go up to my, um . . . let's go up. Yes? And don't worry, will you, about Benny, or anything. He's in very good, um – you know. Hands.'

'I'm sure. They go everywhere with you, do they? Those two women? Sort of armed guard, is it Jamie? Lucas though, I imagine, retains the droit de seigneur . . .'

'Oh God's *sake*, Caroline – don't start up already. You've only just . . . ! *Look*. Let's go up. Shall we? Yes?'

Caroline shrugged, and followed him.

'I'm not saying they weren't *attractive* . . .' she said, as they entered the lift. 'Particularly the child one. With her father.'

'That –' And then Jamie altered it a bit. 'That – was John,' he said.

'Oh *good*, said Caroline, at her most witheringly indulgent. 'I'm so terribly *pleased* for him. That he's *John*, Jamie. How bloody much further? It's like a bloody warehouse, this place . . .'

'Yes well,' said Jamie, as lightly as he could (and why was he gnawing like a lion on this lip of his then, hey? What had this poor sore lip ever done to harm him?). 'That's maybe because it *is*, isn't it, Caroline? Really. A sort of warehouse. It's an old *printing* works, you see, and the storage part is just –'

'Oh *please*, Jamie – spare me the history lesson. Let's just sit down soon, shall we? Then you can say whatever it is you want to say to me and then I'll pick up Benny from Nanny and her cranberry juice and then the both of us can get back to some sort of civilization.'

Jamie grinned and bore it. He ushered her into his space, and closed the door behind them.

'Well,' he said. 'This is it. This is it, yes. Do, um . . . seating over there, look. Yes anyway – this is it. What do you think?'

Caroline glanced about her. Said nothing. Glanced about her.

'Yes . . .' continued Jamie gamely, barely thinking and desperate to calm his rising agitation (God, you know – I really do wish Judy were here). 'So as I say, um – Caroline. This is it. This is where I, um . . . *am*, so to speak. This is it. I think, you know, it's a book title, that: *This Is It* . . . could be wrong. Conned into buying it at Heathrow one time, seem to recall. Could be wrong. Anyway: this is it.'

'Oh Christ's name stop *saying* that, Jamie. I *know* it's it, don't I? I'm *here*. Christ . . .'

And Jamie exhaled in a rush:

'Oh look *please*, Caroline – please. Please don't be angry. All the time. Please try. I mean you're here, as you say. You said it. You've come. I mean – let's for God's sake use the *time*, yes? Yes? Caroline? Hm? Do you want tea? I can make . . . ? Or coffee? Sit down. Why don't you sit, Caroline, hm? Sit here, yes? Or over there, look, if you prefer? Tea, then? No tea? How about some coffee? Yes – that's favourite. I'll make some coffee.'

'What's this.' It ought, thought Jamie, to have been a question, that; but from Caroline it came out as a statement.

254

'That . . .' said Jamie, very quietly, 'is a painting. Action painting. I, um – did it. Painted it. It's mine.'

Caroline nodded. And Jamie regarded her, daring to expect.

'I don't mind tea,' she said. 'If you're making it.'

And for the first time since he left her, Jamie was crushed. He hated the weight as well as the stench of the vile old feeling. But then it eased: it eased, and this pleased him, yes, but also he was filled with a vast relief. The new Jamie – the Jamie he had become had resilience; he took the blow, he bounced right back. Before, he would have been utterly demolished. And just to let her know it, he merely said, quite lightly:

'Is that all you've got to say . . . ?'

And Caroline was all huge and insincere apology:

'Oh God I'm so *sorry*, Jamie – I just assumed that you'd remember. Of *course* I've got more to say: no milk, one sugar.'

Jamie flattened his lips into an acid but tolerant acknowledgement of a nice one. And then he started in on the tea.

'You've certainly . . . !' called Caroline (finally throwing herself on to a sofa: one of John and Frankie's cast-offs – they're so damn kind, those people). 'Can you *hear* me, Jamie? You're already miles away. I say you've certainly got enough *space*, anyway . . .'

Mm, she was thinking: bags and bags of bright-lit space. Christ – you should see where Benny and I are now. Dingy is *kind*, quite frankly. But it's cheap. Dirt-cheap. And that's how it feels. I must say I adore all these windows . . . Like a cathedral, or something. Makes you see colours, for the first time. And God – there are enough of them, aren't there? In that so-called *painting*, there. Pollock thing. And I don't quite know yet what angle Jamie's going to be coming at me from – but I do know he took a wrong turn there. I mean, however great or not great this place may be, there is no way on God's earth that it has made him capable of creating something. Artistic. Even a mess like that. No. So why does he want or expect me to believe that he actually painted the thing? I mean – *what*? He got this huge canvas, did he? And laid it down on the floor and then slapped on all the paint and stood back a bit and then he thought mmm . . . maybe just another splash of red there, possibly – a touch of black, a few more yellow drips and we're done. And then he and a mate set to hanging it up. Ha ha. Very big joke. What – *Jamie*? An artist? I don't *think* so. And there's something else . . . something else is funny here, too. What is it? Something odd. I mean, Christ – it's *all* odd, isn't it? Bloody odd. Like I said at the outset. But it's something in particular . . . something that isn't . . . oh Christ *I* know. Bloody hell. Well now *this*. Jesus – this really *is* odd.

'Jamie,' she said. 'Why aren't you smoking? You're a chain smoker, remember?'

Jamie slammed shut the kettle. Gripped it hard.

'F.A.B . . .' he said.

'Oh *Jesus*, Jamie! You know it just drives me *mental* when you come out with these infantile bloody catchphrases of yours! It's just an excuse not to *think*.'

'Well . . .' he said, as he turned to face her. 'I haven't. Used one. Come out with one. Since I've been here. Not once. And actually, Caroline – I'm an *ex* chain smoker, if you want to know. I'm not saying I'm *off* it, or anything – fact is, I'd murder, kill right now for a fag, if I'm honest . . . but I'm *getting* there. Judy's helped, of course . . .'

'Judy. Oh yes – *Judy*, of course. Another little girlfriend, is she?'

'Oh *God*, Caroline – why can't you *understand*? It's just not *like* that here. It's not how anyone thinks. Everyone's with whoever they're with and it *works*. This is the whole point. This is why I asked you here, Caroline – maybe even, I don't know . . . why you came. No – hear me. Hear me. Please, Caroline – listen. I really do believe, you know, that this place has a . . . *power*. Stop! Don't – don't put that face on, Christ's sake. Just listen. I really do believe, Caroline – I wasn't going to come right out with it this early, but look – it's come up now, so I will. I really do believe that if you came here – if you and Benny were to come and live here, it would . . . we could be *healed*, somehow, Caroline. I'm telling you – I *know*, look, I *know* it sounds mad and crazy and all the bloody rest of it, but once you're here for even a short while . . . things begin to happen. Good things. You begin to change . . . but in a good way. I mean look – never mind the painting: look. On that table beside you. See? See it? Do you know what that is? It's a script. A play. We're doing a play, and I'm going to be in it. *Me*! And I *want* to, Caroline. I really want to. Can you . . . understand?'

'Jamie: hear me. I don't want to be in your *play* . . . !'

'Not my *play*! Not the *play*! Life. My life. *Real* life, Caroline. It is real here, you know. It maybe doesn't, you know – seem it. From the outside. But it is. The most real thing I've ever known. And I want to share it. With both of you.'

Caroline was more than ready with a shotgun, both barrels charged with blasts of jeering and contempt. But something stayed her. What she came out with instead was:

'Well why don't you? If you want one – why not just have one? You've got them, haven't you? They haven't been *confiscated*? So light up. Do it.'

Jamie shook his head.

'I've got them. I've always got them. But I'm not going to. I'm not. I tell you the truth, Caroline – I haven't had a cigarette in nearly five days. Five *days*. When could you remember I could even go five *minutes*? Hey? And I'm not. Going to.'

Caroline looked at him. Jamie approached her, and she watched him coming. He knelt beside her, and he held her hand.

'I've missed you,' he said quite simply. 'Missed you both. Want you back. Want you here. Will you, Caroline? At least think about it? Will you?'

Caroline was surprised to find herself smiling.

'How's the tea coming on?' she asked him.

257

Jamie jumped up to his feet, the energy and hope that suddenly filled him making him grin, making him happy.

'No milk, one sugar?'

Caroline nodded. 'Check,' she said.

'One minute. Coming up.'

Jamie walked the distance, and then he poured out two cups of tea. He couldn't, he thought, carry the two of them over to her (his fingers were trembling and the china would clatter) so he picked up just the one and with both hands clutching the saucer, he slowly walked across to her.

'Welcome,' he said. And then he tacked on: 'Will you?'

Caroline stirred the tea.

'Ought to be getting back to Benny,' she said. 'He talks about you, you know.'

'Benny'll be fine. Does he? Really? He talks about me? But will you, Caroline? Will you?'

She looked at him, and sighed.

'I'll think,' she said. 'I'll think.'

Jamie breathed out heavily.

'Good,' he said. 'That's . . . good. Come on then, Caroline. Drink your tea. And then we'll go and see what Benny's been up to, shall we?'

'These great corridor type things all over the place,' Benny was enthusing. 'Be wicked for skateboarding. Totally cool.'

'Mmm . . .' doubted Mary-Ann (well *someone's* got to put him sort of right about stuff, haven't they? Someone who knows what they're talking about). 'I don't really think Lucas would approve of that, somehow. I mean – it hasn't come up before. Skateboarding. I expect because apart from me everybody here is just so totally ancient. You know? But I'm sure he wouldn't like it. We could ask Alice, I suppose. But I think she'd say he says no.'

'Who's Alice?' asked Benny. 'Is she . . . what, she's like sort of in charge around here, is she?'

'Well not *exactly*. No one's exactly in charge. It's not like school, or anything. I mean – Lucas, he sort of like *owns* it, and everything. But he doesn't go round dishing out orders, and stuff. But people like my Mum, yeah? They don't want to do anything he wouldn't kind of like. So no skateboarding, pretty sure. Anyway – so what then, Benny? You coming to live here, are you? With your Dad? Where do you live at the moment, then? What's your Mum like?'

Benny was still quite struck by the amazing scale of the place. It made the gym at school look like just a, I don't know – ordinary room, or something. It made where he lived look more like . . .

'Oh crap. Place we live,' he confided to Mary-Ann in a sudden slightly guilty rush, 'is just totally *crappy*, if you really want to know. This place makes it look more like a . . . *cupboard*, or something. Box. And it's really noisy because it's on a main sort of, you know – shopping sort of street and we're stuck up above this really smelly kind of takeaway kebab type place. I wouldn't eat anything from there, I tell you. Totally crappy.'

'So are you or not? It'd be good if you did.'

'Did what? Where's this lift go to?'

'*Live* here, stupid.'

'Oh. I dunno. Up to Dad. Well – up to Mum, more like. She sort of says what gets to happen, basically. I wouldn't mind. It's pretty cool. I liked your Mum. She's cool. My Mum's OK. Bit bossy. Who else is here? Where's this lift go to, Mary-Ann?'

'Yeh – she's all right, my Mum. Bit messed up, you know? Cos of my Dad leaving. I didn't like him leaving. It's not great, is it? When they leave.'

Benny nodded. 'No. Except I don't think my Dad really *wanted* to, or anything. Don't know. My Mum says he left us. I don't know.'

'Kimmy is a lot stronger than my Mum. She helps her a lot. You haven't met Kimmy, Benny, but she's really cool. Makes loads of crap for art galleries and stuff and sells them for trillions. Doesn't even *make* them . . .'

'I'm quite good at art,' said Benny. 'Came second in my year. Where's this lift go to, then? It's huge.'

'There's quite a lot of art and stuff going on here, really. Everyone's pretty arty, I suppose. Well – *some*. I actually hate it when I have to go to school because it's so much cooler here. Sometimes I get taken by John, though – and that's just totally cool because of this wicked car he's got. It's like the Queen's. Mile long and totally shiny.'

'Who *are* all these people you keep talking about?' said Benny. 'What is this place actually, Mary-Ann? Don't quite get.'

'Don't know, really. What you'd call it. But it works. It's really good. But you've got to sort of get to know it, if you know what I mean.'

'It's dead quiet, isn't it? You just get this sort of bonk and whooshing type noise in the distance, sometimes. Otherwise you'd think it was empty.'

'It's cos it's so big. Do you want to come and meet Kimmy? She's totally cool, I promise.'

'I don't know. Don't know how long Mum and Dad are going to be. I *suppose* so . . . but listen, Mary-Ann – where does this lift go to?'

'Well all over the place, really. We're quite near the top here, so up is just Lucas's place and the roof and that's about it. Right down at the bottom is the kitchen, and stuff. Oh *yeh*, Benny – let's go down to the kitchen. It's so totally cool down there. And Tubby might be down there – he's great. His voice is really funny and he *gives* you stuff, like chocolate and stuff. Let's go and see if he's there.'

Benny shrugged. 'Cool,' he said, following Mary-Ann into the lift. And as the outer wooden doors slid to and the inner concertina gates clanged shut behind them, Mary-Ann stabbed a large black button and the cage shuddered once and whirred into action.

'It'd be good,' she said casually, as the ragged thicknesses of each successive storey rumbled past their eyes. 'If you came to live here. Be cool . . .'

Benny nodded. 'Yeh,' he said. 'Would. Totally.'

'You know what I reckon,' grunted Biff with some effort, while shouldering another of these bleeding bloody heavy great sacks what he been humping seems like half his bleeding life. 'I *reckon* . . .' he went on – dumping down the thing pretty much anywhere. 'I *reckon*, Tubs, you overdone the spuds. We ain't got no space. We got spuds coming out our ears.'

'Nah,' said Tubby. 'Get through loads of spuds, we do. I'm doing chips tonight, aren't I? You ever seen anyone round here leaving any chips on their plates? No you ain't. This lot'll be gone, telling you, couple days. Plus I got different sorts. These is Marris. Your Marris is a prime chipper – don't go to bits on you, like what some do.'

'Yeh well . . .' mumbled Biff (can't stand it, can I? When he goes all technical on me). 'So where I dump them, then?'

'Just shove them in the corner there, look, and then you can – Oh! Aye aye! Looks like we got visitors. Wotcha, princess! How you doing, girl? All right? And who's the boyfriend?'

'Oh *God*, Tubby, don't be so totally embarrassing, OK?' Mary-Ann was squealing at him. 'I don't have a – *yuck* – boyfriend, do I? This is Benny. Jamie's his Dad.'

'*Yeah*?' went Tubby. 'Oh well then – one of the family. Welcome to my place of toil then, Benny. This here's Biff.'

Benny blushed and looked at the floor and briefly looked up by way of an all-encompassing greeting, and then he looked down again.

'Tell you what, Biff,' Tubby carried on (very much the king of the castle is what I feel down here, I ain't kidding you: my *domain*, yeh? Where I like – belong). 'I reckon them two lovebirds there –'

'*Tubby*!' screamed out Mary-Ann. 'You must totally *stop*, OK?'

'Nah – leave it out, Mary-Ann love. I'm only having a lark, aren't I? No listen – what I reckon is, Biff, that these two here wouldn't say no to a nice bit of Bournville. What you say? Yeh? Nice. Else I got some fudge, you interested.'

'Mm – some choc would be great, Tubby. Thank you,' laughed Mary-Ann. 'Don't like fudge. You like fudge, Benny?'

'Um – not sure. Not sure I've ever had any. Is it, what? Like toffee is it, a bit?'

'Softer, ain't it?' said Tubby. 'Tell you what, Benny old lad – you get your chops round a bit of that, and you tell Tubby what you reckon. Fair?'

Mary-Ann was cramming a large piece of Cadbury's Bournville into her mouth (she didn't used to like this dark chocolate too much, actually, but she's really got to totally love it, now. And Tubby – he's always got just piles of it; uses it for these totally wicked sauces and mousses and stuff).

'Have you two been good boys and learned all your parts?' she asked quite cheekily of Tubby and Biff. 'How's the fudge then, Benny? I so totally don't like it.'

'I learned mine . . .' said Biff, quite gravely. Cos yeh – I have, you wanna know. And yeh all right – I know it's only the two lines, yeh I do know that, smartass, but it's like what Teddy was saying to me that time, ain't it? Like what it ain't the *length* of the part, is it? Nah. Size, like, don't matter. What it is is the, er – what he say? *Relevance*, yeh, that's it – the relevance to the play as a wossname. Whole. And also plus, no one's never asked me to be in no *play* before, have they? Stroll on. And at first I'm going Oh do come off it, Teddy, do please leave it out: you have got to be *joking*, son. But then Paul, he says to me – come on Biff, what's wrong with you, mate? Ay? *I'm* doing it, aren't I? And Tubs – he's well in, ain't he? Mind you, Tubs' case it's your classic bit of type-casting, ain't it? He's only playing the downstairs *cook*, ain't he? Well – that ain't gonna stretch him too much, is it? Me, I'm the chauffeur, I am. Great, I goes – does that mean I get to give old John-John's Alvis a right old seeing to then, does it? And John, he says to me – you so much as even *look* at her, Paul, and I'll have your guts for wossnames. (Way he talks – tell you: breaks me up. Garters.) So look at it, Biff old son: what I'm saying to you, right, is that we all got a slice of this one, yeh? So what you saying No for, ay? Mm, went Biff: mm, he went. Yeh well. You put it like that, well yeh – reckon I'm in, then, aren't I? But I tell you this now, Teddy, upfront and square, like – don't expect no like Oscar-winning performance, nor nothing. Cos I'm telling you, I ain't no Roger Moore, you know what I'm saying?

'Well I got to be honest with you, Mary-Ann,' admitted Tubby. 'I'm so bleeding busy down here – whoops! Pardon me I'm sure, mon-sewer ay mam-zell, for my little bit of French, there. But no – I got so much to do here – no don't *laugh*, don't give me no hard time of it, Mary-Ann. I *mean* it – straight up. I mean – I learned a *bit* of it, yeh sure – but I reckon I bash a few saucepan lids together, it'll sort of cover a multitude, kind of style. I don't got too many worries, that score.'

'I like this fudge,' said Benny quickly. He had been wanting to get it in for just ages because he felt so stupid just standing there and saying absolutely nothing whatever – but as the seconds ticked by, he became quite nervous of speaking at all, and so when the moment came (and it was very probably, oh God, the wrong moment completely, but never mind) he just came out with it in a sort of a blurt, really, because otherwise, well – he just never would have.

'Good lad!' approved Tubby. 'Well I tell you what, me old mate – Uncle Tubs has got a lot more where that come from. Here, Mary-Ann, my little darling – why don't you help yourselves to another couple nice big chunks there, yeh? Then – what? You shown Benny the river side of here, or what? He'd like that, Benny would, I reckon. Sun's out, and all.'

'Mm,' agreed Mary-Ann. 'Yeh – we could do that. Come on then, Benny – let's go for a bit of a walk, OK? Your Dad'll find us when he's ready, should think. OK?'

And Benny, off guard, spluttered through the fudge:

'Mm. Therrr. Leggo. Duh.'

'Pig!' laughed Mary-Ann.

'Aye aye!' said Tubby, wagging at Benny a wooden spoon of warning. 'You wanna watch that one, Benny, I'm telling you now. On at you like a wife already, she is.'

'*Tubby*!' Mary-Ann was shrieking with delight, while deftly pocketing two whole bars of Bournville. 'I *so* won't tell you again! Come on, Benny – let's go, yeh?'

And Benny thought Yeh sure, Mary-Ann: let's go. We'll go wherever you want. Wherever you say. Because I tell you – this place, it's just so totally *cool*.

'Well, Jamie,' Judy was chortling – and lifting up the ends of the heavy Christmas garland as she continued to do so (clearly, thought Jamie, she's terribly tickled by something, here). 'Since you *ask* what on earth this rather wonderful great *swag* of a thing is actually comprised of, I am fortunately in a position to tell you. Now watch very closely – I'll point to each little thing in turn here, yes? Please remember them well: written test in the morning, first thing – write on one side of the paper only.'

'Oh God's sake Judy get *on* with it, can't you?' hooted Jamie.

The back of his head was held by the fleshy cradle of his knitted fingers as he sprawled all over the sofa. He didn't, in truth, actually care too much one way or the other, really: didn't wholly need a detailed rundown of this great long green thing's, um – *ingredients*, so to say (he'd only asked in passing because – well yes because it was different from the usual, but largely because it was, like him, sprawled all over the sofa). But look: Judy, she made such a good *show* of everything, didn't she? Cabaret. Every conversation was a kind of party – and when she was this enthusiastic, well: contagious, very.

'Right, now,' she said, eyeing him closely. 'From the top, what we have here *is* . . . blue pine, yes? That's the, you know – main sort of body of the thing, OK? Then, protea flowers, curly silver twigs, glass sort of drop things – think they're from an old chandelier, or something – tapered white candles, as you observe . . . which are going to be tricky, actually, to get them all upright and lit, but never mind. And these are crystallized pears with the cinnamon sticks, yes? Dogwood twigs help bulk it out – and here, see them? Here, here and here – and then all the way down – yes? See them, Jamie?'

'I see them, Judy – I see them.'

'Right. Good. Well: eucalyptus gumnuts. That's what they are.'

'Uh-huh. Of course. Well face it: what else could they be?'

'Mm. Sarcasm. Nasty trait in a young lad, I think. But seriously, Jamie – don't you just love it? I love it. And there are dozens of them, you know. God knows how he finds the time.'

'Who?' asked Jamie, quite surprised. 'Who finds the time? I thought –'

'Oh God *no*,' Judy rushed to assure him. 'You thought – ? Oh no – this isn't *mine*. I didn't do this. It's Paul. Paul did all of these. I only know all that stuff about what's in it because he told me. I just use holly and berries and all the usual bits and bobs – this is very special. Apparently Lucas thinks it's just genius. That's what Alice said, anyway. Quite believe it.'

'He's pretty amazing, Paul. He's coming round to see me later, matter of fact. I've, um – done another picture, Judy. You know – just a little thing.'

Judy clapped her hands together, once: her customary, always to be relied on (and to Jamie, wholly addictive) quite unfeigned delight.

'Oh God Jamie I'm so very *pleased* – I must come down and see it. Are you pleased? Are you thrilled? Do you love it?'

'It's . . . well – *yes*, I – it's all right, I think. Actually – when I say it's a *little* thing, well – it's not little at all. It's the same size as the last one, actually. Those socking great canvases are all I've got. But I mean it's little in the sense that, well – I'm not making any great claims for it, is all I mean. Oh yes and talking of Alice, you know – she brought over some more red paint for me the other evening – Tuesday, think it was. Love red, get through gallons – and she, er – she seemed to like it, you know. She said –'

'Poor Alice . . .' Judy wistfully interjected.

'Hm? Poor? Why do you say that, actually Judy? Why's she poor?'

'Oh I don't mean . . . I mean just in terms of her *painting*, you know? I mean I really do think that she's awfully good – I love my parrots, love my petunias . . . but she really doesn't get an awful lot of encouragement, does she? Never *sells*, or anything . . .'

'Ah well yes – funny you should say that, because that was her, you know – comment about my . . . what she said when she saw this new painting of mine. Wasn't quite finished then, actually – still on the floor, and everything – and she said Mmm, she said to me: I can really see this sort of thing *selling*. That's what she said.'

'Yes. Well that's kind of what I mean, really. On her mind.'

'Well it never crossed *mine*. You know – selling them, I mean. Although Paul said . . . well, you know he's got this thing called Theme's Schemes? Or he did have, anyway. Sorting out people's places, seems to be. Theme's Schemes: God, what a name. Anyway – he said he thought he could move a few. It's nice to know. I'd like to put some actual, you know – *money* into The Works. Be a bigger part, sort of thing. But I don't know if he's really into all that any more, Judy, tell you truth. Tell you what he *is* into, though: printing. And look . . . I haven't actually, you know, um – mentioned this to anyone, OK, because I said I wouldn't – but I'm telling *you*, Judy, all right?'

'How terribly *mysterious*, Jamie. Very well, then – tell me. What's the great dark secret?'

'Well, I wouldn't say it was . . . it's just, well – when he heard I'd got all of Lucas's presses chugging away, he became most awfully interested. Asked if I'd help him out.'

'Mm. And . . . ?'

'*And*. He came up a little while ago with all these blocks. Old style, you know. Etched and engraved. Very fine work.'

'Well *that* must have pleased you . . . ?'

'Did. In a way. As I say – fine work, lovely. But listen, Judy: one of them was a plate for a fifty-pound note. Twenty, too. And all sorts of documents, deed-type things . . .'

'Wait a minute – wait a minute! Are you telling me these were, what – forgery blocks? Counterfeit money? *Kidding* me . . . !'

Jamie was nodding, and then he was shaking his head; Judy was welcome to pick her way through the bones of either gesture or both and emerge with whatever sort of affirmation she needed, just so long as his sincerity and true intent were both coming over loud and clear.

'And I did – ran off one or two. Samples. Telling you, Judy – they were perfect. Absolutely perfect. Of course, the paper was all wrong, and those, you know – silver strip things weren't there . . . but, um – maybe rather worryingly, Judy – he says that's not a problem. He can get the paper. Get the strips.'

'Good Lord . . .' breathed Judy.

'Indeed,' said Jamie. 'And passports. Had all the pages for passports and special visas and things. Cheques. Cheques, he said – they're the easiest. Not so easy as credit cards. Any bloody fool – this is what he said to me, Judy: his very words. Credit cards, he said – any kid can bang out credit cards. Cash in hand – that's tricky. But here's what's *really* odd, Judy –'

Judy sniffed, but her eyes were bright with intrigue.

'Pretty odd already, I should have said. Wouldn't you?'

'Yup – tis. Tis. But listen, the really odd thing was, he said he'd doubt he'd ever, you know – use them again. Do it all again. But he knew I'd be interested, being a printer and everything – and I suppose he was pretty proud of his work, understandably. Because it really was, you know – very fine. Very fine.'

'So why do you think he . . . ? I mean – why won't he . . . ?'

'Well that's what *I* said. That's exactly the first thing I said. And all he did was, he sort of waved his hands around as if to say, you know – "this place". Here. The Works. I know what he means.

Well *you* do, obviously, Judy. It's here. It's odd. Makes you see things – differently. Head-on.'

Judy nodded. 'And sometimes – for the very first time. Well well. Dark horses. We're all that, I suppose. Who knows what secrets we all have sheltering? Well: another little nugget to tuck away. Oh yes and *talking* of secrets, Jamie – I am just dying to know: tell me. How did it all *go*, hm? Eventually. Has she been in touch again, Caroline? I must say I did find her . . . I mean I didn't really get to talk to her for very long, did I? But she was so very full of *anger*, Jamie. But maybe softening a bit towards the end? Don't know.'

'I *want* to tell you, Judy. Been bursting to. But there wasn't really anything to say at the time. Look, um – can we do the head rub thing now, do you think? It's just that I, um . . .'

'The craving?'

'Craving, yes. Just hit me. Down to one patch. Feel a bit . . .'

'Come over here then, Jamie. Let's see if we can ease away a little bit of that. And then when you're calm, you'll tell me, yes?'

'Mm,' agreed Jamie. 'Oh yes, Judy. Yes. Need to.'

Oh God I do: yes I do. Because OK look – I *think* I've got it all straight, fairly straight in my mind, now (all these changes! So many developments!), but marking it out and pacing myself with Judy close behind me (and ah! Oh yes! Those long and feathery fingers of hers at either temple, working their gentle magic) – this will help it seem more real: batten it down into place . . . make it . . . *crystallize* (a word I don't much use . . . ooh, ooh, my skull is soft, and my mind is easing . . . But I have heard it somewhere recently and . . . oh yes: the garland. Crystallized something, could be eucalyptus, but isn't necessarily . . .). I must, however, focus.

I had taken her around, Caroline. Showed her the place. That day she came. God – but it felt so very strange, you know. Impossible for me to quite get across to you, this one – even get close.

Because look – this is home to me, yes? We know that. This is The Works. So familiar, and so very loved. And by my side was my *wife*, for Christ's sake – so familiar too, then, and *yes* very loved, I'm fairly sure, whether she believes it or not (because once, it is true, neither of us did). But now this is what I told her. Said it outright, when we were both going down in the lift: I love you, I said. I'll tell you how she reacted, what she came out with, in just a short while, if that's all right. Because first I just have to try to convey this *strangeness* I was feeling, walking with someone so known to me in a place that was my home. It didn't, I suppose is what I'm saying, feel *right*, as I had hoped it would do. Didn't immediately gel. But it was only Caroline's resistance, I managed to convince myself, that was making it seem so. Because The Works, as I do not have to tell you – it's not anything to do with *resistance*, is it? Standing back, standing aloof. None of that, no. It's all about mutuality, yes? And the big embrace. Also time, I knew, was ticking away (we were already looking for Benny – a prelude, I was well aware, only to their leaving) and so maybe I rushed it a little bit, did I? When I told her outright. That I loved her.

We were outside, now (bright day it was – don't know if you remember), and she looked at me levelly.

'What, Jamie, you maybe mean, is that you've come to miss the status quo. I mean – *this*, this is now your, if you like, status quo, I suppose – yes, that's what it's become. Your raison d'être, it seems to be now. But there are these other bits, aren't there Jamie? That you want to slot back into place. Benny, most obviously. And, to a lesser extent, me. I'm the other one.'

'Caroline. You maybe didn't hear me. What I just said. I said –'

'I heard. I heard you. I heard what you said.'

'I *said* –!'

'Jamie. Leave it. I told you: I heard. But why did you never say it when we were still together? When we both didn't have so bloody far to *go*? Why, Jamie, when you had some *woman* – why was I always the one to suffer?'

I was thrown. I admit it. Wholly off balance. Completely reeling. Because of all the points I thought she might have raised now – my neglect of Benny, my rose-tinted optimism, all these (as she would see it) hippie dreams – I did not think for a moment that she would rake up something quite so raw, and jagged for us both. And of course of all the javelins she might have tossed at me, of all the reasons she might have mustered why she and Benny should not come and live with me again, here was the sharpest by far. Because I knew the answer to the question, you see: why it was she had to suffer. But it was shameful, this – so very shameful that it could never be voiced. Caroline's suffering had been a necessary and awful part of the – if you can even call it that – *plan*. If I was with a woman – and I did, quite regularly, go with one, yes, for very short periods, why I don't know. Yes I do. They were always pretty, which I rather like. Never beautiful, which I've never had (why I am in awe of Frankie, I suppose). So pretty, yes – and *there*, quite simply. It's not a bit like the old days any more, out there. You don't have to woo – sit there in a coma through endless and expensive, pointless dinners; line the pockets of Interflora – notice new hair and dresses, and comment appropriately. Not any more, you don't. They're just there. These women, vile women. Ranks of them: like cabs. And they get sick of the sight of you just around the time you are wishing to God you'd never ever set eyes on them . . . and so the dance continues. But. I couldn't bear that. That I just was given to picking and choosing because why not? I had to justify it, you see. To myself. So whenever I was in the midst of one of these half-baked, soft-centred and really rather horrible mutual trade-offs, my utter and savage cruelty towards Caroline became quite boundless. I would put on a freshly ironed shirt (a shirt, freshly ironed by Caroline, my wife, for me, Jamie, her husband, Christ's sake) and I would straight away perceive in it a flaw. A slight crease in the collar there, maybe; a loose button (and if there was no loose button, I'd bloody well loosen one). Then I would tear it off – and sometimes it would, quite literally, tear – and hurl it into the corner, cursing her roundly for being the worst wife ever there was. The meals she would present to me, I would ritually spurn; even the very good ones, the teasing aromas tweaking at my nostrils and spiking my appetite even as I scraped it all into the bin. I would discover dirt in far-off corners – locate some bad undercurrent in Benny's character, wholly attributable to her. I pushed her to the point of breaking (avoiding the hurt and bewilderment in her moist and anxious eyes, fearful that such a sight would wound me beyond tolerance) and then she would shriek at me to get out. Get *out*, then, you bastard, if I'm that bad a person! If living here is so very offensive to you – then get *out*, you sod – just get out and *leave* us! And Benny would cry. And I would get out. Find a woman. And tell her, the woman, how I was driven away by the wife who loathed me – driven away by her neglect of home and family. By a mother who could bring my son to tears. Because only if life at home were just, oh – so dreadful, unspeakable, worse than the very worst, could I justify leaving, and seeking something elsewhere. It was, at the very least, upside down. I make no attempt to understand further – and I was, as I say, shocked – so shocked that she should raise it now. You must understand – I have never said a word of any of this before. To anyone. Because how could they accept it, if everything about it perplexed me so? But maybe you, Judy – can understand it? Get from it some sort of sense? Maybe?

'Shhh . . .' went Judy. 'Go on. Go on.'

Well right then: I will. But I can't quite leave her alone yet, Caroline, with all that pain walled up inside her. Because I knew now it was – how terribly cold you felt at your very core, when the person, the one person whom you had no choice but to entrust

272

with not just now but forever, would turn on you. Because, you see, of my father. Who once . . . I have not thought of this for, oh – so many years. My mother had bought me a raincoat for school. Blue gabardine, with a belt and big buttons. My father, he surveyed its structure – explored its texture, as if he suspected a concealment of weapons or contraband. And then he read from the label: waterproof. Nonsense, you know, he said to me idly. You maybe don't believe that, Jamie – that a manufacturer can so brazenly label an item waterproof like this when patently, it is far from being any such thing. Then came the challenge – the dare I always dreaded: you don't *believe* me? he said. I neither did nor didn't – I didn't care: it was a raincoat. My mother had bought me a raincoat for school: why had this become another *thing*? Anyway. He urged me to put it on and step out with him, if I would be so good, to the garden for just a short while. And my mother said Why? What are you doing? The boy's tea's nearly ready – it's cold out there, and practically dark. *Rubbish*, he answered her, angrily: he's a *boy*, isn't he? Not a *baby*. Is he? My mother looked down. I put on the coat (too big – it was much too big) and I followed him into the garden. I stood there. I just stood there as he played the hose up and down and over me; my fingers were hard and blue, and my tears now were mingling with the splattering and ceaseless spray from the hose. When he was satisfied, he turned off the tap and approached me. Take it off, he said, and let's have a look then, shall we? It was a deadweight, that coat now – saturated and dripping, black and gleaming like a beetle's back, the quilted lining stained dark with heavy wetness. My blazer was sodden, as was my shirt beneath it. The knees of my trousers clung and burned, and rivulets of water were chasing each other the length of my spine. *There*, he said – what did I tell you, eh? Nonsense, as I said. People, Jamie, make false claims: learn and learn well. These days you can't, you know: you really

273

cannot trust a living soul. Now. Go in and get your tea, lad: else it'll be cold.

The sins of the father: they never ever leave you. Is it true, that, Judy? Was I with Caroline as bad as he with me?

'Shhh . . .' went Judy. 'Go on. Go on.'

Well right then: I will. But with Caroline, at that very moment, how could I do that exactly? Just go on? She had spiked me, hadn't she? And I stood before her, quite defenceless. So I said with a sigh. 'Lovely day . . .' And then I said:

'I don't know what to say.'

'Change, isn't it?' was Caroline's – surprisingly mild – comment on that. 'Coming from you. But it is, though. A lovely day. The way the sun's just glinting on the water, there . . .'

'I know. You wouldn't believe, would you, that the City's just . . . I mean, we're so absolutely central here, really, and yet it's just so . . . well: as you can see. Peaceful. Look, um, Caroline –'

'Don't rush me, Jamie. Just let me think, OK? Where do you suppose Benny might have got to?'

'Well – all sorts of places, really. And I'm not, Caroline. Don't mean to. Rush you. Could still be up with Dorothy. Dorothy's got a little girl, you know. Mary-Ann. Round about Benny's sort of age, I'd imagine. So. Could be there. With Tubby, maybe. Tubby does the cooking here, thank the Lord. Telling you, Caroline – he's just the best cook I've ever come across in the whole of my life. Um . . . I mean to say, *your* cooking was also very, um –'

'When you ate it.'

'When I, er – yes. As you say. When I didn't go mad, the way I did. And ate it. It was wonderful. But that's just the sort of thing I want you to know, you know, Caroline. I don't – not any more. Go mad. I'm different. Better. I *make* things. I mean to say it's not as if I've fallen victim to some ludicrous sort of weirdo *conversion*, or anything. It's not like that at all. It's more like, well – all the dead stuff, the old stuff, the bad stuff – it's like all that rubbish has been sort of swept away, dissolved ... just bloody got *rid* of, basically. And underneath were mighty good things. Buried. But –'

'Uh-huh. And I suppose Benny and me were –'

'No! No – that's just it. I knew if I said all that you'd immediately think that I meant ... *no*. No no. Some things are lacking. Well two things – just two things, really. You. And Benny.'

'Mm. And if we came here, Benny and me, then everything would be perfect ... ?'

Jamie squinted away from the glare of the piercing sun.

'Yes,' he said, quite simply. 'I truly believe it would. I honestly do.'

Caroline regarded him. 'Well,' she said. 'Well.'

And for a while they just sat there, gazing at the water.

'I'll tell you one thing, though,' said Caroline, then. 'It's very strange to be with you for this length of time and not see you constantly sucking on that endless succession of fags. Have you *really* given up, Jamie? It's amazing. Why don't you – have one now? Hm? It might make you feel better. Might make *me* feel better ...'

'I'm fine. Let's not talk about it. Let's talk about us, hm?'

'Don't you want to, then? Don't you want one?'

Jamie breathed out heavily, and looked away.

'*Yessss* ... !' he hissed out, in exasperation. 'I *do* want one. I want one passionately. That's the whole point. In my pocket, at this very moment, I'm clutching the bloody packet, aren't I? My thumb is rubbed raw from the wheel of my lighter. I want one. *Christ* I want one ... !'

'Well why don't you ... ? I mean, *one's* not going to kill you, is it? Not after the million before.'

Jamie tightened his mouth and looked quite wild. With an effort, he consciously tamed the twitchier of his features, and slowly settled down to some breathing again.

'No,' he whispered. 'No . . . I won't.'

Caroline's eyes were wide as she wagged her head slowly from side to side, as if beholding in a crib the marvellous sight of a quietened infant who could, in the light of appalling evidence, truly be the baby Jesus.

'Maybe you *have* changed,' she said. 'Maybe you *are* different . . .'

Jamie shrugged. 'I told you . . .' is all he said. And then: 'Oh look, Caroline – there he is! See? With Mary-Ann. Yes? Little girl I was telling you about. Dorothy's. Yes? Here they come. Seem to be getting on awfully well, don't they? Chattering away . . .'

'That's because,' smirked Caroline, 'they stroll hand in hand in the groves of Arcadia.'

And Jamie – who didn't know quite how to take that – on balance, left it.

'Hello *Benny* . . . !' he now enthused – maybe overdoing it, in the light of, oh – just everything, really (it was not just the sun that made us spotlit). 'Mary-Ann been showing you round, has she? Been showing him round then, have you, Mary-Ann? Good. Good. So what do you think then, Benny old mate? *Great*, isn't it?'

'Don't,' said Caroline, softly, '*tell* him what to think, Jamie . . .'

'Oh no but I *do*,' rushed Benny. 'Think it's great. *Is* great. Love it.'

'He liked the fudge best of all,' laughed Mary-Ann.

'Yeh!' agreed Benny. 'And the chocolate!'

'Ate masses,' smiled Mary-Ann. 'Utter pig.'

And Caroline was immediately charmed and even excited by the total ease of this silly exchange. A tension in Benny was being released – which *God*, he so much deserved, poor little man, after all we've been putting him through (and not just lately).

'I think, Jamie, I've shown him all the main bits. He says he loves everything. Didn't you, Benny? Say you loved everything. Except for old Stinky, of course.'

And as Mary-Ann and Benny convulsed themselves in a concentrated round of collusive and fizzed-out hysteria, Jamie laughed too – though he was conscious of not being even remotely in on the joke. (And look at Caroline: she's smiling. She's happy. She looks happier now than I've seen her since . . . well, since we *all* were, really: happy.)

'Who or what on *earth*,' Caroline wanted to know, 'is *Stinky*, for God's sake? Jamie? Someone *less* than perfect . . . ?'

Jamie widened his eyes and shook his head with energy.

'I honestly haven't a *clue* – first time I've ever heard the –'

'Oh you know *Stinky*, Jamie!' Mary-Ann protested. 'Though I think I might be the only person who actually *calls* him that. You know! Round the corner! The old – !'

'Oh God yes – I *see*,' saw Jamie. 'The tramp. God – he here again, is he? No but look, Caroline – he's really nothing at all to worry about. Just a tramp. Just sits there. Sometimes I pass him and he seems, well . . . *dead*, or something. Doesn't move.'

'Always talks to *me*,' said Mary-Ann, with a measure of pride. 'Says stuff like . . . Soon you'll be all grown up. Stuff like that. We gave him some fudge, didn't we Benny? Think he liked it.'

Benny nodded. 'Wicked fudge,' he said.

'But he's so totally *stinky*, you know?' laughed Mary-Ann. 'Actually – he's not, really. Sometimes you can smell, I don't know – a sort of perfume on him. But his face is so black and his clothes are just . . . totally *urrgh*, you know? I asked why he was always round here and he said Well why are you always round here and I said cos I love it and I live here and he said Well that's what I think too. He's maybe mad, I don't know. Quite like him, actually.'

'I liked him,' said Benny.

'He's harmless,' said Jamie. And then – more pointedly to Caroline: 'harmless. Really. Just a bit, you know – lost, I suppose. No crime in that.'

Caroline looked thoughtful. Looked quite thoughtful. And then she smiled at me – bit tightly, but a smile's a smile – and then she pretty much just gathered Benny up and in no time at all (didn't see – wasn't wholly aware of its happening) she was . . . they were gone. But I did – I did manage to ask her, ask her again. And I was, this time – this time I was rushing her. Had to know. See? Had to. So I asked her – I said to her, um – *Look*, Caroline, OK? Before you go, tell me – tell me you'll be back. Yes? With Benny. To stay. Yes?

Judy was stroking Jamie's hair, firmly and with even strokes.

'And? Did she? Answer you?'

Jamie turned in the chair – had to *see* Judy, now: behold her, and gauge her response.

'*Yes* . . .' breathed Jamie. 'She did. Answer me. She said yes. She would.'

'Oh *Jamie* . . . !' gasped Judy – and her eyes were glittering.

Jamie beamed. 'I know. And then I said Yes but when? Soon? Soon, Caroline, yes? Will it be? And do you know, do you know what she said to me, Judy?'

Judy nodded – and her eyes now, they were lost into creases of delight.

'*Yes*,' she said. 'Caroline said yes. *Soon.*'

Jamie exhaled, and slapped his knee.

'Yes . . .' he almost sighed. 'You're right. That's exactly what she said.'

And the two of them hugged, each taking turns in letting out a series of yelping noises (sometimes they overlapped).

'Well well!' laughed out Teddy, as he trundled in his empty trolley. '*Some* people are very happy about something! Is it because you've both learned your lines word-perfectly?'

Judy disengaged herself from a still panting Jamie and wheeled around to Teddy, and hugged him too.

'Oh better – better than that, Teddy. It's Caroline. Jamie's wife?

She's coming here to live, with their little boy. Isn't that wonderful?'

'Excellent,' approved Teddy. 'Too late to write them both parts, though . . .'

'Oh *Teddy*!' Judy mock-admonished him. 'You and your *play*. Can't you think of anything else?'

'Um . . . let me see now.' And Teddy narrowed his eyebrows into a great show of deep contemplation. '*Nope* . . . don't think so . . .'

'*You*,' laughed Judy, 'are *awful* . . .'

'The poster's all set up anyway, Teddy,' Jamie enthused (because yes – let's *all* be happy now with the things we love). 'Just needs one more screen, and then I can run off as many as we need. I'm doing it on the big press, you know, so it'll look absolutely stunning. Design's just great. Kimmy got one of her people to do it.'

'Oh that *is* good news,' said Teddy, very much impressed. 'Can't wait to see *that* . . . Um. Tell me, Judy, if you will – why are we knee-deep in *foliage* . . . ?'

'Hm?' checked Judy. 'Oh *this*. Oh yes – isn't it gorgeous? One of Paul's wonderful garlands. I was just telling Jamie – he's done loads of them, apparently. And *Jamie* – won't you, Jamie? Jamie will tell you exactly what it's *made* of. *Well*, Jamie . . . ? Waiting.'

'Oh God, Judy – I can't, um . . . oh well, um – *pine*, wasn't it? Glass bits, obviously . . . And the flowers are, um – *flowers*, of some sort. Oh yes and crystallized *pears* – that's right, isn't it?'

'Bravo. *Protea* flowers. Go on.'

'Christ. Right, um. Twigs. Branches. And those fat things there are, um . . .'

'Dogwood twigs. Cinnamon sticks. And . . . ?'

'Oh God yes – cinnamon sticks . . . and, er . . .'

'Those fat things, as you call them, are . . . ?'

Teddy coughed once, and then he spoke:

'Eucalyptus gumnuts,' he said. 'Are what those are.'

Judy just stared at him.

'Do you know, Teddy – in all the years we've been together, you have never, not once, ceased to amaze me. How on *earth* did you know that they were – ?'

'Eucalyptus gumnuts? Ooh – common knowledge, I would've supposed. Now then – chardonnay all round? Or maybe a drop of burgundy, conceivably?'

As Teddy was pouring, Jamie grasped the moment for a last and hurried word with Judy, in the corner.

'So, Judy – what do you think? Everything's good. Yes?'

'Everything *can* be, now – yes Jamie. You've stopped hating yourself. That's what's happened. You're no longer whipping you.'

'Is . . . that it? God – I don't know. All I *do* know is that we'll all be together again. Oh God how marvellous. And we'll talk – we'll talk. I mean, me and Caroline will talk, yes obviously – but we all will, all together. Because you have to, you know. It's important.'

Judy nodded. 'It is. It is. Oh *thank* you, Teddy. Mm – lovely and cold. Cheers, Jamie. Congratulations.'

Jamie sipped, and then he simpered. Looked at both Judy and Teddy, and just said Thanks. But it is, you know – important. Talking. Because if you didn't, well . . . you'd end up like the Hitlers.

CHAPTER EIGHT

'I always feel . . .' Mike was musing – glancing away towards the farthest picture rail, as if something up there might help him nail it down. 'I mean – this time of year, you know – right on the very verge of Christmas proper, as it were . . . I always feel – in two minds, really, is what I think I mean.'

John accepted the thick and dumpy Duralux tumbler from Mike's outstretched fingers, and happily settled down to being very good-humoured.

'Two minds, ay? Well – doesn't tell us an awful lot, Mike, does it really? Any clues? What's he rambling about, Oona? Any ideas?'

'Oh *God*,' laughed Oona. 'Don't ask *me*. Last to know. But what I *imagine* he means is . . . what's wrong, Frankie? Not like the drink? Bit strong for you is it, maybe?'

Frankie looked up, as if caught red-handed. She had been dipping in a fingernail (it was sort of pale greenish, the drink, but not really very, or anything) and rather carefully licking at that a bit, a frown of doubt already in place, and poised at the fringe of displeasure.

'It's not, um . . .' she ventured, 'exactly *bad*, or anything. It's just a bit . . . what *is* it, actually, Oona? Do you like it, Johnny? What exactly is it we're drinking here, Mike?'

'It *warms* you, certainly . . .' was John's guarded opinion (and he thought Yes yes – warms you: that should do it. Because I take her point, poor little Frankie – it decidedly errs on the side of filthy, this small drink I hold in my hand).

'Well it's actually a sort of gin punch thing,' said Mike, just a touch defensively. 'I quite like it. What do you think, Oona?'

'Oh!' said Frankie. 'Gin. Don't like gin. Could you get gin then, Mike? During the War? I thought they couldn't get it. Didn't you say it was rationed? Whatever "rationed" is. They weren't missing much, if you ask me. What else is in it? Have you not got any champagne? I could whizz up and get some, if you like – couldn't I Johnny? Got heaps upstairs.'

'Ah no well actually this *isn't* a wartime recipe at all. Surprise surprise. Predates all that by, ooh – hundred years, I expect. Comes up in *A Christmas Carol*, matter of fact. You know: Scrooge, and so on.'

Frankie blinked and looked at him.

'Dickens?' he tried. 'No? Well never mind. Anyway, what it basically is is, well – *gin*, obviously, and, um – an infusion of wild berries and, er – water, really. That's it. In a nutshell. What do you think, Oona?'

'I think,' smiled Oona, 'that it's just *wonderful* . . . news that Frankie can whizz upstairs and get us some champagne.'

'See!' laughed Frankie. 'I knew it wasn't just me! Oona doesn't like it either. And I bet Johnny hates it too – he's just too polite to say so. Sorry, Mike – don't mean to be rude. I'll go and get us some fizz then, shall I? Yes?'

'If you really don't like it,' Mike conceded, partly aggrieved, while knocking back his in a show of defiance (his next words as a result emerging rather croakily), 'well . . . then please don't drink it, Gin. John, I mean.'

'Maybe,' suggested John quite slowly, 'a glass of champagne might just be a little more in keeping with the season . . . ?'

'Oh God you're just *marvellous*, you know, you are, John,' cried Oona. 'Our gain is the Diplomatic Corps' loss. He *hates* it, Mike –

plain as a pikestaff. And the reason he hates it – you've just got to admit it, Mike my darling – is because it does rather tend strongly towards the direction of *vile*. Frankie – champagne: *now*. Sorry, darling: got to face facts.'

Frankie was already bumping her way through Mike and Oona's mass of ochre corridors and brown partitions.

'Well . . .' allowed Mike, collecting up the largely untouched glasses. 'It was only an experiment. *Lucas* drinks gin, after all . . .'

'Mm,' grunted John. 'Tanqueray and oolong. Bit different.'

Mike nodded. 'Suppose you're right. Oh anyway – no tragedy, is it? Like I said – it was only an *idea*. I mean that's what I was meaning, I suppose. You know – when I said I was in two minds. I mean, you know – what I mean is, we've all got so *much* here, haven't wc? We're all so terribly lucky. The way Frankie can just run upstairs for cold champagne – and later there's Tubby's nightly feast to look forward to. I mean it's *lovely*, of course it is –'

'Yes,' agreed Oona with alacrity. 'It bloody well is.'

'It *is*,' repeated Mike. 'I know it is. I just said it was. It's just that I can't help feeling that, you know – during the War . . .'

'Ah,' said John. 'Ah.'

'Yup – *you* get it, don't you, John? During the War – this time of year, you know, the housewife will have somehow – God knows how, but she will have squirrelled away maybe a tin of Spam or possibly a decent hunk of cheese, or something. Or maybe she'd done a spot of bartering with a smallholder and got hold of, I don't know – a chicken, or something – couple of eggs, maybe. And she'd be busy planning these pies and puddings and things – all cheap and filling, you see, but it was down to her to make it all really tasty, and plenty of it. Satsumas, if you were lucky, and a bit of coal in the stocking – a couple of sixpences in the pud, if you were really pushing the boat out . . . but the whole family *together*, you know? Well – the ones that weren't actually *fighting*, anyway.

283

At war. And just two precious days to enjoy it all. Home-made toys . . . and then back to work. Back to the big effort.'

'Well,' said Oona. 'I mean, yes – I know what you mean, of course I do, Mike. Well – we've *discussed* it, haven't we? But even that, you know – that's really a rather – well it's all a bit *rosy*, that view, isn't it really? I mean – there truly was *hardship* – absolute agonies. And we don't want that back, do we?'

'Well of course we don't,' Mike readily agreed. 'That's exactly what I mean. We've all gone soft. If anything even a *bit* bad happened to all of us here – I sometimes wonder, you know, if we'd be able to, well – *cope*, basically. I mean – even a *bit* bad. Never mind hunger and blackouts and bombings and all the rest of it. And sitting down to wonder on yet another Christmas Eve whether your husband, son, father – wondering whether you'd ever set eyes on them again. If they'd ever come back . . .'

'*Morbid*, Mike . . .' cautioned Oona.

'Well it is – I know it is. Sorry, and all that. But I do, you know, get just a teeny bit worried, sometimes. I suppose all I'm doing is thanking my lucky stars – I do that every day, if I'm honest – but at the same time wondering what on earth we'd do if suddenly they all winked out and the sky went black. Two minds, you see. In two minds. Which is the only reason I cobbled together this perfectly dreadful drink – yes all right, Oona: I *know* it was dreadful. Sorry, John. Just thought I'd, you know – try it . . .'

And then Frankie was bustling back in (and this cheered up John to a remarkable and evident extent, because look: look, will you, at her perfect skin and her high high cheekbones and that glossy and tumbling mass of hair and those huge, quite huge and glittering eyes of hers. And that's before you even get down to the body – which is, in more ways than one could possibly imagine, altogether extraordinary).

'Look listen: I didn't know which ones to bring, OK?' she was gasping out, as she set down on the table the three green and glistening bottles. 'I don't know why you have all those passages and winding bits, Mike, I really don't. I always bash into something or other and then there's that old man always glaring down at me from the picture. That Churchill man. Anyway – look: I got Cristal and Bollinger and some Asti stuff. I like that one the best, really, Asti. The others aren't sweet enough, I think.'

Mike was bringing fresh glasses (still thick tumblers though, Frankie was crushed to observe).

'You see?' he said – maybe even to himself. 'So much. So much. There's just so *much* . . .'

'Mike,' said John, quite mildly. 'Just enjoy it. It's Christmas.'

'Mm,' agreed Oona. 'It damn well is. Cheers, everybody. Cheers.'

And Mike was nodding with vigour.

'You're right. You're all of you absolutely right. Sorry, everyone – *sorry*. Cheers, then! Gosh, John – how do you always manage to open those bottles so that there's never any, you know – pop and mess, and everything? Mm. Delicious. Yes . . . a decided improvement, I must say.'

'Well,' said John. 'Practice, I think. Done a fair few in my lifetime. Mm. Bollinger's my favourite. Toasty. Cheers, then, all. Everybody happy?'

There were clinkings and sippings and smiles all round: everybody certainly *seemed* to be, anyway: happy. Happiness appeared to have emerged triumphant (which, as just any among them would have eagerly assured you, is at this time of year – along with love – all you need).

'Ow!' protested Benny, as Mary-Ann yet again tightened the string into a rigid little knot around the whitened tip of his index finger. 'Ow ow! My *finger*, Mary-Ann – you're – ow! *Ow*, OK?'

'Well why don't you *move* it, silly? I told you – you only have to keep your finger down on it while I'm bringing the ribbon stuff round again and tying it into a *bow*.'

Benny had retrieved his finger and he sucked it for form's sake, as he eyed her.

'I think you're doing it on purpose,' he said. 'And anyway – how many more of these package things are you going to wrap up? We've done about a million already.' And then he was newly aggrieved: 'You *must*. You *must*, Mary-Ann, be doing it on purpose, you know, because all you have to say is OK, Benny – move your finger out *now*! That's all you've got to say, isn't it Mary-Ann? But you don't. You don't. You suddenly get quicker and you tighten the knot and you just *know* my finger's still in there and –'

'Oh don't be such a *baby*, Benny. Honestly. Look – there's not many more. I know it seems a lot, but you've got to get something for everyone, haven't you? That's a kind of rule here, I suppose – but it's not a *rule* rule, if you know what I mean. Everyone totally *wants* to, you know? And everything.'

'Still seems an awful lot,' muttered Benny.

'Oh and I suppose you don't *want* any Christmas presents, is that it Benny? Everyone gets loads of presents but you just *so* don't mind . . .'

'No no. I didn't mean that. I mean, yeh – *do* want presents. Course. Love getting presents, don't you? Don't actually know what Mum and Dad are getting me. Haven't said, or anything. Do you know, Mary-Ann? What your Mum's getting you? Do you get something different from your Dad? Do you ever actually *see* your Dad, Mary-Ann? Will he be coming? What's he like, your Dad?'

'Got any more questions? Have you? I mean – that's about ten trillion questions you've just asked me, Benny. Like to add on a few million more? Yeah . . . I do sometimes see my Dad. It's a bit of a business. Mum won't come, or anything. She says she's feeling much better about, you know – *it*, and everything, but she couldn't bear now to actually see him. She calls it all "it". So what happens is, John drives me down to a restaurant, or something, and I have lunch with my Dad and we talk a bit – well, *he* does, anyway. Tries to get me to tell him about this place, mostly, but I don't. I mean it's funny – do you get like this, Benny? When you're not here, there doesn't really seem to be anything you *can* say about the place, somehow. Plus . . . it doesn't seem right. Even to my Dad. Anyway. Doesn't happen often, or anything. Me meeting Dad. He gives me stuff. Usually stuff I got sick of last year. He's a bit behind. And then John turns up and drives me back. But no – not seeing him at Christmas, if that's what you mean. Mum says if she saw him at Christmas, she'd just die. She wouldn't really, of course. That's just Mum. But it would be so totally wrong, I think, for anyone to be here at Christmas who wasn't, you know – a part of it. One of us. Like you are, Benny. You're one of us now, aren't you? Pleased you are. Are you pleased, Benny? Are you happy you came?'

'Yes, I – yes I am, Mary-Ann. You know I am. Like it here – love it. And I. Like you. Like you lots.'

Benny looked down, and Mary-Ann stayed silent for a beat before reaching behind her for more red and gold spangled holograph paper and another roll of satin ribbon.

'Better get started on the next one,' she said quietly. 'And don't forget to move your finger out this time.'

'Well I will if you tell me *when*, won't I? But you never *do* . . .'

'And what about *your* Mum and Dad then, Benny? Are they – ? I mean I know *Jamie's* settled in, and everything – but what about your Mum? Are you all . . . ? I mean is it all . . . ?'

'Yeh . . . it's all pretty OK, I think. I mean it's still a bit weird, and everything. The way they go on. Not as weird as it was at the very beginning, though – that was just so *totally* weird, you know? Being nice to each other, and everything . . .'

Yes, thought Benny – had been: really freaky. I mean – pretty odd for us all to be together and in the same sort of space in the first place, really . . . but it was when I heard Dad whispering all this stuff to Mum that I thought yeah, this is really so totally weird. And why do they bother doing that, parents? Whispering like that. I mean why do they think their children don't have ears, or anything? It's like when you're a little kid and they spell stuff out to each other – you know: L.A.T.E.R., and things like that. Mum and your teacher, they spent the whole term making you learn the alphabet, and then they spell stuff out so you won't understand. I sometimes think grown-ups are really stupid. I mean – they *can't* be, I suppose. Really. Not all of them, anyway. But they seem it, pretty often. Anyway – my Dad, right? Whispering to Mum:

'Just . . . make it *natural*, all right Caroline? I mean – oh God don't start interrupting me *now* – he'll be back in a minute and –'

'But it *isn't*, is it Jamie? Whatever this is, it can't by any stretch be said to be *natural*. Can it?'

'Well that's just what I – ! I mean I *know* that – know that, don't I? Bound to be strange, first few days. I'm just saying that if he believes that *you're*, you know – completely relaxed, and everything, well . . . it'll maybe help him, won't it? Ease in.'

'Well obviously I don't intend to be *obstructive* in any way, Jamie –'

'*Shhh*! Shhh! He'll *hear* . . . !'

'Oh don't be so silly – he can't hear us. He's miles away. Now look – like I say, Jamie – obviously I want this to work or I wouldn't be here in the first place, but –'

'You're getting louder! Every word you say, you're actually getting louder!'

'Oh *shush*, Jamie can't you? It's you who's making all the noise. What I just want you to understand is that this is just as much of an upheaval, a leap into the – you know, unknown, sort of thing . . . it's just as new for me as it is for Benny, is all I'm saying, Jamie . . .'

'Well I *know* that . . . of course I know that, but –'

'*So* . . . !'

'Don't shout! Don't shout!'

'Oh shut up and *listen* to me, Jamie! Not shouting, am I? This isn't shouting. I just need you to understand that although I'm not intending to be in any way negative about any of this, I've got to feel good in myself, OK, before I can, you know – be sort of giving anything much in Benny's direction. Right? And anyway look – you're his father. Aren't you? That's why we're here, isn't it? So *you* make him feel secure and loved and easy and all the rest of it and just leave me alone to fend for myself as per bloody *usual*, Christ Almighty Jamie! *Now*! *Now* I am shouting: *this* is shouting!'

And Benny had made himself apparent round about then and said quite coolly Hey you two: what's all the shouting about? And Jamie had groaned and started hissing to Caroline wholly audibly Oh *God*, oh *God*: you see? You *see*? I *told* you, didn't I . . . ? And then, very visibly bucking up and pulling all sorts of parts of himself back together again, he turned on to Benny the full and mighty force of his huge positivity and boundless bonhomie:

'We weren't *shouting*, Benny – no no, not a bit. It's – were we, Caroline? Not shouting. No no. It's – the acoustics here. Very odd. You'll get used to them. Merest sound – just ricochets all over the place. So. Come and talk to me, mate. Laid out all your stuff? Bed nice and comfy? Everything OK?'

Benny flopped down on to the sofa, next to Jamie.

'When do we get to meet Lucas?' he said.

'Ah . . .' was all that Jamie could muster, just for now (because I didn't actually see that one coming, if I'm honest; of all the things he might have asked, young Benny, I wasn't at all ready for that one. Which was stupid of me, really, wasn't it? Because look – he senses, Benny, that Lucas is the pivot here, doesn't he? And I expect he's been told as much too by Mary-Ann, Judy – oh just everyone, really. So it's natural, isn't it? To want to go straight to the heart of the thing).

'I don't think,' said Caroline, 'that Lucas is at all eager to meet *me*, anyway . . .'

'Oh no!' protested Jamie. 'Why do you say that, Caroline? Of *course* he is – both of you, eager to meet both of you. Course he is. Why do you say that, Caroline?'

'I say that, Jamie, because he has made no effort whatever to do so, has he? And when we went up, Benny and me, to say hello, sort of thing, Alice just said to us . . . what did she say to us, Benny?'

'She said,' supplied Benny, 'that we couldn't because this was one of his unavailable times.'

'Ah yes . . .' muttered Jamie. 'He has those. You should have asked me. I could have told you when. Well look – we'll all see him at dinner, won't we? He always comes to dinner, Lucas. Never misses. We'll see him then. Now then, Caroline. Benny. Can I maybe, um – get you both something? Drink of some sort, maybe? Nuts? Think I've got some nuts round about here somewhere . . . cashews, fairly sure . . .'

'Yes! Oh *yes*!' was Caroline's near-crazed reaction to Jamie's mild suggestion – her lit-up face beaming its rays on to Jamie and then on to Benny, each of them in turn, and then back again – to and fro, for quite some time. I am eager, here, is how she was thinking, to project to them both my determined attitude and also a quite irrepressible optimism. 'A drink – glass of wine. Yes! Would be lovely.'

'Excellent . . .' said Jamie, when he had done with flinching (I mean Christ: did you see her just then? Look at her face? Frightened the bloody life out of me, I can tell you. Seemed damned near murderous). 'And nuts? Few nuts for you, maybe . . . ?'

'Mm. *Yes!*' cried our Caroline with zesty and quite undimmed enthusiasm. 'Nuts. Lovely! What about you, Benny? Orange, or something?'

'Yeh,' nodded Benny. 'Great.' (I reckon, he thought, it must be Mum's bad time of the month, or something: she's weird and loud, like she gets.)

'Good good,' approved Jamie. 'And, um – *nuts*, Benny, possibly? Think you could maybe go a nut or two? With the orange? Yes? *Marvellous . . .*'

Jamie returned with two glasses of Teddy's chardonnay and a beer mug full of orange juice, two striped straws bobbing at its rim.

'Can't, um – can't actually seem to be able to lay my hands on the nuts at the moment, I'm afraid. I mean – I know they're around here *somewhere . . .*'

'Cheers, Jamie,' interrupted Caroline, quite swiftly (I'd better, she thought – I'd better stop him now. Because it's just this sort of thing – it's when he goes on like this, quite frankly, that it drives me maddest of all. And that's just not on the menu, is it? At this special time. No – it isn't. So best say Cheers: and then start drinking).

'Oh yes *absolutely*,' Jamie was going – swinging his glass around really quite wildly, but not spilling too much, considering. 'Here's to happiness, yes? Happy happy *happy* – yes? To *us . . .*'

So yes, Benny now was reflecting: at the beginning – totally weird. But it was way better now. Yes. In fact, I think it's actually, yeah – pretty good. They're not pretending quite so much, Mum and Dad. They seem – they actually do seem, well: *happy*. Like Dad said. Which is great. Because I am too.

'*Ow!*' he went. 'Ow ow *ow*, OK, Mary-Ann! You did it again! You did it on purpose! My *finger* . . . !'

And then both of them turned at the sound of Dorothy's voice, as she came through the door.

'What's wrong with your finger, Benny? Here, Kimmy, here – let me help you with all that . . .'

'My *guard* . . . !' Kimmy was going, as she manhandled around the door jamb a carton in danger of splitting. 'I mean, like – my *guard*, you know? Like, if they're gonna deliver, they don't just dump stuff outside, right? What's with these guys? What am I, all of a sudden? Schwarzenegger?'

Dorothy half took the box from Kimmy, and they both edged crab-like in with it – Benny now hovering at the fringes of the action, both hands half-heartedly extended into a weakish demonstration of willingness: he was as ready as anyone to rally round and help, here, though really quite unaware as to how precisely he could sensibly go about it, and at the same time reluctant to actually lay a finger on this big brown box (now being lowered, oh good, to the ground by Kimmy) because it did actually look to be extremely heavy and if he tipped it sideways, or something, and caused any one of them to lose their grip or balance and the whole thing toppled and hit the ground corner first and then tore open and maybe even shattered an idling toe . . . well then he didn't actually need to shoulder even a part of the blame that would surely be coming.

Kimmy now threw herself into a chair, fanning her face with her fingers and rolling her eyes as if dazed by a punch.

'Jeez. Drink, Mary-Ann – yeah? Be a sweetie. And one for your Mom. I get my wind back, I'm gonna call 'em. What kinda delivery service they call it anyhow? Just, like, dumping it anyplace. Hey, Doe – talking delivery, did Tubs tell you bout how he was checking out this new, like, *butcher*? Couple weeks back?'

Dorothy sat down next to her, and hugged a cushion.

'Just Coke for me, Mary-Ann. Goodness – look at all the *presents* you've wrapped! And you've been helping, have you Benny? What perfect children we have here.'

'Hey Doe? Hallooo . . . ? Earth calling Planet, like – Zog, you know? You hear what I say?'

'Sorry, Kimmy – what? Something about Tubby, was it?'

'Right. This new butcher, kay? Listen up, kids – this'll break you up. He goes in, right? Kinda wholesaler, I guess. And there's, like, this real big black guy? And Tubs, he says to the black guy . . . hey, I can't, like, do Tubs' cockney accent, OK? So you have to imagine. So he says, Hey mate, or whatever. Then he goes: do you deliver? And the black guy, he grins at Tubs real broad, you know? And he comes back Sure, man – we do deliver. We also do de kidneys, de brains and de tripe: we do de lot! *Crazy*, huh?'

'Oh *Kimmy*,' laughed Dorothy. 'You made it up!'

'I thought that was really *good*,' said Benny, very eagerly – because he had, he really had got it (first time) and he thought it was really really funny and was already trying to remember it word for word so he could tell all these people, right? Next term at school.

'I did *not* make it up! Ask Tubs!' roared Kimmy. 'Ah – Mary-Ann. My little sweetheart: drinkies. You didn't drown it, did you? You go ask Tubs, little miss Dorothy, you don't believe me. Could be *he* made it up . . . but I look at him, and I kinda don't think so.'

'What's in it?' asked Mary-Ann. 'Look, Mum – I've just got Alice's scarves to wrap up and then that's the lot, I'm fairly sure. Don't *think* I've forgotten anything . . .'

'Good girl,' Dorothy approved, sipping her Coke. 'What's in *what*, angel? What are you talking about?'

'Hm? Oh – I was asking Kimmy. The box. What's in the box?'

'Oh yeh,' said Kimmy. 'The box, right. Well it's paint is all it is, honey. Weighs like a *car*, but all it is is paint. This special stuff I got for the tit pictures, yeh? Comes off real easy. So all these gals I get to do it, they don't gotta spend the rest of their days on earth with green and blue titties, yeh? We don't wanna go screwing with their sex lives.'

'Oh yes I see,' said Mary-Ann, quite seriously. And then, out of consideration, she turned and began to explain it all to Benny. 'You see, Benny, Kimmy is an artist, as you know, but after Christmas she's going to do something new. Different from her usual. She's going to get all these girls, all right? And –'

'Um . . .' interjected Dorothy. 'I'm not actually sure Benny will be – *interested*, if you know what I mean, Mary-Ann. Yes? It maybe isn't the time to, um . . . ?'

'Oh I *am*,' protested Benny. 'Am interested. Tell me, Mary-Ann.'

'OK. Well you know *breasts*, right? On a woman? Tits, yes?'

Benny was two things: paralysed and mauve. Also now sweating: that's three.

'Er . . . well I, um . . . God . . .'

'Yes well you *do* know, obviously. Well Kimmy's going to get all these girls with really big tits and then she's going to slap all this paint all over them, see? Right, Kimmy?'

'Pretty much,' agreed Kimmy. 'Easy on the nipples . . .'

'Right. And then she . . . are you OK, Benny? What's wrong?'

'Nothing. Got to go, that's all . . . told my Mum I'd . . .'

'Mary-Ann,' chided Dorothy. 'I think you're *embarrassing* Benny, aren't you? Are you *embarrassed*, Benny?'

Benny was two things: trembling and practically liquescent. Also bit sickish: that's three. A non-committal shrug was all he felt up to.

'*And* . . .' continued Mary-Ann, fairly huffily (why does Mum just keep on interrupting?), 'she smears the gooey tits all over a canvas and, um – that's it basically, isn't it Kimmy?'

'That's it *totally*, honey,' laughed Kimmy. 'I never been one of those guys who says you should, like, you know – *suffer* for your art. Anyways – that's all New Year. Right now we got the holidays to get down. You all looking forward? Yeh? We gonna have one helluva time, or what?'

And Mary-Ann, just then for the first time, she got the sparkle – felt the fizz of excitement ripple right through her: it's *Christmas*. It really is *Christmas*. God – I'm so totally excited now . . . !

'Yes!' she gasped out. 'Oh yes! This'll be the best. You'll see, Benny – this is going to be just the best Christmas ever. For all of us. Just *totally*.'

I hope it is, thought Jamie: oh God I do – I really do hope it is, for . . . well, I was going to say for, you know – Benny's sake, yes – but it's for all of us, really. Isn't it? Caroline. Myself. Of *course* Benny (goes without saying). But I realize now that you can't just say Oh look, I don't care about me – what sort of Christmas *I* have – I'll just watch the box and drink and fall asleep. And the wife, well – if I bung her a suitably and tear-makingly expensive present (or, failing that, just money) that should buy me at least some peace, if not good will. Because they *sense* it, children, you see – well of course they do. I mean, God – *I* should know that, shouldn't I? Because of my father. I should know that better than anyone, how deeply children feel, and how they brood, and so on. And yet it's funny: although of course one *does* know that – intellectually as well as instinctively (well look – it's just a *fact*) it's still so easy to forget it completely. Or appear to. To convince oneself that because the poor kid's got this year's most fashionable and sell-out toy, he'll have no time to notice, will he, the pent-up resentment simmering in the wings – the stamping and clattering in the hell-hot steamed-up kitchen, the air of tension densely overladen by a much-dreaded and now here to stay thick mantle of disappointment, the brittle bits of another fragmented Christmas ground underfoot like shards of bauble into the carpet's pile.

Like last year. When I wince to tell you that my present to Caroline was an iron. Steam iron. And the reason? The reason I bought the iron is that a week or so earlier I had said to her in passing, oh God look: curse my luck. Got a meeting just off Oxford Street – can you imagine? This time of year. Still. While I'm there – may as well kill two birds, and all the rest of it, yes? So, um, Caroline – is there anything you, er . . . ? I mean – Christmas, you know. Sort of present thing. Anything you particularly . . . ? And she had slammed down hard whatever it was she had been holding, doing, reading, mending – don't know. And said Iron. Iron, she said. And I came back with What – iron, as in Morphy Richards type iron, you mean? Iron for ironing clothes, do you mean? Well, said Caroline (sharp as lemon) – I don't play golf, do I Jamie? So I wasn't meaning a *club*. A club, I feel Jamie, would not be the right thing to get me because I might, mightn't I? I just might be tempted to wrap it round someone's bloody *head*, mightn't I? Hm? And what other possibilities are there, Jamie? And I said Yes OK, mm, Caroline: got your point – an iron, then. And she went (cold as frost) Oh well *done*, Jamie – well *done*. Not a Steptoe cart piled high with scrap *metal*, no no no – but an iron. An ordinary iron. So that I may continue to ensure that all my husband's linen has a knife-edge bloody *crease* in it.

Dear oh dear: you know how she used to be – could have kept it up for hours. Anyway (and it's extraordinary that I used to think like this, but I did, I did – and God, we're only talking last *year*, for heaven's sake) – all in all, I actually figured I'd got something of a result, here: I now knew what she wanted for Christmas. So I had the meeting, whatever meeting it was, and

then (rather nobly, I thought) I braved the crowds in Debenhams
– which was, in truth, pretty empty, really, but anyway – and
bought an iron of some sort which, the woman there assured me,
was chock-full of all the bits and bobs which apparently you really
do want in an iron. And I thought Right, then: that's that. And on
Christmas Day I was going Well *no*, Caroline – of *course* I didn't:
what would be the point? Hm? I mean to say what's the point of
wrapping up an iron and putting a bow on it and everything
when we all know exactly what it is? It's an *iron*, isn't it? It's what
you asked for – what you wanted. So what's the point of wrapping it up? Hey? Why are you looking at me like that, Caroline?
Put the iron down now, Caroline – just put it down, OK? And go
and see how the sprouts are doing.

Well. You think they don't? Kids? Pick up on all that sort of
thing? Course they do. You know they do. But they're very good
at keeping their heads down – literally, very often, as if holding
their futures safe from flares and tracer bullets – and so you
delude yourself into believing that all the hissed-out asides and
pregnant glares and endless silences have all passed them by. But
no. It's there, and it builds. Year on year, it builds. And this year, I
know all this. This year I have bought the most wonderful presents for everyone. Took ages over it. Days. And yes, you might
well ask just where the money came from, and I don't at all mind
telling you: John. Yes, John. Amazing man. Came up to see me
one morning, and somehow he worked the conversation around
to the expense of the time of year, and all the rest of it – but for
him it was not that that was the problem, no no, but his total lack
of imagination. Did I see? Not as far as *Frankie* was concerned, of
course: she was easy – she directed him. And naturally she was
not averse to the odd little extra – trinkets, say, from Tiffany or
Cartier. But as to everyone else, well – totally out of touch, quite
frankly, old man: too damn old. So in the light of this, Jamie dear
chap, you wouldn't, would you, be *too* insulted if I were just to

give you this envelope here? Really would be most awfully grateful if you wouldn't hold my total inability to *project* . . . terribly happy if you wouldn't hold it against me. And after he'd gone – when I'd opened the envelope and seen how much money there was there – I ran up to Judy to ask her if he'd made some sort of a mistake, or something, and should I maybe return it to him? And she said Oh no: that's just John. He always divines which of us are concerned about not being able to treat the rest. And then he steps in, discreetly. Wonderful, isn't it? And all I could do was agree.

So this year, all is good. I've got five things for Caroline – a sort of silky two-piece cardigan and whatever the bit that goes under the cardigan is called, and a rather splendid black fur hat (I assume it's fake, but it looks damn real, believe me) and a charm bracelet with a star on it (I thought that each Christmas – maybe birthdays – I could add a charm: make it a tradition) and a huge box of violet creams, which are very sickly chocolates that for some reason or other she loves to eat. Oh yes – and a big leather diary. *And* I've wrapped them all, yes I have – and every one will be a surprise. Telling you, though – I do: I think of that iron, and I *cringe*. And Benny, well – it would be quicker to tell you what I *haven't* got him, quite frankly. A bit of everything from books to bleeping things with batteries (bought a bumper pack of twenty-four, but you only actually pay for sixteen of them, which seems very good) – by way of a rather smart tracksuit and a watch and his very first mobile phone . . . which may, actually, be a rather silly thing, in the circumstances, but the man in the shop said that the actual, you know – phoning was quite secondary to all the other things it did, like texting. Not quite sure what that is. Anyway – I'm sure he'll love it. Because I really do want this to be – not just the best Christmas for Benny (because let's face it, there's not much of an act to follow) but a Christmas that will in some way make up for not just all the others, but all the times too when he was feeling bad and doing his own sweet best not to show it – and there was I, choosing to be duped and feeling easy in my grown-up certainty that what he felt was nothing at all. No more. The time for tricks is over.

I was going to stop there. That was going to be it, for now. Because I've said all I mean to, really. But it's just . . . my *father*, isn't it? Mentioned him very briefly, just a short while back – and I felt pleased, quite proud of myself, that I didn't enlarge. Because why should he, frankly? Always come back to spoil things. Anyway, look – I'll just get this last little niggle out into the air – flush it away from my system, and then we can all settle down to enjoying our Christmases. Because tonight, you know – did I mention this? I don't think I did, did I? I can't imagine how I didn't. Because tonight's the big night – the night we've all been waiting for. Christmas Eve. Yes truly. The play. The exchanging of presents. And the dinner! Tubby's been working away at all sorts of things in secret, Judy was telling me. He's saved the biggest guns for tomorrow, of course (when I expect we'll get the works), but apparently tonight too is destined to be very special indeed. And Teddy – he's pulled out all his very best wine; he's eager, he says, for everyone's views on the claret in particular, because this time he's slightly upped the proportion of cabernet, I think he said. But of course it's mainly the play that's on his mind. God – he's put so much into it. Do so hope it all goes well. Paul's created the most wonderful set. And Judy's done most of the costumes – though John went and hired a few, the more extravagant. It's odd, really, this play, if only for the reason that the audience is outnumbered by the cast by about seven to one. Because it's just for Lucas, you know, this play. Lucas will sit with Alice beside him (the king with his honorary queen, if you like) and we'll all be putting on a sort of a Royal Command Performance. Extraordinary. But then, everything is now, isn't it? Everything is.

So. That's all to come (and God – just can't *wait* to see Benny's face! And Caroline's: Caroline's too). But first, just this one more childhood memory (get it out of the way). At Christmas, my mother will have somehow managed to save from whatever my father got away with giving her, and she would have wrapped up for me a pair of shoes for school, maybe (each of them filled with fruit and sweets, to lessen the blow), or possibly a set of books she considered improving. Here – this is fond: with the shoes, I remember her smiling with love and saying to me Oh my *goodness*, Jamie – what do you think you're doing, look? You've got them on the wrong feet! And God how she laughed when I looked up at her, genuinely perplexed, and started to cry – because I *can't* – I *can't* have them on the wrong feet because look, Mummy, look: they're the only feet I've *got*! And my father, even he, I think, nearly smiled. Anyway. Sometimes there was a biggish toy – a fort, I remember one time. Which I loved. My father had made it clear to me (and he had been very stern) that this was to be my present for this Christmas *and* next, this arrangement to take in too my intervening birthday. And he kept to his word. But I did love that fort, with the little drawbridge on chains. Didn't have any soldiers, so I had to use spacemen instead. I later found out that the fort had actually been built by old Mister Dimmock from just next door but one (I think by trade he was a pattern maker, or something, whatever a pattern maker was) and that my father had promised him in exchange a slap-up meal at the local pub, accompanied by as much as he could drink. Old Mister Dimmock had laughingly confided in me, oh – years and years later (when I was clearing out my father's stuff after the final stroke that did for him, my mother having passed away as a result of heart failure brought on, I am sure, by the stress and pain and sheer horse work of coping with him, after the first) . . . yes, anyway, old Mister Dimmock had his arm across my shoulder and he said to me I'm still waiting, you know – still waiting for the slap-up meal, never mind as much as I can drink! I was ashamed, and offered him money – which I saw at once had offended him. He said to me God, Jamie – I was only joking: Christ. I wish I hadn't offered him money. Benny didn't take to it, the fort; and Caroline, later, she gave it away.

Anyway. One of the first Christmases I can remember, my father surprised both my mother and me by emerging from the gloom of his study with a wrapped-up globe-shaped thing, football size. He presented it to me. I eagerly tore off the wrapping (it had holly and robins on it) and then I ripped away the paper under that (the *Daily Express*). I soon knew that here was no football – and as more and more crumpled sheets of newspaper fell away from the kernel of the thing (my hands were smudged and inky) even a cricket ball was looking extremely unlikely. I was breathless – caught between laughter and fear, not at all sure how I was meant to be behaving. The parcel became smaller and smaller until finally I could feel at its centre something hard, something I could tear towards. It was a whistle. A heavy, chromed policeman's whistle – which I *think* I loved (I still can't decide). My mother seemed relieved, if a little uncertain. 'Let us hope,' my father said, 'you never need to blow it.' And thereby, he had created a tradition. The next Christmas after that – when I had done with admiring my predictable Start-Rites and was sated on satsumas – my father would bear in triumph his ball-shaped trussed-up present. I ripped it apart. I now knew it would be nothing large, so I beavered away to the core. And this year, at its centre, lay nothing. Nothing at all. The frittered paper gave way to a void. My mother looked at him, and so did I. It was a lesson, he said: never expect the expected. I said nothing. The following year, my mother and I looked very solemn indeed as my father presented me with the paper ball. This year what I expected was nothing. And I was not wrong. And every year after, without exception, the ball was empty. Ah *yes*, he cried in sheer delight, my father – empty *again*: but who knows what the next will bring? Exciting, he said: isn't it?

Well. That was then. But look at us now: just look at us. All that is no more. The time for tricks is over.

'People starting to come down now, Pauly,' cautioned Tubby – his eyes still darting around from saucepan to silver dome, from grill to gently warming skillet. 'Don't you wanna go sort out your doings, or what?'

'All sorted, ain't it Tubs? It's you what wants looking to your wossnames, mate. All of us depending on your famous Christmas Eve nosh-up, ain't we? Ay? Don't want no cock-ups.'

But Tubby (and bleeding hell – you wanna see him, you really do, no straight – I ain't kidding you: just watch him go, son – all decked out in these real kosher chef's whites, he is – great tall hat like a factory chimney . . .). But Tubby (and across his left tit, look – see what it says? In all, like, red and swirly writing? 'Tubby' is how it goes: 'Master Chef'. All right, ain't it? Had it done for him, didn't I? Proper catering place, down Soho: seven sets). But Tubby (OK – I got to it now) – he's only belting off down the other end of the bleeding kitchen, ain't he? What's he up to, silly old sod. Oh yeh – it's Biff, ain't it? What it is – Tubs has gone off to give old Biff a right old ear-bend on account of . . . oh Gaw blimey, he's only giving him a slap across his wrist, look. It's times like this you want one of them video wossnames about your person. Posterity, and that.

'Here!' protested Biff – withdrawing his hand and shaking it a bit – and his face, look: it's well aggrieved. 'What's your game, Tubby?'

'*My* game!' hooted back Tubby. '*My* bleeding game! Oh yeh – that's well choice, ain't it Biff, ay? Coming from you. I laid out all them canapés nice and proper, ain't I? And I don't want your greasy great mitts all over them, OK? You gone and ate one, entcha? You only bleeding gone and *ate* one . . . !'

'Well don't go getting all in a twist, son!' laughed Paul. 'I mean – scuse me if I got this all wrong down the years, but canapés – they're like meant for eating, yes no?'

'Yeh but I got them all *symmetric*,' continued Tubby, unabated. 'For like when I bung them on the table. Have to rearrange all the prawny ones, now . . .'

Biff just wagged his head in wonder.

'Bleeding hell . . . he's just like bleeding Delia, this one.'

'Oh yeh?' Tubby rounded. 'And what bout you, then? Ay? You was polishing them floors and getting all the tablecloths just bang right, wasn't you? You wouldn't like it if I go pulling all the cloths about and dropping muck all over your floor.'

'Bleeding top you, mate,' said Biff, quite shortly.

'Allo!' hooted Paul. 'It's *two* Delias we got here now.'

'*And* you, Paul!' cried out Tubby. 'It's you and all! I seen you – fussing about with your curtains and the lighting and the flowers and all them swags and all. We all want it *perfect*, right? So just don't go messing up the fucking canapés, is all I'm saying. And bloody hell – look at the bleeding *time*. I can't be sodding around like this no more. Go on – off out of it, you two. Go and get drinks for people, or something. Make yourselves useful. I got to glaze the sauce, and then I got a bit of basting to see to.'

'Yeh OK,' agreed Paul. 'Fair do's. Come on, Biff – let's leave little Delia to it, will we?'

'Yeh,' laughed Biff. And then he put a couple of fingers into his mouth. 'Here, Tubs – you want your canapé back, do you?'

'Yeh yeh . . .' Tubby muttered back (his hands were flying, now, from surface to surface, his mind on a thousand things). 'Dead funny, Biff. Dead funny. Now shift yourselves, OK?'

Paul and Biff ambled away – and they was having a right old chuckle, the pair of them.

'Blimey,' said Biff, as he swung open the door to the dining room. 'He was right about people coming down, and all. Teddy's here, look. Frankie and John-John. That John-John, he ain't half got some lovely whistles. Look at that jacket, Paul.'

Paul was nodding. 'Lovely,' he agreed. 'Got to be Savile Row, ennit? I mean – where you gonna get velvet and frogging and all that flash lining nowadays if it ain't Savile Row, eh? Here, Biff – I just gotta check about Lucas's chair, OK? Bit of a surprise. I borrowed this sort of great gold sort of throne thing off of a decorator up Pimlico way. And a little one for Alice. Reckon they'll be well chuffed. Not sure if I take the covers off of them now or if I hang about for the play, like. What you reckon? Hallo – Judy's here. Hallo, Judy girl! All right? Doing good, are we, Judy my love?'

'*Frones* . . . !' marvelled Biff. 'Blimey. Here, Paul – that velvet jacket of John-John's, yeh? It remind me of the time Tubs and me was drinking up West one time and we was in this real classy place and they was all, like, eyeballing us, and that, on account of they must of thought we was dead common, or summing. And there's this bloke, OK? Really like glaring, he was – and I goes over and I says to him: love your blazer, mate. And he goes all sneery, don't he? And he says to me Yeh well that just shows how much *you* know, don't it? This ain't a *blazer*, he's going – it's a smoking jacket. Yeh? I goes. Well I tell you, son – it may have been just a smoking jacket before, but it's a bleeding blazer now, I'm telling you – cos I've only just set *fire* to it! You shouldda seen his face! He leaps up and he starts beating away at it and all the tarts there, they starts squealing and all. Magic – telling you.'

'Hello, Paul,' smiled Judy. 'Merry Christmas. Merry Christmas, Biff.'

'Wotcha, Judy my love,' said Paul, kissing her twice. 'Yeh – compliments of the wossname. So what, um – Biff? Hang on just a bit, Judy, eh? Listen, Biff – so what: you did set fire to it, did you?'

'Oh *yeh* – not many! Tubs and me was gone – but the screaming, telling you! They all got hysteric. Me and Tubs, we was creasing ourselves. Yeh. It's stuff like that what I miss . . .'

'What *are* you boys talking about?' wondered Judy, roguishly. 'No – don't tell me. I feel I don't really want to know at all. Come on, you two. Champagne. Everyone's here, pretty much. Let's all take our places. Isn't it *exciting* . . . ?'

And Paul grinned broadly. 'Yeh,' he said. 'Yeh. It is.'

'I see you got the chairs you were talking about,' said Judy. 'What are they like, Paul? Are they *very* grand? Can't wait. Look – I've put Lucas's present just in the front, OK? On that sort of stool thing. *God*, I hope he likes it. *I* think it's just wonderful. Very special. Anyway. He might open it tonight, you know. Or maybe he'll leave it till the morning. Oh God. I just don't know if I can *stand* it, if he leaves it till the morning . . .'

'Don't you worry, Judy love: he'll love it. Promise you. Now look – I'm off to have a little bit of a mingle, all right? Love the *dress*, Judy, I got to tell you. Sucker for lace, I am.'

Judy was flushed with delight.

'Really? You really like it? You don't think it's too – ?'

Paul was shaking his head, as he stooped to kiss her cheek.

'It's only *perfect* . . .' he said.

But now his eyes were flicking this way and that. The decorations were lovely, not much doubt about that. I fixed up this dimmer, didn't I, on the main lights there, look – but I reckon we won't go lighting all the candelabra till we're all properly, like, seated and that. Did you clock them? The candelabra? They're all baroque and they weighs a ton, I can tell you. They come from my mate up Pimlico and all. He goes in for all the big stuff, he do. Does good with the movie companies. Yeh. Anyway. Stage is all set. Judy's got the costumes on a rack at the back – alphabetical, like, so there won't be no messing. Posters for the play all over: Jamie done Trojan on the presses. So. Reckon I'll have me a quick word with the kiddies, is what I'll do now – little Benny and Mary-Ann, there. It's lovely to have them here, I'm telling you – cos no matter what you, like, got laid on of a Christmas time, it don't mean Charlie, do it? You don't got a couple kids about the place. But hang about – what's this now, then? Oh my Gawd – it's only Frankie, ain't it? Come right up to me, she has, and it's all with the arms and the mwah-mwah kisses all over the shop. She do look well turned out. Lovely scent coming off of her. Telling you – not long back, I could of gone for this one, big time.

'*Paul*!' Frankie was squealing delightedly – the white gleam of light in each of those huge eyes of hers, they look as if they've both been painted on there by some sort of make-up expert, or something. Telling you, though – never mind all the glamour, she's that young and excited, our Frankie, she'd be best off down the end there with Benny and Mary-Ann, squeezing all them wrapped-up presents under the tree. Yeh. So I'm a bit put out then, aren't I? By what she's coming out with:

'*You'll* tell me, Paul – won't you? Tell him, Kimmy – tell him what we're talking about.'

'Tits,' said Kimmy. 'Tits is what we're talking about. Jingle Tits.'

Paul wasn't sure he cared for this. Tried to keep the smile on, though.

'Oh yeh . . . ?' he said, quite evenly. 'Thought I'd just go and have a little word with Benny and Mary-Ann, look . . .'

'Oh no but *listen*, Paul – oh, Merry Christmas and all that, by the way, OK? No listen. Kimmy's going to do these *breast* paintings, OK? Well – not, you know – *do* them, exactly – but what it amounts to is I could have these painted impressions of my breasts in all those art galleries, and things. Cool, no? Anyway. Look. Kimmy asked me, OK? But I don't think my breasts are really *big* enough for that. That's the problem. So what I want to know is, Paul . . . I mean: you're a *man*, aren't you?'

'Hope so, love,' winked Paul. No . . . don't care for it. Not happy. Want to go and talk to Benny and Mary-Ann, now.

'Well . . .' prattled on Frankie. 'What I want to know is, OK – where do you stand on breast implants, Paul?'

'Oooh, Frankie,' laughed Paul (doing my best, doing my best). 'Well to the side, I reckon. You don't wanna go *standing* on them, do you? Ay? Might fall off.'

'Oh God you are *awful*!' gushed Frankie. 'But *seriously*, Paul. What do you think?'

'Well . . . I don't reckon I'm the bloke what you should be asking, Frankie. I mean – it's John, ain't it? Wouldn't he, er – mind, like?'

Frankie reflected for a second or two.

'Oh no I shouldn't *think* so . . .' she said. And then she flattened both her hands across her chest. 'After all – it was he who paid for *these* . . .'

'Dolly Parton,' said Kimmy. 'She's the chick I need. Hey you guys – this'll kill ya. Read someplace she got this, like – *theme* park? Dolly Pee? In the U.S? Now hear this: nooze is, next she's into, get this: "global expansion"? Like – we didn't *know* this? Yeh – sweet lil ol' Dolly and those two real smart missiles she got on her: she's the chick I need.'

Paul was beginning to edge away: felt just a touch iffy, you want the truth.

'Oh God well if *that's* how you feel about it, Kimmy . . . !' Frankie now deplored, 'well then I've just *got* to have them, haven't I? New ones. But maybe there won't be *time*. How long do they take? Do *you* know, Paul? No – suppose you don't. My first lot were done quite quickly, but they were only small. When're

you doing the pictures, Kimmy? Hey, Paul – where are you going
. . . ?'

More a case, love, of where I gone. See? Cos basically I'm outta
here, sweetheart: what I feel is, like, enough is as good as a
wossname, you take my meaning. Reckon what I'm needing now
is a right good dose of festive feeling. And where you go for that
then, ay? Yeh – right on the button, mate: kids. It's the kids what
you look to, ennit? Every time. So I'll just get meself over there,
then. Wotcha Mike, is how I'm going now (cos he's waving, look):
all right, my son? Lovely black suit he's got on him – real smart:
not unlike the Armani I'm wearing meself, truth be told – but I bet
you a dollar to a bob that his is off of some old undertaker, or
something, what died in the Stone Age. Got some great gear, Mike
has: never get enough of it, I can't. And look at Oona then, while
you're about it. Her sort of face – them wide cheekbones, and that
– really do suit all the perm and the rouge and them little dingly-
dangly earrings and all; real skinny eyebrows she got too, but I
reckon that's down to the tweezers, I'm any judge (they're all
arched up: make her look dead amazed about just all sorts). Got a
mauve and red quite tight sort of party frock on her, she has, with
thousands of them little sparkly doo-dahs all over – not your
sequins, nah: what are they? Just little glass beads, could be. Any
road, I'm torching up the candelabra now, aren't I? And they
don't half twinkle bright, all them little glass beads. Could be
what we got us here is your actual Christmas glow.

'You've done the tables just beautifully, Paul,' said Oona,
clutching at his sleeve as he was easing past them. 'Everything
looks simply gorgeous. I'm really feeling jolly Christmassy now. It
only really gets to me at the very last minute.'

'You look fab, love,' smiled Paul, patting her hand. 'I was only
thinking. So tell us then, Mike – what you got wrapped up for
your lady love here then, ay? Zeppelin? Cod Liver Oil, is it?
Spitfire, maybe?'

'Don't you be so damned cheeky!' laughed Mike. 'I'm not going to tell you, am I? Presents are a surprise.' And then he became quite abstracted. 'God, though,' he whispered. 'I'd just *love* to have a Spitfire . . . *die* for one of those . . .'

'Dear oh dear!' hooted Paul, ruffling Mike's hair. 'He don't get no better do he, Oona my lovely? How you put up with him, ay?'

'Dunkirk Spirit,' grinned Oona. 'Make do and mend. Close your eyes and think of England.'

'Why's everyone being so terribly *rude* all of a sudden?' Mike, wide-eyed, wanted to know.

'It's only a laugh, mate,' Paul assured him. 'You know that. Now listen, I'm gonna take meself off and get the rest of these candelabra sorted out, OK?'

'They're beautiful,' sighed Oona. 'Really lovely.'

'Prime, ain't they? Like what Buck House got, geezer was telling me. And I got to get a quick word in with the kids there, look – and then I don't reckon it's too long till the off, look of things. Hope you learned all your lines, you two – else Teddy'll have ya. Old Tubs – he's raring to go, tell you that much for free.'

'Yum,' said Oona. 'Can't wait. Starving.'

'Me too,' said Mike. 'Talk with you later then, Paul.'

'You got it,' agreed Paul – pointing at each of them in turn a cocked thumb and finger in the form of a pistol well ready for the business.

Aye aye, he was thinking now: them two kids is well down the road to exploding, looks like to me. Chattering away they are with old John there, see them? Little red faces, they got: look like the Bisto Kids (as Mike has probably said to them about a thousand times, shouldn't wonder). But you get that often, don't you? The kids linking up with the oldies. Nice, of a Christmas, that is: all the, like, generations and that having a good old natter. Yeh – telling you: I'm getting a right good overview of the whole scene here now, I am, and what I reckon is, the stage is well set for a

Christmas to remember, you want my opinion. Now: I got to be quick. Tubby's bringing out the first of his doings now, look – and yeh, he got helluva cheer, didn't he, like what he always do, silly old bleeder. And Alice, I reckon she's well due any time now – and we all know what that means: what happens then. (Blimey: bit got the willies, I have now. I mean – I *know* I know my lines, don't I? No fears. Been over and over them with Jamie and Judy I don't know how many times – but right now this minute, like, I can't hardly recall a single bleeding one of them. It's nerves, that: it's nerves what does that to you, you know.)

'Wotcha, John-John old mate. These two villains bothering you, are they?'

'Ha!' laughed John. 'Quite the reverse, Paul, my very dear chap. They're keeping me young – aren't you Mary-Ann? Right, Benny?'

They both chortled delightedly by way of excited reply.

He's a lovely bloke, John-John is. Tell you what, though: we missed a trick here, we did. You get the old red cozzie on him – slap on the big white beard and I'm telling you: you ain't gonna find a better Santa nowhere. Gawd: it's really *nice*, this is. Just look around you. Go on. What you see? I'll *tell* you what you see, son: what you see is a roomful of very happy people – everyone gagging for Christmas to get up and running. Well. I say 'everyone' . . . There's the *Hitlers*, of course . . . just bleeding sitting there in the corner, look, as per bloody usual. Just staring down at the table like something's *wrote* on it, or something. It's funny about them two, you know. First time you clap eyes on them you think Oh dear me no – they're gonna kill what we got stone dead, them two are. But you get to not seeing them, after a bit. It's like they're the sort of shadow on the wall – not, like, part of it – but a shade of what just was, or something. Can't explain it. Yeh but: clocked them this time though, didn't I? Well sod 'em, that's what I say. Let's get ourselves back to these two kids here, will we? Have us a bit of a laugh.

'We got off to something of a false start though, didn't we, pets?' smiled John. 'They wanted to know, Paul, what the *Sixties* were like – didn't you? Hey?'

'And *he* thought – !' interjected Mary-Ann – pointing at John and holding on tight to her nose.

'*I* thought . . .' chuckled John. 'Well – I said to them, hm – Sixties, hey? Well, first thing is you slow up a bit, you know? Knees get a bit creaky . . .'

'But *we* meant – !' laughed Benny.

'Yes yes,' agreed John. 'They meant not *my* sixties, good God no – but *the* Sixties, you see. Beatles, and so on. I was more of a Presley man myself, I have to say: more my generation. And then I said . . . what did I say to you then, Mary-Ann, in fact . . . ?'

'You got to talking about Santa Claus,' said Mary-Ann. And then she swung up her bright and urgent eyes and focused their beam full on to Paul. 'Gosh, it's all just so *exciting*, isn't it Paul? Can't wait. Just can't *wait* . . . !'

Paul grinned at her. 'Won't have to, will you princess? Ay? Not long now, love.'

'Oh *yes*,' remembered John. 'Santa – that was it. I said I hoped they both believed in him, didn't I?'

'I said I didn't . . .' admitted Benny, quietly and rather shame-facedly.

'But *I* told him he *had* to,' insisted Mary-Ann. 'There are some things you've just *got* to believe in, Benny, and Santa Claus is one of them. He's nearly at the very top of the list.' And then she was reflective: 'It's not a very *long* list, actually . . .'

Paul didn't ask who or what was top; nor did John. Even Benny seemed to take it for granted.

'Funny, though, you know,' John was musing. 'About the Sixties. I didn't catch up with them, really, until well into the Seventies when I was already far too old to catch up with anything at all, really. Well – anything *fashionable*, anyway. Do you know, Paul – on the strength of that rather feeble song . . . God, could even have been the *Eighties*, now I come to think of it. No, as I say – because of that really rather dreary pop song, I actually did – I went to San Francisco. *And*, I am ashamed to tell you, I, er – wore some flowers: in my hair. Which was thinning even then. God.'

'Yeh?' laughed Paul. 'And what? Was a gas, was it John-John? Get high, did you, you old rogue?'

'A gas . . . ? Oh no. Never felt so stupid in all my life. Everyone just *stared* at me: most embarrassing.'

'What a guy!' marvelled Paul. 'Listen – I'm just off for a quick word with Jamie: see I got my lines right, and everything. Alice'll be in in a jiffy, should think. So later, yeh kids? We'll pull a cracker.'

Jamie was already waving around a napkin in greeting, as Paul approached. Had actually been watching him for quite some time, as a matter of fact, had Jamie – aware of an almost proprietorial (and quite unjustified) glow of pride within him: he really is so very *suave*, our Paul, you know. The way he just glides from person to person, always seemingly saying to them just the right thing and at just the right length before easily moving on, leaving them with a touch to the shoulder and a smile on their faces. Now me, I'm not quite up to that standard myself – no not yet. But I do feel I'm very much on the right track, you know. It's all within sight. Because it seems to me that that poet, whoever he was – the one who went on about man not being an island – you know the one? I'm sure you do. Could be one of the metaphysicals; it's so long now since I actually read any poetry, you know. Could maybe get back into all that. Used to love it – much better than novels, I always thought: truer, somehow. Calmed me. Excited me, too. Did all the things that poetry's meant to, in short. Got all the old Faber and Penguin paperbacks, somewhere. One of my boxes. Must dig them out. Anyway – what I'm meaning is, he was spot-on, the poet, really. Wasn't he? Marvell, was it? Because speaking for myself anyway, I really do seem to be, well – not *comprised*, exactly, but certainly defined, though, by the people around me. My wife, fairly obviously – sitting right beside me now, and wearing a really rather beautiful conical paper hat (gold and holographic; Kimmy got one of her people to make up one for each of us). She actually seems to enjoy being with me. These days. Which is pretty amazing. Enjoys being here. It's Benny, of course, at base. She can see how much he loves it. Thank God. And then there's all my friends, of course – Judy, Paul . . . everyone, really. And constantly hovering above and around us, the masterful comfort and presence of Lucas. The founder of the feast. It all goes to building within you great confidence, you know – backing of that order. I think it was Donne: that man and island thing. Anyway – not quite up to Paul's standard (and here he is now, smiling his smile) but I really do feel I don't have far to go. Oh yes: and while I'm in this rather festive and mellow and . . . yes, I suppose it is a rather self-congratulatory mood (well: why not?) I might just fill you in quickly on the cigarette situation, yes? Last one smoked – up on the roof, while Alice was fooling with rats and cursing the owls – sixteen days ago. Sixteen *days*. God Almighty.

'All right yeh, Jamie? Hey Caroline. Doing all right are you, love? Feeling all merry and jolly, are we?'

'If I drink any more of this champagne I will be,' laughed Caroline. 'And I don't want to eat any more of these olives and canapés and things because they really do fill you up, you know, and I want to be ready for Tubby's special. I'm *starving*, actually Paul. Isn't Alice due down? Absolutely starving . . .'

'I was wondering that . . .' mused Jamie.

'Yeh,' agreed Paul. 'Reckon she's a tad behind schedule. Well –

Christmas time, ennit? She's entitled. I tell you why I come over, Jamie – I was right bothered about my lines, but they all come back to me now. That's definitely nerves, that is.'

'You!' hooted Jamie. 'Nervous? I don't believe it. I must say, Paul – you've done all the decorations quite beautifully. Hasn't he, Caroline? Just beautifully. Look at it all.'

And they did, the three of them – Jamie, Paul and Caroline. They cast their eyes upon the scene – the candlelight glinting on the silver, the glossy crackers and hats and quite spectacular flowers and fruit. Those extraordinary swags. And best, best of all – the sheer ease and pleasure on everyone's faces. Teddy was saying to Dorothy (just caught the end of it) that if Tubby didn't serve us up some food jolly soon, he'd have to open another dozen bottles, the rate they were all cutting into it. And then Tubby himself was peering around the door – a touch of anxiety about the eyes: there was no mistaking it.

'I wonder . . .' said Jamie. 'Do you think I ought to, you know, um . . . go and see everything's all right, sort of thing? Alice, I mean . . . ?'

'Well . . .' demurred Paul. 'They know the routine, don't they? Ay? Alice and Lucas. They invented it. Been doing it every night. Maybe cos it's, like, Christmas, they wanna beef up the tension, like? Mind you – I take your point. It's well late, innit?'

Jamie nodded. 'So what do you think? I mean, I don't want to appear, you know – rude, or anything . . .'

'Well tell you what then, Jamie – you go off and see what's going down, and I'll get Teddy to read us out something Christmassy or do us a little carol, or something. Keep people's minds off the grub. Reckon you'll meet them on the way coming down. You can say you was just off to the kazi.'

'Mm,' thought Jamie. 'Maybe I will. All right, Caroline?'

'Well if you *want* to, Jamie. But I'm sure they'll be here in a minute. They know what they're doing, don't they?'

'You're probably right. Still – no harm, is there? Little check.'

And Jamie eased back his chair, and slipped out quickly.

It's strange, this, he thought – padding in silence down the endless corridor. Never wandered about at this time of the evening, for obvious reasons: all of us down there having dinner, right? And God – now that the sounds from the dining room have faded to nothing, the silence, you know, is absolutely total. And the lift – the lift seems to be making the most deafening row. I suppose it always does; I've just never noticed it before.

Well, Lucas's floor now, and still no sign. I'll just go up to the door very quietly, because I don't want to interrupt anything. You know – if they're talking or . . . anything. Actually, the door is just ajar, I've only noticed – so it looks like I'm about to walk right into them, which is going to look a little odd. No – worse than odd: embarrassing. Maybe I'll just go back down. Will I? Don't know. Oh God – I just don't *know*, now. What to do. Really. Well look – now I'm here, I might just as well – have a *peek*, so to speak. Don't you think? Well right, then. OK: I will.

Hm. No noises that I can hear. It seems rather wrong to be standing in Lucas's place, when he's not around. Maybe . . . oh God: maybe they've gone down by the stairs and I passed them in the lift coming up and right now he's saying his few words to us, Lucas, or maybe already everyone's clapping and cheering old Tubby as he wheels in the first of his trolleys and here I am all alone five floors up and sneaking about Lucas's space like a – *burglar*, or something, and then someone is bound soon to say . . . God, maybe even Lucas himself might look around and say Oh: where can young Dear be? Where has Dear got to? And he'll think me most terribly rude for not being there when everyone else is there and you know I really wish I *hadn't*, now – done this. Come up here. Why couldn't I have sat tight along with everyone else and just waited? What on earth am I *doing* here, actually? Sneaking about . . . like a *burglar*, or something . . .

Well look. I've walked the length of the main room, now (all three printing presses gleaming proudly – God I'm so fond of them), and I'm straining still to pick up any sort of noise while feeling wholly stupid because I just *know* now that they're all downstairs – they're all downstairs, every single one of them, and here I am trying to hear noises from non-existent people. Now the bedroom door's in front of me. Never been in here. Don't think anyone has. Well – Alice, presumably. Well I can't go in. It wouldn't be right. And what's the point anyway? There's no one *here*, is there? No there isn't – because they're all *downstairs*, aren't they? Yes they are. God – what's wrong with me at all? Why don't I just go back down? Because it will be just too awful if, you know – Lucas sends someone up to *find* me, or something. Oh look – I'll just put my head round the door, and then I'll get back down. Can't harm. I'll just open the door a crack, and if there's no response (which, of course, there won't be) I'll just say his name, Lucas . . . just once, I'll say Lucas . . . and then I'm gone.

'Lucas . . . ? Lucas . . . ? Hallo . . . ?'

Damn. There. Said it twice, not once. And added on a foolish 'hallo' for good bloody measure. And I'm walking in now, which I didn't plan to do. What a fine big room. Superbly done. Huge four-poster, look: all the hangings. Purple velvet. It's dark in here. And I've just noticed something else. At the window. Do you know what? Curtains. Well well. Hm. I think I'll go now. People will definitely be wondering. Oh look – there's another door there – that's ajar too. Light on in there. I'll just . . . oh look I'll just put my head around it, shall I? Turn off the light, maybe . . . or maybe I'll leave it on, I don't know. There's a smell – aroma. Can't quite place it. Anyway: quick look, yes? And then I'm gone.

And God. Christ. This is a bit of a shock. Because Alice – she's here. Just sitting in a chair. Oh my God – she's looking right at me. She's not amused. I've walked into something – I've interrupted something badly. Oh Christ I wish I wasn't here. Oh Christ I wish

I hadn't come. Should I speak? Should I leave? Can't just leave now, can I? Got to say *something* . . . God: she looks as if she really . . . *hates* me, or something. I just can't stand the look she's giving me.

'Alice . . . ? Hello. Only me. Look I'm sorry if I've, um . . . Are you, er . . . ? Look – don't be angry, Alice – I only came to see if you . . . Lucas about, is he? Not ill or anything, is he? Can I, um – do anything, or anything? Alice . . . ?'

It's like she's in a trance. I go a bit nearer. She's not moving, or anything. She just stares at me. I'm getting a bit rattled, you want to know the truth. And Jesus. It's only now I see what it is she's, um – *wearing*, Christ's sake. Some sort of cinched-in sort of corset, looks like . . . long legs, the sort you don't, you know, associate with Alice, no not one bit – stretched right out before her, they are, the curves made shadowy by those sheer black stockings, look. God oh God I so much wish she'd speak. Because I can't now, can I, pretend I haven't *seen*? She's there before me, and wearing secret things . . .

'Alice? Hallo? Anything I can, um . . . ?'

And then I think I flinched quite badly, because suddenly her arm flies up and it's some sort of gesture she's meaning, I think – arching her wrist, snapping it back and forth, though seemingly behind her. She's still just staring, though: staring right at me. And it's only now I get the smell – the aroma that suddenly thickens and seems to be all around me: it's cigar, that's what it is. The unmistakable waft of fine Havana. Well. Well well.

'What, um – is it, Alice? Something you need . . . ?'

But no: no word. I follow the trajectory of her now quite manic and insistent wrist. I make to walk around her. Scared? Of course I was. But almost beyond it, I think I must have been: through the glass, and out the other side. I felt as glazed as Alice.

But. Whatever I thought I might see next, it was not this. Because on the window seat that up till now had been concealed

317

from me, there lay sprawled out and in some considerable dis-array – jarring so vilely with all these surroundings . . . the tramp. The vagrant. Quite beyond belief, oh yes I do know that – but Mary-Ann's Mister Stinky was here, and I could scarcely give credit to my senses. I stepped back – looked away and in alarm to Alice, but she had not turned. Her arm stayed twisted behind her back, and still she was repeatedly jabbing at the air. I swallowed once and approached this sight with care. His long and matted hair was strewn across his face – and without at all wanting to, I found myself clawing it back and away from his eyes. Several things, then, happened at once. The half-smoked cigar was still between his fingers, and the hair – it slid too far beneath my trembling hand: it was as if I had somehow and unwittingly dislocated this man's skull. The skin beneath was white and waxy – and then as the hair tumbled down and then away from him completely, I saw with a thrill of sickness the sweet face of Lucas, his tender expression arrested by surprise – caught in appalling wonder, and utterly amazed by death.

III

. . . and an end

CHAPTER NINE

So. What can I say? Even now, when time has passed, what can I usefully say to you? People struggle – I know I do – to express, to come even close to conveying (to others, those outside) the real extent of a personal disaster. The reason, I think, that it is all so very hard is because the actual passing, cold and stark, of just one single human being is not (to others, those outside) so vast or even compelling a thing. People die, they will gently explain, all the time, each and every minute. Which is true, yes – true to the point of worthlessness, as far as I can see, because it does not begin to make provision for the cruelty of *effect*. It is the endless ripples (at first, when you still can't believe it, there comes a succession of these insistent and boilingly caustic ripples, ceaselessly lapping at the edges of you, and you wince at the sizzle of the steady corrosion). These are followed – and for some it comes quickly, very quickly – by a total shattering of not just you but everything that touches: this is appalling – it leaves you stranded and shivering, strung out and laid siege to by the wholly satanic and impossible twinning of a swaddled thick-headedness and irregular though quite vicious incursions of salvos of arrows, each tip finding its target and making you gasp and then cry out before the wounds, they briefly cease to torment you, or else become horribly inflamed, and then you are stormed by an enveloping fire that can have you shrieking and flailing and desperate to be rid of your very own self. And . . . during the periods of relative calm (softening you up, are all the little devils, prior to the next and imminent onslaught) . . . there then comes the fear. The fear, oh yes: this utter fear. It had me by the throat, and it wouldn't let me go. But for others, the effects were . . . different. Varied. So. I'll try to take us through. Will I? Somehow. I'll try to somehow take us back to the moment. That moment I discovered him – when Lucas and I were briefly together, and locked in astonishment. I was already filled by illness, and yet I heard straight away my bombardment of Alice – the gabble of frantic enquiry, made more dreadful by my horrified exclamations.

'Christ! I mean – Jesus, *Jesus*, Alice! What can – . Oh *no-o-o-oo*, Lucas – please! Please don't be – ! Dear man . . . ! Alice! Talk to me! Come and . . . oh *Christ*, oh Christ I'm – !'

Crying – crying, now: thick and hot it came – squeezing its way through screwed-up melting eyelids. My lips were hard, and pulled right back from teeth that seemed unyielding and defensive, while set in horror. I felt a hand, then, clutching my shoulder – Alice had come up behind me, and I took the heat of her breath made bad by the choke of old tears, the still rasping gargle of just stopped-up grief.

'*Help* me . . .' she whispered. 'Oh God please, Jamie – help me. *Help* me.'

I must have just shaken my head. How in the world could I help anyone now?

'Have you . . . ? Called someone? Does anyone . . . ?'

I tried: tried to be calm and practical, here. All the *words* were dancing around me: ambulance, doctor, police – all quite vital, and yet so wholly and blatantly not. A fresh wave of spasm and shock and jarring hurt, then: it racked us both – it juddered right through us. And her silence told me No, in answer to all my husked-out and stuttered questions.

'How is he . . . ? Why is he *dressed* like . . . ? How come he's . . . ?'

I turned to face her – and already she was coming alive now, Alice: she picked up something and wrapped it around her – a gown, it could have been . . . yes, I remember, because she was wearing it later. Later, when everyone knew.

'Help me, Jamie – change him, will you? Get him out of all that – *stuff*. Help me do it.'

I just stood there, not really believing even any small part of it. Already, though, Alice was bustling about – scurrying into the dressing room (her spike-heeled shoes she had kicked aside) and emerging quickly with yet one more of Lucas's beautiful suits – dark wine it was, this one: dark wine – and now she was tugging at the turned-up collar of the mouldy coat that shrouded his shoulders – plucking at the knot of this rotting old muffler. I knelt to help her. I felt, if I was feeling at all now, that I truly had to. She was alarmingly efficient in all of this, Alice. I averted my gaze as she set to his trousers, but then I just had to turn, and found myself looking. His legs were strangely brown: this is at once irrelevant, and something I shall never forget.

'Put this shirt on him, Jamie – please do this. Please do it.'

Lucas's arms, they were not stiff. And their soft insides – underneath and close to him – I felt them spread out to me the last of their warmth. I maybe must have missed completely whole parts of all this amazing endeavour (flown away, or else blanked out) because soon – as I continued to gulp and yelp, as I wept and flustered – Lucas, my Lucas, was sitting before me, dressed like a prince and suffering Alice to care for his hair with two silver-backed brushes, easing gently the wings over the tips of his ears. She stooped then and scooped up the bale of old rags that were strewn about the floor (the tangled wig, the laceless and burst-open shoes) and seemingly made them in an instant vanish: she came, she went – she darted about. My senses were caught in a tornado, and my knees were shaking and cold. I sat in a chair, nearly next to Lucas.

Alice, now, held out to me a telephone. She clutched it tight in both her white and bony hands, her arms stretched out stiffly as she jerked it towards me repeatedly. Her eyes, as I glanced up in panic, were struck wide (wet and urgent) – and oh God, just like Lucas's (and mine, I'm sure – like mine as well) they still were quite astounded.

'What . . . shall I say?' I faltered. 'Hm? Alice? Who am I ringing? How did he . . . ? Don't you think *you* ought to, Alice? No? As you were the one who – ? What am I calling, then? *Doctor*? Surely not a doctor? Ambulance? Yes? OK, then. I'll phone an ambulance. Christ.'

So I did that, somehow. Got through that. Had to turn away (from him, from her): could not now be a witness to the terrible fact. They asked me cold and foolish questions. My name: I told them. And The Works, I said: The Works, yes. Right. Is where we are (said a bit more: whatever she asked of me). And you are quite sure, are you (this woman, she wanted to know), that the man in question, he is dead? So I sucked in my breath and did my best to respond like a human, but all that came out of me was the grunt, first, and then squeal of a cornered pig who knows its time has come. Did I (the woman, she wanted to know) have any idea as to the cause of death? I stared at the phone, and held it away from me. And I looked then at Alice as we both heard her say again (this woman, this woman, who wanted to know): Hello? Caller? Mister Dear? Are you there? I say are you aware at all as to the actual cause of death? I looked at Alice still, and I felt myself blinking repeatedly as she bit down on her lip and then closed tight her eyes.

'He simply . . .' she breathed (and her stomach was fluttering), 'ceased to *exist* . . . !'

I too, now – I had to close my eyes. I sighed out once, and heavily, focusing hard on just the surging and restless redness before me. 'Caller? Hello? Mister Dear? Are you still there?'

And I sort of came to. I sort of did.

'He simply . . .' I breathed (and my heart, it was broken), 'ceased to *exist* . . . !'

And then came the fear – oh yes, this utter fear. It had me by the throat, and it wouldn't let me go.

Paul, I must say, was an absolute brick. Which didn't surprise me, or anything – but God, I was so terribly *grateful* for it. I mean to say the astonishing thing here is that I felt, what? I don't know – responsible, somehow: in charge, if you like. Which is, I maybe don't have to tell you, new to me, very. Much more likely, I've always been, to duck out of anything going – and I mean *anything*, even trivial little silly sorts of things, anything at all that could later be put down as having been my baby. Whereas *this* was . . . oh, just so mindbendingly colossal as to bring me close to the point of passing out (the swimming of the eyes: I experienced that) and yet somehow I felt throughout that I just had to *deal*. You know? Understand? I don't think I did – not at the time. But it was partly because Alice, by now, she was quite useless. Not her fault. Well I mean *obviously*, you know, not her fault in the . . . Christ: circumstances. Jesus, oh Jesus. But when the ambulance team had finished, um . . . *woof!* God oh God. *Seeing* to things – gone away. Taken him. A doctor arrived, not at all sure on whose volition, this, nor even quite when in the time frame, but anyway: he gave her something. No. Wait a bit: that's wrong – the order of this: it didn't go like that. The doctor, this doctor – he must have come *with* them, did he? With the ambulance people? Now I think of it – the ambulance might well have gone away. Is that possible? Don't

325

know. The doctor, anyway – he spent a while with Lucas: undid all his clothes again. Coronary, is what he said. Massive and sudden (he simply ceased to exist). Then maybe something, someone – others arrived. And Lucas, he was taken away by them. Why didn't I go along? Don't quite know. Where, in fact, had they taken him? Didn't quite get. Oh look – it all took years and no time, this: I felt just so *confused* . . . Anyway. I don't know what it was he gave her, this doctor, but she barely had time to stretch out, poor Alice, before she was gone, lost to the world. And he offered it, whatever it was, to me as well. I said no. I mean I envied her, if I'm honest – this new serenity that had overcome Alice: could easily have embraced a good dose of oblivion, right then (because I was alive with just hurt and a crushing regret and even my limbs, they felt so strange), but then how would she feel, I caught myself wondering – how could she cope all alone when eventually her eyelids flickered back into life, and truth seeped in and then invaded her? So no: I declined the doctor's offer of a knockout. Because also, look – who if not I was going to *deal*? Hm? Who else was going to handle it? Hm? If not me. Alice was out. Judy was elsewhere. And where, in fact, *was* Judy, now that I needed her? What was going on? Hm? Why could she not be here? Hm? Oh yes . . . Of course. I remember now – of course, of course. Paul, here, he has quietly reminded me. She is still downstairs, isn't she? Judy. With the others. Of course she is. Still, I imagine – although by now she will certainly be smothered by anxiety – in a state of, well – not ignorance, exactly (suspicion will have begun to spin a narrative of its own), but growing uneasiness, that was for sure. Paul – it was Paul who now pulled me together (I was, he told me later, shaking quite badly) because he was, you know – an absolute brick, but so tender in his handling of me. Couldn't have made it, wouldn't have done it, don't think, if he hadn't turned up when he did.

'Paul. Christ. Thank Christ you're here.'

Lucas – he was still just sitting there, when I first became aware of Paul beside me. I had, I could barely believe it, only just helped Alice in changing his clothes. His tie knot looked less good, less fat, than usual. I suppose because I had done it.

'It's Lucas . . .' I said. Stupidly.

'Paul held my shoulder, and he nodded.

'Yeh. I got the gist. Christ Almighty. I come up earlier Jamie, yeh? Heard you, like – talking and that, so I goes away again. Didn't, like, want to . . . you know. Or nothing. It was Judy what says to me, Go back up, Paul. Something wrong. So I come back up. Here, now. Christ Almighty. How'd it – ? I mean – ! You OK, are you Jamie? Alice, love – you all right, are you? Yeh? You called someone, have you? Do something, can I?'

I just shook my head again and again. Couldn't answer, couldn't respond. I shook my head – and my eyes, I think, implored him to ask no more. I think, as we sat there, the three of us – Paul was gripping me as I trembled badly, Alice still was just staring, her eyes now wild – there was a bond between us, a reluctance to ever stir again. This state of suspension seemed good for now, but even then I knew it was far too fragile a thing to, oh – *sustain*, or anything: I knew that, of course, even before Paul started in on his insistent whispering: telling me so, with urgency.

'Jamie . . . listen up mate, yeh? Downstairs. I got to tell them. They got to know . . .'

This time I nodded. He made to leave me, Paul, but I tugged him back. I needed him to hold me some more – keep me together, from falling apart. And so we stayed – for a while, for a second, don't know how long – and then the wail of the siren, the ambulance arriving, I suppose . . . that, we knew, now put paid to everything.

'Jamie. I got to now. They'll be all over now, they hear that. I got to get down now, Jamie. They got to know.'

And he did, this time – I was going to nod him away, assent to

327

that, but he was gone before I even got around to it. Didn't feel strong again until they had, you know – taken him. Felt even more so, once Alice was unconscious. My thoughts then were with Paul, and how he was doing. Got to get down there – shoulder my share. Because I felt, as I say – *responsible*, somehow: in charge, if you like.

I walked down the stairs. Six flights. Later, much much later, I decided that I had maybe done this for one of three reasons: the shrinking away from enclosure, solitary confinement in the dark and clanking lift. That was one possibility. Or else here was simply a way of prolonging the journey: deferring the moment when I would be confronted by whatever it was that might await me. The third explanation was rather more noble: I was maybe sounding out each floor as I trudged on down – ready to round up any lost or maddened runaways who had fled to their nests, shattered beyond repair by what Paul by now will have told them. All was silent, though: no one was around. It was only when I finally crept down the corridor in the basement that the muted whispers reached me: the stirring just-hum of a critically injured and stunned community. (But I think now that all I did was I walked down the stairs – just that, and quite thoughtlessly: six flights.)

I believed, as I hugged the wall now, that I was still out of sight, and striving to glean some little particle of what was going on (just how bad it would be) before I braced myself to enter. But I can't have been – I must have made myself instantly apparent because a whoop that cracked went up from Judy, and she rushed at me headlong – a bottle, I recall, was sent spinning in her wake and it smashed into pieces on the floor and the rivulets of red were streaming away and making for my shoes and all I could do was just stand there as she clutched at me, so hard she was hurting me badly, and I felt each racking jolt of her sobbing – it throbbed into the side of my neck and her mouth there was wet and ajar and so beyond any sort of control. As I dumbly patted her hair, I dared to look over her shoulder and beyond, and the scene that met my eyes I'm afraid will never even slightly diminish in my memory.

John, I saw first. When at last I began to focus on anything at all, it was John who caught me. And I was grateful. I had to, I think, narrow down the vision – because the huger sight of all my friends, the whole of my family, laid so low – the glaze of tears grafted on to so many faces, each made sparkling by the luscious ochre of candles and the wink of silver (the frosted glinting spangles on the tree, the gleam from the conical and jaunty paper hats that still were perched grotesquely to the sides of so many heads) . . . well . . . this new and quite severe shaft of pain was shocking (it came so close to felling me). I hugged and hugged her – Judy, then: I think to keep me upright. But it was, as I say, John that I saw – hunched over in his chair like a great defeated bear, his head just hanging low between his hands: he looked so very very old, now – old like John had never truly seemed. 'Dear oh dear oh dear dear . . .' is what he kept on saying, softly. Frankie, she was on the floor, her arms about his waist and her face deep into him, protected by the looming of his deadweight bulk. 'Dear oh dear oh dear dear dear . . .' he still went on muttering, as his heavy head kept on swaying in dismay from side to side, the candlelight etching deep and dark troughs into the caved-in flanks of his face, his eyes quite lost in all those folds of exhausted flesh.

Mary-Ann. Little Mary-Ann. She was on her mother's lap and staring with almost accusation right into her eyes (her own were hard, and quite unblinking). Dorothy just gazed out ahead of her – not at Kimmy, who sat before her, fiddling idly with her unresponsive hand. 'Shit . . .' spat out Kimmy, now, with fat disgust (just a few eyes idled her way: not many). 'Shit oh shit oh shit . . . !' Dorothy hadn't looked, though: all I saw in her were

329

spreading traces of the fear that was now, I shudderingly acknowledged, just darting all over me. In Oona's face, there was an inexplicable terror of a different nature – she was almost literally white, despite the gentle lighting, and had about her the air of a culprit. Without, I felt sure, meaning to, she met my eyes and she flinched almost convulsively. She fumbled to the side of her – making, maybe, to clasp Mike's hand – but she was inches away from where they gripped the table's edge, and she explored no further. Mike himself was curled up and small – now he was twisting both his fists hard and deep into the sockets of his eyes, wringing out of them the ceaseless tears, baby's tears, that ran down into the soft and wet corrugations of his quite distorted mouth. Teddy was looking in earnest maybe not at me at all, but at Judy who was still wrapped tight around my neck: he needed her back beside him, I thought: he needs her, yes, and who can blame him? He had a finger, Teddy, stuck deep into a tumbler of something, and he agitated it thoroughly as he spun it with determination, round and round in a clockwise direction – and then he stopped dead, took stock, and churned it up now (round and round) the other way entirely. And always looking with yearning at Judy.

Tubby was wearing his tall white chef's hat, though it was slumped now, and fell across his eyes. His face was red and without expression. One hand kept picking at the breast of a golden goose – he tore away strips and flicked them away: tore away more. Biff, alongside, tipped wine into his mouth with a practised and steady hand. It was as if he was committed to some morbid obligation: as each successive measure was knocked right back and drained to his utter satisfaction, he would purse his lips in mute consideration and then calmly fill the glass to the brim – doggedly and quite without emotion, pressing on. Paul – he was the only one in motion: gliding silently from body to body – holding a shoulder, touching an arm. A terrible parody of just how he was caring for everyone earlier. How much earlier? Hour? More? Earlier, anyway. When things were different.

I had to, now (just had to), sit. It took both my hands and all my strength to first peel and then tug away from me the clinch of Judy's strangling arms. I sat down wherever, and she crouched beside me. It was only then (I don't try to explain: I am merely saying) that I remembered that Benny and Caroline were here. Up till now it was as if my roll-call was complete: everyone present who ought to have been. So I had to seek them out. Oh. There they are. Near the back, and close to John and Frankie. Why had I not seen them, then? When I latched on to John, at the outset? I do not know (I don't try to explain: I am merely saying). Caroline was maybe – wistful, was she? She looked . . . *resigned*, I think is the closest I can come. As if marooned in the waiting room of a doctor's surgery, adrift among so many much sicker people, all with an earlier appointment. Or maybe – her flight, they have just now announced, has been indefinitely delayed, and it is beyond her power to do anything at all but . . . if not quite grin, then bear it. Benny was on the floor and to the side of her – driving up her leg a red and yellow car, bus, lorry . . . some or other rolling thing that clicked in a high-pitched and rhythmic way at every revolution (and in a lower and much lustier tone, whenever he hauled it back). Around him lay quite deep drifts of ripped-up wrapping: Benny, it seemed, was alone in having opened his presents.

I was sitting, now, across the table from Judy – still near the door and rather detached from the rest of them. She made as if to speak – and I had to look away. How long could it be, I had wondered, before all the questions started? If Judy were to pierce the dam, I would soon be pounded into bits by the coming inundation. And then she checked herself, Judy: thought better of it. Soon, though, her eyes and lips were making themselves ready: getting round to it again. I braced myself (had to). Because it was only (I had known this – the minute I entered, of course I had known this) a simple matter of *time* – well wasn't it? And the time, it seemed, had come. But what she said, I had not at all expected. I was, in truth, dumbfounded. She reached out her hand to me, Judy, and she touched and then grabbed at my knuckles.

'Don't . . .' she whispered. 'Don't, Jamie . . . Put it out.'

I jerked up my head and spun around to look at her – the whirl of motion made me lose my balance.

'What . . . ?' I murmured, quite perplexed, as I tried to get steady. '*What* . . . ?'

The meaning in her eyes seemed to lead to my fingers – and the cigarette burning between them. Just alongside of my pale and jumpy hand stood two bent-up ground-out butts driven hard into the table's surface. I looked up to the vaulted ceiling, and I felt rushed then by a mad new sort of wonder. Crying – crying, now: thick and hot it came, squeezing its way through screwed-up melting eyelids. I stubbed out the cigarette (one of three, then, I was unaware of lighting), for I needed both my hands, now, to cover up my face. And in the very brief moment before I closed down my eyes, I caught just this glimpse of the Hitlers: never before had I seen them smiling.

'Was it now . . . ?' asked Judy – in a soft and faraway voice. Jamie was straining to hear her. It was as if with every word, she was apologizing for speaking at all, and maybe even being there. 'Is it now you're going up?'

Jamie swivelled under the touch of Judy's fingers as she stood behind him and much more mechanically than he was used to, it felt to Jamie, she kneaded his scalp around the temples. He looked at his watch, knowing the time exactly.

'A few minutes,' he said. 'A few minutes more.'

Judy nodded. Her hands stood still – and then she seemed to recall what she was doing, and they sluggishly resumed their duties.

'I don't know where Teddy's gone. Haven't seen him this morning. Don't know where he is. He didn't sleep a wink. I don't suppose any of us did. Because we're all . . . we're all out of kilter, aren't we? Hm? Jamie? Christmas morning . . . it wasn't meant to *be* like this . . .'

Jamie reached back, and he patted her hand.

'You don't have to do this, you know Judy. If you don't feel . . .'

'Hm? Do what? Oh – your head, you mean. I will, actually, stop now, I think. If you don't, um . . . I'm not really doing it properly anyway.'

Jamie was up and holding her the second he heard the first sharp inhalation, prior to her latest dry and aching round of sobbing.

'Oh Jamie. Oh Jamie. I am shocked by my weakness. This is so beyond . . . *endurance* . . .'

Jamie, as was usual with him now, had nothing at all to say – to her, or to anyone else. He gently withdrew, and Judy looked up at him imploringly. He tapped once the face of his watch, and pointed to the ceiling. Judy nodded her sad understanding.

'I hope she's . . . give her all my *love*, won't you Jamie? Poor Alice. Poor Alice. I should have gone with her, really. But I couldn't. I just couldn't.'

No well, thought Jamie. You wouldn't have been allowed to. I offered. To go with her. But no – Alice was having none of it. She woke, she told me, feeling just terrible, around about dawn. She felt, she said, disgusted with herself for having slept at all.

Why did you *let* them, Jamie? Why did you let them *give* me that stuff? My place was with *Lucas*. Where did they take him? Where did you *go* . . . ?! And Jamie had coughed quite briefly, and looked down and away: would love to have fled. Well the truth is, Alice, I, er . . . didn't, actually. Go. With him. I know I should have. But I didn't. I just – can't explain it. But I know – I do know where he – oh *God*, Alice, please – don't, please, *look* at me like that. I just wasn't *thinking* straight – you can surely understand that? Hm? Look – look: papers – they left . . . papers. He's here. We'll go. We'll go now. Yes?

But no. She was having none of it, Alice. *She* would go. Alone. But Jamie – I want to talk to you as soon as I get back. Yes? Twelve. Shall we say twelve? Jamie nodded. Twelve, then. Because the old Alice had returned, but even more so – brisk, unnaturally bright-eyed and very responsible – in charge, if you like. Which came as a relief, of sorts; though in other ways, very much not (it seems just to heighten my fear).

So. Anyway. Twelve, now. Twelve noon, on Christmas Day. Good God. It is, I notice, as I walk the walk, very hot in here. The whole of The Works seems overheated. I should maybe mention this, should I? To Biff. Because it is Biff, you know, who generally takes care of . . . things like that. But I don't suppose it matters.

And. Once more I find myself standing in Lucas's space, among his things. I pat the presses, each in turn, and I walk into the back room where I can hear the dart and swishing of a dedicated woman with many things to *see* to. And I am aware too of a smell . . . an aroma that I can't quite . . . oh yes. I have it. I had it the second before I confronted Alice, and she waved me towards a cluster of chairs. The cigar looked large and strange as it was held unsteadily between such slender fingers; I took in the waft of fine Havana, as I sat and waited. Plucked at the piping at the edge of the chair. Went on waiting. Alice stood over me constantly, jerking the cigar between and away from her lips, seemingly surprised each time to find smoke in her mouth, and expelling it rapidly and with a pronounced distaste. It was I who spoke, eventually:

'How, um . . . was he? Oh *Christ* . . .'

'Lucas?' checked Alice. And what did she expect me to do? Nod? Protest with vigour that oh no *no* – I was talking of someone else altogether . . . ? She blew a funnel of smoke in my direction. 'How was Lucas? Oh – beautiful. Cold. *Lucas*, you know . . .' She pivoted sharply and fell into a chair, I think intentionally. 'Do you want a drink, or anything?'

I shook my head. Drink? No. I seem to be content with this cigarette I am apparently smoking.

'Listen, Jamie – there's a lot to see to. Get over. I don't know if I can. I mean to try. So. I think it's better if everything happens very *quickly*, now – yes? I don't want – I don't think I could bear, and nor could anyone else, I imagine, if we . . . I don't know . . . forced ourselves back into some form of – *normality* . . . God – and then had to suffer yet more – *upheavals*. Yes? You agree? We can't afford to draw this *out*.'

Jamie raised his hand and his eyebrow in a gesture of utter acquiescence. At that moment, Alice could well have suggested a mass and immediate suicide, and Jamie felt sure he would have eagerly endorsed the idea (at least in principle).

'Good,' nodded Alice. 'So. I'll talk. You have, I daresay – certain, um – *questions*, Jamie. Don't ask them. I'll talk. Don't interrupt – and *listen*, yes? Because I only say it once.'

Jamie watched her as she eyed, now, the furious tip of her cigar.

'Why do you actually *like* to smoke, Jamie? I think it's vile.'

'Well,' said Jamie (lighting another), 'I wouldn't say I do, really – *like* it. It's just something that creeps up on you. It's hard to shake off. Although I *have* done – did do, once. Shake it off.' It is easier, you know, to talk about this, than whatever might be coming. 'And of course a Havana, well – different, very. Particularly if you're not used to it, and everything. Why *are* you, in fact, um . . . ?'

Alice dropped the cigar into a large smooth crystal ashtray.

'For the smell. Around me. Just before, I made myself a gin and oolong. For the smell. It was disgusting. I don't know how he – !'

And Jamie stiffened, now, as Alice seized up and she closed her eyes. Christ: if Alice breaks, I'm truly done for . . .

She sniffed, and with the back of one finger eased up and away her eyelash from its sticky lid.

'Sorry. Sorry, Jamie. All right, now. Right. Talk. OK. When you . . . found us . . . we were *dressed*, yes? In a way you maybe thought . . . ? Well – me, that's quite easily explained. He liked it. Plain as that. He liked me, at certain times of the day – just before his unavailable times, as a matter of fact – to dress like that. For him. Many men, I imagine, entertain similar ideas. Variations, I suppose, on a theme. Only a few, though, even think to see it through. They need, of course, a willing accomplice. And I was that. So. We move on. You didn't know, did you? That the tramp was really Lucas? No. You didn't. No one did. Except me. And the Hitlers, of course. Yes yes – I know, I know: you have questions. I told you – don't ask them. I will talk. More about them, I promise, later. Are people still puzzled by them? The Hitlers? Or don't they even see them any more? Anyway. He was very proud, you know, Lucas, of that disguise. It was one of the things that thrilled him. He got the idea, he told me once, from those stories, what are they . . . ? Sherlock Holmes stories. I don't actually know what he meant by that – maybe you do. I haven't read them. I don't think they're me. You neither? Well there you are. Anyway. I asked him – of course I asked him why he did it, and for a long time he told me nothing. So . . . I tried to work it out for myself. And couldn't. You get like this – you maybe understand this, Jamie: I think you do. You live . . . closely with someone, someone such as Lucas, you lose the will, the talent, the know-how . . . if you ever had it at all. To think. To work things out. For yourself. Because you know, don't you, that all the thought, it has already been done for you. All worked out. So. I got nowhere on that front. So I just waited for him to tell me. He always did, eventually. Tell me. Things. If he wanted me to know them. Only then. God, you know . . . I did it again, just there. Did you hear? Did you catch it, Jamie? When I said "someone such as Lucas" . . . ? As if. As if . . . Anyway. He said that being the vagrant . . . released him. Got him through to the other side. And don't please ask me the other side of *what*, because I don't know and he never said. Also, he loved to look into the eyes of people here when they weren't seeing Lucas in front of them. It taught him, he said, more about us. Generally, he saw tolerance. Only Frankie, he used to say, is disgusted – afraid. Why is that, I asked him. And he said Oh – do you really not know, Alice? No, I said – no, Lucas: I really don't know. And that was that: he never told me. Do you know, Jamie? Is it just because she's young and beautiful? Does that make sense? Maybe it does to you. I don't know. Anyway. It was the Hitlers who made all this possible, you see. They live down in the tunnel. Did you know? No? No well you wouldn't. You maybe didn't even know there *was* a tunnel, did you Jamie? No. I thought not. Well. They live down there – it's not at all as grim as it sounds – and they made sure that he got in and out of The Works without anyone seeing. There's a special lift. And the tunnel, you see – it more or less leads to where he used to stand. You know: his pitch. Where he was, as a matter of fact, during most of his, you know – unavailable times. And also, they used to see to the *laundry* side of things. Which I know sounds . . . you see, although he always looked so filthy and dreadful, all those clothes . . . well, last night, you possibly noticed. Or maybe not. You maybe weren't thinking. Understandable. But although they were marked and tattered, those clothes, they were always quite scrupulously *clean*. Well obviously. This is *Lucas*, after all . . . God. I never thought I'd be saying all this. Talking about him. Talking about him. Are you sure, Jamie? That you don't want a drink? I can't decide if I do or not. Maybe some champagne . . .'

'I'll open some,' said Jamie. 'For you. If you want . . . ?'

Alice shook her head, quite rapidly.

'No. I'd be sick. Let me finish. Let me say it all. There's so much to be *done*. Now . . . where was I? Oh yes. The Hitlers. I'd better say a bit more about them. They were the very first to come here, you know. The very first, after Lucas and me. I was amazed – amazed that he'd asked them. Because right from the beginning, you know – Lucas, he always told me how people would *need* to be here, and that I would know them when I saw them. Well. The Hitlers, so far as I could see, needed nothing. Nothing at all. Except money, of course. In addition to letting them stay in the tunnel, he paid them, you know. Dave Hitler, he used to work at old Covent Garden, apparently, and then somehow graduated to being front of house – well, glorified bouncer, really, at one of those clubs. You know – Ragout, Blue Angel . . . one of those. Wife oversaw the unofficial and rather more sordid aspects, I understand. Not at all like the sort of club *I* used to work in, but there. And believe me – even now I don't *know* them, or anything. Never really spoken. So why then, Lucas, I asked him. Why them? And he said it again: the other side. The other side. They will be a constant reminder to me, to all of us, of what it is like on the other side. A shadow, he said: a shadow, looming. The serpent in Eden. Our past, and maybe futures. Memorized it. Don't really understand. So. That's all I have. Make of it what you will. It was always to me just a puzzle. And their *name*, I said – their *name*. Is it real? I mean – are they German, are they? Of the actual *family* . . . ? Or what? Lucas was amused. It makes people, he told me – pay *attention*. Along with their silence, it makes them unignorable. Oh yes – the silence. The silence, I have to tell you, was not of Lucas's doing. They just were. Silent. He did tell them, though, to always be aloof – apart from us. I don't really think they needed to be told . . .'

'And,' muttered Jamie, 'was it? Did he say?'

'Hm? Was what? Was what it? What do you mean, Jamie?'

'Their name. Real. Was it?'

'Oh. No. That *was* down to Lucas. He laughed when he thought of it. Their real name is Slingsby. Oh God: it's so *mad*, isn't it? Oh now look, Jamie – I ought to have said when I – right at the outset. All this is absolutely strictly between us two, yes? Understand? I'm still not sure – I just can't think if Lucas would have approved of me telling even you, but I can't . . . I don't see why I should have to carry it all on my own. I can't. It's not fair. And if I had to tell someone, I think . . . I think he would not have minded too much it being you. Because, you know – he loved you, Jamie. In his way. He really did love you.'

Jamie stared down at the floor. He was aware that the end of his cigarette was burning his fingers; aware too that he really should – he ought to put it out.

'I am . . . so pleased to know that. I wish he had told me. I loved *him* – I did, Alice. Still do. Still do . . .'

Alice nodded once, and sucked on her lip.

'Yes,' she said. 'Yes.'

'I wish . . .' whispered Jamie, 'I had told him.' And then his face just crumpled, and he gripped the chair-arm, hard.

'*Please* . . . !' begged Alice. 'Please don't, Jamie. Let's get through this. There's not much more. Let's please just get through this.'

Jamie closed his eyes and breathed in deeply. He looked at Alice now, and tried his hardest to convey to her how brave he was soon going to be. And Alice nodded.

'Right,' she said. 'OK. Now, Jamie – I have to tell you about the . . . I'm going to tell you what's got to happen next – and you, yes? You'll tell the others. Because I have to speak now about . . . saying our goodbyes. The funeral. We have to speak about that.'

'Of course,' said Jamie. 'Of course, of course. You want me to, um – arrange it? Yes, Alice? Make a phone call?'

Alice shook her head very briskly, one hand quickly waving aside the very notion.

'Done. Arranged. All arranged. It's today. This afternoon. It's all arranged.'

Jamie stared at her. The speed! Oh God – the *speed* of all this . . . ! I still haven't even come to terms with . . . ! (I think I just must be bowled over.) But still I find myself speaking in what is, to my ears, a rational manner:

'Are you, um – sure, Alice? I mean I don't mean to, er . . . but are you sure you have arranged this for today? Have you not forgotten, maybe – what day it is . . . ?'

'Oh *God*, Jamie! Credit me with something! That's why it *has* to be today – don't you see? It's maybe *you* who doesn't remember, Jamie. Yes yes – I know it's Christmas, I know that of course. But it's *also* – !'

. 'Ah!' understood Jamie immediately. 'Of course. Of course. Yes. Of course. His birthday. Of course.'

Alice nodded. 'His birthday, yes. Officially. I think he'd appreciate the . . . neatness of it. He also – he'd be upset, you know, if he knew what he'd done to our Christmases. It might please him, maybe, that now we've all got something else to do. Instead. Does that sound crazy to you, Jamie?'

Jamie did his best to lob her over a sort of smile. Shook his head.

'No. No no. Not a bit.'

Well *yes*, if you want the God's honest truth here, Alice. But never mind. It's not at all easy, this: not a bit easy for any one of us.

'So where, um – where is it being held then, Alice? I didn't know they worked, these people, on Christmas Day. Are they sending cars? When should I say to everyone to be, you know – ready, and everything?'

'They do work, they do. If you pay them enough, they do. The hearse will be here by four. We won't need any more cars, Jamie. It's happening here. The funeral's happening right here. This is where he is to be laid to rest.'

Once more Jamie was knocked horribly askew. He forced his face to retain at least some of its composure as he rubbed the palm of a hand all over his mouth – was surprised to encounter this cigarette just hanging there, and then knocked away (he picked it up quickly, felt and heard the sizzle of a burn).

'Oh don't look so amazed, Jamie. You maybe forget that it's *Lucas* we're talking about. He had prepared it all. It's all in his will. Something else we have to discuss – important, actually. But not now. He didn't expect it to be this soon, of course . . . but he had it all prepared. It shows you, though, doesn't it, Jamie? Proof. That he did not in fact think himself immortal.'

'I did. Think he was. Oh God I wish he had been . . . Christ. So anyway, um – where, then, Alice? Exactly? Where are we going to . . . ?'

'In the tunnel. It's all arranged. Just tell everyone, will you? Four. Four sharp. We'll meet in the dining room, and I'll take us down.' Alice sighed. 'I think, if you don't mind Jamie – I think I'd quite like to be alone now, if that's all right . . . ?'

Jamie was on his feet and batting at his jacket pockets and making for the door.

'Oh God *absolutely*, Alice – *absolutely*. You must be totally – God: worn out. Leave it to me. I'll, um – you know. Pass the word.'

Alice stood too, and now she came towards him.

'Thanks. Thank you so much, Jamie. I don't think I could – do all this. Without you.'

'Oh. It's good of you – good of you, Alice, to say that. But I think you could. I think you could.'

Alice put a hand on his shoulder, and gently moved it higher until her fingers lay across the side of his throat, and they both now felt the throbbing there.

'Do you know . . .' she said so softly, 'the thing about this that amazes me most?'

Jamie looked down into her eyes, which were suddenly calmer – and beautiful, now, they seemed to be.

'What? What, Alice? What?'

And Alice nearly smiled.

'The fact that he . . . had no control. No control whatever over his very own life. The fact that he simply . . . ceased to *exist* . . . !'

Jamie shook his head; he dared to look at her, now, expecting her face to be a helplessness of tears. But no: her eyes were still full on him – her lips just poised, he saw and dreaded, upon another, yet one more confidence:

'We didn't, you know, have sex. I might as well say. Despite the way I – you know: dressed, and everything. We didn't. Have sex. I used to – relieve his tensions. Part of what I was for. But we didn't. Ever. Have sex. And along with my Jezebel costume he sometimes liked me to wear a . . . I don't know how it sounds, but anyway: a hat. Bowler hat. Little grey one, with a narrow band. Other times a topper: black silk. That's the one he liked best, I think.'

Jamie was torn between looking away, and not wishing to appear to. Alice kissed him, then – quite firmly, and on the mouth. She withdrew briefly, checking up on his eyes. And then she brought back down her lips on to his. Jamie made to touch her shoulder – but she was gone from him, Alice: she had spun away from him now and left him groggy, and reeling quite badly.

'Do you know . . . ?' she asked him – and she seemed quite eager (whatever Jamie could mean by that). 'Do you know . . . ? Well of course you don't – but I'll tell you, shall I? Shall I tell you, Jamie, Lucas's very last words?'

And it was Jamie, now, who was keen, so eager: he very much wanted to know this.

'Yes. Oh yes, Alice – yes. What? What – oh *God*! What did he say?'

Alice looked dead at him.

'*Jizz* . . .'

Jamie just gaped.

'Sorry, Alice – what? What did you say . . . ?'

'*Jizz* . . .' said Alice again. 'Was his last word on earth. He had just come in. From being – you know: the vagrant. Because he went out every single day, you know, Christmas no exception. And I served his gin and oolong, in all my pretty lingerie. It is pretty, isn't it Jamie? And he lit a cigar. Which he loved to do. Not so much the cigar, I think, as breaking yet another of his own self-imposed rules. Same with the curtains. Anyway. He was just about to change for . . . well, you know what for. His suit and so on I had all laid out. The wine one, the dark wine one that he's wearing now . . . and he told me what he had heard when he came back through the tunnel. You can hear, you know, a lot of what's going on in the dining room, down there. He always used to listen. Everyone, he said, seems in such good spirits. He said to me: Alice – this will be a Christmas to remember. And then he put down his glass, and he drew on his cigar – and then before, just the second before he shuddered, shuddered with such terrible violence and then simply ceased to exist . . . he said to me: "Mm, Alice: *mm*", he said. "Do you know – I really am very much looking forward to all this . . . *jizz* . . ."'

Jamie was aware of Alice's steady gaze. And then came the fear – oh yes, this utter fear. (It had him by the throat, and it wouldn't let him go.)

'Now come on Oona, love . . .' Paul was gently urging. 'Gotta get something down you girl, ain't you? Ay? You know it makes sense. Kimmy's had a sandwich, ain't she? Ay? Ain't you, Kimmy? Go on, Oona love – have a sandwich: my sake, ay?'

Oona looked up and right through him. Reached out and took a sandwich. Anything, really, to stop him talking. (Still, thought Jamie: she still looks quite terrified; Mike – he's, um, resting. And after what's just happened, I'm not too surprised.)

'Teddy . . .' said Judy, quite weakly (can't actually see where he is, you know, Teddy – but he must be round here somewhere because we all are, aren't we? Round here somewhere. He's maybe gone to get more wine, or something. Or possibly he's just slipped away to the kitchen bit, for a moment. Don't know the *layout*, you see: can't remember the last time I was here, in Kimmy and Dorothy's place. It's all full of boxes and mountains of cans; paint, I suppose. Must be maybe paint. Oh. I do so hope *John's* all right. Oh God – it was *awful*, what happened: just so awful. And Frankie – she was *beside* herself, poor little thing. Oh. As if all this wasn't *enough* . . . And what of Mary-Ann? Too young – much too young for all of this: at least now her mother's with her. Wherever they are. Oh. Where's Teddy . . . Ah – he's there. There he is. So I'll say it now, will I? Yes I will: I'll say it now). 'Teddy, my sweet . . . maybe people would like some more . . . ? Maybe just a drop of . . . ?'

'I've got,' said Teddy, placing an assortment of bottles on the table. 'I've just been to get.'

'Anyway . . .' resumed Alice, from her place of authority at the desk by the window. She laid down the papers and took off the gold-framed glasses that Jamie, anyway, had never seen her wearing. 'That's the . . . essence of it. The whole of the will, well – it runs to volumes, as you might expect. But that's the part that affects you all directly.' She gestured towards a heap of thickish envelopes to the left of her untouched glass of chardonnay. 'If you remember, everyone – please do take with you, will you, the letter. When you go. All your names are on them.'

The silence fell again. Tubby was well over to one side, continuing to pile up more and more sandwiches that nobody wanted. He passed out platefuls of them to Biff, who handed them to Paul who was trying his best to make people take one.

'It's all . . .' said Judy, quite suddenly, 'so *much* . . . isn't it? Hm? It's just all so *much* . . .'

Jamie, beside her on the sofa, nodded and gave her bunched-up fingers a momentary squeeze. Yes it is, is what he was thinking. (That, and Jesus: just you look at Alice, will you? Sitting there now, and apparently calm. She kissed me, Alice – she kissed me twice.) But whatever way Judy had meant it, it was, it really was – just wholly overwhelming. The fact that it was now early evening, and still Christmas Day; that they had all just been party to the funeral of . . . Christ: *Lucas*. (And God Almighty: what a thing that had been.) That just twenty-four hours ago . . . Oh God. And so on. On and on. All the stuff that would eat at you for ever and ever. And now this: the latest detonation. Lucas has bequeathed to us all the unhampered ownership of each of our spaces: to do with as we choose. And even through the thick and thinning mists, the waves of shock and pain and the overlay of a sort of derangement – minds, I can only assume, will be working away, working away. It is, as Judy said – just all so *much*. Too much, really: too much altogether. I'm glad, though, at least, that Caroline has gone. This would have been, oh God – it was bad enough, wasn't it, for Benny, I should have said – just seeing us all, as he did last night . . . but Jesus, if he'd had to go through – suffer all of this as well . . . well: too much. So yes, Caroline had been right in her decision to leave, and quickly. Although something – there's something about it that tugs at me, somehow. Normally, I'd talk about this (normally!) to Judy – but just take one look at her, will you, poor love: she's in no state, is she? No state at all.

'So you do see, don't you Jamie?' Caroline had said, over her shoulder, as she continued to bundle things into a bag. 'Why I'm doing this? It's best, isn't it? We'll be at my mother's, so you know where to . . . you know: if you want to.'

Jamie had just nodded. Said 'of course, of course' maybe a hundred times in total. They packed up all their presents, Benny and Caroline, and one or two other things maybe, as well. They both were gone in no time. A relief, if I'm honest, in one way – because family or not, they weren't in all frankness, were they, part of the hard core, here? They did not have to deal with a disembowelling.

'Bye then, Jamie,' said Caroline, at the door. 'You will be all *right*? Benny – say goodbye to your father.'

And he did. It wasn't his fault (look – he's only young) that he tacked on 'Merry Christmas'. Roger, Jamie had mumbled, as he waved them away: roger, wilco, and out. He had breathed deep and heavy, then – as if trying to dislodge from his nostrils something very stubborn and maybe malignant. Right, now (he thought): right, now – I've got a funeral to go to. But first (I've just got time – if I really put my mind to it, do this quickly – then I've just got time, I'm sure) I'm going all the way back up to Lucas's space and I've got to get the small one, the smallest of the presses, clanking into action. I'll print some cards. That's what I'll do. Some memorial cards. Something else for people to take away with them and have for ever (from all of this). And I did: set it up – boxed up and banged in a border, guillotined the pasteboard – just enough to go round. And then I borrowed from Mike a black silk tie (he seemed to have dozens – brownish and thin, compacted with age) and attended a funeral. A funeral, yes. And God Almighty: what a thing that had been.

I don't at all know quite what it was I was expecting from this tunnel of the Hitlers (maybe a sort of bunker?) but when Alice ushered us all through this door I'd never noticed (You ever seen this door, John? Have you? This little door? No, he said to me: I must say, Jamie, this one's new to me) and then on down a curved and narrow flight of smooth stone stairs, I remember thinking – when at the bottom it all opened out before me (and yes I thought this, despite just everything) that it really was, you know, a very grand and handsome space. What we had here was more, much more than the word 'tunnel' implied – it was not unlike the dining room we had all just left, shuffling and mute. And God, how it all had jarred – the swags, the still glistening tree, the curtains and the posters, the still glistening tree and the thrones, those magnificent sconces, marred now by the frozen spillage from the cold and guttered candles: and the still glistening tree, with Lucas's present just lying before it. Arched and uplit, this low broad cellar – ranks of squat and massive pillars, the stonework scored in a criss-cross trellis pattern, the capitals thick with densely worked vine leaves, looked like to me. Extraordinary, isn't it? The workmanship, such attention to detail, the sheer bloody quality of a hidden and windowless undercroft, deep beneath a printing works. Extraordinary too that I should notice it at all. I caught Paul's eye once, though, and he had too: taken in all of it. I think we were the only ones. Everyone else was dumbed by shock: the sight of the dark and quite plain coffin lying unadorned on this series of trestles, down there . . . it was, it was oh – wholly shocking; and weeping came – it was Mike who was weeping.

'Oh *God* . . .' he moaned. 'It's all just so *quick* . . . it must have been just like this, Jamie – in the War, you know. All was fine, and then bang! The bombs fell – or the telegram arrived – and – and – !'

'*Mike,*' said Oona – her voice was low and surprisingly stern. 'Stop. Stop it right now.'

And he did, Mike, to give him his due: he did his very best to stop up the seeping tears – beat them back and subdued them into no more than grizzling, now.

'Alice . . .' I whispered. 'Where are the . . . ? Have the undertakers . . . ? Are they gone?'

She nodded. Only then I noticed the black and gauzy veil she had lowered down over her face; each lacy intersection was stuck with a velvet dot.

'Gone, yes. They've gone. We didn't need them any more. I wanted this to be – just for us.'

'And . . . the Hitlers?'

'Gone too. I paid them. Them we don't need at all, now – not ever again. They're gone for good. Now, Jamie – are you ready? Shall we begin?'

And it overtook me again now, the fear. Not that it leaves you: it recedes, for a while – regards you with malice and an ironical grin as it pays out a little slack, allowing you, for now, to begin to cope; but at times like this, it gleefully rallies its forces – storms back in, takes you over (leaves you quaking).

'Am I – *ready*? Ready for what, Alice? What is it you want me to do?'

Mike was mewling again now – but Alice talked to me over all that in a just faintly louder and more insistent whisper.

'We need pallbearers, Jamie. Six, I think. The straps are there, but he needs to be lowered, you see. Lowered. You see?'

And then I did. A vast and thick slab of the floor had been lifted and swung to one side; a hole was revealed, a great gaping chasm leading on down to unutterable blackness. Christ. My God. Lucas has prepared his very own crypt.

I nodded briefly, and turned back to the others. Right, then: six. Paul, obviously – Tubby and Biff. Me – that makes four. John . . . no, too old: wouldn't be fair. Teddy – that's five. And Mike, I suppose it's got to be. Christ – I hope he can pull himself together, just a bit. Christ, I hope he can. So. Anyway. Had a quick word with Paul, now, and he's passing the word. Teddy's just come up to me, look: You tell me where and what to do, is what he's just said to me: dear old Teddy. Dear dear fellow.

'Oh *no-o-o-oo* . . . !' Mike was wailing, now – and the noise, my God – it swooped and boomed around all the pillars and up over the arches before curving back with violence to hit us all again. 'Oh I'm so *sorry* – so *sorry,* everyone – but I just, oh – *couldn't* – I – I just – oh, *couldn't* . . . !'

'*Mike* . . . !' hissed Oona. 'Just stop. *Stop* – do you hear me?'

John, now, was by my side.

'I'd – like to,' he said quite gently. 'I should regard it as a signal honour, Jamie. If you think I'm worthy . . .'

'Oh Johnny . . .' whispered Frankie, as she clutched his arm. 'Are you sure? Are you sure?'

I looked at John: yes, he was – sure, oh yes, very much so.

'All right then, John. It's not too far. Just a few yards.' And then to Alice: 'I think we're, um. Set, now.'

Kimmy had her arm around Dorothy's shrunken shoulders (Mary-Ann, thank the Lord – they've left her upstairs: I expect she'll be OK there) and they both sort of shimmied forward to huddle alongside Frankie and Judy – she beckoned them on, Judy, and then embraced them when they got there. Oona stayed over to the side with Mike, which was maybe just as well. And still she simply stared ahead of her – careless, it seemed, of Mike's now continuous short and breathless sobbing. Paul and myself, we stooped down at the head of the coffin – squared ourselves to take the heft of it at the shoulders of the thing. Tubby and Biff were right behind us, and John and Teddy I'd positioned at the foot (I suppose I figured that down there, it would be that much less of a burden). We all, now – the six of us – were caught in a pose of deep genuflection: heads hung low, and awaiting ... well, *my* word, I suppose – to take the strain, and rise and lift.

'Right ...' I said softly. 'Ready, everyone? *Now*, then ...'

And we rose slowly as one – halfway up, knees still dog-leg bent, the concentrated weight close to crushing us. And then – !

'Wait!' called out Alice. 'Wait! Stop. Go down. Not yet!'

I glanced with anxiety across to Paul, my face colliding with just this coffin. We all now stood there – bowed and crouched and frozen to the spot, our legs and backs simply killing us – all I could hear was the gasps and grunting (a lot of it mine).

'Right ...' I said softly. 'Ready, everyone? *Down*, then ...'

And slowly, slowly – and there was a creaking now very audible from some joints or other – we eased this monster back down gently, and then we just stood alongside of it. We looked at Alice. Teddy coughed once (which was booming). We waited.

'Doesn't anyone ... ?' she faltered. 'Want to say a few words ... ?'

Judy stepped forward – eyes shining brightly, though each was tipped down at the corners; her mouth was already ajar and she appeared altogether well down the road to saying maybe quite a lot more than just a few words ... but then her lips were trembling, and her eyes, they just gave in. She stepped back and looked down, her fingers and wrists so agitated – wrestling, it seemed, within a despair of their own. I glanced around from face to face – and what I saw in each of them was maybe reflected in my own. There was, we maybe all were feeling, just *so* much to say ... and yet nothing, really: nothing at all. Just being here like this – it sort of put paid to words. And it was then I remembered the cards in my pocket: I had kept it simple, very simple – cream card, black border, and a stark and humble tribute. I solemnly handed one to each of them. These, I whispered, are maybe words enough. Most people glanced down at it, the card. No one spoke. Paul sucked his teeth, and Alice – she looked at me rather wildly, is how it seemed. And then she said *Christ*, Jamie . . . All right, then: let us continue.

I passed my palm across my face (noticing idly as I did it that I was badly in need of a shave: so envied Teddy that thick beard of his; and a good deal less idly that I so much now needed the collective hit of maybe five or six cigarettes, all dragged down at once). The glimmer of Paul's eye was telling me he was ready: we knelt to our task.

'Right . . .' I said softly. 'Ready, everyone? *Now*, then . . .'

And more smoothly, this time, we had it up and on our shoulders – it was so much less crushing when you were finally upright. We walked the few paces to the brink of the grave (and these straps, I don't know – I think they must have been attached to the underside, or something; they were anyway dangling down, which didn't seem at all right, somehow). We had it now in a position, I was judging, where we could safely begin, inch by inch, to lower it down – then we could get a firm grip on each of our straps and – Ooh! *Whoa*! Oh! Oh! Something wrong, now – something's gone awry at the back, look – the whole thing's tipping away and shearing to the left – but I've got it, I think, oh God I hope so – and Paul, yes, he's brought up his other arm now, and Tubby and Biff, they're bracing themselves – so we've saved it, I think, oh God I hope so – but I heard a clunk from somehwere, way to the rear, and a crumpling of sorts and female gasps and a sudden and very worrying increase in the volume of Mike's no longer stifled bleating – and I half turned when I knew we had the coffin secure and it's then that I saw poor John there, collapsed on the floor with Frankie squealing and Kimmy doing her best to shield Dorothy's eyes and Judy bending low, her shuddering fingers tugging at his tie. There was a gash on his forehead (blood dripped down) – and even now as I was preparing to take the strain of the straps (signalling with my eyebrows to Paul – and Tubby and Biff, they were both rallying round) I was running through the possibilities: he had lost his footing, maybe tripped over a strap, and the coffin had tipped and hit him hard on the head. He was moaning, John, as the five of us remaining began to lower the coffin, slowly slowly, bit by bit, into the seemingly bottomless void. *Oh–oh–oh–oh* . . . ! is what Mike was near screaming, now: I blame *myself*! I blame *myself*! Oh God this is my doing . . . my doing! Me! It is *I* who should have taken the strain . . . ! I put this fairly and squarely at my door . . . ! And John was grunting now as Oona was shrieking out OK that's *it*, Mike! That's just fucking *it*, OK?! You just shut it right this bloody *minute*, you bastard *bastard* or I'll fucking kill you *now*, all right?! I was sweating badly, I don't mind admitting it – and the helpless gratitude and relief that I think we all felt when at last the coffin was heard to hit base, well – it just visibly flooded all over us.

'I think . . .' said John – and he was trying to get up, and not at all making it – 'I think . . . I'm quite fine, now . . .'

'I'm not!' yelled Mike. 'I'm very far from it! It's a judgement! A judgement! I am *so-o-oo* unworthy . . . !'

Alice was muttering something, standing quite still at the edge of the grave, but I couldn't begin to make out even one word of it.

Then John slumped back to the ground and he seemed quite out of it and Frankie screamed and Mike quickly became quite delirious and was babbling like a run amok lunatic and a harshly shrieking Oona was beating him savagely and Judy was roaring at Teddy to make everyone *stop*, just make it all *stop* for the love of God in heaven – and I more or less sprinted to where Alice was standing now and I said to her Jesus, Alice – oh God *Jesus*, Alice, I'm so very sorry about, oh Christ – all of this – and what was it, Alice? What was it you were saying? I'm sorry I just couldn't catch it . . . ? And she said to me something and the noise and mayhem behind us now had reached the point of near-hysteria and she had to shout at me quite loudly that all she had uttered was her tender parting message to the loved one: all she had said was that the rest was *silence*! Did I hear her *that* time?! Yes, Alice, yes – I did, I did. And I had to step over a prostrate and curled-up Mike who was yelping and covering his face with stricken hands – Oona was kicking him and spitting as she did so – just to get close to the huddle of anxiety that hovered over John, because we just had to now, didn't we, get him medical attention, that much was clear – and so much more so as I stooped down now and saw for myself how very pale he had become. And as I briskly instructed Teddy to go, go now, you must phone an ambulance (quick: we must lose no time) I was flexing my aching back and still rubbing with care at my strap-burnt palms and fingers because I tell you now: that coffin, I am not joking – it was an absolute deadweight.

So. As I say: what a thing that had been. And we had barely even begun to recover from all of it (and do you ever, I wonder? Really recover from something, God, such as that? I don't think Mike will; do hope John does, though) when Alice whisked us up here and as we reeled before her she told us quite matter-of-factly that as from today we were all now men and women of property. I don't quite know why it was Kimmy and Dorothy's place we ended up in – no conscious decision, I think; it's just that we couldn't all gather in the dining room, could we, as once we might have done. Not with all the . . . well, you know – all the trappings of merriment, just blatantly hanging there.

The ambulance, rather surprisingly, arrived very quickly. Maybe red-letter days are favourite, if you plan on dying, or a collapse. I didn't recognize him . . . well of *course* I didn't recognize him – but one of the paramedics made it plain to me that he had been part of the team that had come here yesterday to, um – attend to Lucas. As he closed the rear door on a still unconscious John and a halfway composed and quite determined to be grown-up Frankie (she insisted – was very firm on the point that it was her place and hers alone to accompany him) this ambulance driver, he tipped me a wink and said quite jokily Right, then – be seeing you again in the morning, will we sir? Which I thought not remotely amusing, and actually in the very worst sort of taste (as I hope I made plain to him).

When it became clear to us, though, that this latest bewildered gathering of the just about walking wounded had pretty much run its uncertain course (the stragglers were limping to the finishing line, which was not so much breached, then, as tumbled over, falteringly) there maybe hovered in the air an overlay of giddy alarm. The realization, possibly, that after the shock of the news and its consequent night (wide awake with disbelief) – following a hasty entombment and now this dispersal by proxy of gifts so hugely in excess of anything that might gaudily remain beneath the still glistening tree (in the reflective festive paper and drifts of coloured ribbon) . . . that now, as real and endless time lapped at the fringe of us and seeped back in, there would soon come a need to, Jesus – apply oneself to something else, then . . . because here was the first appalling intimation that life was meant to go *on*?

'Jamie,' said Oona, as people began to blindly drift away (Jamie could hear Judy in the distance – and she looked so distracted – calling out softly: 'Teddy . . . ? Teddy . . . ? Ah *there* you are, Teddy . . . *There* you are . . .'). 'Can I – talk to you?'

'Hm? Oh of course, Oona – of course. How's old Mike now, do you think? He's taking it so hard, isn't he? Poor old Mike.'

'Poor old Mike,' Oona said evenly, 'behaves like a *prat*. Listen: I really do want to talk to you, Jamie.'

'Well – as I say, Oona: fire away. If you think I can, you know – do anything, or anything . . . ? Fire away.'

And even as Jamie was being at his, he rather had to think, very best and most expansive, he was aware of Alice's imminent and determined approach. He had a feeling, somehow, that whatever it was Oona felt she really wanted to say to him, it would just have to wait (like it or not).

'Oona,' said Alice, really quite magisterially. 'I'm sorry to have to take Jamie away from you, but I just must speak with him. You do understand? Important.'

Alice took Jamie by the shoulder and piloted him away towards the door, leaving Oona just standing there and open-mouthed – maybe about to respond, and then maybe not: either way, Alice surely didn't mind.

'Just follow, will you Jamie? Come upstairs with me.'

In the lift, Jamie heard himself say to her:

'You are suddenly, Alice, behaving very . . . responsibly. In charge, if you like.'

'Mm. I suppose I am. I expect because there's now room to. You too, Jamie – don't know if you've noticed, but you are assuming a . . . what is it? A sort of – *presence* that you surely didn't ever have before, you know. Even the way you talk – it might just be me, but I don't think you were like that. Before.'

And as Jamie followed her into what now, he could only presume, he must refer to as Alice's space (and Alice's alone) he found himself reflecting that you know, all in all, she could be right.

'Cigarette, Jamie? There are some Turkish, somewhere . . . oh – you've already got.'

Jamie glanced at the Gitane in his hand. 'So I have,' he said.

'Drink, then? Do please sit.'

Jamie perched on the arm of a sidechair. He shook his head.

'I'll be fine with the fag. Seem to have got out of the way of drinking. And eating. And sleeping. Most things, really . . .'

'And sex? What about sex? I think I must open some champagne . . .'

Jamie regarded her, as she strode across the room. She opened a low and highly polished mahogany cabinet, which turned out to be a little fridge. She walked back towards him, holding out before her a bottle of Bollinger.

'Jamie? Would you mind? I'm not very good at it.'

Jamie jammed his cigarette into the corner of his mouth, and set to twisting away the wire.

'You're different, Alice. Already . . . you're so terribly different.'

'But maybe only because I can be. You didn't answer me, Jamie. What about sex? Have you given that up too?'

'Well . . .' said Jamie, simply, as he eased away the cork. 'I wouldn't say that, exactly. At least not in theory. Sex, though, has rather given me up, is closer to the truth. Caroline . . . you know: Caroline. When she was here . . . where are the glasses, Alice? Got glasses round here, have you . . . ? Ah yes – there. Right. Maybe I will have just a drop, actually. If you don't mind.'

'Not too much, Jamie, because you're driving. What about Caroline? What about her?'

'Hm? Oh well – just that she . . . I mean she came to live here, as well you know – but she didn't feel . . . she apparently didn't feel that all that side of things was, um – right, yet, I can only assume. Anyway – we didn't, if that's what you mean. Here you are, Alice – maybe the champagne will make you feel . . . I don't know. Not better. Better would be silly. Did you say I'm *driving*, Alice? Did I hear that right? Sorry – I've dripped it over the sides, just a bit . . .'

'Thank you, Jamie. Mm. Delicious. Yes . . . The Works, it wasn't very conducive to sex, on the whole, I think. Odd, really. I imagine anyone outside – you know, outsiders who might have heard of us . . . they would have assumed that it would be one non-stop orgy, or something. Given the – constituents.'

Mm, thought Jamie: well I *think* I know what she must be getting at. I mean: *God* knows, frankly. All my judgements are at least unsound. My sensibilities, well – they are battered beyond recognition. But surely she can be meaning only one thing? She did kiss me, after all: she kissed me, Alice. Twice.

'And the way you're talking,' she had suddenly resumed. 'The way you talk, now. Do you know . . . it almost, just almost reminds me of –'

'Oh *don't*!' rushed in Jamie. 'Don't even think it. I'm quite unworthy. But listen, Alice – what were you saying about . . . *driving*, was it?'

'You're avoiding the point, Jamie.'

'No, Alice, no. I'm coming back to one of yours. It was you who said it, Alice. Can I just top you up, there? Yes? Drop more?'

Alice sighed, and put down her glass. Whatever she had been pursuing, if pursuing she were – Jamie honestly, believe him, just doesn't *know* any more – she would seem to have abandoned, anyway. As well, he thought, she may. Because I've been trying, I think – I have in a way been striving to beat away the fug of all these vapours and find myself inflamed by if not outright rude and hard-on lust, then at least the need to deflect or numb these pinpoints of shock, latch on to maybe something that would help to peel away the layers from my face, the damp coils of misery, that make it hard to sometimes breathe. (And she does have a point, Alice – I used not to talk or think like this.) But I look at her now, and it can't be done: I think she knows this. Though she does not, I'm sure, know why: I've only just got it all clear in my mind, and she'd hate it, Alice, to know. It was when she said to me (was it yesterday? Was it during this lifetime?) that she and Lucas . . .

didn't. Have sex. Ever. They just didn't. Well. I think . . . if they, you know – *had*. Then. I might be very keen, very keen indeed, to get . . . close. To be as deeply inside her as it is possible for . . . one man to go. But if Lucas left it; so, I think, can I. It is he I would have followed.

'Jamie,' said Alice – brisk, now: she was back to being brisk. 'Here. Take these keys. I want you to go and get Frankie. I don't want her staying there all night. She's not used to . . . anything like this. It's all written down here – where she is, and everything. St John's Wood, I think – miles away. Private clinic. Well of course. It is John we're talking about, isn't it? So. Will you? Yes?'

Jamie set down his glass and took from Alice the fob of keys and a piece of paper and fought at the same time with all the business of lighting up another.

'Well . . . yes, I suppose so. Um – these keys . . . ?'

'Spare set. He kept it with . . . He kept them here.'

And Jamie's eyes were wide.

'Is this . . . the *Alvis* . . . ?'

Alice permitted herself a brief and rather bitter smile.

'The first, Jamie. The first. That is the first light of excitement I have seen in your eyes. Yes, Jamie – it's the Alvis. As opposed to the Alice . . . Why don't you just go downstairs and *fuck* the bloody thing?'

She was angry, now – you just had to look at her.

'Oh and Jamie – do take with you this very bad *joke*, will you?'

And she thrust into Jamie's overflowing hand . . . what now, exactly? What was this, then? Oh it's a . . . Christ. Well that's bloody odd. What's she giving me this for? And what's wrong with it? What's upsetting her? Bad *joke*, did she say . . . ?

Jamie left her (didn't say any more: her eyes were blazing) and in the lift on the way down, he began to try to unravel the thing. He unbent the corners of Alice's personal memorial card to Lucas, one of the cards he had only that day and so lovingly printed.

Smart black Roman border. 'Lucas', it read: 'The Founder Of All Our Feasts'. Rather good that, no? And then, beneath a sober and dignified cartouche: 'His Inspiration Will For Ever Bear Fruit. May He Rest In Peach'.

What? Wait just a minute: *what* ... ? Oh *Christ*, no – I couldn't have, could I ... ?

Jamie – cold, he was: clammy, decidedly, as the lift reached the ground and juddered to a halt – had to pass a hand across his bristly cheeks as he felt in his pocket for a cigarette. I burn – I burn I burn I, oh Christ – *burn* with shame. I had wanted to dispatch him to heaven – but I find myself, now, so well down the road to the other place altogether. I have contributed to its paving with this gross and offensive slab of good intention.

Oh well. If one truism has recently emerged, it is this: what's done is done. Right? So. Where did she say the Alvis was? Hm? Because what I think I'll do now is just go and *fuck* the bloody thing.

Waiting. I'm waiting, now. Put my head round the door of the clinic place (found it quite easily, rather surprisingly) – and my God, I'm telling you, it's a very far cry from the sorts of hospitals I've been used to. More like a hotel. And all the Christmas decorations in the foyer thing, there: put Harrods to shame, I'm not kidding you. And um ... sorry, bit distracted. Just to be sitting in this car ... it's sort of taken over from everything else, if you want me to be honest with you. I mean I *know*: you could say Oh *Christ*, Jamie – get a bit *real*, can't you? In the light of just, oh – *all* of it, for

God's sake, it's only a *car*, when all's said and done. Well yes – I can see that that is a perfectly rational attitude – and one, I assure you, that if the option were open to me, well – I'd rush in head-long and share it. But . . . certain things, as we all understand, take different people in different ways, don't they? This is known. And this car . . . well, you've got the hang of me by now. I'm either in or I'm not. Compulsions, you see. And this car, this absolutely gorgeous, gorgeous car . . . well: let's just say I'm in, and leave it at that, shall we?

So . . . sorry, sorry, bit distracted, like I say (every time you move, you know, you get these leathery wafts, rising up to meet you . . .), but the position is now that I've spoken to the reception sort of person and she phoned up to I suppose the room they've got John in (she wouldn't tell me how he was, or anything: I don't suppose she knew or cared) and Frankie rang her back just a minute or two later and she said she'd be down. She said there was not much more she could usefully do here and that she was dead on her feet and that soon she'd be down. So. Waiting. I'm waiting, now. I keep firing the ignition, and then turning her off. It doesn't kick into life, or anything – you're just aware of a gentle purr . . . and then when you kill it . . . well you don't, really: it just sweetly expires. I was maybe expecting her to behave like a bit of a tank when it came to the corners (because she's elegant, yes, but a big girl nonetheless) . . . the power steering, though – it does all the work for you. God, she's a dream. Just perfect. I can so understand John's love of her. I mean, just sitting here – it's a bit, in a way, like The Works, in miniature: you feel so safe. Well. Like The Works *used* to be, anyway – God knows, now. I think . . . I think what I must just quickly do now is I'll fire up the ignition, and then I'll turn her off. Take my mind off the fear of fear (it lurks, in the too close distance).

Dark. It's dark, now. Must have just crept up on me, this winter's night. All the way here (trying hard to remember how to drive) I was aware of just a rather still and constant eerie greyness all around me – could easily have passed for just pre-dawn or twilight instead of – what was it? Mid to late afternoon. And there seemed to be absolutely no one on the streets. Well – it is Christmas Day, as I keep on having to remind myself. One or two lone men in cars, their grim expressions fixed – getting away from what, I wondered. Going where? No: I don't think there was purpose, there. Just killing a little bit of the endless time on this day of the year.

God, though – what it must be to own a car such as this. I cannot conceive of ever being in anything like such a position. I mean – car like this, you presumably own all sorts of other things – property, women, those sorts of things. But then John is rich, isn't he? Yes he is – rich like Lucas. Probably the only two men I've ever met in my life to whom money, the spending of it, simply does not seem to register. Well. I have *had* cars, of course. I've owned the odd runabout. Not recently, though (one of the many bones of contention with Caroline, as you probably don't recall – why on earth should you? Who I haven't, you know, given a single thought to, since she left. Still: she's at her mother's. She'll be fine. I wonder if Benny scooped up a handful of those rather wonderful-looking crackers, before he left . . . ? Because he likes crackers, Benny: well – all kids do, I suppose).

Of course . . . it has just occurred to me (this is, I promise, the first time the meaning has actually dawned) that I now too am a man of property. Those thousands of square feet that I rattle around in . . . are mine. I wonder what Caroline would make of that. If she knew. Not that she really ever liked all the space. Why don't we divide it up, she asked me quite often: like Mike and Oona have done. Also: why don't we take down those horrible pictures, while we're about it? *Sorry,* Caroline – sorry, didn't quite catch? Excuse me? *What* did you say? These canvases here, are these the ones you are referring to? The grand-scale action paintings just here and here, do you mean? My sole endeavours into the world of creation? Those the ones you mean? Well *yes* Jamie, frankly: I mean – I don't mean to, you know – hurt your *feelings*, or anything, but they really are so awfully big and bright and, well . . . it's not as if they're *real* pictures, is it? I mean it's not as if they *mean* anything, is it? So why don't we take them down and then we can go out and get something really really nice instead. Mm, I went: mm, Caroline – mm. Well. Didn't actually see the point in saying any more. That they meant something to *me*, she either got or she didn't (didn't, plainly) – but what I was actually thinking is Hey – slow up here, Caroline: less of the 'we', OK? This is my space – mine. You – you've only just *arrived* . . .

Miss him. I miss him, you know. No: not miss him – too small, too trivial an expression. I am . . . *holed*, is the truth. When a train is driven through you, it takes time, you know, to even gather up your scattered parts, let alone set about the business of shoring up even the tattered edges of so catastrophic an eruption. And no time has passed – no, none at all. Jesus – this time yesterday, he was *alive*, you know. Christ's sake. We all were.

I've just been . . . while I've been sitting here and doing my best to cope with all of this (trying to not let it twist me up too badly: it's not good, you know, to be alone at times like this) . . . I've been rootling around in the glove compartment, look . . . because it's always interesting, isn't it? What people actually do stow away in there. Well – I almost laughed, I really nearly did: if someone had been sitting here beside me, I certainly would have gone through with the full, fat chortle, for form's sake. Because what did we have here, then, but a perfect pair of caramel and butter-soft top-stitched leather gloves: never worn, it looked like, but in their rightful and designated place. And also . . . what's this . . . ? Oh *great*, actually – yes indeed, this is a bit of a godsend, this is. Didn't actually know I needed it until it rolled out into my hands: a full and unopened bottle of whisky. And not just any old whisky, either: twenty-five-year-old Macallan. Well. That should do. And yes – it did: the first jolt, mmm – wondrous, actually. Smooth as cream, but packing all the hit you needed. (My usual hits, by the way – the fags . . . well I haven't in truth been even mentioning them, lately. There is really no point, so utterly constant have they become. It would be like saying to you, now listen: I am now breathing in . . . I am now breathing out; I am now breathing in . . . I am now breathing out. You see what I mean? You take it as read. It is a given. Yes. And talking of that – I was quite lucky to find a funny little foreign sort of shop open, not too far down the line. Forty Gitanes, please, I said to the man there. Sorry – don't stock them. Camels? No? Gauloises? No? OK, then – what have you got? Oh. Yes. I see. The usual. Rothmans, I suppose then, yeh: give me eighty Rothmans. Hundred: what the hell.)

And then I was startled beyond belief – froze right up and briefly went to pieces (I think I even cried out) – when the car door beside me was suddenly wrenched open and the glimpse of frightening night brought along with it this rush of cold air and then the scented and fabulous Frankie was swishingly all over the place with her legs and her hair, her scarves and her fingernails, and the door clunked softly shut and she smiled at me then and she said to me Oh Jamie thanks *so* much for coming and I'm *so* sorry you had to wait so long and Jesus, Jamie, the smoke in here, it's just so *choking* . . .

'Oh God *sorry*, Frankie – sorry. I'll, um – open a . . . but you might get cold if I, um – open a . . . ?'

'Put on the air conditioning, Jamie. Here – this button here.'

'Oh right: air conditioning. Check. F.A.B. Excellent. How, um – is he, Frankie? Hm? All right? Not too bad, is he? God, you know . . . I haven't said that in ages . . .'

Frankie sighed, and looked up at the soft and biscuit-coloured roof.

'I'm absolutely *exhausted*: do you know that? Ooh – is this whisky? Oh give me a swig, will you Jamie? Said what? Said what in ages?'

'Hm? Oh. Nothing. F.A.B. Nothing. Forget it. Here – I'll just wipe the, you know – neck, and everything. Didn't know you drank whisky, Frankie.'

'You don't have to wipe it, Jamie. Actually there are glasses in the back, but I just can't be bothered. I don't, much. But it's such a funny time. What's F.A.B.? Fab, you mean? Like in the Sixties and The Beatles and things? See? I do *know* things. I'm not *stupid*, like everyone seems to think.'

'I don't, Frankie,' Jamie said quickly. 'I think you're just . . . I think you're . . .'

'God – it's really *strong*, this stuff, isn't it? Nice, though. What do you think I am, Jamie?'

'Oh . . . just really – *nice*. And obviously far from stupid. So tell me then, Frankie – how, um . . . ?'

'Johnny? Oh – not too bad, thank God. Very very very mild sort of concussion thing, doctor said. He's asleep, now. Poor thing. God though, Jamie – what a thing to *happen*. It was awful trying to explain it all to them, and everything. I mean – hit by a *coffin* . . . they just sort of look at you. The doctor said, was it a *full* coffin, was it? And I said yes it was, it was . . . do you want another gulp of this stuff, Jamie? Here you are, then. Anyway – yes, I said, it was. It was full of Lucas.'

'Jesus . . .' breathed Jamie, as he slowly unscrewed the cap on the Macallan.

'Well I *know*,' agreed Frankie, with vigour. '*Exactly*. And the doctor said well no wonder he's got such a bruise there because they can be very heavy, you know: full coffins.'

Jamie twisted down the whisky into his throat and his wide-open eyes were fulsomely concurring with that.

'Well I'm sure that's *right*,' he exclaimed. 'Shall we set off now, Frankie? Get back, will we? I mean – I've never actually, you know – *been* hit by a coffin, or anything. If I'm honest. Not even a, you know – *empty* one . . . but I'm sure he's right, the doctor. They must be pretty weighty brutes either way, I should have said.'

Frankie looked at him.

'Is that all?' she asked, quite simply.

'Hm? All? Sorry, Frankie – not quite, um . . . Is what all, actually?'

'All you think I am. *Nice*. Just – *nice*? Is that all you think?'

Jamie leant his elbows on the steering wheel before him and rested his chin in the heel of his hand as he blew through this cluster of fingers that now seemed to be covering a fair deal of his mouth.

'No . . .' he said slowly. 'That's not all, Frankie. Far from it. If you really want to know . . .'

And he turned to see: if she really wanted to.

Frankie blinked as she said to him Yeah? So? Yeah?

'Well . . .' resumed Jamie – and his voice, now, it seemed to him to be husky, maybe. 'From the very first moment I set eyes on you, I thought you were . . . well, I was going to say simply *divine* . . . but it's more than that, Frankie. I thought you were the most beautiful person I had ever seen in just the whole of my life. That's what I . . . thought. And I do. Still think it. Yup.'

Jamie looked away from her, and out of the window; he saw there only a glimmer of his own grey-ringed and hangdog eyes. During the silence, now, he thought he might bite into his lip. So he got on with that, while passing on to her at the same time Oh yeff – by the way, Flankie . . . Lucatch gim ush, left ush, our er . . . (and then he thought Christ, you stupid sod – you sound like a fucking imbecile: cut out the chewing immediately) . . . um, flats, spaces, places. Whatever. In The Works.

'Oh,' said Frankie. 'John'll sell it. He'll sell his.'

A jagged shudder of ice went right into Jamie: he was pierced from head to toe as another set about him, slicing thinly from side to side.

'What? Really? Why? Why do you say that? How do you know?'

'He will. I just know. Do you – like that, Jamie? I'm not – bothering you, am I?'

Jamie looked down at her hand, laid flat on his thigh: presumably what she was talking about now.

'No I – *yes*. Yes, it's good. Not bothering me at all. Well – bothering me in one way, of course . . .'

And then he just fell on her: Christ oh Christ – just couldn't even begin to save himself, now. He had her – Christ, that beautiful beautiful face of hers, he had it between his hands and he sucked so deeply at the sweetness of her lips – and as she gasped, just slightly, he felt charged by a blood-heat he could barely remember, and it made him strong and trembling. He felt her cool fingers at the back of his neck – the talons at their tips were agitating his hair now, and making his skin both red and alive.

'*Frankie* . . . !' he panted – and the way her creamy shoulders just ran down and into and *became* her breasts, as his liquid hands were rippling all over her. ' . . . I think you are just, oh – so perfect – perfect – *perfect* . . . !'

'Gently . . .' breathed Frankie – a collaborator's gurgling just stopped up, now, at the back of her throat, as her dazzling eyes were dipping and dancing before him. 'Your face is all so . . . *bristly,* Jamie . . .'

'Sorry – sorry – oh Christ let me *hold* you – *feel* you, Frankie . . . !'

'I like it,' she whispered. 'I *like* it, Jamie . . . the bristles . . .'

And now she was guiding his hand over the smoothness of her knee and way on up into dark and plumper secrets. She paused, then – stopped it (which caused him anxiety) – and then she drew his hand further and then to the absolute limit where the heat was quite furious and then covered it, his hand, with her own, quite tenderly, as it nestled like a tired and grateful beast in the soft and seething depths and folds there. And then. He felt another sort of warmth – it burgeoned towards him, his cupped hand easing over this round and growing, tight silk-held bulging as he looked for, craving, the light in those eyes and he giddily missed them and he was breathing so hard now at the harshness of the kicking that his heart was putting him under but he had found this face, now, and the small specks of fear that were sparking there, they with ease and warmly dissolved as Jamie and Frankie both then knew that this was fine, oh yes, quite fine . . . but more, thought Jamie – it was *more* than fine, is all Jamie could think, now, before practically swooning . . . it was . . . this thing, it was all just *perfect* . . .

Later, they had kissed and licked each other's hands; then again their lips were softly together. Jamie slowly drew away, and he hung and wagged his head in delighted disbelief. His brain seemed newly tuned, alive with the shot-out tingles from this awesomely whole and utter revelation (they are reaching now for every part of me – and getting there, yes: they are getting there). Of Frankie, Jesus: who could have known this? And as to myself, well – I would never have truck with murky stirrings: such soup I never stirred. Even the faintest squeak of suggestion I would snub for the unthinking upstart it oh please God just had to be. It needs thought – some thought, this; but not, you know, really too much.

Jamie gently beat the steering wheel just once, and then he fired the engine: the Alvis slowly drew away (it would maybe haul them both to somewhere else). Jamie swung the great car around the bollards of the black and deserted car park, the sullen beam of the headlights transforming before his eyes this rain-slicked tarmac into a deep and boundless sea of crushed-up coal and diamonds. And then his heart stopped within him as the farside wing now jarringly crunched into a bloody low wall he had not even seen coming and then both he and Frankie winced and clenched their teeth at the tinkle of glass and the clattering roll (as some bent part was sent spinning away).

Oona, she caught me as I was just about to make my way up in the lift (Frankie I had only now just torn myself away from). Jamie, said Oona – can we talk now? Yes? No, I said – sorry, Oona, but no, not now, can't talk now. And I couldn't. I had to lie down on my bed and cradle my head and gaze up at the ceiling. Which now I am doing. And do you know what I feel? What I am? I am suffused – suffused is what I am: suffused with the flush of shame. I have betrayed a trust. What *happened*? To my resolutions? They have all disappeared. Why am I now a – *violator* ... ? Because no matter how lovely – how well it fits my hand (how right it might seem) ... this just isn't yours, is it? It is *John's* – you know it is, you know it is. Oh Christ, Jamie – there's no excuse: you can't feel good about this one. As he lay there, John – injured, yes, and miles away – you simply invaded, didn't you? And the very purity we all of us loved, it's now just spoiled. And so as a result of one more useless good intention – *damage* has been caused, and it'll hurt John, this, it'll hurt him badly. Because Jesus. A whole new wing and a sidelight: cost a fortune, car like that.

CHAPTER TEN

Paul and Biff and Tubby were all huddled close to the deep and wide-brimmed copper casserole on top of the vast steel range at the far end of the kitchen (and I can't hardly remember, was Tubby's rueful thought, when I last had this lot all going like the wossnames: them three ovens, the grills and rings, yeh? Doing all the business. People here, they don't seem to wanna eat no more: I was going, give it a week and they'll maybe get a bit over it, yeh? But they never).

Paul now loosely draped his arms across Biff and Tubby's shoulders.

'Tell you, Biff me old lad – one day, straight up, you're gonna get down on your knees and you're gonna thank old Pauly from the bottom of your heart. That's if you got a heart, Biff. Come on, son! Don't be looking like it's another bleeding funeral. It's only paper, ain't it? Ay? It's only *paper*, son, is all it is. Ay? Am I right? *Course* I am: you know it makes sense.'

Tubby crossed his beefy arms and very much said nothing: just let Paul get on with it, is the way I look at it. Old Biff, though – don't seem too far this side of tears, by the sight of him. Right choked he is, look.

'Christ's *sake*, Paul . . .' Biff was moaning. 'Please don't do this. I'm begging you, ain't I? Just give it me, like I said. Ay? I'll sell it – I know I will.'

'And *I* know you will and all, Biff,' Paul was now gently insisting. 'That's why it got to be done. How many times we been over all this, ay? I give it over to you, you'll shift it in no time – yeh, to some dumb blind loser, and then you reckon you're laughing. Well I tell you this, son – you won't be laughing when the Old Bill give you a little knock, will you my son? Your previous, you're looking at a twelve stretch, this little lot. I'm saving you from yourself, Biff, ain't I? You don't reckon I'd go torching up good gear, do you? What you think I am, Biff? Ay? *Stupid*, or something?'

The corners of Biff's mouth turned down as he shrugged his inevitable acquiescence. Because yeh, it got to be right, all Paul's saying – and yeh, we been over it a thousand bleeding times. But I'm telling you, I dunno if I can watch this – I dunno if I can stomach it. But I got to see it happen, if you know what I'm saying to you. Nah – can't explain it, nor nothing. Let's just get it done, if we got to.

Paul, now, was unzipping the blue vinyl holdall, and out they came: thick and virgin stacks of beautiful (oh *fuck*, thought Biff – they're beautiful, they are) fifty-pound notes – like bronze and copper paper-bound bricks. Paul dropped them into the pot (and don't – don't try to work out how much we got here: telling you – it'd break your heart) and now he was spraying them with lighter fuel and then very quickly (cos Paul, he'd like to be honest with you – he ain't enjoying none of this neither) he dropped in a match and the three of them stepped back at the sound of the muted roar, and the flames were leaping and vertical as they audibly engulfed the blocks of notes. The smell that came off them was both vile and seductive – the conflagration quite shockingly brief. Tubby was already poking at the blackened and crispy ashes with a wooden spoon, a flurry of rising smuts attaching themselves to the sides of his hot and sweaty nose.

'Well,' he said. 'That's bleeding that . . .'

Yeh, thought Paul: yeh it is. But it's right, what I done – and I'll tell you for why. Biff, right – he been on at me for how long?

Before the, like . . . well blimey, what you supposed to call it? Ay? The *incident*? That do you? (Anyhow – you know what I'm saying – when Lucas, he snuffs it.) Before then, I could kind of keep it down, couldn't I? Handle it, like. Look, I says to him (you maybe heard it going off), we got it sweet here, ain't we? We don't need it no more, do we? Hey? The old life. And he kept sort of schtum – but I knew, didn't I? I well knew. That it was all still bubbling away, there. And lately, he been going Well tell me Pauly, where's the good life gone now then, ay? I'll tell you where, Pauly – it's gone down that hole in the cellar along with Lucas, that's where it's bleeding well gone: no one else ain't gonna run this place, are they? Geezers like Lucas – they don't come in pairs. Yeh. And I don't got to remind him, Biff, that by rights he's due a third share in the property what we all come into (and even now, you know, it chokes me, that: that Lucas, telling you – what a diamond. Cos no one never give me nothing before). Nah – he's got it well sussed, Biff has. I want out, he says to me. I don't want to go on being a bleeding cleaner and heaving around Tubby's fucking fruit and veg. Yeh? I goes: *yeh*? Well I didn't see you minding none of it before. Maybe, he come back to me: but that was *before*. And yeh, he got a point, old Biff has: it's well different, now.

'So come on, Pauly – give us over my third, and I'm gone. I mean – don't get me wrong: stay in *touch*, course I will. But I reckon I got to get done a little bit of work, now. Know what I mean? Keep my hand in.'

'Well you please yourself, Biff – but I can't hardly give you no third of something I ain't yet sold off, can I? Ay?'

'Well break out the bleeding *notes* then, can't you Pauly? Bleeding hell – we been sitting on it long enough.'

'We got to sit on it. You know that. It's too new. Dangerous.'

'Well I'll take the bleeding risk. Just give it me, Pauly, and I'm gone.'

And I tell you straight – I thought of it. I thought yeh, maybe it's right what he's saying here, old Biff: maybe we sat on it long enough. Punt a little out, bit by bit . . . yeh, maybe we could. So I hauls it out and I has a good, like, look at it and Christ Almighty – I'm telling you, son, it's just as bleeding well I did. Cos it weren't right. None of it. I never noticed it before – never clocked it for a moment. But somehow (and I ain't never cocked up on this scale before) I left off the serial number, down the bottom. And you can't go back on them, you know: once they're done, they're done. I tell it to Biff and . . . I don't know, at first I reckon he thought I were feeding him porkies, or something. When he sees for hisself, he's nearly going barmy, Biff is. Then he says it don't matter – his fence, he says, he won't notice nothing till Biff's well clear. Yeh? I goes. And what when he do, Biff? *Think*, my son. Either Old Bill's gonna get a bell or else the Maltese or the Chinks – one of them's gonna come and slap your wrist, ain't they? Ay? You got to *think*, my son. Yeh. So. We burn them. And that's it. We done it, now. So what I'm gonna do is, I'm handing over to Biff all the, like, passports and IDs and the other odds and sods what I got (they're kosher, they are – they're the business) and then I'll slip him his share when we got rid of the gaff. Cos I got to flog it, really; Tubby, he's getting itchy and all. Says to me, he says – there ain't no call now, Pauly: there ain't no call for me here no more. Poor old sod: got all sad when he said it. And me? Well I'm well torn, I don't mind telling you. Cos I love it here, don't I? But I got to sell up, like it or not. You see how it is. So I dunno, is all I can give you, just now. And I ain't the only one, I reckon. There's a funny feeling about the place, these days. We got a new year on us now, see – and people's getting jumpy, you ask me. Like Mike. Old Mike. Had a word with him, just lately (didn't let on to him what's going down with Oona: course I didn't – what you take me for?), and I'm telling you, he's in a right old tizz, Mike is. Says to me, he says:

'I'm *shocked*, Paul. Thoroughly shocked. By . . . God – who I *am*.

I mean you never, do you – really ever *know*, or anything? Till you're tested. You just go through life with all your little foibles and your hobbies and your file-indexed opinions and your favourite books and all your silly little pet likes and dislikes and all the bloody rest of it and you get to, I don't know . . . you get to thinking that these things, they *define* you, or something. That these things *are* you. You get smug, is what I'm saying, Paul. You get smug and fat and idle. And so bloody bloody *pleased* with yourself. That's what happened to me. Cocooned by all this . . . *stuff*. All these relics from lives that were actually *lived*. By people who were worthy of the *name* . . .'

'Now come on, Mike – don't go being too hard on yourself,' said Paul, quite mildly. 'We's none of us perfect. And you don't wanna go knocking all this top-class gear you got, neither. Ain't never seen such a lovely collection.'

'Yes but that's *all* it is, isn't it Paul? Hm? I mean it's just a bloody great collection of *stuff*. Secondhand old stuff that's . . . well, it's all *outside* of me, isn't it really? It's amazing I never ever *saw* this. None of it actually pertains in the slightest to my actual *being*. I mean . . . look, Paul, I'm sorry if I'm going on a bit – you know, putting it all over a bit strong, or whatever – and don't please worry that I'm going to start *crying* again, or anything, because I honestly don't feel that I've got a single tear left in me, quite frankly . . . it's just that . . . well, I feel I can *talk* to you, Paul – that you understand, well – at least *some* of all this. And I know you appreciate all the – things, stuff. Clutter. That's what Oona called it, you know. Just the other day. Clutter, she said. After all these years surrounded by it – *living* it, if you like . . . she just turned round to me and said Well what are you going to do now, Mike? With all this *clutter* . . . !'

'Nah. You don't wanna be worrying your head about Oona, Mike old mate. She loves it all, Oona does.'

'Well. That's what I thought. But you saw, didn't you? How she

– hit and kicked me. Bruised all over, I am. You see, I think it's maybe *me*, Paul. Not the stuff. Maybe . . . before, well – I was a worthy custodian of this old generation, the great generation: the people who fought the War. Me, I can't fight *anything*, Paul. I just go to pieces. I just can't *bear* what's happening to us all here, now. I don't know what's going to *become* of us. Christ – if I'd been alive in the War, well – I *wouldn't* have been for long. They would've shot me for cowardice. And rightly. Rightly so. I feel *empty*, Paul: empty inside.'

'So. You talked to her, have you? Oona? Bout how you feel?'

'No. Not really. I haven't.'

No, thought Paul: didn't think so. Cos I have. And what she says, Mike, you really don't wanna know. Oh dear oh dear oh dear . . .

'I don't think she's really with me any more,' went on Mike, quite miserably. 'God. I never . . . I never ever thought I'd hear myself *saying* such a thing. And physically, you know – oh God I'm *sorry*, Paul – I'm so sorry. I really shouldn't be telling you – burdening you with all of this, but . . . well . . . I won't, you know, go into *details*, or anything, but Oona and me, well – we have our little, you know – *rituals*, if you like. Little sorts of – games we like to play. I'm sure you – you know: understand. Anyway. Lately, well – nothing. Not so much as a dicky bird. I think it's because she senses – she just must sense, Oona, that I'm simply – empty. Last night – Jesus, I was sleeping on my own on the couch thing – you know, the couch thing we've got – and I tried to work hard on my favourite fantasy of all . . . I'm just so embarrassed to be saying all this to you, Paul, but . . . well, you know Frankie? Yes? John's Frankie? Well of *course* you do – of course. What am I thinking about. Well anyway, what I do is . . . I sort of picture her as one of the Andrews Sisters – you know, American uniform and so on. Pencil skirt. Tunic. Little hat. That just *always* gets me going, if I'm honest with you, Paul. And. Last night. Nothing. Absolutely nothing. Not so much as a dicky bird. Empty. I'm empty, you see. I'm utterly utterly *void* . . .'

Hm, thought Paul: not only you ain't talked to Oona, Mike old son, but you ain't had no word with Jamie, neither. What I hear, you get that American uniform off of her and you're sure of a big surprise, son. Way you're looking, I reckon it'd finish you off for good and all, mate. Yeh. And in case anyone's wondering how it come about that Jamie let on, like – well, I reckon he knew. That I could be interested. Jamie and me, we got a bit of an understanding (my way of thinking). But to get us back to what Mike was on about, well – like I say, when I looks at what Oona had to say to me, I don't reckon the poor old bastard's too far short of the mark.

I was just come back from this mate of mine's, see – body shop, he got, down the Mile End Road. Says to me Yeh – he can fix up old John-John's Alvis, no problem at all – good as new in no time, is what he says to me. Cos Jamie, dear oh dear – he were in a right old twist about it (hopping up and down, he were). 'He'll go spare!' is how he was going. 'John comes back and sees it – he'll lose his mind and who can blame him?!' I says to him Relax, my son: I know a bloke, all right? Good as done, mate. And don't ask me how old Jamie, he come to prang it in the first place, cos he's staying well schtum on that one. Anyway – don't matter. My mate, he says give us a couple days (three tops) – and I goes Yeh well that's favourite as it happens on account of John-John, he's in one of them fancy sort of rest places now, out Surrey way – coming out on the Friday, Frankie was telling me. He's all right, though – he bounced right back, did John-John. Telling you – he'll see us all out, that one will.

So. Like I say, I'm just back in, see? And I'm thinking to meself, mm – I go down the kitchen, Tubs down there maybe he can fix us up a plate of something a little bit tasty – cos I were starved, tell you the truth. Hadn't had diddly since me Coco Pops of a morning time. Yeh. And so anyway, I'm walking along, yeh – and suddenly it's all Oona. all over the shop, she is, with her Come in Paul – please Paul – I got to speak to *someone*: all grabbing hands and her eyes like hubcaps, they was (could of been I just seen a wall of them hung up down my mate's place). Yeh all right then, Oona, I goes – don't go getting yourself all in a lather, gel: your Uncle Pauly's here, ain't he? Ay? Get the kettle on, love, and you can tell us all about it. OK? Prime. You know it makes sense.

So she's clanging about in her little kitchenette, and she hands us a cup and saucer (the Clarice Cliffs, point of fact, which I don't reckon is for using, but I says nothing). I were just giving the cup a little bit of a wipe over with my hanky when she come back in with the pot and all the doings, like.

'Oh. Yes. Sorry, Paul – sorry. I haven't been – you know. Dusting, or anything like that, lately.' She gestured around the makeshift parlour. 'There's just so *much* of it . . . all this clutter.'

'Little bit of dirt – never hurt nobody. Sit yourself down, love, and tell us what's got up your nose. Mike not about then? No?'

'Mike? No. Don't know where he is. He might be down in the cellar – prostrate on the tombstone and weeping his bloody heart out, for all I know. I just can't stand the way he's – *gone*, Paul. Just looking at him now – it just drives me crazy, somehow. He just looks soft and apologetic all the time – like a sheep, or something. I think that's why I just *went* for him, actually. He was just asking to be *beaten* . . .'

'Yeh well . . .' allowed Paul, fooling around with his undrink-able tea (she stewed it, is what she done – and where's the milk and sugar then, ay? She just ain't thinking). 'He been through a lot, ain't he? I mean yeh – don't go jumping down my throat, Oona love: we *all* have, we *all* have – yeh yeh, I know that. But Mike, well – he took it special hard, didn't he? Not his fault.'

Oona just shrugged. 'I hope you don't want milk . . . we haven't got any. Can't seem to lay my hands on the sugar . . . Actually,

Paul – it's not really Mike I want to talk about. It's . . . it's . . . well it's *tea*, actually. Tea.'

Aye aye, thought Paul: aye aye. Reckon she gone funny and all on us? Couple forks short of a fondue set, you reckon? Soon find out.

'Tea, ay? What – tea as in, like – *tea*, is it here? I mean – this ain't some new buzzword we got? Meaning, like – something else altogether?'

'No no: tea. Tea. *Lucas's* tea, actually, Paul. The oolong.'

'Oh yeh – that stuff he has with his drop of gin. Had. Yeh. So – what about it then, Oona?'

Oona looked down to her knees. She carefully placed her cup and saucer on top of the doily on the side table, just alongside the brown and mottled ashtray with the central match dispenser.

'I – poisoned it,' she said.

Paul was looking at her, now: looking at her closely.

'You – done *what*, love?'

'Poisoned it. Put poison in it. I have this awful feeling, Paul – that I might have *killed* him . . . !'

Paul just went on blinking. Bleeding hell – whatever the mad old crow was set to come out with, I wasn't was I? Ready for this little lot.

'Except – I don't think I can have, really, because it wasn't really very *much* poison and I crept in – God I was so scared – and put it in this caddy he's got, ooh – weeks and weeks and weeks ago now and the doctor's report said he died of a massive and sudden heart attack and I don't think that this poison could really have done that because all it was *meant* to do, according to this chemist, was make him sort of *sick*, you see – and the only reason I wanted him to get a bit sick is because this chemist, you see, he also gave me the antidote. The stuff that makes you well again if you take the poison – and I was going to be the one, you see, who made him all better and then I thought he might finally come to *love* me.

377

Love me, yes . . . Oh Paul – this must all sound like mad talk to you. Do I sound mad, Paul?'

'Nah – get out of it, love! Course not.'

Yeh, he thought: you're coming over loud and strong, gel, like a numero uno lip-strumming fruitcake, you want the God's honest truth. And look at you now: you gone all dreamy on me now, you have. Hey up: you woke up again, have you? Yeh: great big nutter eyes is what we got – and off we go again:

'You see . . . I've always loved him, Lucas. From the very first moment I saw him in the bar. Seems a lifetime ago, now. When he'd gone – when he'd bought us drinks and smiled at us kindly and spoken so beautifully . . . just beautiful . . . so deep and gentle . . . Anyway – when he had made us this most amazing offer to, you know – come and live here, well . . . I had already, by then, fallen deeply in love with him. I didn't even try to hide it. I just turned to Teddy and I said to him Teddy, I said: that was the most amazing man I have ever met in the whole of my life. And then when he –'

'Er . . . hold up a bit there, Oona. Sorry to, like – cut in and that, but um . . . did you say Teddy then, did you? Was that one of them wossname slips, was it? You're talking Mike now, are you?'

Oona just stared at him.

'Oh of course . . .' she said softly. 'You don't know, do you? Well no. Nobody does. You see, Paul . . . at that time, I was having an affair with Teddy. This was ages ago. Run its course, pretty much, even by that time – but I went on with it because, well . . . we both *drank*, for a start, and Mike – he was always so terribly disapproving. And I like actors generally – they're pretty good fun. Anyway . . . Lucas, he obviously assumed we were, you know – properly together, I suppose. It was Teddy he invited, really. It was Teddy he was looking at. Anyway – I was married to Mike. Mike and me, well . . . we lost a child, you know. Years ago. I couldn't have any more . . . and I sort of – lost interest, basically.

Mike, he just threw himself into a sixty-year-old war: seemed to keep him happy. Anyway . . . Teddy, he said to me Look, Oona – we'd be mad not to take him up on this, you know, if he really does mean it, this Lucas person, whoever he is. He was broke, of course – completely broke at the time, poor Teddy. Couldn't get a part because he was always so smashed. So – he came here with Judy . . . who of course I'd never set eyes on before. I mean I knew he was *with* someone, and everything – but I never sought out any details. And I came with Mike and all the . . . clutter. I suppose Teddy's idea was that we could keep up our drunken and lusty meetings even more conveniently than before . . . that, of course, and a roof over his head, poor sod. Me . . . I just wanted to be near Lucas. Because I loved him. And when I met Alice I just thought Huh! *She* won't be a problem – get rid of *her* in no time flat. But then . . . then . . . the funniest things started happening. Teddy stopped drinking – amazing in itself, that: I'm telling you, Paul – God: the amount of booze that man could put away . . . ! I wasn't quite that bad, but after a bit I'd pretty much kicked it too. And – he started getting on really well with Judy again, Teddy – and me, I really liked her. Still do, she's lovely: everyone loves Judy, don't they? And then . . . I started getting into all of Mike's wartime obsession, much to my total amazement. Really enjoying it, I was, for a good while – saw for the very first time what it was he got out of it. And Alice . . . suddenly wasn't an enemy any more. I *envied* her, of course I did – I think we all did, actually – but I came to see that she was in her rightful place, I suppose – mainly because, well . . . Lucas had *put* her there, hadn't he . . . ? Teddy and me, well – it'd pretty much fizzled out anyway, like I said. The Works, you see . . . it just started weaving its magic, I suppose. But of course it *wasn't* The Works, was it? Now we know. Because The Works, well – it's still here, isn't it? Still standing. But Lucas – Lucas isn't. And without him . . . everything's just falling apart . . .'

'Yeh but no listen . . .' put in Paul (and he was thinking it's bleeding weird, ain't it? Ay? The way it all, like, links up). 'I got all that – but what's all this gubbins about the tea then, Oona?'

She seemed a little distracted now, Oona – going over it all, she could well have been: over and over it, again and again.

'Hm? Oh the tea, yes. Oh God I can't *tell* you what happened to me there Paul, really . . . I just must have gone a little bit crazy, one day. Mike, you see – he'd bought all this stuff from this old chemist shop in Clerkenwell – Stockwell, I think it was – and I just got talking to the old man there, that's all. I had this sudden vision of me being the healing angel – that was it. Mad. Quite mad. So I sneaked up and . . . oh it was crazy, crazy. And anyway, the stuff was so bloody *old* and I only put in about a teaspoonful. I've got a whole great *jar* of the stuff: I doubt the lot would harm a flea. So I don't *really* think I, you know – killed Lucas, or anything. I just . . . loved him, that's all. And you do, you know. Go a bit mental, sometimes. When you love someone.'

Paul put down his tea; he didn't fancy it before, and it seemed even less appealing now.

'So, Oona,' he said to her softly. 'What's going off next, you reckon?'

'Hm? For me, you mean? Well – Mike, he's talking about selling up here and buying some perfectly disgusting little semi somewhere vile on the North Circular Road. Somewhere untouched, he wants – no new porches, no double glazing, none of that. Good luck to him. I sort of understand . . . I sort of do. He's got all this stuff – it's his life, now. And we can't stay here any more, can we? It seems somehow . . . stupid, now.'

'Yeh. Maybe. And what about you, Oona? Going to be happy, are you? In your semi up the North Circular Road?'

'Hm? Oh God *no*, Paul – *I* won't be going. Oh no – I thought I'd made that clear. This stage of my life, well – it's just got to be over, hasn't it? That's all finished. Done with. I don't at all care about the *money*, or anything: he's welcome to whatever he can get.'

'You told him . . . ?'

'No, I – no. Haven't, yet.'

'Going to soon?'

Oona nodded. 'Have to. Joe – he's coming to pick me up in the morning. I don't have much to pack. All this stuff . . . it's all Mike's.'

'Who's this Joe then, when he's at home?'

Oona smiled, quite roguishly.

'Oh well – it's really quite *amusing*, in a rather twisted sort of a way. You see I always used to make out that I had this sort of imaginary wartime boyfriend – my G.I. Joe. It was one of our games. Not one of Mike's *favourite* little games, but still . . .'

'Only . . . he weren't imaginary – this Joe.'

'No. Quite real. God – so many times . . . because Mike would go Oh *really*, Oona – what do you have to go calling him *Joe* for? It's just *so* unimaginative. Yadda yadda . . . and so many times I just yearned to tell him that the reason I call him Joe is because that's his name, Mike: that's his *name*. He's a nice guy, actually Paul. A really nice guy. I mean he's no *Lucas*, but . . . Got a proper job. Computers. Earns. A twenty-first-*century* job. Be nice . . . Sex is great. Because I shouldn't say this but, well – Mike, he's a bit of a wanker, really. I mean I don't too much mind all the Onan thing, not per se. Not really. It's just that, well – the spilling of seed . . . I'm just like everybody else, when it comes down to it. You just don't want to be the one who's always wiping it up.'

Mm, thought Paul: play safe, I reckon.

'And this Joe – he's, what – a Yank then, is he?'

Oona smiled, and nodded happily.

'He is, actually. Yes he is. It's quite poetic really, isn't it? In a ghastly sort of way.'

And it was only after he's left her to it that Paul managed to pin down yet one more thing that was different about Oona: her hair, much shorter and coloured, and she had been wearing a brand-new and very fashionable trouser ensemble – which (she could have told him, if he'd asked) had been bought just that morning in the January sales.

'Well well well well well, Jamie!' Teddy was hailing him brightly. 'I must say you could barely have timed it better, your little visit – if visit it be. Come in – come in. Judy and I were just on the very verge of offering up a little toast. Sit down, Jamie – sit yourself down. A glass, if you will Judy, for our guest, I think . . .'

Judy rose and walked the few steps over to Jamie – fixing upon him her very bravest smile of all. As she kissed his cheek, Jamie whispered to her – didn't really know why he thought he should – Are you sure it's OK, Judy? I mean I can always come back another time . . . ? She just shut her eyes briefly in her Don't Be So Silly way (much more like the old Judy, this; much more, yes – but not, if he was honest, nearly enough, from Jamie's point of view).

Teddy poured red wine into the larger than usual goblet Judy had set before Jamie. His care was almost priest-like.

'To – the new year,' he said. 'That we can all maybe find it within ourselves to . . . start afresh. Finally, to put all these terrible things behind us. Cheers, friends . . . your very good health.'

Jamie nodded to that, and brought up the glass to his lips. Think I'll just light up a fag: don't imagine Judy'll mind too much – take it personally, or anything like that. I think she knows the score.

'Mmmmm . . .' said Jamie, with deep appreciation (all thoughts of fags gone from him, for the moment). 'My God, Teddy – you've *really* cracked it with this one. Jesus – this is just – !'

Teddy allowed himself a low and secret chuckle.

'Ah – alas, Jamie, alas! If only I could find the short cut – the quick and easy recipe for *this* little tincture . . . ! Wouldn't that be the answer to one's prayers . . .'

He brought the bottle over and presented it for inspection. Jamie craned himself forward and dutifully read from the label.

'Christ – I see what you mean, Teddy. Château Latour 1961. But that's – that's meant to be legendary, isn't it? Goodness. I'm honoured.'

'Tis. Tis indeed. But here is a tribute to not just this noble wine, but to its bestower. The benefactor to us all. Lucas, you know – he gave me this bottle, ooh – ages . . . just ages ago. With the apron, yes? See it? "Teddy: Winemaker". What a day that was . . . what a day. Anyway – now seemed as good a time as any to open her up. Lovely, isn't it? Quite puts all my efforts firmly in the shade where they very much belong, I have no doubt. Talking of which, good people, I now must take my leave of you. Just the one box of Teddy's no doubt perfectly odious chardonnay to convey to the nether regions. We're all so out of kilter these days, aren't we? No regular mealtimes, or anything . . . Anyway – empties have been piling up, Tubby was telling me. It's as well to keep everything tidy, isn't it? Go through the motions, as it were . . .'

Even before Teddy had manhandled the box of bottles out of the door and away, Judy had her big and sad and now rather old-looking eyes (they had gone a bit milky) hung level at Jamie. Well: no surprises there. She'd said to him quite urgently earlier that morning that she so much wanted to – needed to – talk to him (come around twelve, she had earnestly implored him: Teddy will be gone by then). Obviously I got here just a little bit early. Caught sight of Oona, briefly, just as I got out of the lift; I think I must have started, shied away a bit – with guilt, or something – because it had clean gone out of my head, you know, that she had ages ago seemed dead set on talking to me too (and God knows why any of them should feel like this, these women – it's not as if I've got anything to *say*, or anything; I am hardly the fount of wisdom. It's not, Christ, is it – as if I'm *Lucas*, or something). Anyway – once I'd stuttered out all my apologies to Oona for not having come to her, well – I was just left standing there feeling like a perfect fool because all she had to say to me was something on the lines of Oh yes, Jamie, yes – I remember now: yes I *did* want to talk to you at some point, confide in you – but that was then: ages ago. Past. I've now talked to someone else, so it's quite OK. Ah, I said – right, then. Well – didn't give two hoots about it one way or the other, if I'm being perfectly frank with you. Because there's enough, isn't there? Quite enough. To think about. Without getting saddled with all of Oona's cares and woes. Well look – there's Judy here, for a start . . . and God knows I owe her. To Judy, I owe just anything, really, she cares to name.

'Well Jamie,' she said to him, quietly – one of her fingers very intent upon tracing and retracing the rim of her glass – round and round, round and round. 'You see the problem.'

Jamie had just lit a cigarette. He blew out the first deep exhalation in a long and blue, hissing plume, nodding with energy as he did so.

'I do, Judy, I do . . .' And then uncertainty flickered in his eyes. 'Um. Well – there are all *sorts* of problems, aren't there Judy? So many. I mean – what exactly did you, um . . . ?'

Judy glanced at him sharply, and then she set to shaking her head from side to side.

'You didn't see, did you? You didn't notice. The wine . . . ?'

Jamie looked into his glass. Empty, predictably. I do that a lot, you know, just lately: glug it right back. And it's a crime really, isn't it? With wine like this. Last few mouthfuls – I completely forgot to taste them. Mind you, with the fag on now, even this stuff would have its work cut out for it.

'Well of course I *noticed*, Judy. I said so. It's wonderful . . .'

'No no no no *no*, Jamie. Not the bloody *wine* – the fact that Teddy was *drinking* it . . . Oh God. Oh God oh God.'

Jamie was all understanding – but he immediately felt both stupid and ashamed. He should have noticed: should have. Of course he should. Didn't, though: didn't.

'Oh well look, Judy – it was like Teddy was saying, wasn't it? Hm? New year . . . special bottle . . . just the one glass, after all . . . a sort of *cleansing*, possibly . . . ?'

Judy threw back her head in maybe disbelief at what Jamie had just come out with. She stared on up at the ceiling so fixedly: it was as if she was marvelling at its very existence.

'You don't *know*, Jamie – you simply have no idea. Just the one *glass*?! A sip – the merest sip would be too much. Too much. He's an *alcoholic*, Jamie – you heard him say so yourself. I just – I just don't *know* now what on earth is going to happen. This – this on top of everything. Because he wants to move, you know. Go.' And now she brought back her eyes and trained them full on to Jamie again: he could barely stand the well of tears, there. '*Leave* . . . ! He wants to *leave* here . . . !'

And her own appalling words set up all sorts of alarm and sent it ringing around the room and clanging right back and cuffing them both in the face quite roughly and setting off in them a heightened and unnatural panic. It was Judy, though (of course) who eventually stretched out to Jamie the pat of a calming hand (and he clutched at it with gratitude).

'The awful thing is,' she continued sadly, 'is that I think everyone's talking about leaving now because – well, simply because just everyone's talking about *leaving*. Oh dear. Anyway. He's quite set. Wholly determined. Do you know what he told me, Jamie? Just last night. Why I had to talk to you, you see. So urgently. The drink, well – I hadn't seen it, before just now. Just then. I had suspected, oh yes – he hasn't for days been eating any Fruit Gums. But I put it aside. Like you do. But today, well – I was meant to see it, you see: I am now meant to know. So . . . this, this is new. But last night he told me that during the last year he had actually turned down three West End parts. Three. Turned them down. Why, I asked him: why, for God's sake? Because, he said, of here. This place. How could he be on the stage every evening, if every evening we all had dinner here? He knew, you see, how important it was. Anyway. He says that now he will – take any part that's offered. The trouble is . . . if word gets out that he's just as unreliable as he was before, well – he's not going to get anything, is he? Back where he started. And word *will* get out, won't it? Because it always does. Oh dear. Oh dear. And the theatre, you know – it's been consuming him lately. It's all surged up in him again – taken him over, like it used to. You know, Jamie – it sounds silly, silly in the context of, oh – that terrible, terrible Christmas Eve, but . . . he never quite got over, you know, not having his play performed. You know: The Works. He'd just put his heart and soul into it, you see – and it was rather good, wasn't it? Didn't you think so, Jamie? I did – I did. I really thought it was rather good. Anyway. By hook or by crook, he seems quite determined to get back into the theatre *somehow* – says he can't go on living in isolation. Isolation! Jesus, Jamie – the whole point, wasn't it, was that it – this – was the reverse of that! Isolation . . . Anyway . . . he says we have to now be closer to where . . . real people are. Real people. Is what he said. Well. I'll go where he likes, of course. But if he's drinking . . . well, there's just no point. And it could kill him, you see. Any more rejection. He so needs something – he even went to Oona, you know – and she's made it quite plain she wants nothing more to do with him. And God – she could hardly have put it to him more cruelly. She said she had no desire to – listen to this, Jamie: no

386

desire to "open old wounds". Oh God. Just *imagine* how he felt
. . . ! He was mortified, when he told me . . .'

Jamie was confused. Felt he was witnessing an outpouring –
endorsing a monologue – rather than even slightly participating
in just anything at all, really.

'Sorry, Judy – what exactly – what's, um – Oona got to do with
any of this?'

'Hm? Oh Teddy and Oona, they had a little thing, once. Not
here, of course – oh no, not here. But before. She wasn't the only
one. In his drinking days, there were many. Boys too, sometimes,
as a matter of fact: not unknown in the acting profession. Something else I suppose I'll have to try to get used to. Oh dear. Not
sure I can. Not again . . .'

Judy looked deeply sad and reflective – but then she snapped
back almost immediately, as if she had suddenly recalled to mind
something most terribly amusing.

'Oh yes, Jamie – and another thing: he's finally decided, Teddy,
to change that name of his. Well – shorten it, really. He said to me
– if it's true, if you really do believe it, Judy, that one day I'll have
my name up in lights, well – it's just got to be a better one than
Lillicrap, hasn't it? He's got a *thing* about it, you see . . . Anyway.
He's going to be called Teddy Lilly from now on, he says. Or even
Ted. Ted Lilly. He hasn't quite decided . . .'

And then she crumpled – so thoroughly and immediately that
Jamie could not possibly have seen it coming. He managed to
steer the burning fag end well out of the way as she fell quickly
into him, and he was amazed now to feel his torso jerking hard
and in rhythm to Judy's hacked out and deep-felt sobbing.

'And . . .' she managed, after a while – her face still buried deep
into Jamie's shoulder. 'I've got a . . . lump. On my breast. Lump.
Teddy says I'm imagining it, but I'm not.' She raised up her wet
and red, puffed-out and yet still intense and white-blue eyes. 'Do

you want to, Jamie . . . *feel* it . . . ? My lump? Will you *feel* it, Jamie
. . . ?'

Jamie just sat there. He continued to smooth the palm of his
hand up the plane of her back and down again and he shushed
out maybe consoling noises. He still was focused on a far part of
the wall: he fixed intently on just where the light, look, struck the
flat of a window ledge.

'No . . .' sighed Judy. 'You won't. Teddy won't either. Well.'

She drew herself away, and slid her hands all over and around
her soft and pale and sopping face, sniffing and gulping as she
did it.

'One reason, actually . . . why I go on with the Samaritans. It's
sometimes . . . the only way I know . . . to connect. I am quite fully
aware, of course, why they call me, these men. Ask for me – you
know: specifically. Why Teddy doesn't like it. They talk about sex
– their, you know – sexual so-called problems . . . all made up, I
shouldn't wonder. And then they wait for me to talk back to
them.'

Judy, now – to Jamie's considerable consternation – seemed
almost like she always did: the competent Judy – the one in
control. The old Judy: the old one, the one I needed.

'Have some more of this delicious wine, won't you Jamie? It's a
shame to leave it. Teddy, I feel sure, will now be at the back of the
kitchen and close to the bottom of possibly his second or third
bottle of chardonnay, I should think. Unless he's found the
brandy. So . . . he won't appreciate this, the Latour. Do, Jamie –
please do. Pour. Pour, for both of us.'

Jamie did as he was told. Sipped his wine – passed over to Judy
her glass.

'They get off on it, of course,' she resumed, quite matter-of-
factly. 'Yes of course they do. Why they ring. These men. Much
cheaper than the Phone Sex lines. Much. But the point is,
Jamie . . .' And now she was fixing him again with that sort of all-

consuming stare that Jamie, frankly, could have well done without. 'The point is, you see . . . that I do too. Yes I do. I need it. It is, as I said, the only way I know . . . to connect. You see.'

Jamie stared down at his hands. Wanted a cigarette: didn't somehow feel it was maybe the time. Judy sighed.

'I expect,' she said, 'you would like to be off. I don't, believe me, in the slightest bit blame you.'

Jamie grinned almost right at her, feeling so terribly awkward. And then he put down his glass, stood up suddenly and walked to the door as if his limbs were of timber. Judy came over, and placed one hand on his.

'I know we all have our . . . doubts and secrets, Jamie. It's just that after so long sealed up, well . . . they're all emerging, now. They were always *there*, of course – it's just that now, we can see them again. And we maybe don't care to. Like your marriage, Jamie, yes? Don't let it upset you. I don't, I have to say, think that it does for a moment. Living with a woman . . . it's not for every man. It's really just a question of knowing what it takes to get you *through*. *My* greatest anxiety, of course – I might as well tell you: I've told you everything else. Is leaving here. I don't mean, you know – for *good*, not in that sense . . . although that is, in itself, quite paralysing. No . . . I mean just setting one foot outside. Even as far as the river. Because I don't know if you know, Jamie, if you ever noticed – no reason why you should – but since we came here, since Teddy and I first came here, apart from the Samaritans – and John, he used to drive me straight there, and then straight back again – I haven't – not ever, not even for a moment – ever left the place. I just simply do not know any more what the world outside is *like* . . .'

Jamie looked down at the ground. Thought to touch her shoulder, but he didn't go through with it.

'And . . .' concluded Judy. 'I'm *frightened* . . . frightened, Jamie.

Very. But. All it is, I suppose – is knowing what it takes to get you *through . . .'*

It's the smell of the morning, Jamie had now concluded: it's the smell of the morning rather than its brightness, that reminds me. Mm – there's a sharp tang of newness and excitement in the dapplings of the sun and the sparkling reflections. Misplaced, now: quite wrong, oh yes wholly. Because on the morning I am recalling, the day I first came here, there was about me a heightened awareness of a different order: the anticipation of a sort of future – maybe even the outside chance of permanence. But my unloading those pitiful and few, quickly grabbed-at possessions from the back of that perfectly maddening person's cab (the declaiming idiot who for all his blather didn't even know where he was meant to be taking me) – it's rather different, isn't it, to the sight of this swarm of sturdy and unsmiling professional movers stowing away seemingly mountains of stuff into this vast and cavernous van. They have an economy of movement, these intent and burly men – no brief journey is wasted, each squat and lift quite tight and controlled. They heave things with ease that it makes me near faint to even contemplate. Like that deeply panelled and elaborately pedimented armoire there, look – which Kimmy has just told me is packed to bursting with cans of paint and a stacked-up series of three-sided boxes, I think is what she said to me, that once were destined to form the basis of some installation or other – one more heap of crap, was Kimmy's eventual and dismissive summing-up – but now just so much lumber that it was easier to move en bloc than go jerking around with all the hassle of judicial assessment and careful disposal.

'How do you feel, Kimmy?' ventured Jamie (she was watching and berating all the movers – and loving it, seemed like). 'Now that, you know – you're finally doing it. Leaving.'

'Look at it, Jamie, kay? Everyone's like *talking* about quitting, but they all just hang in there. Not my style, baby. When you gotta go, you gotta go – you know? Hey! Hey you with the klutzy cap! Yeh you – I'm talking to you. Go easy, kay? These babies are *art*.'

Yeh, thought Jamie: she's right. Most of us, we're just now loitering, basically – hoping against hope that quite soon (maybe tomorrow?) everything's suddenly and rather wonderfully going to get back: to be just the way it used to.

'Still. It's quite a decision. Anything, um – I can do, or anything? No? Something?'

'You could haul your butt up top and see how they're dealing, Jamie – Doe and Mary-Ann. They're taking it kinda hard. But it's those two guys I got to think of here, you know? Me – I can settle most anyplace. I only came here on account of Doe. You know that? Oh yeh sure. She was all set to move in here with Mary-Ann and the putz she called her husband – all real cosy, it was gonna be. Then putzo, he gets to thinking otherwise, so me – I just came along for the ride. That, plus I love her. She maybe don't know . . .'

Jamie looked at her. 'You mean . . . ?'

'Yeh. Yeh. *Sure* I mean. Crazy about her. But I ain't, you know – pushed it, or nothing. I figure, she comes to explore her seck-shallidy, she'll maybe like, you know: see it. One day. Hey – who knows? Maybe once we get outta the shadow of this place, it'll all come good. Hey you! Not you, mister – you! Yeh you! Nix with the cigarette, OK? There's canvases in there! *Art*, honey!'

This reminded Jamie that his fingers were singeing. He dropped the fag end to the ground and swivelled his toe hard into it a couple of times, as his hands were busy seeking out another.

'We're going to, like – *Chelsea*?' resumed Kimmy. 'You know Chelsea, Jamie? I kinda like it. The address I gave to Alice. Maybe you can come visit?'

Jamie nodded. 'Maybe,' he said.

'I think . . . you know what I think, Jamie? Me and Doe, we can bring up little Mary-Ann real good, you know? Between the two of us. I can, like – *provide*? Who needs a schmuck with stubble and a schlong? You just gotta believe in what you got. And could be Doe, she one day lets *Cheeses* into her life, who knows what's going to happen? Jamie – you go see what's keeping those guys? Yeah? Me, I'm kicking ass, here.'

Jamie smiled and leant to kiss her lightly.

'I'll see you, Kimmy,' he said, while thinking it unlikely, very unlikely that he ever would again. (Ern, his name was, that blighted cabbie – been in the game for twenty-two years, come Christmas; twenty-three it would be now, then.)

It was quite a jolt, seeing the place empty, like this (again the reminder of when I first came here). I mean, these spaces – well yes, we know that they're immense, granted – but when all the bits and furniture are suddenly gone . . . And I hadn't even noticed that Kimmy and Dorothy even *had* that much stuff (but just look at the van: it's the size of a house, and already pretty packed). Is there anyone here . . . ? Ah yes – Dorothy is sitting on a bentwood chair: she's way down there under a towering window, and idly entwining her fingers into and around Mary-Ann's thick and tawny, loosened-out hair (crouching tightly and very close to Dorothy, Mary-Ann is, seemingly intent upon the blankness of a wall, and nothing else at all in the whole wide world).

Jamie approached, cursing each clunk of his heels on the endless runaway flooring.

'So, you two . . .' he said softly, as he neared them. 'All right, are you? Ready for the, um . . . ? Kimmy's, er . . . Actually, do you mind if I – ?' He then just lit one quickly, and inhaled very deeply.

'Well . . .' he said. 'Well.' He even considered attempting a laugh: soon abandoned that idea, thank Christ.

'Did Benny like his presents?'

Jamie was momentarily stilled. Fine rays of cold sun were streaming unhindered through so many windows, and as Jamie now doggedly continued his clumping approach, the vision of the two of them (still way down there at the end) would keep on whiting out, before he was briefly dazzled by a glaring light that then darkened. And Mary-Ann's voice was whip-thin and reedy – it just about made it into the air before being wholly engulfed by the sheer and booming volume of space all around her.

And still he hadn't responded, because he didn't in truth know quite how to (keep on sucking on the cigarette: Christ they're a godsend, in more ways than one). He had spoken maybe twice on the phone to Benny (since). His mother had spoken tersely and passed him over (Here Benny, here: talk to your father). But presents . . . they hadn't come up. I have entirely forgotten all those things I gave him, even their nature – and he had said nothing about any of them. Or, indeed, about anything else; had simply grunted 'Hi, Dad', and left it to me to get on with it. Caroline had said that she had decided it would be best to stay on at her mother's until, as she put it, Jamie saw fit to shift his arse and get something *sorted*. Quite the Caroline of old, in short (those briefly gaudy colours streaming away from a lance of her own erection now not just tattered or threadbare but gone, quite gone: torn away and blown off into hell). She had heard, of course, about Lucas's will; news like that, it travels on the wind.

'He *loved* them,' said Jamie, who had reached them both now (which felt a good deal less unsettling, let him tell you). 'And he said to say a very special hello and big hugs to you, Mary-Ann. Yes indeed.'

She was still just staring at the wall.

'But not,' said Mary-Ann quite starchily, 'in those words, I guess.'

Jamie glanced over to Dorothy for maybe just a little bit of help, here: wasn't any.

'I'd like to talk to him again,' went on Mary-Ann, rather dreamily. 'He was nice. Don't suppose I'll ever see him again now, though . . .'

'Oh *nonsense*,' blustered Jamie. 'Of *course* you will, Mary-Ann. Be *great* friends, the two of you will . . .'

Mary-Ann shook her head, quite firmly. Wouldn't look up, though: still just mooning at that blank bit of wall.

'No. It doesn't happen. When people go, they just *go*, you see. I've watched it. I told him to believe in things, you know. But only the things that are *here*. When they're gone, they just don't matter any more, really. It's just like they die, or something. Everything good is dead, now.'

Jamie didn't really need to hear any of that, to be perfectly frank with you, and so he felt on the whole rather relieved to see Mary-Ann unfold herself from the floor now and say to her mother that she'd be downstairs with Kimmy, if she was wanted. She didn't look once at Jamie, and then Mary-Ann just turned and ran the length of the echoing room and heaved open the door and let it slam shut behind her. Which is sort of fine, thought Jamie. Except that now there's just Dorothy to deal with. Right, then:

'*So*, Dorothy . . . this is, um – sort of it, then, hey? How do you, um . . . ? Nothing I can do, I don't suppose . . . ?'

She turned to face him.

'Do you think that's true, Jamie? Is it true?'

'Er . . . what's that exactly, Dorothy? True?'

'What Mary-Ann just said. That when things go, they die.'

'No! No no no no no. No, Dorothy: no. Not at all.'

Well *ye-e-e-ss*, I suppose so. I mean – not maybe literally, but to all intents and, you know: what is it? *Purposes*, they do, yes they do. Really.

'But it's funny, you know though,' went on Dorothy. 'When Lucas was . . . well – you know. When he was – *here*. I barely saw him. I mean – dinner, of course, when we all did. But at other times, well – whole days could pass and . . . But now I just know he's not here at *all* . . . you know: *gone*. Well, there's just no point any more, somehow. No point in any of us being here. I suppose that's why we're going, really. Probably best. Kimmy thinks so, anyway. If it had been left to me, well . . . I would've done nothing, I expect. Which is what I do. Nothing. Nothing at all. Perfectly useless. I'm the only one here, you know, who never put a single thing back into the place. Passenger. That's all I was. It's Kimmy: she's the one who does things. Gets things done. Odd to be leaving . . . though in many ways, of course, I never should have come here in the first place.'

'She's very – fond of you,' muttered Jamie (I want to go, now: want to go). 'Kimmy is, you know . . .'

'Oh it's more than *that*,' protested Dorothy, suddenly quite animated. She stood up now and rested her hand on the back of the bentwood chair. 'I suppose I ought really to take this down . . . it's the very last thing . . .'

'I'll take it,' said Jamie immediately. 'Give it to me, Dorothy. I'll take it down.'

'She *loves* me, is the point,' said Dorothy, quite earnestly – wide-eyed and full into Jamie's unsuspecting face. 'I have to always pretend to not know how deep it goes . . . because much as I just totally adore her, I'm not ready for anything, you know: more. Just not into it. Although many people *are*, aren't they Jamie? That sort of thing.'

Jamie lit a cigarette. Had to crush the last butt rather painfully between his finger and thumb and lose it in a pocket: didn't like to drop it on the floor.

'Are they?' he said.

'It seems so to me. Jamie – can I tell you a little story? You maybe might like to know it.'

'Won't, um – Kimmy be waiting, Dorothy? And Mary-Ann . . . ?'

'It won't take long. Listen. Once . . . ages and ages ago, it seems to me now, but it wasn't really. My very best friend in the world sat me down and said to me Listen: listen, Dorothy – listen to me, will you? Yes, I said: what? You can tell me – I am listening: you are my very best friend. You can tell me anything. And at last I hear it – because it took some coaxing, in the end. It turns out that the night before, as I lay asleep, my very best friend was being raped. I was shocked. You must report it, I said: I'll come with you to the police. But no: didn't want to. But why *not*? I was going. Why *not*? You *must*. Why *not*? And then I got my answer: because . . . and I'll never forget the words . . . because I *liked* it: really *enjoyed* it. I just stared. You *liked* it? But how is that – ?! I mean how *could* you – ?! And then . . . I understood. Had to. It was maybe time to stop being stupid. So I said Well then, Anthony . . . if you liked it so much . . . *enjoyed* it . . . I suppose you are saying that's the end of us. And of course it was. You see, Jamie – Anthony, my husband, he used to go to all these rather strange clubs and bars. I don't know if I was meant to know or not. I think so. He left all the matches lying around. Anyway. Where he met Lucas, in point of fact – in one of those places. And John. Well John – he owns them all, you know. The Ragout, The Blue Angel – dozens of them. Where all the money comes from, I expect. They were all great friends, you know. Anthony . . . and John, really . . . they would only come here to be close to Lucas. Mary-Ann and me, we were just baggage. What I mean when I say I never should have come. And then . . . soon after, John met Frankie – who seemed to be the answer to his dreams. Understandable, I suppose. If – you know – that's the way you think. It was Lucas who introduced them. You know about Frankie? Yes: I thought so. And Anthony, well . . . we were no sooner here, the three of us, and then he met . . . someone else. And he left me. Left me and Mary-Ann and set up home with, oh God: *Nelson*. Can you believe it? Lucas was so upset, when he left. I think there was talk of me and Mary-Ann leaving and this Nelson person taking our place . . . but nothing came of that. And me, I don't mind telling you, Jamie – I was just *that* much away from an insane asylum. If it hadn't been for Kimmy, well . . . But you see I know why she came to me so, oh – *absolutely*. I knew it then and I know it now. But – I just can't be what she needs me to be. You see? I've tried: just can't.'

Dorothy glanced up, as Jamie continued to gaze at the floor. She breathed in once, and thought she might try to be brave.

'The joke is . . .' she continued – putting all she had into a very frail show of lightheartedness, but faltering quickly ' . . . the really daft thing about all of this is that after all this time I still love him, Anthony – and he, he's in love with *Nelson*. Lucas too – I love him as well, rather oddly. Like we all did. And now he's with God in heaven.'

Dorothy now set to striding with purpose the length of the room and Jamie tagged on behind her, the bentwood chair dangling lightly from three of his fingers, as he swung it to and fro.

'Oh Jamie!' she called. 'Is my jacket down there? I need it to cover my arms. Can't bear them. The sight of them. Isn't it odd? I keep being told they're no worse than other people's arms, but still . . . Lots of us, I think, have bits of ourselves that we find embarrassing. Oh God I'm going mad, look! I've got it. I've been holding it all the *time* . . . !'

She turned at the door, and faced the space.

'So,' she said, quite finally. 'One last look . . . You know, it doesn't really have the feel any more of where I've been living.

You know: home. With all the stuff out, and everything. It's just – empty, now. Nothing, really. Coming, Jamie?'

Jamie lit a cigarette, hefted the chair, and followed her out.

He blinked at them, he hoped politely – this man, this woman – as they wandered down the broad and resounding corridor – and she, this woman, would often break away from the side of him, this man, marvelling at all the features – the windows, the beams, the light, the space, yakety yak – just as everyone always did. He was in truth caught unawares, Jamie, this time; he hadn't been told that a new lot was expected – but the stream of people, God, it was becoming near constant, now. The agents seemed to just send another gang of them round whenever they damn well pleased: formal appointments had become a thing of the past. Yet one more.

'I find this the hardest bit, really,' he said to Paul – relaxing slightly, now that he knew the outsiders were gone. 'You know: strangers. New people. Walking about the place. It sort of brings it all home. As it were . . .'

Paul nodded as he handed to Jamie a green and fluted glass, filled up to the brim. (Mike – he give me the set of them, the glasses. 1950 is what he reckons. Dear oh dear, poor old Mike: don't know if he's coming or going these days, Mike don't.)

'Yeh. Know what you mean. Here, mate – get this down your screech. My very last bottle of old Teddy's chardonnay, this is, son. Cos I don't reckon he gonna be turning out no more, do you?'

Jamie smirked, and sipped the wine.

'Christ . . .' he said quietly. 'If the state we found him in last night's anything to go by . . . Jesus. It's all he could do to get the bottle up to his mouth. Poor Judy. Last thing she needs. Did they like it, Paul? Those people? Think they were interested? I expect they were. Everyone seems to just love the place on sight. Understandable . . .'

'Yeh. I reckon we'll get a good offer there, Jamie old mate. It'll sell fast, this place will. And you, son – you don't wanna go hanging about no longer, you know. You got to put it on the market. I mean – it ain't as if you got to leave The Works, or nothing, is it? Ay? I mean – we got it all worked out nice, ain't we? Ay? But we'll need the dosh, Jamie, however you wants to look at it. And I wouldn't go worrying yourself too much on Judy's account neither, mate. Anyone handle it, she can.'

'Yeh yeh – I know that, I know that Paul . . . it's just that, poor Judy – that's all she ever seems to do, handle things. It's about time she got a bit of a break, that's all I mean. She's just so scared about leaving, you know – and now with Lillicrap back on the bottle, well . . . She really helped me, Judy. With my life. Marriage. And the fags, and everything . . .'

'*Yeh* . . . ?' laughed Paul – watching Jamie pointedly as he stubbed out about the seventh, his fingers scrabbling away at the packet.

'Yes, well . . .' allowed Jamie. 'Wasn't her fault I went back on them. Or that Caroline . . . But she's really special, Judy is. I think there's a genuine healing power at work there, you know, Paul. Think she's got a third eye. Truly do.'

'Yeh?' sniffed Paul. 'Well you'd never know it – not to look at her.'

'You being funny?'

'What – me?! Leave it out. Ain't never made a joke in my life! No but straight, Jamie old mate – I do know what you're banging on about with old Jude. Reckon she could've done me a bit of good and all, things hadn't gone the way they did. I went to one of them one time, I did – therapist, healer, whatever it is they wants to call theirselves. Didn't even last out the one session. I mean – I weren't that frantic, if you know what I'm saying, when I come in. Time I leaves, I were a bleeding head case. It's all of that "relaxing" music what done it for me. Took me right to the edge, that lot did. All birdsong and babbling brooks, it were – lots of violin. Tell you, I was all up for strangling the birds with a length of catgut – else drowning the sods in all the tinkling bleeding water. So nah – didn't really do it for me, none of that. I mean – what's it all about, ay? But listen – no listen, Jamie, listen to me, right? Never mind laughing – ain't no good just sitting there laughing, is it? I meant what I said about getting your gaff sold off, you know. Got to be done, son. Alfie. Ay? You know it makes sense.'

Jamie nodded. He was right, Paul, of course he was. And yes, they'd been over the idea again and again and it worked, so far as Jamie could see: yes indeed, it could be very good. So why am I dragging my heels? Oh God – obvious, really. My usual sad and feeble dread of change – that, and a natural idleness. But unlike a lot of us, I've got a real option, here – thanks to what I think of now as Theme's scheme. Because it was he, you know, who came up with it all. I don't know what I would have done otherwise, if I'm perfectly honest. Hung on as long as possible, I suppose, surrounded by builders and strangers and alien noise and bad *intrusion* – and Caroline on and on and on at me all the time for money . . . and then I would've just sold it for next to nothing during a trough in the market and thrown at her just all of it – and then what? Nothing. Drifting. Lost. Again. But this . . . is really good. Or could be, anyway. Either way, this is the plan:

Um. First, though – let's get all our dependants out of the picture: you know – the people Paul and I used to live with. Well on Paul's side, Biff has already left us, of course (I hope, is all Paul said, he goes easy – whatever that might mean; I don't inquire into any of that). Tubby, well – he's sort of in and out. Gone for a few days – back for a meal and a change of clothes. Seems in two minds. Paul, he reckons Tubby could get a really good job in a restaurant somewhere (and God, if I owned a restaurant, Jesus – I'd make him head chef just like *that*) but he's not sure the money would suit him (Tubby, he's more used to lump sums, is all Paul's said – whatever that might mean; I don't inquire into any of that). And on my side, well . . . Caroline and Benny, they're renting somewhere, just at the moment. Caroline, she phoned me and she said it's in Belsize Park and it's very nice. And then she told me what the rent was and I said Yes, yes I see – well I *hope* it's very nice, anyway, because for that sort of money, it bloody well should be. And it's Alice, actually, who's helped me out, here. Went over with her the plan – well, Theme's scheme, as I say – and she seemed . . . well do you know, I didn't expect her to be so terribly *pleased*, but she was, she really was seemingly delighted. So Alice, God help us (how do these things come about?), is currently subsidizing Caroline's rent: another good reason why I've got to get my dear old space on the market, just as Paul says – because I don't want bloody Caroline's rent to drain me white. And plus I feel quite strongly that I have to get square with Alice eventually, whether she's in need of the money or not. Which of course she isn't, but that's neither here nor there. But I might as well say: Lucas, you know – he left her just everything. Not just the obvious, the whole top floor, but everything he owned. Well – who else, I suppose. In fact, that's exactly how she put it when she told me. She looked rather sad. She said that Lucas had not so much left it to her, as *not* left it to anyone else. Well, I said to her – at least now you're a millionairess, Alice: it's not, is it, a bad beginning, if one is faced with beginning again. She smiled at me and said A millionairess, yes – what a wonderful word. I am, Jamie, a millionairess many many many times over: I alone form a

401

sorority of millionairesses, yes; but as to beginning again, I'm not sure one can – I think you can only begin once. I think there can only ever be one beginning. It's the nature of the thing. (And she still looked sad.)

So. Anyway. Back to the scheme. I was in quite a state when I first spoke to Paul about it all (we meet in the evenings; his is a very soothing presence). So Paul, I said – this is the situation. The reality. We've got to sell. Got to get out. What are we going to do about it? And much to my complete surprise, he told me.

'Well see, Jamie – what we got to do, like, is get together on this one. Me – the reason *I* got to sell up, well – fair do's to Biff and Tubby. And you, mate – you're in for a two-thirds glassing and all, ain't you?'

'Two-thirds? You don't know Caroline. Way she sees it, she's due for half, and her son – that's how she's taken to calling him now, Benny . . . her son – anyway, Benny she reckons is also due half for his future, and the rest I can do what I like with. It's not easy. Being married.'

'No, mate. Why I never done it. But nah – she'll settle on two-thirds, course she will. I mean look – she's a lucky cow, ain't she? Ay? No offence, nor nothing.'

'None taken. Yes she is. It's not as if she's done anything in return for it, or anything. Christ – she didn't even *like* Lucas, Caroline. I was amazed, you know, in one way, that he let her stay here. Well – he wouldn't have *not* let her, of course: not his way. But I don't think he was ever that keen . . . Anyway. She is. You're right. A lucky cow.'

'Right mate. Now look. If what we both want is to, like, stay on here – cos you do, don't you Jamie? You don't wanna jack it in?'

A light had stirred in the customary hopelessness of Jamie's beaten eyes.

'Oh God *no* – I mean yes, yes – of *course* I want to stay here, but – ?'

'Yeh well listen. Your third and my third – we still a bit short, right? Of the full monty. For our own gaff, like. But listen – I been having a quiet word with Alice, ain't I?'

'Have you?' checked Jamie. Have you really? Oh. I thought that was me: I thought I was the one who had the quiet word with Alice.

'Yeh I have. And listen. The cellar, right? And the tunnel? Plus the old dining room and kitchen what they leads off of? Well, that's all Alice's, that is – loft is, and all. Anyway – cut it short, she'd be well pleased flogging it to us for what money we got. And I got it checked out: worth a pile more, telling you. So like I say – you wanna go getting your skates on don't you, my son? You know it makes sense.'

So there were the bare bones of it. We've talked in more detail about it all since, of course – how it would work, what we'd be doing. And now the sight of that pair of interlopers, newly done with sniffing around and pawing at Paul's great space and obviously loving it – this and his repeated urging – has finally determined me to do it: I'll put my place on the market first thing in the morning. Jesus, the time is more than due: if we're going to do this thing, well then let's just get down and *do* it. Because Killery – you know: Mike, Oona's Mike – he's just accepted an offer. Buying a little house in I think he said Pinner, or somewhere, apparently, to keep all his stuff in. He threatened to get rid of it all, you know – the whole caboodle: said it was all dead and gone and so should he be and why was he still hanging on to all this debris when Oona, his Oona was *gone*?! Because she has, it seems: left him. Paul appears to know a good deal more about all the ins and outs of it, but I don't inquire into any of that. Not that interested, to be perfectly frank, whatever it is other couples get up to. Although I do confess in this case to surprise: I really did think they were utterly together, those two, you know, in spirit and mind. But there. You never know anything, do you really? About two people. By definition, one has never been alone with a couple, has one? No. And therefore it follows: you know nothing whatever about it. But he seems to have rallied a bit lately: seems very pleased with the house he's buying, anyway. He says it's got the original stained glass in the front door panels and the plumbing hasn't been touched since before the War; wiring's a death-trap – he's completely delighted. So, I said – you've got what you want, then: well – not too *bad* anyway, is it? There's only one thing I want, he said quite mournfully – only one thing I want in the world.

'Oh yeh,' said Paul, when I told him. 'I know – a Spitfire, right?'

'No!' protested Jamie. 'No no. Not at all. What Killery said to me was that all he wanted in the whole wide world was for his Oona to come back to him. Sad. Think she will?'

Paul's lips were clamped tight as he shook his head with emphasis.

'Not a chance, way she was talking. But listen – they ain't the only ones neither what's on the move. Judy's just took an offer and all, what I hear.'

'Really?' said Jamie. Really? Oh. She never told me. Was a time, me and Judy, we used to tell each other everything . . .

Paul nodded. 'What I hear. She leased up a flat down Drury Lane way. She says to me it might help old Teddy if he's near the theatres. Yeh, I thought: dream on, lady.'

Jamie shook his head. 'Poor Judy. She was telling me – oh God, it's tragic, really . . . she was saying that he's so determined to make a go of it on the stage that he's finally going ahead with changing his name. Well – cutting it in half, is what he's doing, really.'

'Yeh?' said Paul. 'Well I can't see that Ted Crap's gonna get him too far, but there you go – just let him get on with it, ay? Bless.'

'Oh *God*, Paul – honestly. I don't suppose he *will* get a part, or anything . . . ? No, he won't. Of course he won't.'

'Too bleeding right he won't. Face up, Jamie – the only thing old Ted Crap's gonna do on the stage is to bleeding fall off it again, ain't it? Ay? State he's in. Still – give the lad his due: it were a nice little play what he wrote us, weren't it? Ay? Shame we never done it.'

'Mm. That's what he thinks too. So. They'll be off then, soon. And, um – John, you know. Did you know? Alice was telling me. John's as good as sold as well. He's not been back once – did you know? No. Not since. Got his lawyers to handle it all, apparently.' (And yes, I've wondered about this. I mean there are many reasons, aren't there, why John would be, um – disinclined, as he might himself put it, to come back and be confronted with all these disparate and bubbling sets of turmoil, where before we all huddled beneath the one great blanket of harmony . . . yes yes, I see that there are. But could one of those reasons possibly be that Frankie told him about *me* . . . ? What little there is to tell. And John, he thought me, my presence, could be just slightly *dangerous* . . . ? I would, you know, quite like that. Because I have just lately felt, oh . . . so very tame.)

Paul looked at Jamie for only a short while, maybe knowing that here were the warm and raw edges of a thing that had yet to be handled.

'All right now, is he? John-John? Doing good?'

'Far as I know. Yes. I mean, there was no lasting, um – you know, damage, or anything. Shock, I should think. More than anything.'

'Uh-huh. And, er – Frankie . . . ?'

Jamie looked down; looked across briefly to Paul, and then he looked down again. The strong exhalation of smoke from his nostrils was mingled now with a sigh.

'God, you know, Paul . . .' is what he eventually came out with. 'I just . . . from the moment I first set eyes on . . . Frankie . . . I just, well – I thought: perfect. This is just perfect.'

'Mm. And still? What – you still think that, do you?'

'If I'm completely honest with you, Paul – I do, I do. Even more so, if anything. Less frightening. Much. I, um . . . oh God, I suppose I might as well tell you, Paul. Haven't said this to anyone else. I actually, er – I've made a bit of a fool of myself with Frankie.'

'Yeh,' said Paul, quite shortly. 'You already told me. In the car.'

'No – no no. After the car – after. I couldn't – I just couldn't get it all out of my mind. I went dizzy. Dizzy. Bit mad. I thought and thought of . . . touching – touching, yes, and the smell. The smell and the feel. And then I remembered when she kissed my knee . . .'

'Oh yeh? Kissed your knee, did it? What – that in the car and all?'

'No – no no. Before the car – before. And why did you just say that, Paul? Hm? "It". What did you say "it" for, like that? I hate that.'

'Did I? Dunno. Weren't aware. For that matter, since you're getting all wossname – what you say "Lillicrap" for? And "Killery". Ay? What's all that about, as if I didn't bleeding know.'

'What? I don't know what you – ! Did I? I didn't notice. But that's not the point, Paul, is it? You deliberately – !'

'Oh *can* it, Jamie, Christ's sake. I deliberately done *nothing* – that's what I done. You got the hots for Frankie – and so what? Ay? You ask her, did you? *Her*, hear it? *Her*. OK? Choice. So – you asked her How About It, did you? Say to her – here, Frankie, tell you what: you say so long to old John-John and shack up with me? Yeh? That it? That what you done?'

Jamie was shocked, now, and not at all enjoying the blaze in Paul's eyes and the friction in the air. He had never before seen him angry like this.

'I wouldn't . . .' started Jamie, purposely slow and quietly ' . . .

quite have put it like that . . . but yes, I suppose so. More or less. I did. Yes.'

'And she says no, don't she?'

'She, um – did, yes.'

'Well of *course* she bleeding did. What was you expecting? Ay? Course, if Lucas had gone and left to you all what he give to Alice, well – then we got a tale with a very different ending.'

Which was, Jamie acknowledged with shame, not just the truth of the matter, but pretty much exactly what Alice had told him too. Because it's not true what I said to Paul earlier: I had spoken to someone else – I had told it all to Alice. I have seen, she said, the way you look at Frankie. Lucas – he did it too, in just the same way. When he dressed . . . you know, when he became the vagrant, yes? He particularly enjoyed it when Frankie came along. Found her most deeply exciting. Told her so, I gather – but only, of course, when he was dressed. He said to her quite baldly how much he wanted her – what he would do to her. All the things men say. Why she was so terrified of him, I suppose, our local tramp, poor Frankie. It amused Lucas most awfully, of course, because he knew so well that as *Lucas*, well – she was his for the taking. As, of course, was anyone. All you men here feel the same about Frankie; well – not Mike, I shouldn't have said. And it doesn't surprise me one little bit. (And even now, thought Jamie – feeling low and almost in disgrace – I do not know how much of all this Alice is truly aware of: it can only be an assumption, then, but I suspect she has it all quite firmly in her grasp.) *But*, she concluded, you have to understand, dear Jamie: a thing such as Frankie, well . . . only a Lucas or a John could possibly hope to afford it. You do see?

Jamie was aware of the first of the tears rolling away and on down his cheek only when he felt first the firm grasp and then the steady patting rhythm of Paul's hand on his shoulder.

'Sorry, mate . . .' he said so softly, 'if I come over a wee bit strong there, Jamie old son. It's just . . . I care about you, that's all. And that – that with Frankie, well – it's the old old story, ain't it? Ay? It ain't just always about two people. Sometimes, it's the money what makes up the menage-ah-wossname. See? Same old story. With, yeh – a bit of a twist there, granted. And I'm telling you, son – you listen to your Uncle Pauly, ay? All that paint and dresses – you get sick of it, you do. After a bit. Trust me, yeh? You know it makes sense.'

Jamie closed his eyes and gave himself up to a relief of sorts that was washing all around and into him. (I do not know how much of all this Paul is truly aware of: it can only be an assumption, then, but I suspect he has it all quite firmly in his grasp.)

Jamie spread out his arms and widened his eyes – a superfluous gesture, as far as Alice was concerned. She was very well aware – had been for days, since the packing began – just how vast and now empty was all this space around them. Nothing much at all here, now, to stand even mute or blind testimony to her and Lucas's union (the time they spent amid it all). The presses, of course – they still stood four-square and defiant – but little at all of a personal nature. The very smells had faded back into nothing – there was no longer an aroma of even day-to-day confidence, let alone the deep-scented wadding of infallibility that had been invisibly spun here, the spores spreading outwards and down; no lingering traces were remaining of this warm insulation's quite captivating fragrance – God, it had so much pervaded, and now the very nature of it Alice was finding so very teasingly elusive, impossible to conjure. The essence of place (and this was quite plain) had now been forever dispersed.

'Where was it you said you were going?' asked Jamie, his voice sounding both reedy and needless. (And yet when the time rolls round for the last rites to be – again – administered, a few words, surely, seem in order.)

'I told you,' said Alice, quite carelessly. 'Didn't I tell you? Cheyne Walk. Very beautiful. Where Lucas used to live before. He never sold it. There are other houses he never even mentioned. The ins and outs, you know, of all his holdings and so on . . . like a maze, I'm telling you. I had to go begging his old firm of solicitors to guide me through it. New lot hadn't a clue, basically. Been dealing with this person called Duveen. Clearly didn't like Lucas a bit. Can you imagine that? But people, you know – *outside* . . . didn't, often. Adored his father, though. Everyone seemed to love Lucas's father. I quite did myself. Everyone, mm . . . not Lucas himself, of course. He killed him, you know. His father. Did you know? It's rather shocking. Well – I say *killed* him . . . he didn't, you know – just sort of *kill* him, kill him . . . but certain drugs were withheld, others boosted, a few from outside added to the mix. You know the sort of thing. He told me all this quite dispassionately. Rather proud of it. Otherwise, he said to me, the man could have lingered on for just *ever*, and then how could we all have come to be in The Works? He saw it as simply a practical solution. For the higher cause, I suppose. Do you want tea, Jamie? Everything else is packed, I'm afraid.'

'I wonder . . .' said Jamie, slowly, 'if I would have done. You know – if I'd been given the chance . . . Tea? No no – no tea, thank you, Alice. Killed my father, I mean. I wanted him dead often enough, that was for sure . . .'

And never more so, maybe, than on my twenty-first birthday. I had just that day been told that I'd got a half-decent degree from Exeter (God knows how I pulled it off) and my mother, dear old thing, she was so very happy, that day. Just think, she kept on saying delightedly – my little boy is now a full-grown adult man and a Bachelor of Arts to boot! And my father, he'd smiled and said to me Indeed, indeed . . . I've got something for you, Jamie my lad: I've been waiting a long time for this day to dawn. And my mother – she beamed and nearly wept with first relief and then pure pleasure as my father handed over to me this rather large and stiff-backed envelope. That she had not the slightest idea what it might contain soon became quite plain – and I didn't, I never did tell her because, well . . . why add more, hey? Why add more? But what he had presented me with was a scrupulously accurate record of the total expenditure incurred on my behalf since a few weeks before I was born. Everything: clothing, food, schooling, travel . . . everything. Even to a proportion of the rates, electricity, gas (telephone was separate: pretty much every call I'd ever made, somehow logged). Old bulldog clips held together wodges of yellowed receipts. 'After the tune,' he smiled, 'we must always attend to the piper!' And I did. Paid him back. Every penny. One reason I've always been so bloody broke: I had to have it over with as quickly as possible – get clean again – although I never, of course, breathed a word of it to Caroline. And when he died, he left nothing. I think that any money he had he would have preferred to destroy, rather than to give it away. Anyway. That was my father. I maybe should have. Killed him. What do you think?

'I have been trying,' said Alice – pouring out tea into a smallish cup – 'to get to like this oolong. Or even stand it. It makes me feel rather ill, if I'm honest. It's got a very funny smell, but I imagine it's meant to. Sometimes it gives me palpitations. Other times I just get sick. And don't say Well why drink it, then, because you know why. You know why.'

'Maybe you should just take the gin. But listen, Alice. Tell me. Why do you think Lucas did what he did? I mean – leave us all a part of the place. It's puzzled me. I sometimes think I sort of see, and then I just don't at all. I mean – it was so terribly important to him, wasn't it? Keeping it – us – all together. And yet he must have known that if he gave something valuable to people, well . . .'

'Of course. Of course he knew. I talked about this briefly to the man Duveen – the lawyer man – and we sort of agree. You and I, Jamie, will understand rather more because we loved him. Lucas, you see, had naturally to be the overlord here: he needed that, and so, of course, did we. This was meant. How it should be. But he would not have wanted The Works to have continued without him. I mean, it *couldn't*, obviously – not just from the financial point of view, but . . . well . . . it just couldn't. You understand that, Jamie. And of course it hasn't. But the only way, I think, he could have ensured that we wouldn't all just go through the motions – or worse, root out some other benefactor or mentor – not me, he knew I wouldn't be game, but maybe John, say, or someone – was to guarantee its break-up, after he was gone. I sometimes think he would have quite liked to have sealed us all in, like the Pharaohs did with, you know – what're they? Word's completely gone. Pointy things. *Pyramids*, yes. So that we all would have died slowly and horribly at the foot of his sarcophagus. But even Lucas had his limits. Of course, if he *had* lived for ever . . . well then we all would have stayed. Of course we would. But in the light of how things have turned out for everyone, well – would this in fact be a wholly good thing? That said, it was perfectly clear from the wording of the will, according to Duveen, that he fully anticipated a good fifty years more. He didn't expect to go, you see. He foresaw practically everything, Lucas . . . but not that. Not just – ceasing to *exist*.'

Yes, thought Jamie: I understand. Now that Alice has set all this before me, I see, I see it. I wish, however – I really do wish I was the sort of person who could work it all out without, oh – even *hints*, let alone such pre-packed solutions.

'It's quite a thought, that, isn't it Alice? That if he had lived for ever – or even fifty years . . . that we all would have stayed. That we all would have been here for ever as well . . .'

'Mmmm . . . well that's not quite right, actually. We wouldn't all have been here, no. I wouldn't, for a start. And nor would Judy, or Oona. And certainly not Dorothy and Mary-Ann. You see, after a while, the women – they would have been gently eased away. They would not have known this, of course. That a process had occurred. They each individually would have been under the impression that they had come to an independent decision, but that would have been an illusion. And one by one, they would have gone. Lucas would never have suggested such a thing – and nor would he ever have dreamed of preventing their coming in the first place. Like your Caroline, Jamie. He wasn't that keen, you know, but he never would have said no, would he? Not his style, is it? Not his style at all. But eventually, given time, a natural evolvement would have taken place here, I feel quite sure of it. A shedding of skins. Because – being here, however it might have looked to us at first, whatever people might have thought they *wanted* it to be, well . . . it was never about couples. Not in the, you know – traditional sense, anyway. Hence, I think, the Hitlers: always something there to remind us. And, of course, he had all the time in the world, Lucas. There was never a rush. The right moment would in each case present itself. No hurry. Lucas . . . he had all the time in the world.'

Jamie just watched her, not caring to move. He was surprised when suddenly she smirked and laughed quite shortly.

'One thing he said to me once. I remember it. He said to me You know, Alice – it's a myth, a myth that women live longer than men, as everyone says. It's not that. It's just, he said, that they take longer to *die* . . . Yes. Didn't get what he was on about, at the time.

Do now. Ah well. This tea, you know – it really is quite horribly filthy.'

'Will you go on with it?'

'The tea? Do you mean the oolong, Jamie? Or just – more generally? The tea: no. Other things, well . . . I shall probably become that typical unexpectedly liberated woman – and one with money, as well. I shall have my hair cut short, buy clothes I will always think would look far better on other people and no doubt attract all sorts of unsuitable men. Well – they're all that, really. None of them – there aren't any, are there? That would suit me. And you, Jamie? What about you? Happy with your arrangement? I'm pleased, you know, that Lucas . . . well, that he won't be alone. You and Paul – you will be his sort of custodians, I suppose. Odd to think of it. Bit queer, really. Oh and *yes*, Jamie – I knew there was something else. In the trunks I've sent down, I've also put in –'

'Oh yes – I meant to say, Alice: I meant to thank you. For all that.'

'Hm? Oh don't be silly. I'm just pleased they'll be getting some use. They're such terribly beautiful suits, you know – and he only ever wore them a few times each. Any decent tailor can shorten all the legs. It's just such a shame the shoes are too large for you. Anyway, listen: I hope you don't think it's pushy of me, or anything, but I've also put in those two little pictures of mine. You know – of The Works. I mean for God's sake do feel free to chuck them if you simply can't bear the sight of the things, but –'

'No. No no – not at all. I'd love them. I do love them. Thank you.'

Alice simpered: she looked quite fond.

'How sweet you are, Jamie. Judy too – she was always so sweet about my useless little pictures. I had a sort of amour with an artist once, you know: an architectural painter, as a matter of fact. Country houses, that sort of thing. He taught me a bit. Once, he asked me to sit for him in this rather lovely garden of his. And I did. Wearing not very much. When I looked at the canvas, I really did get such a terrible shock. He'd simply painted the building behind me. I wasn't there at all. So I left him. It was soon after that I met Lucas, as a matter of fact. Ooh – and thanks so much, Jamie, for seeing to those beastly agents, and things. They measured up the loft – did I tell you? Said it would convert beautifully and they would sell "as is". They talk like that – perfectly beastly. Anyway – I nearly was sick when they told me: found two dead owls up there. They'd been trying to break through the roof, poor things. The owls, I mean – not the agents. Completely forgot about them. Lucas said to me: the owls, they need looking after too, you know. And I didn't. Ah well. Gone now. Just two more things that are gone.'

And then she was – Alice: gone, in a final flurry of kisses and promises (kisses not at all like those others we fleetingly shared – that day, that day). She was both convinced and determined, Alice, she said, that from now on we would find it so much easier – yes, each one of us – to at least attempt to smother all bad memories and then: who knows? Maybe even achieve great things. I don't really think she believed it. Our individual peaks of achievement, if that's what they were, had already been reached by means of instinct and Lucas, so long ago. It was now more a question of surviving the comedown – facing up to working with what there is left to us. Like Judy said to me that time: all it is, I suppose, is knowing what it takes to get you *through* . . .

Well. A couple of minutes or could be simply ages have now passed by, and Paul and myself, we're a bit more settled, for better or for worse. He's tried to coax me back to painting, but I honestly can't be fagged, to tell you the truth. And he's doing his best to get Theme's Schemes up and running again – though I can see at times that he aches for an easier route, like he maybe used to pursue (though I do not dwell upon any of that). Something's got to be done soon, though. It's not as if we've got any money, or anything. Paul says not to worry – he'll print some. God – I think he's joking, but it might even come to that, you know; I just find it physically impossible, these days, to even think of *looking* for a job . . .

What has shaken Paul quite badly, though, is hearing that Biff, poor old Biff, is . . . er – helping the police with their inquiries. Paul just shook his head in sorrow, when he got the news. 'I told him – didn't I tell him?' he kept on asking me (as if I knew). 'He just had to go *easy* – that's all: he just wanted to treat it a little bit *easy* . . .' Tubby seems OK, though – working in the kitchens of a big hotel in Park Lane, I'm pretty sure it is: you know – one of the big ones down there. They'll only trust him with the vegetables, at the moment – but he's quite determined, Paul was telling me, to get right to the top so that he can make a fortune doing adverts for Sainsbury's and get other people to write all his bestselling books. Sort of Kimmy-style, was Paul's comment on that. And talking of Kimmy – she was all over the papers, you know, just a week or two back. Her breast paintings exhibition caused a predictable stir (we got invitations to the opening, Paul and me; we didn't go, though). And then she must have decided to up the ante rather by performing them live, as it were – slamming these naked women all slathered in paint against a vertical canvas (and we got invitations to that as well, Paul and me; we didn't go, though). All the critics were rather sneering – talked of someone called Eve or Yves Klein, I think it was (and God knows who he or she might be) having done it all before. You can imagine Kimmy's reaction to that: two fingers to the media, followed by a total sell-out of all the pictures. Well good. Dorothy and Mary-Ann could be in a lot worse hands than those, you know, whatever the eventual outcome.

The big event for me was just last weekend, when Frankie came round. Not to see me, you understand – just to pick up the last of her things. John was parked just round the corner, apparently: he wouldn't come in. She said to me Sorry, Jamie – you know: about everything (it was maybe just whisky and fear, made me do it). And then she said You see, Jamie – so many men want me, looking the way I do: I think because on the whole I am less trouble. But still I am, Jamie, one of the freaks . . . and disguise, it is *expensive*: do you see? I said I did (well what else could I say?) and I wished her well and I kissed her cheek and the touch and the scent of her had me nearly swooning. I must have seemed different for the rest of the day because Paul, he got quite cross with me (but I think he's wrong about one thing, you know – I don't believe I would have got sick of them: all the paint and the dresses). One of my few abiding memories, now, is of Frankie and me in the leathery insides of the dark blue Alvis: it was a coming together.

What else can I tell you? Oh yes – I got a letter from Judy. It's hard to tell, of course, quite how she's feeling – because naturally she was putting a terrifically brave face on things. They are living in two rooms in Covent Garden, she and Lillicrap – and even that, she said, took up most of the money they made from the sale. She's doing much more for the Samaritans, she says, and undergoing a course of treatment for the lump in her breast; but I mustn't tell anyone. She actually put 'treatment' in inverted commas; I don't know what it means, and I just can't go into any of that. She has developed agoraphobia, which does not in the least bit surprise her, and if it were not for Teddy she would now seriously consider getting herself off to a nunnery, assuming one would have her. And, Jamie, she added on in brackets, you might think that funny, but I'm not, you know, actually joking. Oh yes and talking of Lillicrap – he's shaved off his beard and he did, says Judy, get an audition for an upcoming I think Ray Cooney sort of farce, but he fell off the stage (Paul laughed, when I read him out that bit). At first, the knot of people in the pit were happy to give him the benefit of the doubt – demonstrating his ease with a pratfall, maybe – but then he was sick, and so that was the end of that. Poor Judy. She's racked with guilt too, now, because during a recent session at the Samaritans she recognized Lillicrap's voice on the other end of the line, and without thinking she hung up. This, she said, not only breaks the big and golden Samaritan rule, but also now she'll never know, will she, whether he was just trying, rather heartrendingly, to keep her from talking to some other man, or whether he was in genuine need, and driven to call out of sheer desperation. Oh dear. She asked us, Paul and me, to dinner at the weekend. They'd both, she said, love to see us. Lillicrap, he doesn't make wine any more, fairly naturally, but by way of making up, Judy says, he 'tastes' for England. I said yes to the dinner, but on the day I'll cancel. Can't explain.

Oona? Not any more with her G.I. Joe, from what I've heard – he was more of a means, apparently, rather than a destination. (Judy, in the letter, said that she sees her from time to time and that one day soon we must all meet up for a grand reunion: that's one day, I can tell you, that will never dawn.) Killery, meanwhile, is still reliving the Blitz in his semi in the suburbs: I hope that's all he needs, because I think that for Killery, there can be no more. He remains quite bitter, apparently. Is given to muttering things like 'You don't just *surrender*, if the going gets tough; what you do is you see it *through . . .'* He's got an old army revolver – said he'd shoot himself, if only he could lay his hands on some ammunition. Yes well. Poor old Killery.

And then there's Benny. My son. He told me . . . oh God look – we meet, every other Saturday: it feels so wrong – I can't even explain what I mean by that. Whether I should be with him always, or never at all. Anyway. He told me . . . oh God look – I'm no sort of *father*, am I? So maybe he's better off this way. Anyway. He told me . . . they've bought a new place now in Belsize Park (I did give them all the money, in the end – all of it. Paul was very · angry. But Alice, God bless her, just reduced the price of the cellar to virtually nothing, so it turned out all right). Anyway. He told me . . . that she's seeing someone called Donald, Caroline is. His mother. And that he seems OK, this Donald. So that's . . . OK. Inevitable, I suppose. Can't, can you – *blame* anyone? I'm just not the right man for the job.

So. The place – our place, our little cellar and tunnel (not so little, actually), is looking very smart and cosy, I have to say: it's amazing, you know, how Paul has this ability to create a true home out of really very little. I miss all my fabulous windows though, if I'm honest. Sometimes, down here, you can forget what season you're in, let alone whether it might be night or day. He didn't want me to hang up Alice's pictures (said they were 'right manky') but there I had to put my foot down. And just underneath, I've got the silver model, which she gave me too: I found it in one of the trunks. Ah . . . you maybe don't know. You see, for Lucas's present – Christmas, yes, and also his official birthday – the thing we all clubbed together to get for him was a little silver model of The Works. Kimmy got one of her people to do it.

The detail is remarkable. All the stone dressings are in gilt, and everyone here – they engraved their names on the underside: a memento and an heirloom. Alice had scribbled in a note: He would have loved it – and you, Jamie, are the only other person who will love it also. And she was right: it's where I *belong*, you see. I do.

The smallest of the presses I've got down here, now. It had to be dismantled and reassembled (Paul says it's a good thing to have). The others were sold at auction. The V&A got the huge one, which is a result of sorts, I suppose. The dining table – because we eat together every single night, Paul and me; he's not in old Tubby's league, Paul, but he's not a bad little cook. And the dining table, you know, we have placed on top of the tomb. It wasn't, as it turned out, a special crypt that Lucas had had excavated. There are several deep chambers rather similar, down here – once used for Christ alone knows what (I can't imagine). Nice, in a way, to know they're there. So anyway – that's where we eat every night. So that he can share our evening meal. And we always have fresh flowers on the table – Paul sees to that. He gets them in the Columbia Road. In fact the other day, he came back from there and he said to me Here, Jamie, you'll never bleeding Adam and Eve it! (I love the way he talks: love it.) What, I said to him: what? Well apparently, down the far end of the road (and, he said, he ain't never before clocked it) there's a flower shop called Slingsby's and it's run by – yep, you got it: the Hitlers. And get this, says Paul: that Dave Hitler, he's only gone and grown a little square moustache there, look – you couldn't make it up, could you? (Funnily enough, I've grown one myself. Not that shape though, obviously. It's a bit gappy. Paul says it ages me. I doubt I'll keep it.)

Another thing I found in one of the trunks of suits (and Alice was right when she said they were beautiful: I wear them all the time, now. Paul, he took up the hems for me. I don't know, by the way, what happened to the tramp clothes – and yes, since you ask: I would have been quite tempted). Yes – the other thing I found in one of the trunks . . . and I'm not quite sure if she knew it was there or not, Alice, because it was right at the bottom, and tucked away. Anyway – it's Lucas's journal. I know. I never suspected he kept one. To be perfectly honest with you, I have yet to pluck up whatever it is I need to pluck up in order to read it. I have peeked at the opening, however. It starts off like this: 'My father is dead. I simply can't tell you how happy this makes me.' Yes. So I know I'm going to like it; it's just a question of finding the right moment, really.

Anyway. That's about all, I think. It's quite a nice afternoon, actually, so I think I'll just walk outside for a little bit – have a stroll around. Maybe smoke a cigar. I mix in the odd one now, in between the endless fags (because Alice, she gave those to me too: boxes and boxes. They're good, but I expect I shouldn't inhale them. But what the hell – I'm a chain smoker: it's what I'm programmed to do. If it kills me, it kills me. Paul hates it when I talk like that). And you know it's rather tricky, these days, to make one's way about out here because they're full of parked cars, now, all the cobbled walkways and the darkened bays (and God – the builders' skips!). All but the unconverted loft has now been sold, you know, and still the place is a forest of estate agents' boards. Paul and I, we escape the worst of it because of our special entrance via the tunnel (the one Lucas used in secret); the noise of developers, the unsettling sight of people, and so on. Hardly ever use the big main double doors, now. But the old lion, though – he's still there, looking down at it all with both calm and dignity. And the sign too – no one's taken it down, or anything: Trespassers Will Be Prosecuted. Quite a laugh, that, really: the place is packed full of them. Anyway.

You know . . . I have tried to be a little bit upbeat, here, but just seeing all this, now . . . it's rather hard. It's rather hard. Oh dear. I think I might be in for one of these moods I get now. When I simply stand here, marooned – clinging with a sort of desperation to no more than the vestiges . . . The air is still – some would say peaceful, but no. It merely hangs limply across a jagged discordance, tuned in to maybe my ears only. It is rather as if after so many years of regular care and service, the back has been ripped away from a fine old clock – a hammer taken rudely to the works. The face, of course, remains placid and the same, masking all signs of evisceration, betraying no hint of the pain. The vital throb is gone, though – and we need a steady beat, just to know that we are here, still. But let's be clear: it is not that heaven has been lost. He never gave us that. He simply acted as the suppressor of the source of anguish that led us to him: he kept us out of hell. To all refugees, I think, there comes a bonding at the moment of solace. The instrument, some will view as only chance, others as their destiny. When you're a child, you maybe think of Daddy. Most will talk of God, or falling in love. And we . . . we just called it Lucas.